CHEYENNE LANCE

He'd left the East a boy—and met the West a man. Once a trapper, now as crafty as any Indian, mountain man Zachariah Dobson had made a life for himself among the Cheyenne. As the most famous of their Dog Soldiers, he had fought many a Kiowan brave. Now his own Indian Family was threatened and he would have to lead the Cheyenne into the worst war yet—against the Comanche, the most fearless tribe of them all.

MEDICINE WAGON

McGill, Lila and Zeus, a motley trio of entertainers, traversed the Great Plains on the traveling medicine show circuit, hustling their happy audiences before moving on to the next town. But when they holed up for the night on Jonathan and Emma Whitlock's ranch, they got more than they bargained for. Daughter Martha was sick and gun-toting Jonathan suggested that "Doc" McGill stay awhile to help find the cure.

CHEYENNE LANCE
and
MEDICINE WAGON

JOHN LEGG

LEISURE BOOKS   NEW YORK CITY

A LEISURE BOOK®

July 1990

Published by

Dorchester Publishing Co., Inc.
276 Fifth Avenue
New York, NY 10001

CHEYENNE
LANCE

*For the former Karen
Eileen Murray, without
whose perseverance and
loving peskiness this would
have never been written.*

PROLOGUE

The man pushed aside the flap of the tepee and stepped out into the pre-dawn chill. His breath plumed in the cold air. The light coating of frost crunched softly as he limped slowly across the grass.

He paused, standing in the wide lane between the two rows of lodges, breathing deeply of the cold, crisp air. He watched the faint splinter of light in the east grow minutely. Spring was coming. Despite the chill, he could feel it coming: the slow awakening of green, growing things and that certain tint in the sky.

He walked again, the stiffness in his joints lessening and loosening as the blood flowed in his veins. He halted again, this time at the edge of the stream, checking to make sure the thin coating of ice that often covered the water at this time of year was gone. He was glad to see the stream free of ice. Dropping the breechcloth and stepping out of his moccasins, his only garments, he plunged into the frigid water.

By now, the sun was rising overhead and fog, caused by the difference in temperature, swirled. He knew it would be gone quickly, as soon as the early May sun grew strong enough to burn it away. But for now, he was glad it lingered to mask him from the world. He did not want to be seen yet.

He could hear the sounds of the awakening village—the yapping dogs, the wailing children, the neighing and shuffling of the horses, the hoarse shouts of the men. He heard it all.

He climbed out of the water, his muscles cramping from the cold, and dried himself as best he could with the breechcloth. He listened to the sounds of the village. They were warm and familiar, and they comforted him. Standing naked in the early morning sun, he examined his body. The scars still stood out pinkly against his dark, toughened skin, the puckered flesh stark in contrast to the otherwise smooth lines of his figure.

Still shivering a little from the coolness, he flopped down, stretching himself on the grass to bask in the warming sun. He gazed up at the brightening sun through the fog. Listening to the sounds of the camp behind him, he thought back to the reckless, restless past that had brought him here to the banks of a small stream near its confluence with the Arkansas River.

CHAPTER 1

Zachariah Dobson rode out of the rendezvous in high style, accompanied only by one of the beaver men who trapped alone high in the mountains and his lightly loaded pack animals. His hoarse bellow as he spurred the horse in a reckless race through the camp had almost taken off the top of his throbbing skull. Two weeks of cheap *aguardiente*, the highly potent, home-brewed whiskey favored by trappers, gambling and too little sleep had left his insides churning and his head splitting.

It had been a fine rendezvous, he thought, eying the ground before him with clouded eyes. Even now the park-like glade straddling the Continental Divide between the peaks of the mountains held a fascination for him. But this morning he had fought back the nausea and the agony searing through his head to leave the rendezvous in true mountain-man style. Painstakingly he dressed in his finery in the rear of the make-shift saloon. He was almost through when Moses Smithfield poked his head around the hanging canvas that separated the saloon from what passed as a store-room.

"Whar away, amigo?" hollered Smithfield. Both men had been in the mountains so long that the only speech they now knew was the bastardized English most of the mountain men used. That highly colorful

7

language was further enhanced by phrases, or some-times just single words, from the French and the Span-ish who roamed through the vastness.

Zachariah finished pulling the long-fringed shirt over his head and looked at the best friend he had. Though they no longer trapped together, the bond be-tween them remained strong. He saw his friend's bloodshot eyes and hoped he looked better than Mose.

"North of the Arkansas," said Zack. "An' a leetle south of the Big Sandy, I reckon." Zack watched Mose as he settled himself down on an empty cask. Denying the sourness in his stomach, Zack thought back on the days when they had trapped together.

It was the spring of 1818 when they left the Missouri settlements with a large trapping party led by a man known only as the Captain. Zack had been 19, Moses 20. Zack came from the forests of Virginia; he'd run away from home, where a stepfather had taken to regularly beating the boy. He lived with kinfolk in Kentucky before drifting west toward the Mississippi. Mose had left his home in New York state, looking for the adventure and excitement that he heard was the lot of the fur trappers in the Far West.

Zack had ridden into the Captain's camp with only his horse, a twenty-year-old rifle and the clothes on his back. He hadn't eaten in two days. Seeking out the leader of the outfit, he said to him, "I'd like to sign on as a trapper, sir."

The Captain glared at him balefully. "How much experience ye got, boy?"

Zack tried to embroider the truth a bit. "I been trappin' since I was four years old. Beaver, mink, otter." It was true that he had learned trapping at a young age. But not quite four. And he knew nothing of the ice-cold, bitter rivers that he would have to wade through; or of the frozen nights and blizzards and hostile Indians he would have to face.

8

"Whar'd ye do all this trappin', boy?"

"In Virginny, where I'm from."

"How old are ye?"

"Twenty-one," Zack answered without blinking.

"Ye're lyin' to me on both counts, boy. But I like yore spunk. 'Sides, out hyar we don't ask too many questions. It's a sight more comfortable that way. But I suppose ye ran away from home." The last was a question.

"Yes, sir." Once the truth was out, Zack's shoulders slumped and his weariness caught up with him.

"How long's it bin since ye et somethin', boy?"

"Two, three days, I reckon. I don't rightly remember."

"The cook wagon is over yonder," said the Captain, pointing. "Go fetch yoreself somethin' to eat. Tell the cook I sent ye and that ye kin have as much as ye want. Ye'll start out as a swamper with the outfit, an' if'n ye're lucky, ye'll work yoreself up to bein' a trapper. If'n ye don't git kilt fust."

It was the first time Zack had really heard the argot of the mountain men. But before too many years passed, it would be the only speech he used.

"Does that suit ye?" asked the Captain.

Zack nodded his head, not so weary now, knowing he'd soon be filling his belly. He had no real idea what a swamper was, but it was a job, and he readily agreed.

He would soon come to learn that it was a harsh, brutal life; the work was endless. But he would get used to it.

"What's yore name, boy?" asked the Captain. When Zack told him, the Captain said, "Ye'll work hard with this outfit, Zack. Ye'll work till ye feel like droppin'. But keep yore scalp outta trouble, and we'll git along jist fine. Understand?"

Zack nodded again and turned, leading the horse over to the cook wagon. He spotted another youth, about the same age as he was. When he filled his plate to brimming, he sat down by the other young man. "I'm Zack Dobson," he said perfunctorily, and began wolfing down his food.

The other youth, eating more sedately, said, "Moses Smithfield." He continued eating without further comment. Zack, usually outgoing, was ravenous and so did not mind the silence. He preferred to keep his mouth stuffed with food.

The two young men, thrown together by circumstance, became close. They hauled wood together, stood guard over the horses together, worked pelts together. And when the party reached the Spanish settlements, they got roaring drunk for the first time together. Over the years, they would develop a bond to withstand the tests of time, distance and misfortune.

For two years they worked as swampers, doing all the work the trappers would not do. "This hyar's wimmin's work," Zack had grumbled more than once. But both of them followed the trappers closely, pestering them almost constantly with questions. They finally felt it was time; they drew straws, and Zack won the privilege of talking to the Captain.

By then, Zack had not only picked up most of the habits of the trappers, but also their jargon, which he used as frequently as they. It had been easy for him to slip into using the polyglot language of the trappers, because it had its roots back in Virginia, and the old frontier states of Kentucky and Tennessee.

He confronted the Captain in the leader's tent one evening shortly after his many chores were done. The sounds of the trappers arguing, gambling and swapping yarns could be heard faintly. He poked his head into the Captain's tent. "Kin I have a word with ye, Cap'n?"

The Captain looked annoyed, but relented. "Shore,

10

Zack. What's on yore mind." He set aside the ledgers he had been working on and sat back. It was the book-work that had caused his annoyance. Keeping books was not a chore the Captain relished, but when he was at it he hated being disturbed. The only way to do it, he knew, was just to go ahead and get it over with.

"Well, I bin thinkin', Cap'n," started Zack. He faltered then. He had thought of doing this for months, but now that the time was here, he wasn't sure. His nervousness showed.

"Go on, Zack," said the Captain.

"Well, Cap'n. I bin thinkin'. Me'n Mose bin with ye fer close on to two years now, and we're still pork eaters." The Captain overlooked the French term of derision for swampers. "I figger we bin hyar long enough and know enough to be trappers."

His speech was not elegant, even though he had practiced it often enough with Mose. But he couldn't help it. Finally he blurted out, "If'n ye don't make us trappers, we'll jist have to go somewhar else." Tongue-tied and embarrassed, he stopped.

The Captain looked at him seriously for a moment and then grinned. "Wall, boy. Ye shore done yore part of the work now, or I wouldn't say so. I figger we kin find a place fer ye an' yore friend on the trap lines. Go draw yore supplies, ye both kin start to-morrow."

The youth, still gangly with young manhood, let out a whoop that echoed through the camp. He raced back to tell his friend, heedless of the amused looks on the faces of the other trappers.

That friend's voice now brought him back to the rendezvous in South Park. "When're ye leavin'?"

Zack finished tightening his dress moccasins, the

ones bleached almost white, decorated with beads, pieces of metal and painted porcupine quills. Like the rest of his fringed buckskin outfit, they had been made with loving care.

"Soon's I git ready. Any minnit now."

Brushing some imaginary dirt off the front of his fancy silk shirt, Mose said, "Mind if I ride along with ye fer awhile, amigo?" They usually left together, and the question was just a formality, as was Zack's answer.

"Be pleased. Whar ye headed fer, Mose?"

"West of the Green, I reckon. Up toward the Snake. I kin ride a ways with ye. Mebbe as far as the mouth of the Big Sandy afore I head west."

An hour later they were packed and ready to go. They paid a young Indian boy to take their pack animals a mile or so outside the camp so they'd be unencumbered when they left. Slowly the two men rode to one end of the temporary village through the dust, noise and high odors that accompanied a mountain rendezvous. As they walked the horses down the makeshift street, they saw a crowd that had gathered around a snake someone had chopped in half. This late in the rendezvous, with most of the men jaded, almost any diversion was welcome. The trapper who had caught the snake, had drunkenly hacked it in two with his tomahawk.

Now the knot of half-wild mountain men intently watched the reptile's squirming death throes. Their shouts of encouragement were loud, and the few that had any money left placed bets on how long the wretched thing would last.

As Zack and Mose walked past the milling crowd, Zack said to his friend, "Looks like we'll have a right fine send-off with all these folks up and about, now don't it?"

12

Mose only grunted, squinting his eyes against the biting glare of the sun.

At the end of the camp, Zack looked at Mose. "Ready, amigo?"

Mose grunted in assent, and they gave a last check to their appearance and horses. Mose rode a tough prairie mustang he had caught and broken himself. His feet dangled well below the horse's belly. But the mustang had speed and stamina, and Mose would not part with it.

Zack's horse was a big-boned, powerful appaloosa stallion he had taken from a fallen enemy. It was an excellent mount, sturdy and fearless. Most of the other trappers had, at one time or another, tried to buy him from Zack. But he steadfastly refused all offers.

Mounted, they looked at each other and smiled. Then they let out a bellow that shook the camp. They fired their heavy rifles and spurred their horses. Still yelling, they raced through the camp, scattering men, women, children and dogs in their headlong rush.

Halfway through the camp, they fired their pistols, the shots accompanied by the firing of numerous guns by the other men in the temporary village. Visiting Indians and their wild white counterparts lent their voices to the race. The roar was deafening.

The two mountain men finally slowed their speeding horses half a mile out of camp. The few men reckless enough to try to race with them had turned back with final shouts of good luck and encouragement.

At a trot, they reached the meeting place where they met the young Indian. They paid him off and stopped just long enough to change their clothes. Off came the fancy moccasins Zack wore and Mose's tooled leather boots with the jangling silver spurs. The soft linens of delicately beaded buckskin shirts, embroidered with exquisite designs, were carefully packed away, as were

the fringed, supple buckskin trousers. In their place went soft, comfortable old clothes made of greasy, soot-blackened buckskin that was no longer used for tepees.

"Wall, amigo," said Zack. "It's bin a right long time since we got us a send off like that 'un."

"I reckon," said Mose.

Zack looked at his friend, amazed again that they had become so close, since the two of them were so different. Zack was the more outgoing and outspoken of the two; he was always talking, spinning tales, discussing. Mose, on the other hand, hardly ever said a word that wasn't necessary. When they trapped together, Mose almost always let Zack do the storytelling around the campfire at night. Zack smiled, thinking that maybe this was why they had remained such good friends.

The differences between them were also in their builds. Zack was short and stocky, with a barrel chest and broad shoulders. Despite his lack of height, his arms and legs were thick with muscle. With his pitch-black hair hanging past his shoulders and the darkness of his weather-beaten skin, Zack could have almost passed for an Indian. But the mustache and full beard gave him away. The mustache was long and flowing, drooping thick and bushy over his mouth. He kept the mustache all year long, but the beard was usually reserved for the cold winter months, both for convenience and comfort.

Mose, on the other hand, was long and lean. His skeletal figure, though, belied a steel strength from tough, leathery sinews. His face, too, looked skeletal, with its pointed chin and nose. And Mose, though older than Zack, could scarcely grow facial hair. His beard, left to grow during the winter, was patchy and sparse, light brown, almost blond, like his hair which he also wore long and straight.

14

Mose climbed back on his horse and waited patiently for Zack. Quickly tying his sack closed, Zack remounted. Without a word, the two set off, traps clanking and leather saddles creaking. The late summer sun beat down on them, hot and blinding. But both knew it would not be too many more weeks before they broke out the thick buffalo robes or Hudson's Bay capotes.

CHAPTER 2

As the horse plodded across the broad, grassy plain, Zack mumbled to himself, "Damn. 'Shore hope Mose is feelin' some better'n me." He took a sideways glance at his friend, who rode quietly, his head up, his face in deep shadow, protected from the sun by the large, floppy-brimmed leather hat. In the monotony of the ride, head hurting, stomach aching, dull from tiredness, heat and hangover, Zack looked over his past with Mose. "'Member," he asked, "when we furst got to be trappers?"

Mose grunted another assent. Then he smiled.

Their first year as trappers had been almost more than they bargained for. The work was hard, long and often boring. The mountain streams were usually frigid, and they would wade out of them with legs that were blue from the cold. The food was sometimes bad, and there frequently was not enough to go around. He remembered talking to Mose about two months after the Captain had made them a part of the trapping party itself.

"This party's too damn big," he complained to Mose one night across the campfire. "That's jist too many folks hyar. Trappers, pork eaters, drovers, cooks, scouts, hunters. Hell, they cain't even keep us all fed. They kin kill off the game faster'n we kin trap

16

the beaver. An' that don't take but two, three days. It warn't so bad last year when we was swampers an' the party was smaller.''

''Ain't much ye kin do 'bout it,'' commented Mose.

''Guess ye're right,'' Zack said miserably.

And there were other problems. Since they had bought all their supplies on credit from the Captain, they were indebted to him. Every pelt they took went to the Captain to help pay off what they owed for the traps, horses, ammunition and the protection offered by the large trapping party. By the end of the first half-season, they were still in debt to him. But there was nothing they could do about that either—for the time being. Their chance came many months later. Before that, though, they had to become men. And they did that within a week.

They were out riding across the vast emptiness of the prairie, coming down out of the mountains to trade with some of the numerous tribes of Plains Indians. The party was strung out, stretched over a mile or more, when a large war party of Blackfeet were spotted. The Indians, knowing other trappers would be coming soon, charged, hoping to take some scalps before rescue came.

The column of trappers burst into action. ''Hyar's damp powder, boys, or I wouldn't say so,'' hollered one trapper. ''Lit's go git 'em, stid of waitin' hyar to be took.''

The mountain men raced off in a headlong dash toward the charging Indians. Zack and Mose, scared like they had never been before, were swept along with the tide.

Zack entered the swirling, frenzied fray, not knowing what to do. Fear clutched at his stomach and he had trouble breathing. He saw the other trappers ride into the surging cluster of Indians with rifle in one

17

hand and pistol in the other. He decided he should do likewise.

He almost choked on the dust that clogged his already constricted throat. Guns were going off and people were screaming. It was difficult for him to distinguish between the screams of pain and the war cries. He found he couldn't differentiate between the shouts of the Indians and those of the trappers. They all sounded alike.

He fired off his rifle needlessly at nothing, just to be doing something, to make some noise himself. His throat was too strangled for him to yell, and he was afraid of his own silence. He could barely see the other battlers, though he knew they were all around. Out of the swirling dust came an Indian hurtling toward him, coup stick raised, ready to strike.

Almost by instinct, Zack raised his pistol and fired. Hit at point blank range by a ball from Zack's horse pistol, the Indian was blown back off his mount by the force of the blast. The coup stick fell harmlessly to the ground.

Zack stopped his horse, and the full realization of what he had done hit him. Leaning over his horse, he vomited, retching until there was nothing left, heedless of the frenzied battle surrounding him.

Finished being sick, he looked up dully and realized the fight was over. The smoke and dust were clearing, and he could see the remaining Indians fleeing, pursued by the rest of the trappers. An older trapper Zack had come to know, pulled up beside him and said, "Nice goin', boy. I seed what ye did to that redskin." He looked over at the body. "Ain't ye gonna take his scalp?"

Zack smiled weakly. "Don't know's if I kin, Jim."

Jim Clancy was a large, jovial, red-faced man, whose boyish countenance belied his years and ex-

18

perience. "Feelin' poorly are ye, boy?" After Zack's affirmative nod, Clancy said, "I know how ye feel, Zack.'Felt the same way myself, first time. But ye'll git used to it. Ye'll have to, if ye plan to last out hyar. It ain't no place fer faint hearts. C'mon now, boy, go'n git the scalp. Once it's over, ye'll not feel so bad."

Zack again nodded, then dismounted. With faltering steps he walked toward the still-warm body. Looking down, he saw a youth not yet as old as himself. He again started to retch, his empty stomach refusing to quiet. He stumbled away. The other, older trappers roared with laughter. The only one not laughing was Mose, himself pale from sickness.

Later that night, as Zack talked with Mose, Clancy walked by and dropped a glistening, wet bundle at his feet. Zack picked up the bloody scalp and immediately dropped it.

"What was he?" asked Zack, still too squeamish to touch the fresh scalp.

"Blackfoot," answered Clancy, squatting down on his haunches. "Meanest, most orn'ry bunch of savages ye ary laid eyes on. Hate everbody, 'cept theyselves. Most Injuns ye kin usually parley with if they give ye a chance. But not them heathens. Ye gotta watch 'em all the time, boy."

"I'll do so," said Zack. He thought a minute. "Was arybody kilt?" he asked.

"Naw. Jist a couple of scratches on one or two of the boys is all."

"How many of 'em did we put under?"

"Don't rightly know. At least eight. But Injuns, all Injuns, try harder'n hell to git back their kilt and wounded. An' they take crazy risks to do it. Say the daid won't git to the happy huntin' ground 'thout a proper burial."

Clancy stretched himself up. "Ye larned a valuable lesson today, boys. Don't ye fergit it, neither." He walked away, muttering to himself as he always did.

The scalp lay for an hour at Zack's feet before he picked it up. The next morning he stretched it over a willow hoop to dry. When it was ready, he wore it proudly, dangling from his rifle, the old musket his father gave him so long ago.

Zack and Mose finished their entry into manhood less than a week later.

After the fight with the Blackfeet, the trappers headed south, keeping near the foothills of the Rockies. Early one afternoon, they spotted a group of Southern Cheyennes. Leaders of the trapping party went out to talk to the small group of proud warriors. And that evening the trappers camped about a mile or so from the Cheyenne village.

It was the first time Zack had ever been so close to a group of Indians except for the battle, and he was amazed. Now that he was a full member of the trapping party, a man who had counted coup and carried the scalp ripped from the head of an enemy, he went to the Indian village to visit, to sit near the large fire and watch the trading going on. He even traded a little on his own, passing out handfuls of beads, some awls, a couple of knives and other small trinkets in exchange for a few furs and a new buffalo fur cap he would always wear.

That night he got roaring drunk with Mose and a young Indian warrior. They had a fine spree, whooping and hollering and attempting to follow the Indian dances. They fell asleep under a tree.

"Damn," mumbled Zack the next morning, waking up where he had fallen the night before. Every muscle in his body ached, and he felt wretched. Even the icy cold water of the stream could not slack his thirst. But with some help, and the resilience of youth, the two recovered by the evening and were ready for another visit to the village. Today, they knew, would be another big parley and trade. The celebration of the night before, they were told, was to welcome the white mountain men. Tonight would be more serious business.

Zack and Mose rode into the village with a rickety-looking old trapper named Jeremiah Witherspoon. They sat and watched the trading, listening, trying to learn the Indian language, helped a little by Jeremiah. The old trapper had sparse hair on his head and a grizzled beard. By his own admission, he had been in the mountains forever. And he was a wonderful encyclopedia of useful knowledge. Clancy stopped over for a while, and between the two veterans, the young men soaked up a wealth of information.

Clancy and Jeremiah finally left the youths to themselves and, in an unusual display of patience, they sat unmoving, emulating their older counterparts, listening and watching. Later, the Captain and Jeremiah, along with Clancy, stopped by. "I got a surprise fer ye, boys," said the Captain. "Come along."

Zack and Mose hesitated, looking at the three mountain men. They shrugged and stood up to follow. They stopped at the opening of a small tepee.

Jeremiah cackled, "Go on in, boys. They's two squaws in thar waitin' fer ye. Ye have me blessin' and that of their fathers."

The two young men shuffled uncomfortably. "Wall, what are ye waitin' fer?" asked Clancy. "They's all ready fer ye, nice'n formal. Ain't nothin' to worry 'bout, 'cept makin' a leetle love to these hyar fine squaws. Ain't no Injuns gonna come bother ye. Now go on, git in thar."

The older trappers stood laughing. Zack, always the

more impetuous of the two, muttered, "Hell, why not?" and stepped through the opening.

Inside the dark tepee he could see two huddled figures, one on each side. It was the first time he had been inside an Indian lodge, and he was surprised by its size, cleanliness and comfort. Everything was in its place; the buffalo robes that served as bedding were neatly arranged along the skin walls; the full parfleche bags, the cooking pots—all the tools of an Indian's everyday life were carefully arranged in place.

One of the women beckoned to him shyly and addressed him in Cheyenne. He could hardly understand her. Putting on a brave front, he said, "Speak American, girl?"

"A little," she whispered. "And some Spanish."

He went to her and knelt down. He heard Mose enter the lodge and go haltingly toward the other woman. "What's yore name?" asked Zack.

She said it in Cheyenne, and Zack was able to make it out. She had given him the formal name used by the villagers: "She Who is Wind in the Morning." Then she asked, "And you?"

"Zachariah Dobson," he said softly. It seemed not the time to speak loudly.

The Indian woman, whom Zack now saw was quite young and pretty, had trouble with his name, the syllables foreign to her tongue. Zack laughed at her attempts at pronunciation. "Jist call me Zack," he finally said.

She had trouble with that name, too, but managed to at least make it understandable.

He took her in his arms. She smelled sweet to him, like herbs or something he could not quite recollect. It surprised him, as did many things these days. He had always thought Indian women would smell of bear grease and smoke and sweat, like the men had last night. He didn't know it then, but the Cheyennes were

22

a clean people and bathed often in the clear, cold streams. The women, and the men too sometimes, used herbs and plants to give themselves a clean, fresh odor.

Things became more urgent then, and he forgot about all the mysteries and surprises and abandoned himself to the pleasures of the woman.

He stayed with Wind-in-the-Morning until the trapping party left the Cheyenne village and headed back west toward the mountains two days later. He left, promising Windy, the name he now called her, that he would be back.

Zack's senses, always alert, brought him back from those long-gone days. He saw a small herd of buffalo grazing about half a mile away. Day's end was fast approaching, and he and Mose would have to make camp soon. They'd need some fresh meat. Mose had seen the buffalo, too. He pointed his rifle at a small hillock to their right. Zack nodded, and the two men, trailing their pack horses, headed that way at a quick trot. They tethered the pack horses behind the protective covering of the hill, and circled around the other side of it, coming out much nearer to the herd. Approaching the dark mass of beasts from the downwind side, they walked the horses slowly. The herd mainly faced away from them and paid the two no heed.

"Wanna run 'em, or shoot 'em from a stand?" asked Zack.

"Ye kin run 'em, if'n ye want, but this chile's too damn hungover to be chasin' no bufflers. I'm jist gonna git close enough to shoot me some fresh meat."

"If that's whar yore stick floats, I guess mine does too. But let's git a move on. I kin almost taste them roasted tongue and ribs already."

They got to within fifty yards of the herd before the

animals began to get restless. They waited until the bison quieted down, then they dismounted and walked another ten yards closer. "Ye take the shot," said Zack as the two threw themselves prone on the ground. "I don't think my head kin stand the noise."

Mose nodded and sighted down the long barrel of his rifle. Zack, rifle primed and ready to fire, kept watch. Anyone who had ever spent time in the mountains kept a loaded rifle ready in case of unforeseen problems. Zack didn't figure on Mose missing his shot, but there was always the chance that his target would move.

Mose's big rifle boomed, and a large cow dropped in its tracks. The rest of the herd started, but remained standing in their places. "Stupid buffler," commented Zack.

The two moutain men remounted and headed toward the herd. Suddenly they both fired off a pistol and raced screaming toward the shaggy beasts. The buffalo, finally startled, ran, lumbering across the grassy sward, leaving the dead cow to be butchered.

Zack and Mose sat howling with laughter, ignoring their aching heads, knowing full well the herd would be miles away before its members stopped running.

Zack looked up at the sky. "It's gittin' late, amigo. We'd best git some meat and make tracks."

They butchered the buffalo, taking only the ribs, tongue, hump and liver. The rest was left to the wolves, coyotes and the buzzards, already circling above. Indian fashion, they ate the beast's liver raw. And they drank a little of the animal's blood to slack their thirst. As they worked, their eyes and ears caught every movement and sound. Though they were not conscious of their alertness, they knew all that went on around them. Failure to do so could mean a sudden and painful death.

Wrapping the dripping meat in a piece of the buffalo's hide, they remounted and went back to get the pack animals.

"How 'bout we camp by that small grove of trees by the tiny brook 'bout a mile from hyar?" asked Zack. "It's near and downright comfortable."

Mose nodded in agreement. They rode off and were soon at the place where they would spend the night. "Looks like somebody's bin hyar jist a leetle while ago," said Zack as they dismounted.

Mose nodded. "Yep. Looks like a small band of Shoshonis. Hope they ain't lurkin' about. I ain't aimin' to spend this whole night up watchin' the horses."

They started making camp; a fire was built, the horses were rubbed down, fed and hobbled, firewood was gathered. It was almost dark when they finished. Throwing some meat on the fire, Zack asked, "How far ye think we came today?"

Mose flopped down near the fire. Zack did likewise. "Oh, 'bout fifteen, twenty miles, I reckon."

"We made good time."

"Yep."

They were silent, watching the flames flicker around the shanks of meat which dripped into the fire. Soon, the two were gnawing on half-singed ribs, grease sliding down their chins and hands. "R'member when we left the Cap'n?" asked Zack.

"Shore." Mose tossed the bone he had been munching on into the darkness and reached for another rib. "That was shore some years ago now, warn't it?"

"It was. Bin nigh on 'bout eleven years now. We was still some green then, warn't we?"

Mose laughed quietly. "'Bout like the grass."

They had stayed on with the Captain for two years as trappers. But after four years with the party, they were disgusted. Working the trap lines one day, Zack brought it up. "How long we bin trappin' fer the Cap'n now, Mose?"

"Been close to two years now, I reckon. Why?"

"I'm gittin' godalmighty tired of allus bein' in debt to 'em. Ever pelt we take goes to the Cap'n, and ever year we're still behind. He's got us in debt fer the rest of our lives, and that don't shine with this coon, no sirree."

"Ain't much we kin do 'bout it, now is that?"

"Mebbe, Mose. Mebbe." He grumbled some more and went back to his work. But he was always on the watch for an opportunity.

It came a week later. They were out working their trap lines when Mose hissed, "Quiet. I hear somethin'."

Zack knew better than to question Mose's hearing. Silently they climbed to the top of the river bank and cautiously looked around. A short distance ahead, they spotted a war party of eight Crows, almost out of their element high up here in the mountains.

"Hyar's our chance," whispered Zack.

Mose looked at him, puzzled.

"What we're gonna do," said Zack earnestly, "is take them Injuns. We'll kill us a couple, if'n we kin, and then steal their pelts and horses. Then we kin sell 'em to the Cap'n and buy our way outta his contract. It ain't usual to see a war party carryin' so many pelts. Guess they must've jist raided somebody and made off with 'em."

Mose looked dumbfounded at his companion. "Ye're crazy, Zack Dobson. They's eight of them and only two of us. Ye're gonna lose our hair fer us, shore, is what ye're gonna do."

"Naw, I ain't. Ye know's well as I do that Injuns don't like to git kilt any more'n we do. And they like the odds in their favor. If'n we kin kill off that chief

26

thar, the one with all the feathers, and mebbe one or two more, they'll skedaddle, leavin' us with those extry horses which they took from somebody else, and them two horses loaded with pelts.''

''I still think it's a damnfool thing to do, but if'n that's whar yore stick floats, I guess I'll jist have to throw in with ye.''

They killed two of the Crows before the Indians could react. The Indians charged the embankment and two more died. One of the Crows shouted something in his native language.

''What'd he say, Mose?''

''He said he thinks thar's a whole party of trappers hyar, and he's tellin' 'em to git.''

The Crows gathered up their dead and fled, leaving the stolen horse herd and the loaded pack horses. They would, as Zack had thought, leave them all behind so they would not be overburdened in their flight.

''Yahoo!'' shouted Zack, doing a little war dance. ''See, Mose, I tole ye we could do it. We shore made 'em come now, or I wouldn't say so.''

Even Mose was smiling. ''We shore did shine now, yes sirree.''

They each lifted a heavy bundle of furs off the horses and then set about digging a cache to bury some of the pelts. They were experts at it. When they were finished, they themselves would have a hard time finding the spot.

''That's a right smart idee ye had, Mose. If'n the Cap'n knew we had all these plews, he'd never let us be free till he got all of 'em.''

''That's what I figgered. If'n ye go down thar and tell 'em we only got a few, he might let us go if'n we turn 'em all over to 'im. Then we kin come back hyar later and pick up the rest of the pelts. Then either sell 'em at the rendezvous, or down to Santy Fe.''

They split up. Mose was to stay and guard the extra horses, while Zack headed back to the camp and tried to bargain their way out of the Captain's contract.

Zack rode into an almost deserted camp; most of the men were out on the trap lines or else hunting. The few left in camp sat around playing half-hearted games of hand or three-card monte. One or two sat repairing equipment.

Zack handed the horse over to one of the swampers and strode purposefully over to the Captain's tent. He stuck his head through the flaps. "Kin I see ye fer a minnit, Cap'n?"

"Why shore, Zack. What kin I do fer ye?" He put aside the ledger he had painstakingly been filling in with his tight scrawl. It was one of the rare days when he welcomed a break from the tedious bookkeeping.

"Wall," said Zack. "Me 'n Mose bin doin' some thinkin'." He sat on an old stump that served as a chair and pulled out the pipe he had started smoking only a year ago. The Captain waited patiently while he fired it up, deliberate in his motions. Pipe going, Zack continued, "Me'n Mose bin with ye fer 'bout four years now, Cap'n, an' we ain't gittin' ahead a'tall. Ever pelt we take goes straight to ye to pay off what we owe ye. Then we gotta go in debt agin fer the next year."

"Ye git the same contract as everbody else, Zack."

He started to continue, but Zack cut him off. "I know that, an' we appreciate everthing ye done fer us. Now, ye've taken right good care of us whilst we bin with ye; supplyin' us with food and powder and ball an' traps an' all. Yes sir, ye've shore bin good to us, or I wouldn't say so. But we'd kinda like to git out on our own, Cap'n. Work fer ourselves a leetle."

The Captain's face went benevolently stern, like that of a concerned parent. "That's right commend-

28

able, Zack. I'm proud of ye both. But ye seem to be fergittin' that ye and yore friend owe me a heap of dollars fer all the supplies I sold ye on credit fer the season.''

"Naw, Cap'n. I ain't fergittin' that. That's why I'm hyar. To buy outta our contracts.''

The Captain looked surprised but wary. "Whar'd ye git that kind of specie, boy? Ye bin holdin' out on me? Don't ye fergit, everthing ye got belongs to me.'' He looked hard at Zack.

Zack stared right back at him. "Me'n Mose came into some goods hyar a leetle while ago, an' we was thinkin' we might be able to buy our way out.''

"Whar'd ye git the supplies, boy? Steal 'em?'' The Captain's hand clenched.

"Ain't yore concern, Cap'n. Me'n Mose took 'em fair an' square an' we kin use 'em any way we want. We got some horses an' some pelts we'd like to trade with ye, an' I figger we kin do some bizness.'' He paused briefly. "If'n ye're willin', of course.'' But his dark eyes glittered, telling the Captain he would brook no argument.

"How many horses ye got, boy?''

"Enough, I reckon. We gonna bargain?''

The Captain, seeing the look in Zack's eyes, knew he was beaten. "All right, Zack. We'll make a deal. But I hope ye stick with the party till the end of the season at least, an' offer me first chance to buy yore pelts. I'll pay prime fer 'em.''

"I think mebbe we kin do that, Cap'n. But if'n we git a better price fer our plews somewhar else, we'll take 'em thar.''

"Wall, now, Zack, that's only fair. At least ye're givin' me first chance. I cain't ask fer more'n that.''

They bartered and argued good naturedly for more than an hour before the bargain was struck. Zack was excited, but he calmly shook hands with the Captain, thanked him and leisurely walked over to the corral to get his horse. He knew he had won and felt manly pride in the fact. Mounted, he trotted the horse slowly to the edge of the camp. There, the boy that still lurked inside the man, came out. "Yahoo!" he screamed as loud as he could and took off on a dead run for his rendezvous with Mose.

He ran the horse at full speed over the dips and rises of the prairie. As he neared the meeting point, he pulled the horse first to the left and then to the right, back and forth in a zigzag pattern. It was a trick he had learned from the Indians. The fast zigzag was used when there was good news. When there was bad news or danger, the rider would speed to the camp in a straight line. Mose stood on a slight rise, looking toward the trappers' camp three miles away. He had spotted Zack zigzagging toward him at a reckless pace, and knew he was free.

Zack pulled up the horse in a jolting cloud of dust and tumbled off. "We did it, Mose. We did it." He jumped around in a combination war dance and jig, circling Mose and shouting, "We're free, we're free!"

Mose let him get it out of his system. He was excited himself, but too reserved to show it. When Zack calmed down a bit, Mose said, "Tell it."

"Wall," said Zack sitting down by the small fire Mose had built up. He reached into the fire and grabbed a hunk of the rabbit that was roasting there. He yelped when he burned his fingers on the hot meat. But he began eating it right away, the grease dripping down his chin and hands. "He were a leetle upset when I first tole him, but he got used to the idee right quick. I took so long cause we was dickerin'."

Zack ripped off another hunk of rabbit. "Anyways," he continued, "we git to keep the pelts he don't know 'bout, plus two horses each, our traps, some powder and ball and enough small tradin' supplies to last out the season. Barely. We'll have to take it easy on the tradin'. He's almost got us over a barrel. We ain't got nowhars near enough tradin' supplies to trade fer a lot of pelts, so we're jist gonna have to do a lot of trappin' afore the end of the season if'n we want to git enough to outfit us fer next season.''

Zack wiped his greasy hands and face with some grass after tossing away the bones. "I think the Cap'n figgers if we cain't trade fer pelts, an' we stick with him till the end of the season like I tole him we would, then we won't have any dollars fer supplies next year an' we'll hitch up with his outfit again. But I'd ruther work as a clerk back in some store in St. Louis or down in Taos afore I sign up fer another year with that thief.''

"Me too," said Mose quietly. "But what d'ye mean ye tole him we'd stay on with him till the end of the season? I thought we was free now.''

"We are. But I tole the Cap'n we'd stay with his party, as free trappers, mind ye, till the end of the season. I did it fer our protection, Mose. Ye know we'd probably not be bothered by Injuns as long as we're with a party this big. An' I don't reckon we're quite ready yet to leave out on our own.''

Mose grunted. "I reckon ye're right. It's good thinkin', but I don't know's I like it much.''

"Ye worry too much, amigo. 'Sides, I tole him we'd give 'im first crack at buyin' our pelts, but if'n we found a better price fer 'em, then we'd take it. We still got quite a few plews hyar in the cache that he don't know about, an' that'll help us out some.''

Mose cracked a grin. "Wall, ye're right now, or I wouldn't say so. That ole buzzard thinks he's got us in a hole, but we'll show 'im. Yessirree, we will. It's good ye tole 'im we might take our plewssomewhar else. I figger he was gonna try'n take us thataway too. He still might if we ain't nowhars whar we kin trade 'em.''

"I ain't too werried. He needs supplies, too. So I figger he's gotta stop at the rendezvous, or head on into Mexican territory afore the season ends. We kin sell 'em thar, if need be.''

Mose laughed. "That was shore some time ago. We seen a mite of country since then.''

Zack joined in the laughter. "An' The Cap'n was shore some put out when we sold our plews to that Mexican trader fer twice as much as he was offerin'. I reckon we showed that ole coon. I purely loved the look on his face when he saw all them pelts we had hid in the cache. I thought he was gonna go loco on us.''

The two men finished their pipes in quiet laughter. Mose stood and stretched. "Wall, amigo. It's shut-eye time fer this chile. Mornin' comes early.''

They rolled into the thick, brown buffalo robes. Without another thought of the possible danger of lurking Indians, they fell asleep.

CHAPTER 3

They were up and gone before first light. They felt better this day; their bodies were still young and healthy enough to quickly fight off the effects of their spree.

The air on this late August morning was already sweltering. They stripped down to buckskin trousers, allowing the sun and the never-ceasing wind to toughen their already hard skin. They were constantly on the alert, eyes always moving, searching out the slightest movement. The breaking of a twig, the hurried flight of an eagle or rabbit, told a whole story to the trappers. Vigilance was second nature to them now. It was a part of their being.

Despite the unconscious wariness, they were lost in thoughts of their own. The boredom of the ride made them drowsy, and they rode slack-jawed, eyes drooping. But their senses continued working, taking in the most minute signs, interpreting them instantly and correctly. They had seen the results of a trapper's loss of concentration. More than once they had come upon the body of one, stripped naked, scalped and mutilated. They were passing through the country of the hostile Blackfeet, where danger waited at every turn. And, too, they still had to traverse the country of the Crows who, while often friendly to the whites, were known to attack small parties of trappers for their pelts, horses or scalps.

That fact was almost constantly on the minds of the two mountain men, as they rode across the emptiness of the prairie with nothing in sight save an occasional small stand of trees, a herd of fleeing elk, a grazing herd of buffalo and the mountains miles and miles to the west.

"Hear 'bout the Crows?" Mose asked.

"Shore. At rendezvous. They're probably madder'n hornets now, after gittin' whipped by both the Pawnees and the Sioux. I shore ain't hankerin' to meet up with any of them varmints right now."

"They kin be mean's snakes when they's angry," said Mose. "And some of them young bucks is gonna be right bent on raisin' some hair."

But their journey went along uneventfully. They crossed the Absaroka homeland of the Crows and entered the friendly country of the Cheyennes. But still they could not relax. It was also a land where the hostile Kiowas, Pawnee, Osage and Utes were known to roam.

While there, they ran across a small war party of Shoshonis, heading back to their mountain home. They stopped to trade with the Shoshonis and learned that the Kiowas had also counted coup on the Crows that year and had taken a number of scalps from the Utes far to the west.

"They'll more'n likely be peaceable then," said Zack, who knew he'd be skirting Kiowa territory on his way up to the mountains.

Mose grunted. "The Kiowa ain't ever peaceable, but mebbe they won't be so anxious fer blood. They've raised hair, an' mebbe they'll not be on the warpath. But still, they's jist as bad as the Blackfeet. Ye jist cain't be shore of what they're gonna do."

For a week they traveled south before turning east near the head of the Arkansas River. They followed the Arkansas for two days, before turning southward again. Near the headwaters of the Apishapa River, they spotted a small herd of buffalo.

"We'll be goin' our own way soon, Zack, an' I figger we outta make at least a leetle meat now, whilst the buffler's handy and we kin help each other. Jist in case."

Zack nodded agreement. "But this time let's run 'em. I ain't run no buffler since spring."

Mose grinned. "I were thinkin' the same."

They made a small camp and ran the buffalo, shooting more than they could ever use. For a few days they lingered, eating fresh buffalo meat, while strips of the tasty flesh hung on hastily constructed drying racks. The meat would be turned into jerky so the two men would have at least a small supply for the winter, in case their Indian friends did not have too much luck on the fall hunt.

Three days later Mose said to Zack, "I figger we got enough meat fer now, amigo. 'Sides, I'm hankerin' to be movin' on. The cold'll be hyar afore long."

Zack nodded, knowing what was coming, and was saddened by it.

"So I reckon I'll be movin' on tomorrow," added Mose.

Zack nodded again, puffing silently on his pipe. It was always thus, he thought.

The next morning, Zack sat on the appaloosa and watched as his friend rode out west, heading toward the distant mountains. When the other man was no more than a speck on the horizon, Zack turned his horse toward the southeast. He would enter the mountains later. As he rode, he thought of the first time he and Mose had gone their own ways.

They had left the Captain's party near Santa Fe, down in Mexican land. They spent a few weeks in that Spanish town enjoying their freedom and the civilized life; the fine, though burning hot Spanish food; the liquor, raw and undiluted; and most of all, the pretty, dark-haired señoritas.

But the rich life quickly faded with their money, and they left out with a small group of free trappers from Taos and Santa Fe. These were real beaver men, as wild and savage as the Indians and the wilderness they struggled with.

"Jist remember," said the grizzled leader of the party. "Ye're still green, an' we 'spect ye to keep yore place. Jist keep yore mouths shet and listen."

They happily agreed, knowing they'd learn much more by watching and listening instead of talking.

And learn they did. They learned about the Indians—which ones could be trusted most of the time and which ones couldn't; and about the signs of the wilderness, and how to read those signs quickly and correctly, without conscious thought; how to survive a raging blizzard on the open prairie or in a snow-choked mountain pass; and how to ride out one of the sudden, horrifyingly intense rainstorms and the surging, almost instantaneous floods the rains brought. And there were a thousand other minute details they needed to know if they were to survive in the fur trade. They learned more in the first six months with the tightly-knit little group of free trappers than they had in all the time they were with the Captain.

Then the old hands, many of them French Canadians who had drifted down into Spanish territory long before the Americans, began slowly to accept the newcomers. Their tight circle of friends opened briefly to accept Zack and Mose and closed around them again. The two felt secure in that little circle; somehow special, apart from the rest of the world. They had been out eight months when Zack became Old Zack, and fully accepted into the small band of mountain men.

A lone trapper from their party was riding a little ahead of the rest of the men, searching for game. Their supply of meat was running low, and hunters regularly drifted a little ahead or off to one side, looking for fresh meat. The rest of the men plodded along, numb with weariness. The April sun felt comfortingly warm after the bitter winter that still lurked in the mountains.

They snapped to attention when they heard a shout from the hunter who was racing back toward them. When he got close enough to be heard, he shouted, "Blackfeet!" That one word sent a ripple of shock through the men. Zack's heart sank, thuddingly, into his stomach. He had had many encounters with various Indians since his first battle, but none were so tenacious and bloodthirsty as the Blackfeet.

"Damn," muttered one of the trappers. "This hyar's damp powder, or I wouldn't say so. Eighteen year I bin in these mountains, an' now I'm finally gonna lose my hair. Damn Blackfeet, they're out awful early this year, lookin' fer hair."

"I ain't werried," shouted another trapper. "We bin in worse spots than this afore. An' this chile ain't about to lose his hair 'thout takin' some of his own off'n some of them redskins."

"Both of ye shet yore traps," bellowed Jim Hickory, the oldimer who led the group. "We're in a fix, an' they's no use in sayin' nay to it. Was they close, George?" he asked the hunter. Hickory had been in the western mountains more than twenty years, drifting down to Spanish territory with the early French trappers even before Lewis and Clark left from St. Louis on their historic two-year journey.

George, the hunter, was about to answer when he

pointed toward the horizon. "See fer yoreself," he said.

The men looked up and saw about thirty painted Blackfoot warriors grouping on a bluff about a mile away.

"Damn," spat Hickory. "We're in a fix fer shore, boys, or I wouldn't say so. Our onliest chance is to git to them trees yonder an' hope we kin hold 'em off. Gather them pack animals up close together, and we'll make a beeline fer 'em."

The men hurried to tie the pack horses and mules close together and tighten the few loose packs. Hickory shouted, "Let's move," only seconds before the leader of the Blackfoot band let go a war cry that swept over the flat land.

The trappers reached the woods and rapidly hobbled the horses and mules in a thicket. With curses in various tongues, the trappers flung themselves to the ground or behind trees. The Indians raced to within fifty yards of the stand before pulling up their horses in a flurry of flying hooves, dust and war cries.

"Hold stiddy," cautioned Hickory. "When they git close enough, ever other man shoot. Allus keep half the guns ready."

"Ain't no call fer ye to tell us that," said George. "We fought Injuns afore."

"Wall, now," shot out Hickory, "I'm jist aimin' to make shore ye're able to fight Injuns another day."

The Indians pulled back a ways and regrouped. Again they attacked, screeching horribly, the ululating sounds stretching out across the prairie. As they neared, they dropped off to one side of their mounts and rode in close to the trappers, firing rifles and arrows as they remained hidden behind the walls of horseflesh.

They circled around and readied themselves once again for a third assault.

"Hold stiddy," said Hickory again. "They's jist tryin' to skeer us. Next time it'll be fer real."

As the Blackfeet rested their horses, they shouted insults at the trappers, calling them cowards, women and worse. One young warrior, brightly emblazoned with red paint on chest and face, trotted closer to the mountain men. From there, he taunted the white men, shouting for them to come out from behind the trees and fight him.

One of the trappers muttered quietly, "Ride in a leetle closer, amigo, an' ye'll lose yore hair, fer shore."

With a sudden shriek, the Indians charged again, the taunting young brave leading the way. This time they rode upright, unafraid of the men who hid behind trees, unwilling to face the fierce Blackfeet in the open.

Hickory whispered over the din, "Now we'll git 'em. Hold stiddy, boys, till they's closer."

The men held their breaths, watching the charge. The Indians rode closer and closer. Zack could see the hideously painted faces and could almost smell the bear grease rubbed on their bodies. He didn't know what was louder, the pounding of his heart or the thud of the horses' hooves.

Suddenly Hickory yelled, "Now!"

Some of the guns roared and, while they were hastily reloaded, the other trappers took aim, ready to fire. The first volley killed two of the Indians and wounded a few more.

The Blackfeet pulled up in consternation, quickly wheeled, picked up their fallen brothers and rode out of range of the deadly long rifles of the mountain men.

"Now that's fat cow, or I wouldn't say so," whooped one of the trappers.

"C'mon, ye heathens. Try agin, an' we'll take yore hair," shouted another one.

The Indians again charged, this time using their

horses once more as shields. The trappers fired when they could, but with little effect. The Indians rode, circling, never ceasing, not allowing the trappers a clear shot. As they circled, the Blackfeet were more accurate. Two of the mountain men were wounded by arrows. The Indians continued to circle, wheeling their horses, firing sporadically. Mose suddenly collapsed with a grunt.

"Mose!" shouted Zack, kneeling over his friend.

"Watch them Injuns," Mose snapped, "afore ye git yoreself shot." He lay back, gasping for breath.

Zack, anxious for his friend, stood and again took his place behind the tree. Though he was worried, he figured that if Mose could mouth off to him like that, he'd probably make it.

Finally Hickory yelled, "This ain't gittin' us nowhar. Shoot fer the horses, boys. Put 'em afoot."

It worked. While half the trappers kept their guns loaded, the others slaughtered Blackfoot horses. Two volleys were enough. By then the Blackfeet had lost eight horses and another warrior killed. They picked up their dead and dying and fled.

"Wahoo!" yelled one of the men. "That's tellin' 'em. Damned savages. That'll larn 'em not to mess with no Taos beaver men."

The rest of the men threw up their heels in a war dance of their own making. Then they turned to their wounded. The first two had only superficial wounds, but Mose's chest was covered with blood.

"Jim!" yelled Zack. "Mose looks like he's hurt bad."

The other men gathered around, muttering to each other. Mose's buckskin shirt was blood-soaked, and he was having trouble breathing. "Cut his shirt off," ordered Hickory.

Zack sliced through the greasy, slippery buckskin. Mose stayed tight-lipped, though he grunted softly in pain a few times. One of the few Blackfeet warriors with rifles had gotten lucky. The ball had smashed into Mose's breastbone, breaking it, and then lodged in the chest cavity.

"This hyar's damp powder," mumbled one of the men. "He's a gonner fer shore."

Zack leaped up and flattened the beaver man with one quick punch. His knife flashed in the sunlight. "Don't ye never say that. He ain't daid, an' I ain't gonna let him die. Ye understand me?"

The man looked up at Zack towering above him. He rubbed his jaw. He saw the long, heavy blade and Zack's determined face. "Shore, Zack. Shore. Anythin' ye say, amigo. Jist put that Green River back now. I didn't mean nothin'."

Zack sheathed the knife and turned back to Mose. He looked at Hickory. "Kin ye do anythin' fer him, Jim?"

Hickory slowly shook his head. "Don't know's thar's much to do, Zack. 'Cept mebbe try'n git that ball outta his chest. Then all we kin do is wait an' see."

Some of the men grumbled. With beaver still carrying winter fur higher up in the mountains, the men were loath to miss out on the bounty, having to lie in wait while Mose either recovered or died. None liked the idea, either, that they might become sitting ducks for another, larger war party of bloodthirsty Blackfeet.

Zack nodded at Hickory's words. "Ye git that ball outta thar, an' if he's still alive, I'll git him back to Taos or Santy Fe, whar he kin git some proper doctorin'."

"Ye're crazy, Zack," said George. "It's better'n a thousand mile back to Santy Fe. An' across hostile Injun country, too. Ye'll not make it by yoreself, boy."

"He lives through gittin' that ball outta his chest,

41

I'll make it with him to Santy Fe.'' He turned toward Hickory. ''Wall, what're ye waitin' fer? Do it.''

Hickory nodded once, mind made up. He figured Mose would die when he tried to carve the hunk of lead out of his chest, but there was no other choice. If he lived, Zack would get him back to Spanish territory, if he could. And if the two died on the journey, well, there was little he could do about it. He had all the other men of the party to think about.

''All right, Zack,'' he said. ''He's yore friend. Somebody git the whiskey an' dose 'im good. I ain't gonna try an' git that ball outta him 'thout 'im bein' dosed real good.''

One of the men handed over a jug of trading whiskey, not yet cut with river water or sweetened with honey. Almost pure alcohol, it would knock Mose out quickly.

Another trapper said, ''Me'n George'll git some bark ye kin use fer a poultice.''

While Zack forced the whiskey down Mose's throat, Hickory heated his Green River knife in a hastily made fire. Zack finally called him. ''Jim, I think he's had enough. Ye kin start now.''

The operation was over more quickly that Zack had thought possible, and Hickory looked at the small round ball he held in his hand. ''Wall, I got it. Ye kin bandage 'em up now, boys.''

Two of the men quietly and gently poulticed up the wound with crushed, watered-down bark and beaver hair. Then they bandaged it with some of the soft-weaved fabric they carried with them for trading.

They stayed the night there. It was a restless night. Between caring for the injured Mose, who tossed and turned with fever, and trying to keep a careful watch out, should the Blackfeet return, the men got little sleep. But when morning rose, Mose was still alive.

He was mostly unconscious and his breathing was irregular, but he was alive.

"I nary would've believed it," said George. "I thought he'd of gone under fer shore afore now." The others, too, shook their heads in wonder.

The trappers took the time to make a travois for Mose and gave Zack the best pack horse they had to pull it. Gently they tied Mose into the travois. When Zack mounted up, Hickory came over to him and handed him a small package. "Hyar's some extry powder fer ye, amigo. Ye may need it."

Zack mumbled his thanks, and Hickory continued. "Wall, then. Ye'd best not delay too long. The best way to go is down past the Stinkin' Water and then head east of the Wind River Range toward the North Platte. Head south across the Colorado an' then on down to the Rio Grande. Ye git that far, an' ye're almost home."

Zack nodded.

"Ye got enough food to last ye?"

Zack nodded again.

"We'll take keer of yore furs fer ye both. If ye cain't find us afore the season's over, we'll either sell 'em at rendezvous or down in Mexican territory, if we git that fur south. Then we'll bank yore dollars fer ye."

Zack nodded once more and turned his horse toward the south. The shouts of good luck from the other trappers rang in his ears as he trotted away.

Three weeks later he staggered into Taos. He'd made more than 1,200 miles, but he didn't think he'd make the extra sixty miles to Santa Fe. Mose had managed to survive the trek, and Zack handed him over to the care of a Dr. Sanchez. Then he stumbled, bleary-eyed, to the nearest adobe hotel and collapsed. He slept for twenty-four hours. Refreshed, he trimmed

43

his full beard and even decided on a bath, his first of both in some months. Then he went to see Dr. Sanchez.

"How is he, Doc?" Zack asked in badly broken Spanish.

The medical man winced at the crude attempt at his native language and said in impeccable English, "He will live. But it will be some time before he is able to move about. He is a very lucky young man." Only the slightest trace of a Spanish accent could be heard in his speech.

Zack reverted to his normal way of speaking. "Kin I see him?"

"Si. But he is still asleep. Do not disturb him."

Zack stepped into the austere room and gasped. He had been so exhausted at the end of the trip that he had not noticed how Mose had looked. He had only known that Mose was alive and they were in Taos. Now he was shocked to see his friend's condition. The usually gaunt face was shrunken even more. He looked haggard and gray.

Turning to the doctor, Zack asked, "Are ye shore he's gonna make it? He don't look none too good to me."

"Si. He will live."

"Bueno," said Zack. "If'n ye say so, I'll take ye at yore word."

Four days later, Mose was awake when Zack went to see him. "How're ye doin', amigo?" Zack shouted when he entered the room.

Mose's voice, never loud, was a mere whisper. "I'm jist fine. How're ye?"

"Feelin' fat an' lazy now, or I wouldn't say so."

"The doc tole me what ye done to git me back hyar, Zack. He said he didn't know which one of us looked the worse. I shore am obliged."

"Hell, twarn't nothin', amigo," said Zack, shuffling in embarrassment. "Ye would've done the same fer me."

"More'n likely." Mose looked like he had fallen asleep again, and Zack waited patiently. Mose drew a deep breath and opened his eyes. "Look, Zack," he whispered. "I ain't goin' nowhar fer quite a spell. Ain't no reason why ye should wait fer me hyar. Ye need to git back to the mountains and make some dollars, amigo. Whyn't ye go on off trappin' an' come back hyar jist before next winter sets in?"

"Hell, Mose. Ain't no reason fer me to head up into the mountains now."

"Wall, now. It's only the beginnin' of May. Ye kin still catch some of the last of the winter beaver high up. It'll help make up fer what ye lost in bringin' me hyar. 'Sides, ye still got time to make rendezvous. It won't be startin' fer another month or so, the way I figger it."

Zack's eyes brightened. "Ye shore ye'll be all right hyar by yoreself?"

"Sartin. Doc'll take good keer of me."

"All right, amigo. I'll leave what money I kin with the doc to pay fer yore treatment an' in case ye need anything. I'll be back afore the new season starts in the fall with enough furs fer both of us. Then we kin have a right proper fandango."

Mose nodded wearily and closed his eyes as Zack left.

It was Zack's first real time alone in the mountains, and he loved it. He took his time, trapping as he went high in the Sangre de Christo Mountains and then north toward the Wind River Range, but he didn't get that far. This high up, the beaver still wore winter pelts.

Despite his usual love of company and talk, he found that he liked the solitude and lonely splendor of being among the high peaks by himself. He never did make rendezvous, taking time to explore some of the beaver-filled streams he had often heard about or only glanced briefly on his way through, but had never had the time to trap.

He occasionally stopped with a tribe of friendly Indians, to feast a little and talk; to learn the news of the mountains. But he stayed only a little while and then drifted off on his own again.

But being alone also had its dangers. Indian attacks were more likely for a solitary mountain man, and the late spring blizzards that struck suddenly were not safe to weather alone. Zack cursed and grumbled whenever one hit.

As the days grew longer and hotter, he did less trapping. Summer pelts, he knew, would not bring a very good price. It was the thick, glossy winter pelts that brought in the money. So he traveled along, drifting from stream to stream, mountain range to mountain range. He found that he knew a lot more about the wilderness than he had thought he did. Free from the restraints of being the youngest man in a party of experienced trappers, he saw that he knew more and could do more than they had given him credit for.

At the end of the summer, he slowly wound his way back down from the mountains and into Taos. He rode in with only one pack horse loaded with furs. With the pelts he had taken before Mose got hurt, he had had a good season, so he rode into the town in high style.

As he came roaring in, guns blazing, he spotted some of the men from Hickory's party. One of them yelled, "Hey, Zack. Zack Dobson. Hyar's yore amigos. Welcome home."

George called to him too. "Hey, looky hyar. It's old Zack Dobson fresh returned from the mountains."

Zack grinned and waved, but kept riding in. He stopped at Dr. Sanchez's. First, he thought, he'd check on Mose. Then would come the spree.

But he was disappointed.

"Your friend recovered much more quickly than I had expected. I could keep him here no longer. He is truly a remarkable man."

"He say whar he was goin'?"

"No, he just arranged credit with one of the traders, packed up and left. He was quite untalkative, your friend."

"Usually is. Do I owe ye any money, Doc?"

"No, what you left was more than sufficient. What was left I gave to your friend before he left."

"Bueno. Thanks."

Zack traded in his furs and joined the others in their spree. But something was lacking. A feeling of sadness was on him, and he did not enjoy the women, the whiskey or the gambling as much as he had in the past. It was the first time in more than five years that he and Mose had not had a spree together, and he felt at a loss without his old friend.

But it would not keep him from ruffling a few feathers. He reveled in the knowledge that he was no longer considered a greenhorn. The word had already traveled through the mountains. The men knew of his solitary, gut-wrenching trip across the mountains to get Mose to a doctor. Yes, they knew, and he took boisterous pride in the fact.

Zack spent more than a month in Taos, waiting for Mose to return. But it was near the end of August, later than he usually left, and he could wait no longer. Zack figured his friend was planning to winter in the mountains. Most of the other mountain men had either left or were preparing to leave.

Hickory looked up Zack one day in the saloon. "Howdy, amigo," he said, joining Zack at the otherwise empty table. "Ye leavin' soon?"

"Hadn't thought much on it, but I reckon so."

"Wall, amigo. Me'n the boys're leavin' day after

tomorrow, and we'd surely like to have a man like ye throw in with us.''

''That's mighty genrous of ye, Jim. But I think not. Mebbe next season.''

''Sorry to hear it, Zack. But if that's whar yore stick floats, so be it.''

Zack thought about it, and two days later was waiting in the pre-dawn chill outside of town when the trappers rode up, led by Hickory. ''Mind if I join ye fellows?''

''Not at all, Zack. Mighty glad to have ye with us,'' said Hickory. ''Let's ride.''

Zack, considered an old-timer now, was treated with more respect. And he had fewer of the unpleasant chores to do. But it wasn't long before he realized he liked the solitary life rather than trapping with a party, even a small one like Hickory's. He'd travel only with Mose from now on, he decided. Despite his outgoing personality, he realized he disliked the noise and confusion and the constant camaraderie. The flaring tempers, quickened by the bitterness of winter, became a constant irritation to him. He yearned for the high silence of the majestic peaks, the soft whisper of a rushing stream overflowing with beaver.

The desire for solitude became even more urgent when Zack's old friend Jeremiah Witherspoon went under. Jeremiah, too, had finally left the Captain. The old brigade leader headed back east, pockets full of money, to throw in with other rich fur men. So Jeremiah drifted down into Taos, where he picked up with a small group of free trappers. Finally he ended up in Hickory's little group.

''I'd be right proud if ye was to be my partner,'' Zack said as they left Taos that first day.

Jeremiah laughed his high cackling laugh. ''Ye've shore growed up a mite since I last seed ye. By cracky, it'd be me that's more'n proud to work the trap lines

48

with ye, boy. This coon knows a real mountain man when he sees one.''

So they trapped together, quietly and efficiently working the streams. Most often it was Zack and Jeremiah who brought in the most pelts. They had a fine time crowing over the rich, lush pelts they carried into camp.

The six Blackfoot warriors had appeared out of nowhere, charging down the sloping river bank. As usual, Zack was wading in the fast-rushing stream, fishing out the traps, freeing the drowned beaver and flinging it out onto the bank before resetting the trap. On the bank, Jeremiah would quickly and efficiently slice the pelt off the animal and fling the bloody carcass away. From his higher position, Jeremiah was the first to see the Indians. ''Waugh!'' he grunted. ''Head fer cover, Zack.''

But it was already too late. The first arrow caught Zack in the fleshy part of the thigh. ''Damn,'' he gasped through clenched teeth. He heard Jeremiah's gun go off and saw one of the Indians tumble dead to the ground.

''Now, Zack! Run fer it!'' wheezed Jeremiah.

Zack flipped up one of his pistols and fired. He wrenched the arrow out of his leg and splashed sloppily through the water hoping to make it to the bank and his rifle, and maybe even the safety of the cottonwood trees along the bank.

Jeremiah's gun boomed again, and Zack clambered up the muddy bank, snatching up his rifle. He dived behind a tree. Taking a few quick breaths, he checked the priming on his rifle. He edged the gun around the tree. Two of the Blackfeet were dead, but the other four were closing in on Jeremiah, knowing that, because of his age, he would be the most vulnerable.

''Damn,'' shouted Zack as he saw one of the warriors strike the old man with his coup stick. He fired, and the Indian fell. But he also heard Jeremiah's cackling laughter.

"Ye ain't got me yit, ye bastards," the old man yelled at the Indians. "I ain't riddy to go under."

An iron-shod lance caught Jeremiah in the chest, pinning him to the ground. Grimacing in pain, the old mountain man pulled out one of his big pistols and fired wildly.

Laughing, the feathered, nearly naked warrior who had thrown the lance slid off his horse, a scalping knife in hand.

"Naw ye don't!" screamed Zack. "Ye ain't takin' my friend's hair, ye son of a bitch." He fired the rifle on the run, hitting the Indian in the head.

The other three Indians gave it up. Wheeling their horses, they raced off, splashing across the stream.

Zack ran to his friend. As gently as he could, he pulled the long spear from the old man's body and tossed it aside. Jeremiah coughed, spraying blood. He drew a long, deep, ragged breath. "Wall now, old Zack," he wheezed. "This coon's finally goin' under. Nary thought I'd see the day." He coughed again, crying out with the pain.

"Ye ain't daid yet," hissed Zack.

"Wall, now. This hyar's damp powder, or I wouldn't say so. I kin hear them heavenly angels already." He paused, trying to catch his breath. "An' I bin around a right long time. More'n sixty year all tole. An' I raised my share of hair now, or I wouldn't say so."

He fell silent. Zack thought he had died. But he saw the shrunken, blood-covered chest struggle feebly. Jeremiah's eyes opened, but they were glazed. He felt around, looking for something. "Whar's my gun, Zack?" he asked faintly.

"It's right hyar, Jeremiah." Zack handed him the gun.

Jeremiah's withered fist closed around it, and he sighed. With one more great effort, he opened his eyes and focused them.

He held the rifle out to Zack. "Hyar, now, Zack. I want ye to have this."

Zack started to protest, but Jeremiah stopped him. "Ye jist do as I say, boy. I'm gone under fer shore now, an' thar ain't nothin' neither ye nor the good Lord kin do fer me now." He paused, sucking in wind. "Ye bin a good partner, or I wouldn't say so. Ye bin right fair with me an' done more'n yore share of the work. Ye bin almost like kin to me, an' there ain't ary other person I'd like to have this gun more'n ye. She's old, but she still shoots plumb center. I call 'er Thunder."

"But Jeremiah . . ."

But it was no use. The old trapper was dead.

Sadly, Zack gently placed Jeremiah's body across the saddle of his horse and went back to camp. Zack grieved, but death in the mountains was common, and little was made of it. Those who were close friends mourned. But the ceremony was over quickly and simply. Then life had to go on.

Zack stuck it out with Hickory's party through the season. In late May the beaver men headed back toward Mexican country. They camped a last night not too far out of town. The morning they were to ride into Santa Fe, they dandied themselves up fine and proper in fringed buckskin pants that were beautifully worked; beaded shirts and moccasins; and new caps of beaver, raccoon, or even mink fur. Some wore heavy leather boots, finely tooled, with large silver spurs that jangled and clanked.

Zack, freshly washed in the small stream that tumbled icy cold down from the mountains, chose moccasins and soft buckskin shirt and trousers. His old cap, made of winter buffalo fur, bedecked with a

51

feather on one side, was placed carefully on his newly combed hair. "I'm ready," he shouted.

The rest of the men called out their readiness, and they cantered off toward town. At the outskirts of the adobe city, they gave a last-minute check to their appearance.

Then Hickory shouted, "Yee-ha!" and the horses thundered into town, the men firing their weapons and screeching crazily, like a bunch of Indians on the warpath. Spanish soldiers, thinking they had been attacked by a bunch of Apaches, tumbled out of their barracks and the saloons, fearfully dragging their rifles with them. Streams of angry Spanish joined the already thunderous noise as they saw it was no more than Jim Hickory's wild bunch of free trappers.

Pulling up in front of the trading post in a cloud of adobe dust, Zack heard a familiar voice: "Hey, Zack! Ye old horse thief, don't ye even greet yore old friend?"

Zack looked down through the dusty haze and saw Mose leaning against the wall of the trading post, a grin stretched from ear to ear. He started walking toward Zack, who shouted happily, "Who're ye callin' a horse thief? I'm half mountain lion an' half buffler bull, an' I'll whup any man that says nay to it."

He flung himself off of his horse and onto Mose amidst the cheers and catcalls and laughter of the other trappers. They wrestled around in the middle of the dusty street, the other men forming a shouting, laughing circle around them.

Finally Zack yelled, "Enough! If'n ye buy me a drink, I'll let ye be, fer now."

Mose, sitting atop Zack's chest, laughed. "Ye got yoreself a deal, amigo." He jumped up and offered his hand to Zack.

Brushing themselves off, Zack said, "Let me git my pelts traded in, an' then I'll join ye in the saloon.

We kin have a right high ole time. Jist make shore ye got a jug handy."

If may have been the best spree they ever had. They won more and lost more and spent more and drank more than they ever had. They were in three brawls and wooed a number of women, both Mexican and Indian. They outdid themselves.

"We shore made 'em shine now, or I wouldn't say so!" Mose bellowed one night after a particularly high-spirited fight in the saloon.

But three weeks of all-out fandango were all they could manage at one time. They rode north, heading for Taos, to see what kind of deviltry they could get into there. It was a time for visiting other old compadres and holding another spree before heading back to Santa Fe in time to prepare for the new season.

They stayed in Taos almost another three weeks. "That was right nigh 'bout the best spree I ever did have," chuckled Zack one night. But they had had enough, and so rode south out of Taos to a place where they could rest, camping near a small, almost dried-up stream halfway between the two Mexican cities.

"When ye figger on leavin', amigo?" Zack asked across the small fire.

"Gittin' itchy?"

"Wall, now, I shore am. It's three days we bin out hyar, an' I'm gittin' the urge to be movin' on."

"Me, too. I reckon we kin leave fer Santy Fe in the mornin', if'n ye're up to it."

"Reckon I kin be so." Zack paused for a minute. "When ye figger on settin' out fer the mountains?"

Mose was silent, staring at the fire. Slowly, he said, "I aim to head fer the mountains alone, amigo."

"What?" exploded Zack. "Alone? Ye're crazy, boy. It ain't safe up thar by yoreself. Ye'll lose yore scalp fer shore."

"Naw I won't," answered Mose calmly. "Ye

53

trapped end of the season afore by yoreself, an' warn't no harm come to ye. Same with me. I nary saw a bad-hearted Injun all the while I was in the high country. 'Sides, ye said yoreself ye liked bein' alone up thar.''

"But whyn't ye want a partner ary more? We kin trap more beaver that way. 'Sides, I figgered jist the two of us. I didn't want to go with no party this year.''

"I know that, Zack. But I feel more to home by myself. Even two in a trappin' party's too much fer me after I bin out thar by myself. I allus bin more to home alone, amigo. Ye should know that.'' He paused and stirred up the fire, throwing on another log.

He continued: "I don't know what made me leave the doc's house an' head up thar last season by myself, but I was gittin' the itch to move on. Mebbe I jist wanted to see if'n I could do it. I didn't know when ye'd be back, so's I left. When I were up thar, I realized I'd bin missin' somethin' all those years with bigger trappin' parties. It'd be the same even with jist ye, amigo. Allus at the whim of somethin' or some-one.''

"But who're ye gonna swap yarns with over the fire, an' who're ye gonna gamble with, if'n ye're all alone?''

"I kin play hand with the Injuns,'' Mose laughed, "an' I kin swap yarns with a griz.''

"Waugh!'' Zack spit. "I still think ye're loco. 'Sides, what'm I gonna do?''

"Ye're one of the best trappers in the mountains, boy. Ye'll have no trouble findin' a party to join up with. Hell, ye kin even start yore own party, if'n ye had a mind to.''

"Ye plannin' on comin' back to civilization at all?'' It wasn't often, but once in a while a trapper got to liking the solitude and the mountains so much that he never returned, staying in the wilds, living like an outcast Indian.

54

"Why, shore. I figger we kin make plans afore we leave to meet somewhars and mebbe have our own rendezvous up in the mountains afore we head back this way. Or else onto the rendezvous on the Green."

Zack, never one to be kept down in the spirits for long, brightened considerably. "Why shore, amigo. We kin have our own rendezvous an' then head on into Santy Fe."

They left the next morning and pulled into Santa Fe two days later after a leisurely trip. Once there, they outfitted themselves with the little money they had left and with a good dose of credit. It took only two days to prepare their stake. They decided to have one last party before they left.

Just after dawn, with the temperature already nearing the one hundred degree mark on that hot August morning, they rode out of Santa Fe, guts aching and heads feeling like they were ready to burst.

Ten days' ride later, they separated for the first time since the day they had met at the Captain's camp. Mose headed west up into the Uncompaghres country while Zack headed north and a little east, across the plains, to spend some time with the Indians before heading west into the mountains himself. Before winter came, Zack made his way into the mountains, joining up with a small party of trappers from the Mexican territory. He knew them all and had trapped with most of them at one time or another. But after wintering high in the Rockies with them, he decided that he, too, preferred the peaceful solitude of being alone in the mountains. Once more he decided that the only partner he would take would be Mose—if Mose ever changed his mind.

But that conviction would not hold true later. After he started taking She-Who-is-Wind-in-the-Morning with him.

In late May, he met Mose near the Roaring Fork

and they swapped tales of the winter, wrestled and drank what little methiglin, their potent trading whiskey, they had left before making the long trek back to Santa Fe.

It became their pattern. Every year they would either meet somewhere in the mountains, back in Mexican territory, or at the annual trappers' rendezvous. Each fall they left the city or rendezvous in high style, and split somewhere in the foothills of the Rockies, Mose heading directly up into the mountains, Zack angling off to spend time with the Cheyennes.

"It's the same now as it was then," Zack mumbled to himself as he looked across the prairie. "Nary a change from year to year."

He continued his solitary ride, knowing that he, too, liked the solitude of the mountains. But not as much as Mose did. He had found a solution to the problem. That was why he always stopped among the Indians before he headed up into high country.

He always stopped on his way to his rendezvous with Mose, too. The Indian woman, Wind-in-the-Morning, accompanied him on his trapping ventures up into the mountains. So he stopped at the Cheyenne village on his way out to get her and to spend time with the men of the village, whom he had come to admire and respect. And he stopped on his way back to the other land, the land of the Spanish-speaking people. He stopped to drop the woman off at her village. He could not bring himself to carry her into the towns, as some of the trappers did.

But he could not forego her pleasures either. He loved her, in his own way, and treated her well—maybe better than she would have been treated by an Indian husband. He missed her while he was in the city, but still he could not bring himself to become a full-fledged squaw man, carrying his woman, and the inevitable children, with him wherever he went.

So he went back, year after year, twice a year, torn between his feelings for the Indian woman and his straight-laced upbringing back in Virginia.

CHAPTER 4

He made camp that night on the banks of the Purgatoire River. For his dinner he roasted two rabbits and a prairie chicken he had shot earlier in the day. It was, he thought, a welcome change from buffalo meat. After wolfing down the succulent meat, he leaned back against his saddle and lit his pipe. He thought about Wind-in-the-Morning and his feelings toward her.

He would be glad to see her again, and she him. But still he felt he could not bring her with him all the time. His childhood had been too foreign to the idea. It was not done. Although he had been in the mountains for so many years and thought he could forget all those childish ideas, they still lingered.

He remembered back along the years to his home near Dan's River in Virginia, close to the border of North Carolina.

He had been born in the year 1799—the third child of a small-time farmer, etching out a barely sufficient living. His father, Jedidiah, although a man of the land when Zack was born, had been an excellent woodsman in bygone years and imparted much of that skill to his young son, Zack. Jedidiah's other sons preferred the farming life, but Zack took to the woods.

Zack was only ten years old when his father gave him his first rifle. Out of date and worn, it was, nonetheless, accurate, and Zack learned well how to use it. He also learned to trap and how to make his way silently through the woods. By the time he was fourteen, he had the urge to move on.

Jedidiah died when Zack was eleven. His mother remarried a short time later. Zack's stepfather soon took to beating him, trying, through brute force, to bend Zack to the yoke of farm life. But it only served to stiffen the lad's resolve to lead a wild life. By the time he reached his fourteenth birthday, he could see no reason to stay any longer. Over his mother's protests, but knowing he would have had his father's blessing, Zack left for Kentucky to live with relatives. There he was happy for a time. The work on the farm was light and the game plentiful enough to keep the young hunter busy. But even this soon paled.

Almost as soon as he had crossed the mountains into Kentucky, he heard talk of the mountains to the far west. He had heard of the fur trade. And the buffalo were so plentiful, he had heard, that they blackened the prairie with their numbers. He wanted to be a part of the excitement and danger of the fur trade.

At the age of sixteen he left, on his own, for the Missouri territory with the intent of joining one of the fur-trapping expeditions he had heard so much about. But none of them wanted to take on a young greenhorn fresh from the farm in Kentucky. So he made his way, living where he could, paying his way by hunting and with some small trapping on the Mississippi and a little further west, up the Missouri River. Almost two years later, hungry, tired and broke, by lying about his age Zack joined the Captain's expedition to the Rockies.

But for all his wild upbringing, he had still been raised in the East, with its ideas of civilization. There were few Indians left in Virginia by the time he was born; they were mostly dead or shipped out West. But there were stories from the old timers. And there were the black slaves.

He had learned early that he was somehow better than blacks and redmen; the other races were somehow tainted. They were not to be respected as much as even the poorest whites that lived in the area. Living in the wilderness had showed him, in many ways, that these ideas were wrong; that people should be judged by what they did and who they were, not what color their skin was.

But he still could not get the thought out of his head that if he brought a squaw to town with him as his wife, he would somehow be bringing shame on himself and his family back in the East.

"Damn fool ideas," he told himself more than once. Many of the mountain men brought their Indian women back to Taos or Santa Fe, or even to St. Louis. And they also brought the numerous half-breed children that naturally grew of such unions. No one thought the worse of them for it. Even the quiet Mose occasionally rode into Santa Fe with an Indian woman he sometimes called his wife.

Although she had never asked to be taken, Zack knew quite well that Wind-in-the-Morning would have loved to be brought to the big white man's town; to see the lights and the color and the activities of the pale strangers flocking to the West.

He called her Windy, not only because of her Indian name, but also because of her penchant for conversation. And in that conversation, she often hinted that it would be exciting to see the town of adobe lodges. He promised her he would take her with him some day. But he never did.

"Hell," he said aloud to the night sky blazing with stars. "Mebbe I'll jist take her along with me this year." But he still wasn't convinced. He knocked the ashes from his pipe and rolled in his robes.

In the morning he ate a cold breakfast of jerky, washed down with a few swigs of fresh, cold water. He was off early.

The prairie stretched out in front of him for miles, seemingly without end. Only an occasional small clump of trees or a slight hillock disturbed the vast emptiness. In the distance, Zack could see a massive herd of buffalo looking, from this distance, like a brown wave undulating across a wide, golden ocean as the heat made the scene shimmer in front of him.

He often wondered on trips like this whether he liked more the solitude and majesty of the mountains or the long, lonely stretches of the plains. But he had never decided. Each had its beauty. And its dangers. The mountains, he thought, were certainly more beautiful, but they could also be the most dangerous. The high, cold streams could become raging, surging torrents in a matter of minutes. And the snows were frequent, deep, cold and bitter. The snow could be expected in some of the high passes from September to May, with early or late storms occasionally striking.

But winters on the plains were not easy, either. The cold was numbing, and the wind howled like a demon, shrieking and blowing the bone-freezing cold down from Canada. It swept the snow along with fierce gusts that stung the face. And the wind never stopped. It sometimes lost its intensity, but it never really stopped.

The hail, too, could be devastating: huge chunks of ice crashing down from the sky, some of them large enough to knock a horse unconscious. Even in summer, the plains had their own special hells. The wind still whistled and moaned with nothing to slow it, and the heat was staggering.

The game, though, was more plentiful on the prairie, and he often hunted the buffalo, elk, deer and even some of the smaller game animals like rabbits that roamed freely there. His hunting was as often

61

done for sport as it was for the fresh meat he liked to have every day, if he could get it.

Midway through the day, Zack spotted some horsemen trotting toward him. He stopped his horse and shaded his eyes with his hand, standing up in the stirrups for a better look. "Look like Osages," he said to his horse.

It was another danger of the plains. He started slowly forward again and, as he rode, he checked his weapons. Like most beaver men traveling alone or in small groups, he carried his big Hawken across the saddle horn, cradled in his left arm at all times. In his belt were jammed two pistols, big percussion, muzzle-loading pistols with the kick of a mule. He also carried in his belt a tomahawk and the big Green River knife. A pouch of balls and a horn full of powder were slung over his shoulder.

"Hope they ain't gonna act contrary," he said. He had never had any trouble with the Osage, who only occasionally drifted this far into the land that was hunted upon and fought over by the Southern Cheyennes, the Comanches and the Kiowas.

But he also knew the Osages could be notional Indians, and might attack without warning if they were in the mood to take scalps—or if they thought the odds were greatly in their favor.

When they were about one hundred yards apart, Zack recognized the leader as a middle-aged warrior of great reknown. He was known as Slow Dog. Zack had met the brave before and, though they did not dislike each other, they were cautious.

As they drew closer, Zack raised his right hand in greeting. "Hough," he called out, attempting to pronounce the Indian word for greeting. "How be ye, Slow Dog? Bin quite a while since I laid eyes on ye."

Slow Dog responded in kind, with upraised hand.

"Enemy of Kiowas rides alone?" asked the Indian. His four warriors began to circle Zack, looking over his almost-empty packs. Seeing little of value in the packs, they began to enviously eye the pack animals and the big appaloosa.

Zack, who was known as Enemy-of-Kiowas among most of the plains tribes, answered, "Yep. But only till I git to the village of my brothers, the Shyans." He kept a wary eye on the warriors still looking over his animals.

"Has Enemy of Kiowas any tobacco to give to his old friend, Slow Dog?"

Zack almost laughed; old friend, indeed. They hardly knew each other. Zack watched as one of the Indians reached out a hand to snatch one of the few pelts that Zack had in one of the packs and said, "I got a bullet fer ye, old friend, Slow Dog, if'n yore brave don't git his paws off my pelts." To emphasize his statement, Zack lifted the big rifle off the saddle, bringing the muzzle around to face Slow Dog. He had not cocked it yet, but Slow Dog knew he was dead if he did not do as Zack asked.

Slow Dog warned the warrior off with a small movement of his hand; his eyes never left Zack's face.

"Ye jist tell 'em that if they keep away from my pelts an' animals, I may be able to find some terbacca fer ye all."

Slow Dog called his warriors back. He knew full well Zack's reputation for ferocity and thought the odds were not in his favor.

As the braves moved away from Zack, the one who had tried to steal the pelt bumped into him. The mountain man, who often had a plug of chewing tobacco in his cheek, let fly a huge glob of brown juice that landed on the neck of the Indian's horse and oozed slowly down its side, near the warrior's leg. The Indian made a move toward his knife, but Zack calmly leveled the Hawkins at his chest. ''Ye pull that knife, an' I'll blow ye to hell an' back, boy.''

Slow Dog called again to the warrior in his native tongue. With a surly look, the warrior jerked the horse's head around and rejoined the others lined up behind Slow Dog.

''Now, that's more like it,'' said Zack. Keeping an eye on the Indians, he reached into his possible sack. ''Ye should teach yore young bucks some manners, Slow Dog. Thar warn't no call fer him to git so nasty. I ain't got no quarrel with yore people.''

The older Indian looked at him with dignity. ''You are right, Enemy-of-Kiowas. The young one will be dealt with.''

Zack handed out some tobacco and jerky to the Indians. Only the bitter warrior refused the handout, haughtily sitting astride his pony.

Zack shrugged. ''Have it yore way, boy.'' With a nod to Slow Dog, Zack slowly started forward. As he passed the Indians, he heard the young warrior begin to argue, and he knew the brave wanted to kill him. But Slow Dog, with a few curt phrases, quieted the hot-blooded warrior. The braves then wheeled and raced off at full gallop.

As they rode away, Zack breathed a sigh of relief. ''Wall,'' he said to his horse, scratching its broad head, ''that were a close 'un.''

But the rest of the day was uneventful, though he did ride with an extra measure of caution. He was lucky, he knew. Lone trappers were frequent victims of bands of hostile Indians.

That night he camped alone on the prairie, far from any water. He spent a restless night, alert, even in sleep, against the possibility the Osages might return to steal his horses and maybe take his scalp.

In the morning he awoke, tired but ready for the

day. It was cool in the pre-dawn darkness, but he knew it would be blistering hot before the sun traveled a quarter of the way across the sky. Despite the fact that the August sun still blazed almost unbearably during the day, Zack knew it would not be long before the cold would begin blowing down from the north. He shivered a little with the thought that the snows would, within two months, blanket this land, covering it with huge drifts.

But he shook off the feeling. Long before the big snows came he would be wintered in an almost comfortable camp high in the mountains, beside a racing steam teeming with beaver. And there would be Wind-in-the-Morning. He smiled at the thought, giving the horses a little extra time to graze on the sparse, dried-brown grass before setting out.

In two days he would be in the village of Strong Horse. He would be in his own lodge with Wind-in-the-Morning, but he would also feast at the fire of Strong Horse, the village's head chief. He would also feast at the fire of Hawk Wind, leader of the Eagle Clan.

He began to saddle the appaloosa. "I wonder," he said to the animal, "who'll be leadin' the huntin' party this year."

He finished saddling the horse and mounted up. "C'mon thar, boy," he urged. "Lit's go."

Only once was the monotony of the ride broken. A large grizzly, startled in its feeding, charged him. The pack horses spooked and bolted, racing far out over the prairie. But the appaloosa, knowing well the rider on his back, stayed put. His only indication of fear was a nervous whinny and a shuffling of hooves.

"Easy, boy," said Zack. The horse steadied, and Zack raised Thunder. The gun boomed, but at the same instant, as if it knew what was coming, the grizzly swerved and the ball hit harmlessly in the dirt.

"Damn," swore Zack, kneeing the horse into motion. The appaloosa needed no further encouragement and raced off. The bear turned and charged again, but Zack was far enough away that he could take the time to load the rifle again. "Ye'd best not miss this time, ye old buzzard," he said to himself.

Again he steadied the horse and took aim. The grizzly charged straight ahead, and Zack's aim was true. The bear stopped short, reared on its hind legs, then dropped. It rolled over once and lay still.

Zack sat stride the appaloosa, waiting. He knew the habits of the grizzly and knew the bruin could be playing possum. After half an hour, he figured the animal was really dead. It hadn't moved all the while. Dismounting, he walked cautiously toward the supine bear. At arm's reach, he prodded it with the rifle, but it lay unmoving.

He wasted no time in skinning the animal. The skin he would give to Windy to make a fine sleeping robe. And the teeth and claws, he saw, would make a nice necklace for him to wear. He took a hunk of the bloody meat for his dinner and then went in search of his pack animals. He found them before long, complacently chomping the short, brown grass two miles away.

Wiping the sweat away from his face, he looked at the sky. "Damn," he muttered, "that spree done wasted a heap of time. Guess I best be lookin' fer a place to bed down fer the night."

The next day was another of the monotonous rides across the emptiness. Boredom clutched at him. But he was heartened in knowing that before dark tomorrow he would be in the village.

He once more spent the night in the open, using buffalo chips for a fire to heat some of the bear meat he carried. He drank sparingly of the water he had brought in a skin canteen hastily fashioned from the bladder of a buffalo. He camped by a mud puddle that would become a roaring river in the spring thaws. He allowed the horses to drink only a little of the muddy, brackish water at a time.

He was up before dawn, the chill air refreshing. "Today's the day, I reckon," he said to the stallion as he saddled him.

The sun's brightness was just beginning to edge out the inky blackness of the night when he mounted up and rode out. He forced himself to keep the horses in check, anxious to get to the village, but wanting to spare the animals. In mid-afternoon, he topped a small rise in the undulating land and sat up straight. There, arrayed before him, a mile and a half away, was the village. He sat at the top of the rise, hand and buffalo-skin cap shielding his eyes, as they feasted on the conical shapes of the tepees shimmering in the afternoon heat. He could see the vast horse herds, grazing comfortably on the buffalo grass, watched over by alert young boys. And there he also saw the meat racks, heavy with rich buffalo and elk, drying in the sun.

"Yep," he said to the horse. "That's their village. I kin see ole Hawk Wind's lodge. An' thar's the lodge of ole Strong Horse. We're home agin, ole hoss." Even at this distance the distinctive coloring of some of the lodges were recognizable to his practiced eyes.

As he sat there looking down on the village of about forty lodges sitting on the banks of the Big Sandy River, he thought back to the first time he had seen it about ten years before. It was then that he had met Windy and gotten drunk with the young Indian warrior. He and Mose were both still young and with the Captain's party. It had been less than a week since the battle with the Blackfeet when they spotted another band of warriors racing toward them at full gallop.

"Oh, m'god, Mose, they're back," he remembered shouting.

67

But everyone else in the party seemed unconcerned. The oldtimer, Jeremiah Witherspoon, had heard him and rode up alongside. "Ain't nary a thang to be werried 'bout, boy. Ain't no call to be skeered," he said in his high, thin, nasal voice. "Them're Shyans, not Blackfeet. They're friendly toward us. The Blackfeet don't come nowhars near this fur south. Hell, it was might unusual to see them as far south as we did t'other day when we went agin 'em."

"How kin ye tell they're Shyan from this far away?"

"Easy, Zack. Their paint's distinctive. So's the way they wear their hair, and the way they ride. The Shyans're probly the best horsemen on the plains. Better even than the Sioux or the Crows. Most of 'em look like they was born in the saddle." He had paused to watch the Indians' progress, then said, "Ye'll git to know the difference 'tween all the Injuns afore ye're through with us, boy."

Zack relaxed as best he could as he watched the racing warriors heading toward them, howling like all the demons in hell. When they were about ten yards away, they skidded to a halt, foam from the horses flying about, the dust rising.

"Waugh," said the Indian leader to the Captain. "How is my old friend, and friend of all the Cheyennes, Stands-in-Water?"

"Waugh," answered the Captain. "I'm just fine. And how is my old friend, Lame Bear?"

As they talked, Zack asked Jeremiah, "How'd the Cap'n git sich a silly name's Stands-in-Water?"

The old man laughed. "Seems the fust time the Cap'n met up with the Shyans, he was down to 'is bare hide takin' a bath in a stream somewhar. The Shyans came riding up like the devil hisself was on their tail and scared the bejesus outten him. He thought fer shore he was gonna lose his hair. But they jist

68

fooled with him fer a while an' then invited him to their village. They bin friendly ever since.''

Zack and Mose joined in the old man's laughter. Zack turned his attention back to the Captain and the Indian called Lame Bear. They were talking in Cheyenne. Zack couldn't understand them, but he moved a little closer to observe the fully decked-out warriors behind the Indian leader.

He had never been so close to an Indian before, except during the short-lived battle, and then he had been too scared and too involved to take notice of what they looked like.

The warriors were hideously painted. Recently returned from the warpath, they had been celebrating their victory over a group of Kiowas. Dripping scalps hung from lances and coup sticks, the blood glistening in the sun.

The Indians themselves were tall and handsome, with skin the color of a lightly bleached penny. Their foreheads were high and wide, their noses long and straight. Black eyes stared ahead, unblinking. Thick, black, straight hair gleamed from the grease used to keep it in place.

The warrior closest to Zack was a big man, middle-aged, broad in the shoulders. His long black hair was parted in the middle and hung in braids on each side of his head. The braids were wrapped in otter fur, and a number of feathers, loosely tied to the hair and fur, blew softly in the light breeze. Long, looping earrings dangled from the man's ears, and he was otherwise adorned with beads and small glittering pieces of metal. He was naked, save for a loincloth and moccasins, which Zack noticed were undecorated except for small bells that jingled quietly every time his horse moved.

Not knowing the meaning of the warrior's paint, Zack was intrigued by the man's facial decorations.

69

One side of his face was painted red, with a large black circle around the eye. The unpainted side of his face had a yellow circle around the eye and three black slashes that ran across it from nose to cheek.

Even his arms were painted, Zack noticed. Red stripes, like lightning, ran down his right arm from shoulder to just past the elbow. The left arm was adorned with five red circles. The warrior's horse, a small, sturdy-looking mustang, was also painted and decorated.

Zack heard the war chief say to the Captain, "The young warrior seems to have a great interest in my brother, Hawk Wind. Is he preparing to attack?"

The question startled Zack, but the Captain laughed. "Naw, Lame Bear. He's jist a young buck what don't know too much yet. He ain't nary seen an Injun close up afore, an' he's jist intrested. Only Injuns he's seed up close was some Blackfeet that attacked us up north aways. An' we both know they don't rightly count."

Lame Bear looked at Zack, who looked away in embarrassment. The Captain continued, "In fact, this young 'un an' his friend, that long skinny feller over yonder, each counted coup for the fust time on them Blackfeet. They each kilt theyselves a Blackfoot right up close, and took the scalps."

The Captain winked at Zack, covering his small fib to the Indians who, at the news, began to whoop and holler. Zack noticed that Jeremiah rode up next to him, and whispered, "Hold yore head up, boy. Ye're a great warrior, an' ye ain't got no call to hang yore head. Ye don't want them Shyans to think they's something wrong with ye, do ye, boy?"

So Zack raised his head and stared proudly straight ahead, his cheeks still red with embarrassment, while the Indians rode around him screeching. Lame Bear, the only Indian not joining in, smiled at the Captain. "You have some fine warriors riding with you this

70

year, Stands-in-Water. This one will go far.''

The Captain looked at the Indian and said seriously, ''I think ye're right, Lame Bear. I think ye may be right.''

The Indians wheeled and raced off, back toward the unseen village to tell the rest of the tribe that visitors were expected and there would be much trading and feasting.

Later that afternoon, the weary trappers had topped the rise where Zack now sat. It was the first time he had looked on an Indian village, and he was both excited and scared. He could see the women scurrying about, bringing in firewood and preparing the food for the feasting that would go on for days. He could see, then, as he could see now, the racks of meat and skins drying in the sun, the flies buzzing around them. And he could see the massive horse herds grazing under the watchful eyes of the young boys, not yet old enough to go on the hunt or the war path, but old enough for the blood to run high. ''My gawd,'' Zack had whispered to Mose, ''I ain't ever seed so many horses afore.''

He had sat and watched the warriors preparing themselves, too, to greet the mountain men. They were painting themselves carefully and dressing in their finest beaded and feathered clothing for the celebrations. The sight, even at that distance, was somehow frightening to Zack.

Even the dogs of the village felt the excitement; racing back and forth barking raucously.

Zack turned to Jeremiah, ''Are ye shore they're friends of the Cap'n's? They look almighty mean to me.''

Witherspoon threw back his head and laughed his scratchy laugh. ''Why, shore they're friendly. What's the matter, boy, ye skeered?''

Zack nodded, and Jeremiah laughed some more.

71

"Hell, boy, they ain't nothin' to be skeered 'bout. They's jist paintin' an' dressin' theyselves up to look their best fer compny. Same's ye an' me would if'n we was havin' compny come to our home."

"Ye shore?" asked Zack, unconvinced.

"Course I'm shore." He sat, shaking his head in silent laughter.

The men rode a little further, and the Captain stopped them to make camp a half mile or more outside the Indian village. "I thought we was gonna stay in the village," said Zack.

"Naw, nary do," commented Jeremiah.

"Why?"

"Couple reasons. Fust, 'though the Shyans're friendly, they're still Injuns. That means they ain't got no concept of private property. If'n they git likkered up an' start wanderin' 'round our camp, ye'll have to watch everthin' ye got that ain't tied down, else some brave'll walk off with it."

"I thought ye said they was friendly," Zack interjected.

"They are. But they don't consider sich doin's as stealin'. It's jist part of their nature. 'Nother reason we don't stay in the village is that it's jist too damn crowded. Both fer us an' fer the animals. Ye spend too many days in close compny with Injuns and ye'll have lice an' all kinds of other crawly things. 'Sides, after more'n a couple days in a tepee, ye'll not like the odor much."

"I thought the Shyans were clean Injuns."

"They are. 'Bout the cleanest of ary I ever met. But they still git lice. Comes from the way they live I reckon. Hell, we usually wind up gittin' lice ourselves after a winter."

Jeremiah paused for a few seconds to spit a huge gob of tobacco juice on the ground. "We also gotta have grazin' room fer the horses. Them Shyan herds'll crop the grass down to nothin' in a wee bit. Our horses should have enough grass fer grazin' 'thout movin' 'em too much.''

They stopped, and the men dismounted. They quickly began to set up the camp that would be their home for the next few days. The work went quickly; after so many months working together in the mountains the men were used to the routine. When they were finished, Jeremiah strolled over to where Zack and Mose sat cross-legged on he ground. ''Wall, boys,'' he said, ''hyar's damp powder now or I wouldn't say so.''

Worried, the two young trappers looked at him. ''What's the matter, Jeremiah, the Shyans aimin' to take our hair?''

''Naw, nothin' like that,'' said Jeremiah. The fear in Zack and Mose was a joke to the other trappers.

''Then what's wrong?'' asked Mose.

''Wall, as much as I hate to do it, I gotta go take a bath in yonder stream. That's what's wrong.'' He looked crestfallen.

The two young men screeched and hollered, jumping up to dance around the abashed old mountain man. In the few years they had been in the mountains with the Captain's party, they had not seen old Jeremiah bathe himself. They knew he did so once in a while but, like most trappers, he avoided a bath through most of the winter, saying the grime, dust and grease helped keep in the body heat. But they had never seen Jeremiah in the water for a bath. Not even in the summer. During the warmer months the mountain men usually took baths whenever they were near a river or stream. But Jeremiah had never been caught at it. He said the dirt kept the hot sun off him in the summer.

''Hey, boys,'' yelled Zack. ''Look what we got hyar.'' Some of the trappers looked up. ''Ole Jeremiah's gonna take hisself a bath down in the stream.''

73

From a distance away, one of the mountain men yelled, "What? A bath ye say?"

"That's right," bellowed Zack. "Ye best come an' watch. Ye may nary git to see it agin."

The men came running, and before Jeremiah could take off and hide a few of the trappers had grabbed him and lifted him in the air. The men carried the struggling trapper toward the stream with the rest of the men following, war dancing, hooting and just plain carrying on behind them.

The Captain, who had been in the village, came riding up. "What in tarnation's goin' on hyar?" he called over the din.

"Jeremiah's gonna take a bath, Cap'n," yelled Zack. "An' the boys decided to help him afore he changed 'is mind."

The Captain jumped off his horse. "Hell, this is somethin' this coon's gotta see fer hisself." And he joined the parade.

Jeremiah, still struggling, screeched at the top of his lungs, his high voice cracking, "Ye horse thieves. I'll git ye fer all this. I'll not fergit this fer as long as I'm alive. I'll 'specially not fergit ye two imps," he said, staring directly at Zack and Mose. "Spawn of the devil ye are."

But the two young trappers only laughed the harder at his threats. The old mountain man was still hurling obscenities, threats and invective when he hit the water, fully clothed, with a loud splash.

He came up sputtering. "Ye bastards," he called out. "I'll cut yore hearts out fer this." He started heading for the other bank, but some trappers were too quick for him and waded across to the other side to head him off. He saw the waiting men and knew he was licked.

He looked at the hollering, hooting trappers and

shrugged. "What the hell," he said. "I'm wet now, an' I might's well finish the job. Ye needn't stand thar gawkin' at me."

"Kin we trust ye?" called out one of the men.

"Have I ary gone back on my word?" he asked, pulling the grimy shirt over his head.

"Cain't say as ye have," said the Captain. "C'mon, boys. I think the ole coon'll finish what we started fer 'im."

Still laughing, the men headed back to camp.

A while later Jeremiah strode purposefully back into camp, still with sopping hair. But he was clean and freshly shaven. Even his buckskins were mostly clean.

"My gawd," shouted Zack, the first one to see him. "He even shaved."

"Shaddup," said Jeremiah, holding a finger to his lips. "Gimme a break, boys. Everbody'll know soon enough anyways. I took enough ribbin' fer one day."

Zack laughed. No one had heard his first announcement. "Guess ye're right. Ye ain't sore, are ye, Jeremiah?"

"Naw, I ain't too put out. It were all in fun, I guess. But I'll git ye both back some day. Jist be riddy fer it."

"We will," said Mose, laughing.

"Ain't ye gonna take a bath?" asked the clean beaver man.

"What fer?" asked Zack.

"Fer the same reason I did, ye fools."

"What's that? Ye nary did tell us why ye decided to take a bath all of a sudden."

"'Cause I aim to have me a Shyan woman tonight. It's bin a time an' a time since I had me a Shyan squaw."

"An' ye needed to take a bath fer that? I ain't ary seed ye bein' so carin' afore."

"Why, shore. Ye 'member I tole ye the Shyans was 'bout the cleanest Injuns I ever seed?" Both the youths nodded. "Wall, ain't no respectin' Shyan woman gonna come near no ole coon what smells as bad as I were. I were smellin' right high, or I wouldn't say so."

"That's right smart," commented Mose.

"Shore is," answered Jeremiah. "Ye boys ary have ye a Shyan woman? Or ary woman a'tall fer that matter?"

Both Zack and Mose grew red, the embarrassment flushing their faces. "Nary a one?" Jeremiah asked incredulously, a gleam showing in his eye. "Neither of ye?"

"Wall," Zack started to say, but Jeremiah broke in. "Don't ye lie to me, boy."

The red on Zack's face spread, reaching his neck. He fell into shamed silence.

Mose said quietly, "I had me a whore onct, back in St. Louis. Sort of."

"That don't hardly count," commented Jeremiah gleefully. Mose and Zack looked at him, puzzled by the foolish grin the old man was wearing.

Jeremiah grinned even wider, showing his broken teeth. He turned around and yelled, "Listen hyar, boys. We got us two untouched boys hyar, posin' as men. An' mountain men, no less. They ain't ary had them a woman. They's pure as the driven snow." He was laughing full now.

"Shaddup," hissed Zack between his teeth.

Jeremiah looked back at him and, laughing all the more uproariously, said, "I tole ye I'd git even with ye one of these days fer makin' fun of me. I jist didn't think it'd be so soon or so much fun."

Jeremiah hollered, "C'mon, boys. Come lookit what this ole coon's found."

The men came running, laughing and leering at the two red-faced young men who had nowhere to go. The men had a field day. It had been a long time since they had had so much entertainment in one day.

"So ye're virgins, are ye?" jeered their friend Jim Clancy. "Bin all this time in the mountains an' ye ain't nary had a woman?"

Another trapper called out, "Hyar now, Cap'n. How could ye take on a couple of boys to do a man's job? They's still wet behind the ears."

"An' dry somewhar's else," hooted Clancy amidst more shouts and jeers. Jeremiah sat there looking over at the two, a grin spread wide on his face. "I tole ye. I tole ye," he kept repeating, cackling, doubling over in glee.

Zack looked at him. "Ye rotten ole buzzard," he said. "I hope ye git the French disease from yore Injun woman tonight."

Jeremiah laughed even harder. "I tole ye," he said. "I tole ye."

Zack and Mose sat there miserably taking the shouts, cat-calls and abuse that rained down on them for nearly half an hour. Finally the men began to drift off and soon they were alone with the old trapper.

"That warn't very nice," said Zack sullenly.

Jeremiah wiped the tears of laughter from his eyes. "Now we're even," he commented. "Wall," he said after a short interval, "are ye gonna take yore baths now?"

"Wall," said Zack, still morose. "I guess so."

"Aw, hell, boy. Cheer up," said Jeremiah. "Mebbe ye'll git lucky tonight."

Zack, not one to be down for long, brightened. "Mebbe ye're right," he said.

CHAPTER 5

The two young trappers were not to lose their youth-fulness that night. After they bathed, they dressed in what little finery they had.

Jeremiah came along. "Wall, ye boys shore do look fancy. Ye riddy?"

They both nodded and mounted up. Riding slowly toward the village, Zack asked, "What're Shyan wim-min like?"

"Wall, boy," answered the old man. "I've had most of 'em, or I wouldn't say so. An' the Shyans an' the Shoshonis're 'bout the best. The worst're the Crows. Nothin' but whores, the whole lot of 'em. Sell theyselves fer next to nothin'. Ye don't wanna git mixed up with no Crow wimmin."

"From arything I heered 'bout the Crows," said Zack, "me mixin' with ary Crows a'tall don't seem likely."

"Ye jist keep that notion, boy, an' ye'll be all right."

"Ary others we should keep away from?" asked Mose.

"Shore. 'Paches mostly. They's mean most of the time, an' not worth the trouble of keepin' 'em. An' the Utes is kinda squat and dumpy, but they're clean an' faithful. The Nez Perces're good, if'n ye kin git

78

close to one. Their men're purty defensive, but friendly mostly. If'n ye kin win their favor, they kin be the best of friends."

They were on the outskirts of the village now and Jeremiah finished, saying, "But ye'll larn 'bout all of 'em, if'n ye stay out hyar long enough. Now, mind yore manners tonight, boys, an' don't cause no trouble. The Injuns have some ways that're a mite peculiar to white folks, but that don't mean we shouldn't respect their ways."

Zack nodded. "I ain't aimin' to cause no trouble. All I wanna do is have a few drinks an' have me a good time."

"An' mebbe git ye an Injun woman, too, eh boy?" Jeremiah kidded him.

Zack flushed, but grinned. "Mebbe."

Zack, Mose and Jeremiah left their horses in the care of an Indian boy. Jeremiah said to the two young men, "Now mind what I tole ye boys. Jist watch yore manners. I'm goin' off an' leavin' ye to yoreselves. I got me some bizness to take keer of."

"We'll watch it," promised Mose.

"Go on 'bout yore business, ole man. We kin take keer of ourselves," said Zack.

And they did. The two went toward the big fire in the center of the village where the Captain and some of the other leaders of the party were doing a little trading and a lot of talking with some of the chiefs of the village.

They squatted down on their haunches outside the ring of important men. A young warrior joined them before too long, carrying a jug of methiglin cut with river water and sweetened with honey. It could sting like a bee and kick like a mule. It was not a drink to be taken lightly.

The three young men passed the jug around and

talked in a strange amalgam of Cheyenne, English, French and Spanish. Each culture, as it had touched this wide land, left its mark in the language there. Men, red and white alike, talked freely in the strange patois. "Damn," would as easily become "*Sacre Bleu*," "*Madre Mia*," or the glottal clickings of one of the numerous Indian tongues.

Zack and Mose talked with the Indian who was called Thunder Blanket and tried to listen in on the palaver as much as they could. Both proved to be very educational and they would use that knowledge. But it was not long before Zack, Mose and Thunder Blanket became roaring drunk. They wrestled and danced and raised hell without moving far from their seats. They hollered and raved, bucked and snorted, laughed and fell into an untidy heap more than once. Long before the big fire blazed down and the leaders, both red and white, were finished with their business, the three young men had passed out where they sat.

Zack woke up and saw that Mose and Thunder Blanket were already gone. He found Mose down by the stream trying to drink it dry. There was no sign of the Indian.

Zack joined Mose, lying on the bank of the stream, head half submerged, gulping down huge mouthfuls of water.

"Damn, Mose. I ain't ary felt this bad afore in all my days," said Zack when he came up for air.

Mose groaned. "I know what ye mean. I ain't feelin' so good myself." He tried to stand but, deciding it was unwise when his head started to reel, settled for crawling up the sandy bank to rest his head against a tree. Zack followed.

For what seemed like hours, they lay on the banks of the river, afraid to move. Jeremiah, sprightly despite his age, found them there. "Wall, boys," he said jovially, "how're ye feelin'?"

"Not so good," moaned Zack.

"Too much tradin' whiskey, eh?" laughed the old-timer.

Mose just nodded.

"I got jist the thang that'll fix it fer ye. C'mon."

They staggered to their feet and walked sickly back to the village. Jeremiah told them to wait as he entered a tepee. The two recognized it as the home of the Cheyenne medicine man. Jeremiah stepped out after only a few minutes, with two cups of a dark, brackish brew. He handed one to each of the young men. "Here, drink this," he ordered.

Zack took the cup and sniffed suspiciously at the contents. "Don't smell none too good," he said.

"I tole ye to drink it, not stand thar smellin' it, boy. Now drink it up like good leetle lads. All in one gulp."

Zack looked at Mose, and they both shrugged and swallowed. Zack almost choked. "That's awful," he winced.

Mose had a sour look on his face, but he kept his composure. "How long's it take fer this stuff to work?" he asked.

"Not long," answered Jeremiah. Zack should have known something was up when he saw the old trapper trying to suppress a grin. But he was too sick to dwell on it.

"Wanna head back to camp?" Jeremiah asked innocently.

Zack and Mose nodded, cringing at the pain in their heads. They got their horses and saddled up. Seated, they clumped slowly out of the village. About halfway back to the camp, Zack suddenly jumped off his horse and was violently sick. Mose joined him seconds later.

As they knelt on hands and knees on the prairie grass, Jeremiah roared with laughter, holding tight onto the saddle horn so he wouldn't fall off his horse. In between spasms, Zack hissed, "I'll git ye for this,

81

ye ole coot. Ye're no damned good."

The two finally stopped retching and miserably climbed back on their horses. When they arrived back in camp, Jeremiah took them straight to a fire where food was waiting. "Eat," he commanded.

They looked like they would be ill again. "I'm too sick to eat," whined Zack. Mose nodded in agreement.

"Eat," Jeremiah commanded again. "Ye'll feel better onct ye git somethin' in yore bellies."

Too sick to argue, they sat and started to eat. Jeremiah left. As the warming food hit their systems, they felt a little better and began to eat more heartily. When Jeremiah returned, he asked, "How're ye feelin' now?"

"Some better," commented Zack. "What was in that potion ye give us?"

"Hell, if I know. Jist some concoction thunk up by ole Grass Grows. But I ain't ever seed it fail."

"Was we s'pposed to git sick?" asked Mose.

"Why, shore. Cleans the pizzen outta yore system. Onct ye clean out the pizzen, ye kin eat some hearty food, and ye'll be good's new."

"Wall," said Zack. "I am feelin' a sight better. An' seein's it was ye who give us the medicine, I guess I don't hold no hard feelinᴡ . Even though ye did know we was gonna be sick's dogs an' ye laughed yore eyes out."

Jeremiah chuckled at the memory. "Wall, now. It's purely a funny thing to see some 'un take a dosin' an' git sick all over hisself the fust time. Ye'll do it to some greenhorn yoreself one of these days."

Zack and Mose, feeling better by the minute, joined Jeremiah in the soft laughter.

After their repast, the two young mountain men stretched out on the grassy sward and slept, awakening late in the afternoon feeling much relieved.

The Captain strolled up. "Wall, ye boys feelin'

some better now?'' he asked. When they both nodded, he asked, ''Ye ready fer another big night in the village?''

Zack nodded. ''Why, shore.'' But he vigorously added, '''Cept I aim to keep away from the methiglin this night.''

The Captain threw back his head and laughed, then nodded his head. ''Now that seems to be a right smart idee.'' The Captain smiled again, and Zack thought as he left, ''He's up to somethin'.''

Later, they again dressed in their finery, clean now of the stains of sickness, and rode into the village with Jeremiah. As they rode into the circle of tepees, they saw Thunder Blanket looking none the worse for his part in the drinking the previous night. The Indian nodded, grinned and waved as he continued on his way.

They left the horses with the young Indian boy again and parted company. Zack and Mose headed for their position under the tree where they had spent the night before. They had just sat down on the packed earth when Thunder Blanket came up. ''Want whiskey?'' he asked.

Both Mose and Zack shook their heads emphatically. ''No, thankee,'' they said in unison. Thunder Blanket smiled and left.

The palaver ended early that night—much earlier than the two young men thought it would. But the feasting and celebrating lasted well into the dark. Shortly after dark, the Captain, Jeremiah and Jim Clancy, whom they hadn't seen since they helped Jeremiah with his bath, walked up to the two of them. ''Both of ye come with us,'' commanded the Captain.

It was then that he met Wind-in-the-Morning, and he cared for her straight off. In the two days they spent together, Zack discovered many things. He discovered how a good woman could make a man feel bigger than he really was; and how comfortable it could be to have one to take care of you.

He was happy. Wind-in-the-Morning made an excellent wife. Raised since babyhood to tend to a man's wants and needs, she was good at her duties and proud of her accomplishments. When he left, she gave him moccasins she had made for him. They were made, he could see, with loving care, softly comfortable and finely decorated. In exchange, he gave her a bolt of red cloth and two fine, plump otter furs.

He was sad when they had to part, but the pull of the mountains was stronger even than that of the woman. He rode off, promising he would return some day.

He sat on his horse at the top of the rise these many years later and looked down at the village. "That was shore some time ago," he said aloud. "But it won't be long now afore I'm back in yore lodge, Windy."

But years ago, after he had ridden out of the Cheyenne village, it had been some time before he came back. By then he was a free trapper and an old hand in the mountains. He had, as Jeremiah had predicted, learned the ways and comforts as well as the foibles of the Indian women of many tribes. He had taken scalps and almost lost his own on a few occasions. But through it all the thought of the woman he called Windy was often with him. One day, after he had split from Mose, he rode down out of the mountains and across the plains toward the area where he knew the village should be at this time of year. He topped a similar rise and saw the village strung out before him. His heart pounded faster and his breathing quickened. He hoped, an ache beginning to grow in him, she had not taken an Indian husband in the time he was away.

He was quite near the village when a small group of warriors raced out to meet him. He knew they would charge the first time without hurting him, testing his resolve and wanting to find out his intentions. He stood his ground, stopping the horses without showing fear. After they screechingly circled him once, Zack held up his hand, palm outward, in a gesture of peace. He recognized the scowling, fierce-looking warrior leading the little band.

"Thunder Blanket. Remember me?" he asked.

The warrior halted and stared briefly. Then he grinned and shouted in better English than he had used the last time Zack saw him, "Zakria. He who drank with me many winters ago. You have returned. But you have changed. Your face . . ." The Indian tugged at his naked chin and then pointed to Zack's heavy beard. They both laughed.

"I shore have," chuckled Zack. "How've ye bin?"

"Things have gone well for my people, and myself. The buffalo have been plentiful and the winters not so bad. And you?"

"Cain't complain."

"What brings you back to the land of the Cheyenne?"

"I come in peace to my Shyan friends. It's bin many winters since I was last in yore village, but in all my travels, I ain't nary met a tribe as great as the Shyan nation. Nary did I meet sich great warriors and hunters as the Shyans."

He realized, for the first time, that when he spoke to the Indians his speech took on the regular singsong cadence inherent to the language of the red man, whether he spoke in English or in Cheyenne.

"You speak well for a white man," said Thunder Blanket.

"Thankee," said Zack seriously. "There is another

reason why I have come back to my Shyan brothers.''

''Speak,'' commanded the warrior. Zack could see the young man was more haughty than before. But he carried it with much dignity.

''Nary in my travels did I meet sich fine wimmin as the Shyan wimmin. I have come in search of a woman who spent some days in my lodge, those many years back.''

''Do you speak of She-Who-is-Wind-in-the-Morning?'' demanded Thunder Blanket, staring intently at Zack.

''Yep,'' answered Zack, growing excited. ''She ain't bin married has she?'' he asked apprehensively.

''No, my friend,'' said Thunder Blanket stolidly. ''She has not taken a husband. But,'' he said slyly, ''she has had many offers.''

Zack now knew that Thunder Blanket knew Zack wanted Windy and was raising her value in Zack's eyes.

''That's fine. Do'e know her, Thunder Blanket? Is she well?''

''She is well.'' The Indian searched the face of the white man, looking for something which he apparently found there. ''She is my sister,'' he said simply.

Zack was startled. He had not known Wind-in-the-Morning was Thunder Blanket's sister. ''I don't rightly know yore ways, Thunder Blanket, but if'n it's okay with ye, I'd like to win yore sister fair and square.''

''You seem to speak straight, white friend. I will help you.''

''Then I'm welcome in yore village?''

Thunder Blanket wheeled his horse and led the warriors and Zack, trailing his pack horses, into the village. That night they celebrated the return of the white man.

Zack did not see Wind-in-the-Morning that night or the next, except in passing. There was much celebrating to be done. On the third day, he thought he might have to force a confrontation, something he did not relish doing. But before he could decide, a warrior came racing into the village. "Kiowas!" screamed the rider. "Kiowas!"

The camp turned into bedlam. Warriors and boys raced to bring the horses into the village for the warriors to ride or else to herd them further away, across the river, out of reach of the warlike enemy. Women and children scurried about, herded by members of the camp police, forcing them into safer positions, out of danger.

Zack grabbed his big Hawken and ran to his horse. In the milling herd he spotted Thunder Blanket. He forced his way through the people to the Indian's side. "Hyar now, amigo. Whar away're the Kioways?"

"Stay here, friend Zackria. This is a fight of the Cheyenne. It is not your concern."

Zack spit a brown gob of tobacco juice on the dusty ground. "The hell it ain't my fight. Ye've taken me into this village in friendship, an' we've smoked the pipe together. That makes it my bizness."

The Indian nodded. "Again you have spoken wisely. Follow me." The Indian kicked his horse and was off. Zack was only a second slower, as the big, powerful appaloosa caught up with the short-haired mustang ridden by Thunder Blanket.

Two miles from the village the warriors spotted the Kiowa war party and slowed to a walk to prepare. "They look ready to take some hair, amigo," commented Zack.

Thunder Blanket only grunted and began to direct his warriors. Though still young, he was a highly respected war chief, followed by many of the warriors, both young and old. Suddenly, as if by prior arrangement, both war leaders shrieked their war cries, and the two groups of warriors rushed pell-mell toward each other.

The sound was deafening: shrieks, howls and the thunder of many hooves. The battle was furious and close. Zack, from a distance away, had fired the Hawken. The shot was true, catching one of the Indians, mostly by luck. With a whoop, he stuffed the rifle into a handmade leather scabbard dangling from his saddle and raced ahead.

"C'mon ye heathen varmints," he yelled. "C'mon and fight a real warrior." He dropped the reins and let the horse have its head. He pulled out his pistols, one in each hand, and charged recklessly into the thick of the battle.

A large Kiowa warrior, one whole side of his body painted black, loomed up in front of him. The Kiowa raised his lance and pointed the wicked-looking stone blade at Zack's chest. He screeched and charged faster, hoping to count first coup on the white warrior.

Zack's pistol boomed, and the Indian fell, shot in the face at close range. Zack saw the Indian's blood-covered, agonized countenance briefly as he swept past the fallen man. He pulled up his horse, having passed through the milling throng of screaming warriors. He stuck the empty pistol back into his belt and turned the appaloosa to return to the fray. The loud war whoops crashed around him, the din almost drowning out the death songs sung by some of the warriors.

The dust temporarily blinded Zack, and he coughed and choked on its thickness. Vision clearing, he ducked, avoiding a heavy blow from a stone-headed war club that would have crushed his head, had it connected. Zack's other pistol blasted, and the warrior fell wounded, dying under the trampling hooves of screaming, frightened horses.

Zack stuck the pistol back in his belt, knowing it would be of no more use to him in this battle. He drew out his tomahawk. As he did, he saw three Kiowa warriors converging on Thunder Blanket.

With a blood-curdling shriek that rose above the rest of the noise, he raced toward his friend, swinging the tomahawk high and wide, slicking and hacking as he forced his way through the battling warriors. Three Kiowas fell wounded by his onslaught. Then he was at Thunder Blanket's side, and the three who had attacked his friend bore the brunt of his frenzied assault. All three fell dead from Zack's flashing, deadly tomahawk. He was incensed by blood now, and went wild, swinging the heavy little hand-ax crazily to and fro in wide, sweeping arcs. The Kiowas were frantically scattering helter-skelter in an effort to elude the white demon in the midst of the blood-crazed Cheyennes.

It was over. The dust cleared, and the Cheyennes took to scalping the fallen Kiowas that had been left behind by the others. They also set about caring for their own few dead and wounded. They headed back toward the village slowly, allowing a few of the warriors to pass the word of their victory to the criers who would spread it to the people.

Zack joined the victory celebration, becoming as one with the Indians he had fought alongside. He drank a little and learned the steps to the victory dance. And he sang, his awkward voice struggling to mouth the words of the delicate chants. He shuffled around the fire, seemingly hypnotized by the thudding drums and the incessant rattle of gourds and dried buffalo scrotums filled with pebbles. His body, he found, came under the control of the drums and the rattles, and the sing-song intonations. He abandoned himself to the feeling, no longer possessing his own limbs.

He joined the Indian warriors in recounting his brave deeds against the Kiowas, telling of the many he had killed, of the coups he had counted and the scalps he had taken. He boasted of his bravery, unclouded by modesty. The Indians, too, told of Zack's great prowess. Particularly Thunder Blanket. The war chief told the assembled warriors and chiefs that his wife and mother and children would be outside the camp now, mourning him, wailing sorrowfully into the night, slashing their arms and faces and cutting their hair in grief, had it not been for the courage of his white brother.

Zack reveled in it—the dancing and singing and the boasting of brave deeds. Six Kiowa scalps dangled, shining wetly, from his long buckskin shirt as he danced around the fire, a grisly testimony to his abilities on the field of battle.

But even Zack and the strong Cheyennes were not indestructable. After two days of unceasing celebration, they fell exhausted, snoring quietly where they had fallen. Zack awoke almost eighteen hours later, hungry and aching in all his muscles from the unaccustomed exercise. He sat and rubbed his eyes. Thunder Blanket sat nearby, staring at him.

"You are awake at last," said the Indian. "Are you hungry?"

"'Bout enough to eat me a whole buffler, hair and all."

"Come with me," said Thunder Blanket, smiling. "We will go to the lodge of my father, Hawk Wind. There we will eat."

Zack just nodded and struggled to his feet, the effects of the celebration lingering. They walked to a large lodge, painted on the outside, showing of the many deeds of the warrior who lived within. Though Zack did not know what all the pictographs meant, he knew full well that they signified that a great warrior owned the tepee.

"Yore father must be a brave warrior," said Zack.

"He is," Thunder Blanket said proudly. He held the flap of the tepee open for Zack, allowing him to enter first. Zack's eyes took a little time getting used to the low light in the dim interior. At the place of honor sat Hawk Wind, the man Zack had recognized his first night in the camp as the impassive warrior he had stared at so many years before.

Unpainted, Hawk Wind was in the full prime of early middle age, his face just beginning to show a few lines and wrinkles. His shoulders were broad and straight, his chest deep with strength and dignity. The bronze moonface, with its high cheekbones, wide forehead and long, straight nose, looked stolidly back at Zack.

Zack let his eyes roam around the interior of the lodge, taking in the neatness and order. Hunched over the fire in the center was Wind-in-the-Morning. He started. He had forgotten that Thunder Blanket was her brother and Hawk Wind her father.

She looked a little older, but not much, and no different. Still thinner than most Indian women, she was just as he remembered. He started to go to her but was stopped by the hard hand of Thunder Blanket. "Not yet," whispered the Indian.

He nodded and seated himself cross-legged across the fire from the elder warrior. The older man held out his pipe. Zack took it and reverently offered it to the four cardinal directions. Then he took a long pull and blew the smoke in the same four directions; east, west, north and south. Smoke was also directed up and down, for the Sky Father and the Earth Mother. Twice he did this and then he passed the pipe to Thunder Blanket, sitting on his left.

Hawk Wind nodded approvingly at Zack's actions. "You will make a fine Cheyenne warrior," he said, and Zack nodded gravely.

They finished the pipe, and Wind-in-the-Morning passed out bowls of greasy, stomach-filling stew thickened with corn meal. Zack, being the guest, was served

91

first. As the woman handed him the bowl, he looked up at her. She looked briefly. at his face and then averted her eyes, embarrassed.

"She still likes me," he thought. He watched her serving the others, pleasure filling him.

The meal over, Hawk Wind smiled broadly. "You seek to make a wife of my daughter, She-Who-is-Wind-in-the-Morning?" he asked.

Zack now found himself embarrassed. He squirmed a little but stared at Hawk Wind. "If'n ye'd accept me as sich."

Hawk Wind beamed. His daughter, married to a white trapper, especially one who was so fearless, would be rich by the tribe's standards. "She will make you a fine wife," he said.

Now it was Zack's turn to beam. The bargaining was quickly over, and later that day the marriage became official. With gifts he had received from the warriors in the village, Zack set up a small lodge for himself and his new bride. The lodge stood near the one of Hawk Wind.

He stayed in the village near the foothills of the Rockies for some months, joining the Indians in another battle and on the hunt. He learned easily their language and their customs, becoming as one of them. But village life soon paled for him. He longed for the high, clean reaches of the mountains. He wanted to feel the plush pelt of winter beaver in his hands instead of the rough coarse hair of the buffalo. He wanted the fresh, thin air of the high mountain passes instead of the greasy, smoky closeness of the tepee.

He finally decided. "I'm goin' back into the mountains soon. Would ye like to come with me?" he asked Windy.

She was still rather shy around him but answered softly, "Wind-in-the-Morning is yours. She will go where you go."

"Bueno. Good," said Zack, pleased. "We'll leave in a week or so. There ain't no real hurry. Winter's still a ways off yit."

The time was spent preparing supplies of pemmican and some jerky, the food that would sustain them through the long mountain winter when no fresh meat was available. Zack took extra care of his horses, wanting them in the best of health for the long trip and the bitter cold. He saw to his traps, repairing and cleaning them. And he looked to his other equipment: the sharpness of his Green River knife and his tomahawk; he cleaned and oiled the Hawken and his pistols and saw to the robes and powder and ball and a hundred other small items they would need for their time away from the village. Sometimes Zack thought the chores and preparing would never be over.

But Wind-in-the-Morning was efficient. She made them moccasins, soft and very thin, for wearing in the lodge at night, and others, using the thick hide of an old bull, with the hair inside, for wearing outdoors. She made long, heavy buffalo robes to keep the cold from their bodies. And she made buckskin shirts and leggings. And much more. Her fingers were never idle but flashed quickly and almost effortlessly over whatever project she had foremost in her mind.

In two weeks they were ready. They loaded the thick, heavy parfleche bags with pemmican and some lighter bags with jerky and other supplies. Zack, not one to lean on ceremony, just arose one morning and said, "Load the horses, Windy, we're leavin'." When the horses were packed, Zack hoisted Windy onto a small prairie mustang he had acquired especially for her, and he climbed on the appaloosa. Taking only long enough to bid goodbye to some of their close friends, they rode out.

They wintered high in the Rockies, up in the Wind River range. The snow came close to covering their

93

cave. But the cave, with a lean-to to protect the entrance, was large enough to keep the two people and the horses safe and secure. When the snow let up long enough, Zack strapped on snowshoes he had made and shuffled off to check his trap lines or hunted for fresh meat, when he could find it.

The beaver he took were sleekly smooth, heavy with thick hair to protect them from the winter cold and the frigid water.

"Jist lookit these," he said to Windy more than once, holding up the full, finely tanned beaver pelts. "Thar ain't no finer beaver bein' took in the mountains than these."

Yes, Zack was happy. He had his woman and the beaver were plump and plentiful.

The coming of spring, though, was a relief after the monotonous months of cold and snow. The two headed down out of the mountains toward the plains, where the buffalo would be plentiful and on the move north. Zack killed a number of the beasts, huge and shaggy, still covered with their winter fur. They feasted on fresh hump and tongue and on raw liver and on roasted ribs, sizzled over a hot, short fire of buffalo chips.

They lingered on. Zack was loath to leave. The green was coming back; new things were coming to life. He could feel himself opening up to accept the warmth and newness of spring.

But he knew they must leave. Wind-in-the-Morning wanted to see her people, and he needed to sell his furs and resupply. For the first time, his youthful prejudices got in the way of his affection for Windy. He loved her, he knew, and enjoyed being with her in the mountains or on the lonely plains, where no one but the Indians and a few of the trappers knew of their marriage. But he found that he could not bring himself to take her back to Mexican territory.

And so they lingered.

One day, though, he knew it must be done. Mose would be drifting down from the mountains. He had already missed the rendezvous up on the Green. So he ordered Windy to pack.

"We are going home?" she asked.

"I reckon," he said noncommitally.

They arrived in the Cheyenne village and were greeted happily by Hawk Wind and Thunder Blanket. Wind-in-the-Morning would have it easy this night as they feasted at the fire of Hawk Wind's lodge. And Windy would join the other women to tell them all of her adventures they had been on since leaving.

He spent a few days at the village before deciding it was time to leave. "I'm headin' back to Santy Fe in the mornin'," he said to Wind-in-the-Morning that night.

Not as shy as she had been when she met him, she asked flatly, fearfully, eyes averted, "I am not going?"

"Naw. It ain't proper," he said by way of explanation. He tried to explain further. "It ain't that I don't want ye to come along," he lied. "It's jist that it ain't no proper place fer a woman. This's man's bizness, an' a woman ain't got no place thar."

She screeched and scolded him, fiercely accusing him of wanting to go into Mexican land to find another woman. In her anger, she lapsed back into her native language and spoke so rapidly he could hardly understand her. But he did know, quite plainly, that she was not pleased with being left behind.

Finally he yelled at her, "Shaddup, woman!" She kept up with her shrieking, and he raised up his hand to strike her like any warrior would have done with a belligerent squaw. But the same streak that prevented him from taking her to Santa Fe with him also prevented him from striking her now. Angrily he stalked out of the lodge, the woman's scolding voice following him from within.

He walked to the stream and flopped down, back up against a large rock. He still fumed. "Damn squaw," he muttered. "The old-timers was right. They ain't nothin' but trouble onct ye git to carryin' 'em 'round with ye all the time."

The aging Strong Horse stopped near Zack and sat. "You are troubled, my friend?" he asked in Cheyenne.

"T'ain't nothin'," mumbled Zack.

"A man should not be upset so by his wife," said Strong Horse. "You should discipline her. It is not right that a woman should talk to her man so."

"I cain't hit a woman. It ain't right," Zack complained.

Strong Horse sat quietly and thought that over. "Then you should ignore her," he finally reasoned.

"That ain't easy," said Zack, a small smile tugging at the corners of his mouth. "That woman of mine's shore got a sharp tongue, an' it's mighty hard to ignore it, or I wouldn't say so."

The older man laughed. "Most Cheyenne women have sharp tongues, which they know well how to use."

He stood up and grasped Zack's shoulder. Zack looked up at the Indian's seamed face. "Well, I must be going now," said Strong Horse. "I am sorry to have disturbed you, friend Zack. It is not my place to meddle in the affairs of a man and his wife. You will solve it in good time, I am sure."

The Indian pulled his blanket tighter and walked slowly off.

Zack decided he needed some activity to work off his anger. Brushing himself off, he walked over to the corral and saddled the appaloosa. Then he rode out onto the prairie, the tall grass brushing his knees as he rode. He raced the horse around helter-skelter as if the horse were somehow to blame for his anger. After a good run, he and the horse were both panting and sweat-covered. He stopped the horse at a puddle to let him drink briefly. Dipping the battered old buffalo cap in the puddle, he poured the lukewarm water over his head.

Cooled a little, Zack remounted and rode slowly back toward the village. Along the way, he shot a deer that had been unfortunate enough to bound within range of the big Hawken. He rode into the camp and turned the horse over to one of the boys to be cared for. Then he lugged the carcass of the deer across the camp toward his lodge, heedless of the damage being done to the skin.

Dropping the deer outside the tepee, he entered the lodge. He gave the woman no chance to restart her tongue lashing. "Thar's a deer outside fer ye to take keer of right after ye give me some food."

Sullenly she handed him a bowl of stew and stomped outside to clean the animal. He was puffing on his pipe when she returned, a bloody hunk of fresh deer meat dripping in her hands. She hung the meat over the fire and cleaned her hands with sand.

Picking up the empty bowl, she cleaned it too with sand and then some water. She sat beside him, looking contrite.

"That was a fine deer my husband brought home," she said.

"I thought ye'd like it."

"Does that mean my husband is not leaving?"

"Naw. I'm still goin' tomorrow. I jist shot it so's ye'd have enough meat whilst I was gone. It should last ye till I git back, come beginnin' of fall."

"You will be back?" she asked anxiously. "You will not find another woman while you are gone? Perhaps some no-good Apache or Mexican woman who will not treat you right?''

"Naw," he answered seriously. "I don't want no other woman. I got ye. I jist don't feel ye got any place comin' along to Santy Fe. It's fer bizness, and ye ain't got no place thar. 'Sides, I wanna spend some time with my friend Mose. Ye remember Mose, don't ye? He's the one's long an' thin's a lodgepole.''

"Yes I remember him.'' She giggled softly. "He was with you on our first night many winters ago.''

"Yep, that's right." Zack, chuckling, put his arm around the woman. "Wall, me'n Mose're ole friends, an' ever' year we git together in Santy Fe an' have us a real spree. Ye don't wanna be left all alone down thar with all them ferriners whilst me'n my amigo git likkered up an' gamble, now, do ye?''

She shook her head, and he continued. "Ain't it better I leave ye with yore people here in yore own camp so's ye got yore friends an' yore family to look after ye whilst I'm gone?''

She nodded and said, "Yes. It is better. But you will come back?''

"Shore. I'll be back in time fer the fall hunt. After that, ye an' I'll head back up into the high country again.''

In the morning, Windy packed up Zack's furs and, with his string of pack horses trailing behind, he headed off across the plains for his rendezvous with Mose. And less than two months later, he retraced his steps across the land that would one day be Colorado. Wind-in-the-Morning was happy to see him when he returned. But in her Indian way, she hid her joy until they were alone in the tepee that night. His return was also welcomed by the war chiefs of the village. Before he retired for the night, there was much feasting. He had brought in some fresh elk meat himself for the feast.

As he sat near the blazing fire of Strong Horse, his friend, and now brother, Thunder Blanket, said to him, "We are glad that you have returned, friend Zack."

"Wall, now, I shore am glad to be back now, or I wouldn't say so."

"We had feared that Enemy-of-Kiowas might not return to his old friends, the Cheyenne. Your return is welcome more, because we need your help."

"Kiowas on the warpath?" he asked.

Thunder Blanket grunted an affirmative. "Yes, the Kiowas have bad hearts this year. And so do the Osage, though they are not so troublesome."

"Damn Kiowas. They send any war parties agin' ye yet?"

The Indian nodded. "Some small ones, yes. Earlier, in the warm months. But we are afraid that if we go on the fall hunt, they will attack the camp while we are away and the women and children are undefended."

"So ye wanna git them first?"

"Yes." Thunder Blanket spoke slowly, as if reluctant to say it. "The war chiefs and the principle chiefs have decided that it would be better if we send a large war party against the Kiowas and attack them in their own country before they come against us."

"That makes sense." Zack looked sideways at his friend. "But ye don't look like ye agree with the idee."

"I feel that it is necessary."

"Then why're ye lookin' like ye jist swallered somethin' bitter? Ye kin gain a lot of honors with a raid this big."

"Ah," sighed Thunder Blanket. "I am now one of the war chiefs and must lead my Dog Soldiers into the battle."

Zack placed a gentle hand on the man's shoulder. The Dog Soldiers were the elite of the Cheyenne warriors. It was to them that fell the most difficult tasks, the most risks.

"I see what ye mean, ole friend," said Zack. "Ye may lose many warriors. Yore great deeds would then be fergot an' the men ye lost remembered. It's not a life to look forward to."

"No, it is not," said the Indian slowly. "But I am a leader of my people and as such must do what is necessary."

"Ye'll do all right. Ye led warriors on raids afore. Jist take as much keer with yore medicine as ye allus do, an' ye'll come outta this war with all yore warriors intact. As well as many coups."

"I hope you are right, friend Zack." He paused before speaking again, looking thoughtful. "I have a request, although it is a hard one to make."

"Why, ye shouldn't feel bad 'bout askin' me ary favors, Thunder Blanket. Ye'n me're brothers. Anythin' ye need, if'n I kin do it, I will. Jist ask."

"I would like you to ride with me as one of my warriors when we meet the Kiowas," said Thunder Blanket softly.

"Wall, shore now. I wouldn't think of goin' agin the Kioways with ary one else." Zack paused to stuff another hunk of buffalo meat in his mouth. He chewed slowly, and when he was finished with it, he boasted, "Ye'n me'll take keer of them Kioways. Don't ye fret."

"I hope so. Together you and I will make some very bad medicine for the enemy." A fiery little grin lit up the Indian's broad face.

"That we will, my friend. That we will."

Thunder Blanket was amazed by Zack's lack of concern over the impending battle. The mountain man sat happily eating and joking with the other warriors. While fearless himself, Thunder Blanket nonetheless worried about what would happen to the warriors in

100

his charge when the battle was joined.

Zack danced the war dance with the Cheyenne, but that was as far as he would go with the Indian rituals before the battle. He was confident in his abilities and felt the paint and fasting and sweating were unnecessary. But he did not interfere or poke fun at their rituals either. It was not his way. And he was too much a part of the ways of the wild to ridicule them.

When they rode out of camp almost seventy-five warriors strong, led by Thunder Blanket, Hawk Wind and three others, they made a grand spectacle. Most of the warriors wore only a breechcloth and moccasins. Some, like Hawk Wind, had through the years also earned the right to wear the long, flowing eagle feather headdress. And those warriors wore the bonnets proudly, the feathers falling down their backs to the ground.

The paint they wore was varied: from small dabs here and there on the face and arms, to almost completely covering the warrior's whole body. Horses, too, were decorated with splotches of paint and brightly-colored cloth.

Zack rode out as always: in buckskin trousers and shirt, and the battered old buffalo cap with the feather sticking out one side. He would not admit it, but the hat was his personal medicine; he could as little do without the hat as Thunder Blanket could do without his spirit help. He also, like all the other warriors, wore a medicine bag under his shirt. It hung by a rawhide thong under his left armpit. He knew not what it contained; it had been given to him by Grass Grows, the ancient medicine man. He had not wanted it, thinking it was superstitious, but could not refuse it for fear of offending the old man. So he took it and wore it.

It was two days' quick ride for the unhampered warriors. On the second day, the scouts ranging far ahead and off to each side reported that they were close to the Kiowa camp. It would not be safe to go further just yet.

The men camped in a small grove of trees for the rest of the day. Weary from the long, hard ride, they took turns napping, keeping watch and eating buffalo jerky warmed over small fires made from buffalo chips and twigs. Those who stayed awake also renewed their prayers to their spirit helpers. Zack took his turn watching and eating and sleeping, but he made no offerings to the spirits, save for offering his pipe to the four directions a little more often than usual.

Night descended. The men stealthily led their horses through the chill darkness until they were in sight of the camp. "Good," muttered Thunder Blanket.

"What's so good 'bout it?" whispered Zack. "Thar must be nigh on to a hundred of 'em."

"Yes," whispered Thunder Blanket. "But it is the camp of a large war party. There are few, if any, women with them. We will not have to attack a camp full of women and children, as I feared we might. There is no honor in fighting and killing women and children."

"Ye're right 'bout that," said Zack. "I ain't much given to fightin' wimmin an' kids myself."

The camp lay in silent confidence. The Kiowa warriors, with their large numbers, were unafraid. Deep in their own territory, far from either the bloodthirsty Comanches or the tenacious Cheyennes, they felt secure. Only a few sleepy guards kept watch over the few hundred horses the Kiowas had with them.

As they sat in the dark, Thunder Blanket said to Zack, "We will attack just after the dawn. Some of our people will stampede the herd. When the Kiowas come out to see what is wrong, the others will attack, surprising them."

Thunder Blanket's small band of Dog Soldiers would have the most dangerous job. It would be their lot to wait off to one side during the short-lived main battle. Then they would cover the retreat of the fleeing Cheyennes. They would be alone, just a dozen of them, to face the savage fury of the bloodthirsty Kiowa warriors, who had been goaded into fury by the assault.

Just after dawn cracked the eastern sky, one of the Cheyenne leaders screamed his bloodcurdling war whoop and led a band of twenty-five members of the Red Shields warrior society toward the horse herd, only fifty yards away.

The horse guards, groggy from drowsiness, were quickly killed and scalped. The Red Shields shouted and fired off their few guns urging the frightened horses into a run. As the horses stampeded, the Kiowa warriors streamed out of their tepees, grabbing their weapons on the run and shouting hurried orders to each other. Quickly they formed a battle group, some of them mounted on horses the Red Shields had not scared off. They faced the second wave of Cheyennes, members of the Fox Soldiers and Elk societies. Right after them, charging from the flanks, came the warriors of the Bow String Society.

Together these shrieking warriors spread through the Kiowa camp, killing all who crossed their path. The scene, watched by Zack and the Dog Soldiers, looked like chaos. The screams of the wounded and the wild, high-pitched whinnying of frightened horses only added to the nightmarish panorama. Choking clouds of dust made the battle seem almost dreamlike as the fighting men drifted in and out of sight behind the dust.

Zack sat on the bluff watching. His face was set in hard lines. The view he saw was not pleasing. But he remained stern; from all the signs they had seen, this large band of Kiowa warriors had been heading toward the village of the Cheyennes.

"The Kiowas fight well," murmured Thunder Blanket.

A grim Zack only nodded.

The fighting was furious. The sun, now brutally hot, glinted off metal knife and tomahawk blades and off the points of lances. The heat made the ground shimmer, making the battle look like a dream to those who sat apart.

With the whole camp up and fighting, the Cheyennes, out-numbered, began to fall back. The huge horse herd, stolen from the Kiowas, was far out on the prairie now, the Red Shields forcing them into a faster and faster stampede.

Thunder Blanket could no longer stand the waiting and watching. The Cheyennes, facing the larger number, were beginning to fall. With a hoarse shout, Thunder Blanket called for his men to follow him.

Without fear, the elite Dog Soldiers waded into the thick of the fighting, using lance, bow and tomahawk. Zack left the big, heavy rifle hanging in the scabbard on his saddle and his pistols in his belt. They would not help here. For close-in fighting like this, he preferred the heavy-headed, two-foot-long tomahawk that he used so effectively. As the Dog Soldiers charged into the midst of the battling warriors, they shouted for the other Cheyennes to fall back and flee toward home. "Turn back. Turn back!" shouted Thunder Blanket. "Your work is done here!"

The Dog Soldiers took reckless chances to remove their dead and wounded brothers from the field. A Dog Soldier would die before allowing another warrior to be taken or scalped.

Thunder Blanket charged into a group of four Kiowas that had a struggling Cheyenne on the ground. They were about to slice the scalp from the writhing warrior. With a scream of savage fury, Thunder Blanket pierced one of the Kiowas through with his long lance. The other Kiowas jumped at him. With a laugh of derision, he grabbed one by the long, greasy hair. Yanking the brave's face toward him, Thunder Blanket slashed his throat, screeching, "Die, yellow Kiowa dog!"

As he dropped the gurgling corpse, he kicked another of the attacking Kiowas in the face. Pulling the long lance free from the first Kiowa he had killed, he smacked the other Kiowa across the face with the butt end. As the warrior fell, Thunder Blanket punctured the Kiowa's side with the lance. He jerked the lance from the Indian's gaping side. Eyes clouded with pain, the Kiowa and the other that was still alive scattered, racing to escape the demonic fury of the murderous Cheyenne.

Thunder Blanket slid off his horse and grabbed the wounded Cheyenne. Throwing the brave onto his own horse, Thunder Blanket shouted, "Ride!" He emphasized the command with a hard swat on the horse's rump. Now on foot, he let out a piercing shriek of a whoop and shouted, "I am here, eaters of carrion. Come, Kiowas. See what a real warrior is like!"

The iron-tipped lance held in his right hand, Thunder Blanket stood his ground against the Kiowas who rushed toward him. He grabbed a tomahawk from one of the dead Kiowas and held it in his left hand. Hurling taunts at his enemy, he planted himself, unafraid. He began to chant his death song, ready to die for the service of others.

The Kiowas attacked this bold Cheyenne, knowing he was a leader of their attackers. They were fully aware that if they could kill him and scalp him, the other Cheyennes would be demoralized. So the Kiowa warriors, in desperate rage, attacked the brave Cheyenne.

The first ran straight onto the sharp iron of Thunder Blanket's lance, the spear ripping through his body. He yanked the weapon free and split open the head of a second Kiowa with the tomahawk he adroitly wielded. Three more Kiowas rushed at Thunder Blanket while a fourth took aim at him with an arrow and then fired it.

Thunder Blanket staggered under the impact of the arrow that caught him high up in the right side of the chest. He snapped the arrow off and shouted invectives at his attackers.

"Come, yellow-hearted women," he bellowed. "Do you think one small arrow would stop a Dog Soldier?" He laughed and then grimaced in hurt. But he would not give in to the pain. "Come," he yelled, laughing at the enemy. "Try to take me."

He threw the long lance, and it tore through another attacker's stomach. But he had no chance to use the tomahawk again as the two other Kiowas overwhelmed him and wrestled him to the ground.

Zack had helped rescue another fallen Cheyenne warrior, killing two Kiowas in the process. He was continuing his personal battle with the Kiowas when he saw Thunder Blanket go down. "No!" he screamed. He kicked the big appaloosa urging it to speed to his fallen friend.

He pulled the horse up in a rage and swung mightily. The tomahawk cracked through the head of one of the Kiowas. He wrenched the hatchet free and swung around. The other Kiowa looked up in surprise. Zack smashed him in the face with the tomahawk as he swung it wildly from side to side.

The other Cheyenne warriors were streaming out of the village's furthest limits and were racing across the plains. Zack and Thunder Blanket were the only two Cheyennes left in the heart of the Kiowa camp. The

Kiowas, suffering in defeat, were still fighting poorly, uncoordinated. But they were recovering.

"C'mon, amigo," Zack shouted over the din of shrill screams. "Lit's go. We gotta get outta hyar. And pronto."

Thunder Blanket, chest covered in blood, looked ready to argue, but Zack shouted, "Thar ain't nothin' ye kin do hyar arymore. We got all our wounded and thar warn't but two dead. We got them too. Thar ain't no call fer ye to die hyar. Ye're needed to help defend the others whilst they escape."

Thunder Blanket nodded. Grabbing Zack's outstretched hand, he jumped on the appaloosa behind him. The white man wheeled the horse around and, dodging a few wildly-launched arrows, they raced out of the camp.

They caught up with the rest of the Dog Soldiers who were being attacked by a small force of Kiowas who had managed to save some horses and rode out in pursuit. Zack rode up beside one of the riderless horses that ran after the other loose ones, not knowing what else to do. Without slackening speed, Thunder Blanket grabbed the wildly running mount and flung himself across the space, bringing the horse under control.

He and Zack joined the other Cheyenne warriors in routing the last of the Kiowas who had turned back in defeat, gathering their dead and wounded as they went. The Cheyennes slowed to a trot and then to a walk, taking their time heading home. There was no need to fear another attack.

Thunder Blanket's wound was not as bad as it had first seemed. Two days later he rode into the village with the others, weak and still blood-covered, but elated. Young and healthy, the Indian would recover quickly.

CHAPTER 6

The Cheyennes rode victoriously into their village, glistening, bloody scalps dangling from lances, coup sticks, guns and belts. The celebrating was loud, long and continuous, tempered only by the grief of the wives and families of the dead warriors. Their constant wailing swept across the empty land, loud enough to be heard over the din of the celebrations. Eight warriors had fallen to the Kiowas, two of them in the enemy camp. The others died of wounds on the way back to the village. Only one Dog Soldier had been lost.

The large herd of captured horses was divided among the braves who had fought that day. The largest number of the horses went to the war chiefs who had led the raid. Thunder Blanket received many horses. Two of them he gave to Zack, another he kept for himself. The others he gave to the family of the man who had been killed while in his care.

"Ye should've kept another 'un fer yoreself," Zack said to him. But the Indian only shrugged. It was his way.

The Cheyennes celebrated wildly, recounting their brave deeds, strutting, flourishing scalps and newly-acquired feathers. And none was more boastful than Thunder Blanket and the short, stocky white warrior who had fought alongside of him. Zack's woman, She-Who-is-Wind-in-the-Morning, was especially proud of her man and her brother. Out of their hearing, she would often recount their courageous deeds to the other women, praising them boastfully, pride glinting from her eyes.

The men of the village could go safely now on the fall hunt. They no longer feared a Kiowa attack. Or an attack by anyone else; it was late in the summer, and the Comanches had already bested the Apaches and were no longer anxious for war. The Osage had their hands full with the Crows further north, and as for the Kiowas—they would not be bothering the Southern Cheyennes this year.

The camp prepared for the hunt, the village crier announcing all the plans as they were made by the tribal council. As the preparations were being made, Zack also made ready to leave for the mountains. They would leave, he told Windy, as soon as the hunt was over and enough pemmican and jerky made.

He was repairing one of his traps, sitting cross-legged on a blanket in front of his tepee, when Thunder Blanket strode up purposely and sat beside him. Wind in the Morning, seeing the visitor, brought him food. When the Indian was finished, Zack dug his old pipe out of his possible sack. Lighting it, he offered it to the four directions, and then passed it to Thunder Blanket. The Indian also made the offering and then puffed deeply. The two men passed the pipe back and forth until the mild tobacco was gone. Though he preferred regular tobacco, Zack always carried a blend of kinnikinick for his Indian friends, who found regular tobacco too harsh for their tastes.

"I would approach my brother Zack with a request," said Thunder Blanket more respectfully than he had ever spoken to the white man. He waited patiently for Zack's answer.

Zack looked at him directly for a moment before saying, "Ye kin ask."

"My brother, Zack, has fought very bravely for his Cheyenne cousins. He has counted coup on the enemy many times and has gained many honors. He has also saved the life of Thunder Blanket twice. For that I am grateful."

Zack was astounded. Not only was the Indian developing into one of the most highly-respected war leaders, he was also turning into a fine speaker and orator. His speech flowed effortlessly and was always very respectful. He will go far as a chief, thought Zack. Zack also wondered what the Indian wanted, but he was patient enough to sit and wait. One did not hurry these things, he knew from long experience. It would all be done in due time. So he waited.

The Indian finally continued. "Many times my brother has joined the war party with Thunder Blanket. And at all times he has shown his bravery."

Zack sat unmoving, a habit gained from the Indians. Inside he was restless, anxious to get back to his work and wanting all the while to know what the Indian wanted. But he waited like a good Indian—stoically and patiently.

"You have become one of the People," said Thunder Blanket. "Even to taking a Cheyenne woman, my sister, as your wife. This is good. You have taken many of the Indian ways, sharing your wealth when you have it and sharing misery and grief when it is known in our village."

Thunder Blanket paused to gather his thoughts. "It is rare," he began, "that such a brave warrior does not belong to a society of warriors. This is not good."

So that's it, thought Zack. "He wants me to become a member of the Red Shields or something." But he did not speak aloud. Thunder Blanket was not finished.

"I have thought much on this," said the Indian slowly. "And I think you should join one of the warrior societies. I have thought that maybe you have not felt welcome enough in our village to seek admittance to one of the societies."

"That's partly it," said Zack honestly. On the few occasions he had considered joining one of the societies, he had thought they might not accept him because he was not a true Cheyenne. Maybe, he thought, he had been wrong.

"I don't see no reason I cain't become a member of one of the warrior societies. Which one d'ye think I should join? The Foxes? The Bow Strings?"

"I came to see you today, not only to suggest that you join one of the societies, but to suggest which one."

"I will listen, my brother."

"I have come to ask you if you would like to join the Dog Soldiers, to become a member of that society with your brother, Thunder Blanket, and our father, Hawk Wind."

Zack sat shaken. He had thought he would be allowed to join one of the many warrior societies that flourished in the Cheyenne culture. Anyone, that is, except the Dog Soldiers.

"Are ye shore?" he questioned.

"I would not have said it if I had not meant it," said the Indian calmly.

Zack still sat in wonder. The Dog Soldiers were the most elite of the warrior societies and, as such, were entrusted with many duties and powers not given to other warriors. He also knew that admittance to the society was rather restrictive. Membership was limited to those few warriors who were superior in fighting skill and bravery. It was not an easy life, nor one to be taken lightly.

"If'n ye'll have me, this ole coon'd be more'n glad to join with ye. In fact, I'd be right honored if ye'd take me."

"You realize, brother, that it will mean extra duties and responsibilities on the hunt that is to begin soon?"

"I reckon I kin handle it."

Thunder Blanket smiled for the first time. "I thought you would. If I did not think that of you, I would have stayed away."

Their meeting became more informal now, like in the old days, as Thunder Blanket helped Zack check his traps to see that they were working properly. They passed the time in idle chatter, their hands kept busy by work.

A few days later, Zack went through the rites, making him a member of the Dog Soldiers. But he refused to take part in the torture ceremonies of the Sun Dance held a few days later.

The dance was held for luck on the hunt, and Cheyennes from many miles around trekked to the spot where the dance would be held. Zack danced some, but refused to have his flesh pierced as Thunder Blanket had pledged himself to do.

"Ye're crazy," he told Thunder Blanket, "lettin' yoreself git skewered thataway. Only un's gonna poke holes in my carcass's some ole Kioway who gits lucky with an arrow."

Thunder Blanket and Strong Horse, who sat nearby, laughed at his description. "You may just end up that way, Enemy-of-Kiowas," said Strong Horse in Cheyenne. "You have not made many friends in the Kiowa camp."

"Wall now, I reckon I haven't at that. But it'll take a heap better Kioway than I ary seed to take this chile's hair."

"Spoken like a true Cheyenne," said the old Indian, laughing.

"I still think ye're crazy, amigo," commented Zack.

"You will enjoy the Sun Dance someday, my brother," said Thunder Blanket with dignity. "You will find it useful some day. Yes, I think you will."

"I don't reckon I'll need it, but ye nary kin tell." The idea left him uneasy. He was not afraid of the pain. But the significance of it disturbed him.

Sun Dance over, preparations for the hunt progressed rapidly and seriously. One of the duties of the Dog Soldiers was to act as the village police during the hunt, to prevent anyone from hunting on his own or making so much noise that the buffalo might be frightened away, jeopardizing the whole tribe. It was an important duty, one taken very seriously.

When he became a Dog Soldier, Zack joined the other warriors of that society in keeping order in the village during the preparation for the hunt. Like the other Dog Soldiers, his presence was often enough to keep most of the people in line. Punishment, though severe when given, was rarely meted out.

After much planning, the village was ready. The chief chosen to direct the hunt decided that the tribe would leave the next morning. It was early in the Moon-When-the-Deer-Paw-the-Earth, September. The village crier went about the village passing the word to all the families, calling out, "Sleep early. Sleep early. Tomorrow we move the village. Sleep now. Sleep now. We leave for the hunt in the morning."

Zack was glad for the decision. He was anxious to get started and he told Windy so that evening in the lodge. "It's 'bout time we was leavin'. I was gittin' tired of stayin' in the village allus tryin' to keep the rules from bein' broke. 'Sides, by the time we git up to the mountains after takin' the time to make meat, the snow'll be fallin' right reglar. Most of the prime fall pelts'll be took by then."

113

"We can leave by the beginning of the Moon-of-the-Changing-Season," said Wind-in-the-Morning. "It will not be too late."

"Hell, that's the beginnin' of October already," exploded Zack. "By then there's likely to be waist-deep snow on the ground up in some of the high passes."

Her stroking seemed to calm some of his anger. "I think the good weather will last long enough."

"Ye think so?" he asked.

"The spirits tell me it will be so, and the signs say there will be more good weather."

"Damn, ye shore are somethin', woman, or I wouldn't say so." He hugged her, and they rolled closer together. But he was still pent up. "It's too bad we had to go agin them Kioways so late in the year. Now the bufflers've gone so fur south we gotta move the whole village. That's gonna take some time."

Wind-in-the-Morning held him closer. "It will be all right. It will be done soon."

They drifted off into sleep, warm in the chill night air.

The next morning the camp was a bustle of activity as the camp prepared to move out. Lodges were taken down amid the shouts of the men and women and the noisy banter of children. The large herd of horses was rounded up and placed in the care of boys who next year would be able to ride with the men on the hunt. But this year they were still too young.

Zack was up early and, with Thunder Blanket and some of the other Dog Soldiers, mounted up and rode through the village, hurrying the slower people along. Occasionally the flick of a riding quirt was necessary to get some laggard to hurry, but by mid-morning, the camp was ready to leave.

The leading chief gave the command to move, and the village crier passed it along. "Now we move!"

he shouted as he rode slowly down the line of families. "Now we move!"

It would be afternoon before the last families in line, the poor ones, would begin to move. But the first families, with all their possessions, moved out rapidly. They would not go too many miles this day, but by the morrow they would have become accustomed to the travel, and they would make better time. And each day would go a little faster.

A week out on the trail the chief gave the word to halt. The crier once again passed it on to everyone. Buffalo had been sighted, a large herd, and a semi-permanent camp would be made here, close enough for the hunters to gather in the buffalo but far enough away so the bison would not be scared off.

Zack chaffed at the delay. He wanted the hunt over and done with. The battle with the Kiowas had delayed the hunt so long that the buffalo were even further south than the hunt leaders had thought. It was more time wasted. Normally, he knew, the men would have left the village where it was because the buffalo would be close. The men would ride off to the hunt and, when it was over, the women would come with their skinning knives and their horses and butcher the meat, packing it on the horses for the short trip home.

But this year they had to move the whole village miles away to find the buffalo, a long slow trek that galled Zack. It would be at least another week before the hunt would be complete and most of the meat dried. It would be another week beyond that to make the pemmican and jerky to last through the bitterness of the winter. He chafed at the delay, but kept his peace about it, knowing there was nothing he could do. But he grumbled to Windy just the same. Knowing that grumbling was his way, Windy mostly ignored him.

After his lodge had been put up, Zack sat inside,

checking his weapons, when Thunder Blanket entered after calling from outside. He was fed, and they smoked a leisurely pipe, discussing the day's travel. Finally Thunder Blanket said, "Brother, do you think that you can stay awake through the night to stand guard?"

"I've gone without sleep afore," answered Zack. "But why d'ye need a guard all night?"

"The young men are hard to keep still. This will be the last big hunt until the spring comes; possibly as long as the Moon-When-the-Ponies-Shed if we have a long winter."

"Wall, now, I guess ye're right," said Zack thoughtfully. "May is a long ways off. But are ye really afeared the young 'uns'll take off?"

"Yes. Not the seasoned warriors. They are old enough to be able to contain themselves. But the young men, the ones who are on the hunt for the first or second time, they will want to gain honors by getting the first buffalo or the biggest bull or the fattest cow."

"They are gettin' a leetle itchy, ain't they?" laughed Zack.

Thunder Blanket remained stone-faced. "It is not a matter to laugh at, friend Zack. Should one of these young men succeed in getting past the guard and attack the herd, it may stampede. If that happens, we would have to follow the buffalo many miles further south, and winter is fast approaching. One or two warriors, hunting early, could force the village into starvation. That is why our punishment in such matters is so severe."

Zack sobered. "Don't they know that?"

"Of course. But they are young and not yet tempered by wisdom." The lightest smile brushed across the Indian's dark face. "They also consider such

116

doings as part of their training. If they can sneak past the guard, they have shown that they have learned their lessons well."

Zack had not really considered the consequences before, but now he realized the gravity of his position. "Then I guess I better git some shut-eye now, so's I kin watch fer them young coons all night an' still ride on the hunt tomorrow."

"It is wise," said Thunder Blanket. "I will come for you when you are needed."

"Come git me a leetle earlier then ye need me, my friend, an' we kin eat together afore we go on out."

"You are generous, my brother," said the Indian. "I will be grateful to do so." With nothing further to say, Thunder Blanket stood and walked silently out of the lodge.

That evening, just before the sun dipped behind the far-off mountains, Thunder Blanket and Zack sat down to a meal of elk stew seasoned and filled with wild prairie turnips. Finished eating, they shared a pipe in friendship and then went outside.

Zack's appaloosa was saddled. He said silent thanks to Wind-in-the-Morning. Thunder Blanket's pony was also saddled. As they mounted, the Indian said, "You are entrusted with preserving the success of this hunt, my brother. You have the authority, and the duty, to punish anyone who breaks the rules laid down by our chiefs. Do not let your heart grow weak."

"I understand," said Zack. "I ain't about to let no young buck ruin the hunt and endanger everbody."

The night seemed long, but Zack remained awake and alert. Sometimes walking, sometimes riding softly in the shadows, he watched. Near daybreak, he caught three youthful hunters trying to sneak out of the camp to attack the buffalo herd at first light. In shame and embarrassment at being caught, the young men walked meekly back to their lodges, the fire and excitement gone out of them.

As dawn crept slowly up, Zack could hear the camp waking. It was a quiet awakening as Indian villages went. Mornings were usually a cacophonous time, full of arising life and spirit. But today it was not so; mothers stifled crying babies with a quick breast, and the other children, catching the serious tone of the camp, went about their childish business in silence.

Zack rode into camp, watching the women, unusually quiet, preparing a small meal for their families or honing the large, heavy-handled butcher knives for the coming chores. He sat outside his own lodge, and She-Who-is-Wind-in-the-Morning brought him a small bowl of her stew. "Is this all I git?" he asked.

"You will soon be feasting on raw liver and kidney," she said in Cheyenne. "Tonight there will be fresh hump and tongue, roasted the way you like. Or," she said slyly, "are you not enough of a hunter to bring in much fresh meat from the hunt today?"

She sat across from him and began to hone her favorite butcher knife, one he had given her. "Naw I ain't fergot, but I'm hungry. 'Sides, ye must think I'm a good hunter, or ye wouldn't be settin' thar honin' that knife of yores, would ye?"

She glanced at him sideways, a slight smile on her lips. She knew her man would bring in meat. She knew he was one of the best hunters and warriors in the village. She would have much work to do today; there would be many buffalo to skin and butcher. Her man, she knew, would get the most animals of all the hunters. She knew this, and so she readied her tools.

An hour later the hunters mounted ponies, leading their favorite buffalo ponies by a rope. In one mass they headed toward the buffalo. The men were silent, realizing the importance of their task. The well-trained buffalo ponies also remained quiet. As the men spotted the buffalo, they dismounted and handed over their horses to four young men. Then they mounted the buffalo ponies, so well-trained the rider did not have to control it except by gentle knee pressure.

The hunters spread out, closing in on the buffalo herd in a large semi-circle. They edged closer until the leaders of the herd began to shuffle nervously. The approaching hunters halted and sat quietly, unmoving on their mounts until the buffalo settled down again.

When the buffalo had resumed grazing, the leader of the hunt raised his short bow in the air. He let out one piercing shriek and the men, with bows and a supply of arrows already in hand, charged the dumbfounded buffalo. The bison stared stupidly for a few seconds at the racing horde before lumbering off across the grassy plain.

Now that the charge was on and they were bearing down on their prey, the men let loose, whooping, shouting and hollering, chasing the buffalo to where other hunters sat waiting. As the buffalo approached these riders, they, too, joined in the chaotic race across the prairie.

It was bedlarm—choking dust, clots of flying dirt and grass, the thunder of thousands upon thousands of hooves, men yelling, an occasional horse squealing in pain as a wounded bull stopped suddenly and slashed at the horse with his horns.

Zack had fastened on his old beaver cap with a rawhide string tied under his chin so it wouldn't fall off as he sped after the animals. He was no longer tired. He was elated. The blood surged ever quicker through his veins. The rush of the wind, even the cloying dust through which he rode, caused the blood to sing in his arteries. Here was freedom.

The big appaloosa ran effortlessly along, big muscles flexing and stretching, pulling up alongside a large cow. Zack dropped the reins. The horse needed no control, knowing what to do. Zack, the only hunter using a gun, brought the Hawken up and pointed it just behind the last rib on the massive, pounding animal. He pulled the trigger and the gun boomed. The beast kept pace for a few steps before sprawling headlong, blood pouring from its mouth and nostrils. It quivered briefly in its death throes, but Zack was already gone.

He raced on. He would have shouted for the pure joy of it, but his mouth was full of rifle balls, kept there for convenience and speed and because the spit would keep the ball lodged in the gun without wadding as he raced along.

He flew along, loading the big .53-caliber Hawken in the old way—an unmeasured dose of powder poured into the gun, the barrel held straight upwards; then he lifted the barrel to his mouth, spit in a ball and rammed it down only once with the wiping stick. A smack of the gun stock against the saddle served to settle the powder and ball. The rifle was kept upright until the next target loomed.

As he rode up alongside another large cow, Zack poured a small amount of powder in the pan as he brought the rifle up. In the same fluid motion, he brought the muzzle to rest against the broad side of the cow and pulled the trigger. It fell immediately, rolling over and over, legs akimbo.

Zack urged the appaloosa toward a large, rangy old bull. He knew Wind-in-the-Morning could use the bull's tough, thick hide for winter moccasins and for new parfleches.

He went after the beast in the same way, but his aim was off just the least bit. The enraged bull, only lightly wounded, swung his massive horned head around to gore the horse, but Zack's appaloosa was too quick, the bull's horns passing within inches of Zack's leg. The old bull pounded on a few yards further and then stopped. Zack and the horse almost ran straight into the beast's broad, thick forehead. But again the appaloosa was too quick and swept aside out of range of the wicked horns. Bleeding from nose and mouth, the bison shuffled around, snorting, spraying blood as it did. Zack pulled up the horse and faced the magnificent old bull. "Sorry, ole fella," Zack said to the wounded animal, "but I need yore hide more'n ye do."

He took his time loading the Hawken this time, keeping a wary eye on the buffalo as he did. He took careful aim and fired. The bull fell as if pole-axed. Zack again took a little more time reloading Thunder and then took off in pursuit of the herd, now moving half a mile away.

The appaloosa, rested a bit, got its second wind and was soon again in the thick of the herd. Zack fired and loaded, fired and loaded, again and again, not missing another shot. The Hawken began to heat up, and the barrel expanded slightly so a ball would no longer stayed lodged within. It was also too hot for him to be able to spit a ball into the barrel.

Because the ball would not seat properly, the Hawken misfired twice in a row, barely grazing a running buffalo. He knew he was through for the day, and he pulled the foamed horse to a stop. Both man and horse were sweat-covered and breathing heavily.

As he turned the horse to walk it slowly back toward the camp, he scratched its broad head between the ears. "Nice goin', ole boy," he said to his mount. "I guess we showed them bufflers, or I wouldn't say so. Ye did jist fine, an' I'll see to it ye git some extry special feed tonight."

As he neared the spot where the hunt had started,

he saw the women already skinning and butchering the huge carcasses, identifying the animals killed as their husbands' by the distinctive markings on the arrows and lances. The ones slain by Zack were easy to identify—they were the only ones with holes from rifle balls.

He counted the animals he had killed as he rode back toward the women. He could see some of the other men back already, sloppily eating raw innards from the bison. He rode up to where Windy was working on the second buffalo Zack had claimed. She was being helped by her younger sister, Rain Cloud Woman.

"Whyn't ye helpin' yore father, like ye're supposed to?" he asked the girl good-naturedly.

She was shy, like her sister had once been. "Because my fatter is a great warrior and a great hunter and has many wives to help butcher the buffalo he killed."

"Then how'd ye git stuck doin' mine?" He was still joking with the girl, although she did not know it. She was only about twelve, Zack guessed. And she looked much like her sister—a little more broad, and her face was a little flatter, but he could tell they were sisters.

She was embarrassed, but she answered him honestly: "My sister told me that her man is the greatest hunter in the tribe and that he would kill many buffalo. She said that since her man would shoot so many buffalo she would need much help in butchering them. So she asked me to help."

Zack glanced at Wind-in-the-Morning, who was busy slicing large slabs of meat from a buffalo carcass. She did not look up. He did, though, see the creeping signs of embarrassment on her almost hidden face. Face still averted, she hissed. "You speak too much for a young girl. There is much work to be done. This is not the time for talking."

Zack dismounted and touched her cheek. She turned toward him, eyes still averted. "I shot twenty buffler, Windy, includin' a tough ole bull ye kin use fer some new parfleches. I guess ye're gonna have yore work cut out fer ye this day."

She smiled and finally looked at him. "My husband is a good man." She handed him a large, dripping hunk of raw liver. "Eat as much as you like," she said. "There is more. But I must get back to the butchering, because I have much work to do. Yes, there is much to be done."

Zack bit off a large mouthful of the meat, still steaming from the animal's body heat. The juices ran down his chin and dripped onto his caked buckskin shirt. He paid it no heed. "Ye got enough horses to carry all the meat an' skins back to the village?" he asked between mouthfuls.

"There are enough." She went back to her work, humming a little tune of her own making.

Zack picked up more fresh, raw organs from the beast that Wind-in-the-Morning and her sister were slicing quickly and efficiently. Remounting, he rode slowly off, giving the big appaloosa a rest.

The feasting that night in the village was lavish. The women drifted in and out of the camp all afternoon and into the night, bringing in the loads of meat and skins. The men began their dancing and singing and feasting early, and were joined later by the women, after they had finished their work. Most of them, men and women and children, gorged themselves on fresh buffalo meat—raw kidneys and livers and hearts, and roasted hump and tongue and ribs—until they got sick. Then they would vomit and rejoin the feasting to gorge some more.

Zack still felt the effects of his gluttony when he awoke the next day. Wind-in-the-Morning was already up and bustling about. With her once more was Rain Cloud Woman. The two were among the few that did not gorge themselves to the point of sickness.

"Would you like something to eat?" Windy asked Zack when he stepped sluggishly out into the sunshine.

"Ye should know better'n to ask a damnfool question like that the day after a big hunt. I et so much last night, I mightn't eat agin till next spring."

The women laughed and continued working. "Ye git enough meat and skins to last out the winter?" he asked.

"Yes, there is plenty of meat. We will have enough."

"How 'bout skins?"

"We have many furs and enough robes. I will make new buckskin shirts for you and many pairs of moccasins for us both."

"Anythin' else we need afore we leave?"

"No, my husband. Everything will be ready. I am drying some of the meat for jerky and I will make pemmican with some of the cherries, chokecherries and blackberries I have picked and saved."

The pemmican, Zack knew, would be thick and rich with fat, a mixture of buffalo fat, mashed buffalo or elk meat and squashed berries all mixed together. It was a high energy food, good for the bitter-cold mountain winters.

"Bueno," he said, "When kin ye be ready to leave?"

"By the beginning of the Moon-of-the-Changing-Season."

"Wall now, that's kinda late, but if'n it's the best ye kin do, so be it. We'll jist have to make tracks when we leave. So ye best be ready to move."

"I will be ready." Wind-in-the-Morning went back to her work with more concentration. Over her shoulder she said to Zack, "Now go off and join the men. There is much to be done before we can leave."

Two weeks later Zack and Wind-in-the-Morning rode out of the Cheyenne camp on the Arkansas River and headed west up through the lower Rockies and then north toward the headwaters of the Platte River.

Zack trapped many of the streams and rivers leading up to the higher reaches of the Rockies, lucking out with the leavings of the larger parties that had already drifted through the area. He got a number of high-quality, early-fall pelts. Already they were becoming thick and rich in preparation for winter. With Windy's expert hands working the pelts, he knew he could get a prime price for them.

But they did not dally. They never stayed longer than a day or two in any one place. Zack wanted to be wintered-in before the big snows came. It had started snowing their first day in the mountains, but it lasted only briefly. Zack knew, however, that before long the heavy snows would come, and he wanted to be settled in before that time.

They wintered near several small streams heavy with beaver. They made the camp, half-cave and half log-and-sod house, near the Yellowstone's confluence with the Stillwater, high in the Bighorn Mountain Range.

Their first day in camp the snow fell, thick and wet. "Damn," snorted Zack as the white blanket fell, settling on their heavy outer robes and in their hair. The snow melted and trickled down their backs.

"Damn stuff could've waited a few more days till I got the shelter built," he grumbled.

But the snow continued, day after day for nearly a week. When it finally stopped, it was almost six feet deep in some places. The horses, inside the cave with the humans, had subsisted on branches and tree bark that Zack cut down and brought in to them. But already they were beginning to gaunt down. When the snow stopped falling, Zack led them out of the cave, flattening the snow with his body so the horses could walk to a small stand of trees nearby without bogging down.

The few stunted trees stood out grotesquely from the white cover, but the horses were able to strip off the bark or to munch the few hardy strands of grass that had survived, clear of snow, beneath the tree.

As the gaunted horses grazed, Zack walked back to the cave. "I wanna git us some fresh meat," he said to Wind-in-the-Morning. "I'm already tired of jerky and pemmican. I'm gonna go out a ways an' see if'n I kin git a mountain sheep."

The woman nodded. "I will look for roots where the snow is not deep. They will help to thicken the stew we will make with the meat you bring."

He grunted an affirmative and picked up the snowshoes he had made during the week of snow. "I also gotta check my traps, if'n I kin," he said. He strapped the snowshoes on his back and, picking up the Hawken, he mounted the appaloosa Wind-in-the-Morning had saddled for him. He wrapped the heavy buffalo robe around him and nodded to the woman. "I'll be back soon," he said. He turned the horse and walked slowly out of the desolate camp. Windy watched as he left, her spirits dropping as he grew smaller.

The hunt was long and hard, although it covered but a few miles. He walked successfully back into the camp leading the big horse loaded with a dead mountain sheep and six thick, large beaver pelts. He dropped the pelts on the ground and pulled the animal carcass after it. Exhausted, he sank to the ground, gratefully accepting the cup of steaming boiled coffee that Wind-in-the-Morning handed him. Wordlessly, she unsaddled the horse and led it to the stand of trees to graze on what little feed was left.

Coming back to the fire, she began to skin and butcher the mountain sheep. Finished, she spread out the beaver pelts as well as the mountain sheep pelt to begin working them. Using the mashed brains of the sheep to soften and clean the furs, her short, thick fingers kneaded and prodded. As she worked, she asked, "Was it very hard?"

"Purty bad," he answered. "I had to tramp more snow fer the horse than I did fer me. Damned beast jist sat thar eatin' tree branches, whilst I cleared a path fer him."

"Were the mountain sheep far?"

"Naw. But wadin' through that snow made the goin' purty rough. 'Sides, the damned thing didn't want me to git a shot at it. I must've laid in the snow fer an hour or more waitin' fer a decent shot."

Zack pulled out his old pipe, filled and lighted it. "Then when I did shoot it, the damned thang fell in a gully, so I had to go in an' fish it out. It was plumb wearisome, I tell ye."

He puffed quietly on his pipe for a few minutes while Wind-in-the-Morning worked silently over the hides.

"I gotta git this shelter done afore too long. We cain't stand too many more of them storms 'thout better cover."

They were lucky. Good weather prevailed. He cut logs and some hunks of sod where he could find them to form a rudimentary shelter. He chinked it with mud from the stream bed that he hacked out and melted down over the fire.

The good weather also brought a breath of Indian summer and the warmer temperatures that went with

127

it. Zack knew it wouldn't last and worked feverishly to get everything done. Finishing the shack, he gathered together enough feed that, along with the bark and tree branches around the shelter, would be enough to keep the horses alive until spring. He and Wind-in-the-Morning also gathered what roots and other tubers they could dig up to supplement their meager diet.

Zack grumbled at the extra work, but Windy was adamant. "We will grow sick with nothing to eat but jerky and pemmican," she scolded. So he dug.

Zack also worked his traps, gathering in the fine, heavy pelts of the winter beaver. He was careful not to trap any one area overly much, so he alternated his traps from stream to stream and from location to location among the many streams and brooks that ran nearby. Soon the cold and snow came to stay. Within a few weeks the ice was too thick over most of the small streams to allow Zack to set his traps. So he concentrated on trapping the larger, free-running rivers which did not freeze over.

The snows came, too, with days going by without the two people being able to see the sky because of the clouds and the swirling, wind-swept snow. Zack had tried to pick a spot well sheltered by rocks and trees, but the mountain wind still found its way into the crude shelter. The nights were bitter cold, the temperature usually hovering well below zero. Bones and skin ached from the frigid air.

The days were hardly better, with the temperature only rising a few degrees. Their life was a hell of monotony. Zack grumbled and cursed and fidgeted. Day after day they were unable to leave the shelter because of the snow or cold, and when they could leave the cabin, they could not travel far.

The horses gaunted down slowly but steadily, despite the efforts made to feed them. Zack and Windy were well-fed, but the diet was boring, and Zack grumbled about that too. "I cain't wait till spring," he said more than once. "Then we kin git us some fresh buffler. Some roasted hump or tongue."

To break the monotony of eating, Zack once in a while brought home a whole beaver when he could get one, and they feasted on roasted beaver tail.

In mid-March the weather broke. Although the cold was still numbing and often below zero and the snow still fell regularly, they could somehow feel spring coming in the afternoon air. Gradually the ice began to melt on the streams, each day growing a little thinner. The snows began to fade. One morning Zack came back from his trap lines to find the horses outside. The snow in some places was patchy, and new grass was beginning to spring up. The horses munched greedily at the sparse vegetation.

"It's good ye got the horses out fer some fresh feed," Zack said as he dismounted.

The woman, working over a beaver pelt, nodded. "We cannot afford to lose any more animals," she said.

"Wall, now, that's shore true, or I wouldn't say so." During the winter Zack had had to shoot one of the horses that had gaunted down so much it was suffering. "I ain't much fer horsemeat," said Zack, "An' I shore hated to shoot that horse. But the leetle extry meat did come in handy. I were really afeared we was gonna have to kill a few more of the horses if'n the weather hadn't started gittin' a leetle better."

Zack unsaddled the horse. "The river's risin' right quick," he said. "The snow further up must be meltin' right regular durin' the day now."

"Are we safe?" asked Windy.

"Wall, shore," he answered, walking over to the fire. He sat and stretched wet pants legs toward the heat and dished up a bowl of the stew that simmered there. "I got us far 'nuff back so we ain't gotta werry 'bout the river less'n it gits real bad. If'n it does, we'll jist skedaddle outta hyar."

The days grew warmer and the snow melted faster. An occasional snow or hail storm drifted by, but the effects of these storms were temporary. The cold was still often bitter at night, but the days were warm, and the sun was higher in the sky.

With the disappearance of the snow, grass and other foliage began to sprout. The horses were left outside all day to graze and fatten and gain their strength for the journey home. Zack was also busy with his traps, catching the last of the winter prime. Wind-in-the-Morning was kept busy with the beaver pelts Zack brought in. Her work on them was the finest he had ever seen. When she was finished with them, they were soft, full and luxurious.

Zack also brought in two bearskins from grizzlies he had killed while on his trap lines. With the advent of spring, the bears, who had hibernated much of the winter, were active and often mean. Being lean and hungry, they were prone to attack. And the females, having recently given birth, were even more inclined to attack, both from hunger and in defense of their cubs.

Zack sat by the fire one night, carefully cleaning the Hawken, while Wind-in-the-Morning sat nearby, patching one of his buckskin shirts. He looked up and asked, "What day is it?"

Wind-in-the-Morning, who had her own way of keeping a calendar that Zack always found exact, said, after some figuring, "In three more days it will be the beginning of the Moon-When-the-Ponies-Shed."

"Almost the first of May already. I was hopin' to be out afore then. Think ye kin be ready to leave then?"

"I will be ready if you wish to leave."

"I think it. The horses're plump enough, an' I wanna git back to the village fer the spring hunt. If'n they ain't already had it. 'Sides, I ain't hankerin' to cross Crow or Blackfoot country on the way south, if it's after the hunt an' they're out to raise hair."

The woman nodded in agreement, but she thought of the many things still to be done before they left. She thought of all the hides she would have to have prepared and of the packing she must do. She thought of the fine clothes she must still make if they were to have a proper entrance to the village.

"Yes," she said to herself, "all these things must be done before the trip. It will not be right to see my people if I am unprepared."

Wind-in-the-Morning took pride in her work. She was a fine cook and was one of the best at dressing hides. She had few equals in the Cheyenne village in the way she decorated the finely made, soft dress clothing she made for herself and her man. Like most Cheyenne women, she took pride in the way her man dressed. The better he looked, the better was the reflection on her. She was looked upon with respect. Her man was aware of this. Zack took pride in the wearing of the finery Wind-in-the-Morning laboriously made for him. He also liked her to look good, and he showered her with foofooraw brought back from his trips to Santa Fe and Taos.

She also knew she must now take more care of herself; to protect the life growing inside her. She remembered the night she had known for sure and had told Zack. She was scared, frightened he would not want her or their child. But she got his attention after they had finished the night meal and he had lighted his pipe. She knew this was the best time to approach him. The long day, with its abundance of chores was over, and he would be relaxed.

131

"Have you ever thought of having a son?" she asked him innocently.

"Naw. Not really. I ain't ary give it much thought. Why d'ye ask?"

She looked down at the hands held in her lap. Quietly she said, "Because you are soon to become a father."

He let out a whoop and jumped in the air, dropping his pipe. "Wall, I'll be damned," he shouted. He grabbed her and swung her in the air, spinning her around. "I'll be damned," he said again. "I'm gonna be a papa."

"Put me down!" she shrieked, laughing.

"Yep, that's right," he said, stopping. "We gotta watch out fer the baby now." Gently he set her down.

"You are not angry with me then?" she asked.

"Angry?" he grinned. "Hell, no, I ain't angry. I'm gonna be a poppa. Why should I be mad?"

"You never mentioned having a child before. I thought you might not want to become a father."

"I jist nary thought of it afore," he said. "But it's purely fat cow now, or I wouldn't say so." He again lost himself in joy, dancing around the fire, whooping and hollering until the horses shuffled uneasily, spooked. Laughing, he went back to quiet them.

Zack now treated Windy with more care. Over her protestations, he helped her in gathering firewood and in caring for the horses. She often argued with him about it.

"What will the other women think?" she demanded. "They will think that I am lazy and cannot do my own work. They will laugh at me for being unable to do what is necessary. And the men will laugh at you for doing women's work. It is not right."

He just laughed at her. "They know better'n to laugh at me," he said happily. "I'll whomp 'em good, they laugh at me. I jist want the baby to be all right, an' I ain't takin' no chances howsoever.''

They left the winter camp on the first day of May, the over-laden pack horses winding their slow way down out of the heart of the Rocky Mountains into what would someday become the state of Colorado. They stopped briefly to trade with the Shoshonis for more horses to take the strain off the ones they had.

Late in May they came within sight of the Cheyenne village. Scouts had spotted them, and riders were racing out to greet them. The young warriors rode out and wildly circled the man and the woman. They shouted and whooped, dancing their ponies, calling out warm greetings.

Zack and Windy were dressed in their finest clothing for the ride into the village, and they rode in with dignity, straight-shouldered, heads held high, but grinning broadly. Windy's bulging belly was the subject of many jokes and laughter.

They rode to the lodge of Strong Horse. With the old man stood Hawk Wind and Thunder Blanket. The three stood in front of the lodge, blankets held decorously around them, feathers blowing in the slight breeze. Stolidly disguising their grins of welcome, they waited as Zack rode up and dismounted.

Zack greeted the three men and entered the tepee to smoke the pipe in welcome. Windy, proudly boasting of her obvious pregnancy, was happily led away by the other women.

Inside the lodge Zack and his three friends, as well as some of the other leading warriors, passed the smoking pipe in silence.

When the pipe was finished, Strong Horse asked in Cheyenne, ''Well, my son, how have you fared over the winter?''

Zack related the experiences of the winter, including

133

the killing of the horse and his impending fatherhood. This last bit of news elicited cries of happiness from the warriors.

After reciting his narrative, Zack asked, "Brothers, have my people, the Shyans, made their spring hunt yet?"

Strong Horse answered, "Not yet. The planning is done and the hunt is to be held within the next few suns. We have waited for all the people to come together. Some were delayed further north by the long winter."

"Have ye bin on the warpath yit?"

"No," answered Strong Horse. "Only after the hunt is over and we have meat can we think of making war on our enemies. The hunt is more important. The people are hungry after the winter moons. The hunters have brought in a little elk and deer, but we need the buffalo."

"When're ye leavin'?" asked Zack.

"When the chief of the hunt feels that the time is right," answered Strong Horse once more.

"Who's leadin' it this year?"

"I am," said Hawk Wind with solemn dignity.

Zack grunted and left it, saying only, "It's a right wise choice." He would talk to his father-in-law later. But he knew the time would not be easy for the older man. The leader of the hunt had an awesome responsibility. The well-being of all the people rested on his shoulders. If the hunt was a success, the leader was revered and honored. But if the hunt was a failure, thought Zack, he would be a broken man. He would never be able to hold his head up again in the tribal council. He would be scorned.

The talk turned to other matters, and Zack pushed the thoughts of the hunt from his mind. Although the annual hunt had not yet been made, the young men had brought in enough elk and deer meat to provide a feast for the travelers.

The feasting and yarning lasted until the moon was high in the sky, and it was well after midnight before Zack rolled into the robes where Windy already slept. She grumbled sleepily when he clumsily woke her while getting comfortable. But she got up and helped him get undressed. There had still been a little of the trading whiskey left. Tired, he murmured his thanks and fell soundly asleep.

He awoke groggy from the previous night's gluttony. But after a plunge in the still ice-cold river, he felt better. He walked to the lodge of Hawk Wind, who sat outside patiently chipping an arrowhead from a small piece of stone. Zack sat silently next to the Indian and waited. After a short interval, Hawk Wind put down the finished arrowhead and nodded toward Zack. The mountain man said, "Father, it makes my heart glad to hear ye are gonna lead the hunt. But it also makes my heart sad."

"Why do you say that?" asked the older man in Cheyenne.

Zack could not speak for long in the flowing tones of the Indian, so he alternated between the jargon of the mountain man and Cheyenne. "Cause ye kin lose yore shirt on a gamble like that is why. Ye kin gain many honors, but ye kin lose everthing ye got."

"It is an honor just to be chosen to lead the hunt," commented the Indian wryly. A small grin tugged at the corners of his mouth. "It is an honor to be chosen, and the risks must go with the honor. Without the risk, there would be no honor in leading the hunt."

"But what about yore family? Yore wives and children?"

"The welfare of the village is more important than my family. My wives can find other men to keep them, should they choose to, and my sons are grown warriors proven in the hunt and on the warpath. My two daughters, She-Who-is-Wind-in-the-Morning and Rain Cloud Woman, I need not worry about. One is in good hands already, and the other can take a husband any time she chooses. Already the young warriors, and some not so young, are flocking to my tepee." He smiled at the last.

"I guess ye're right," Zack said doubtfully. "But if thar's ary a thing I kin do fer ye, ye jist lit me know."

"Thank you for your offer of help," said Hawk Wind. "But you will be busy. Or have you forgotten your responsibilities as a Dog Soldier?"

"Naw, I ain't fergot. But ye jist 'member what I said."

"Thank you, my son," said the Indian simply.

Zack nodded and rose. He paused and opened his mouth as if to speak, but decided against it. Without another word, he left, seeking Thunder Blanket to plan for the hunt.

CHAPTER 7

The celebration was wild in the Cheyenne village near the southern bank of the Arkansas River. Hawk Wind had never been in such high spirits. The hunt had been a complete success; not one life had been lost, and the village was now well-supplied with meat and furs. Only three hunters had been injured and those only slightly. Yes, thought Hawk Wind, as the honors were heaped on him, life is good.

Zack joyfully joined in the celebrating. He was happy for his father-in-law. But he, too, was honored for his bravery and marksmanship.

The feasting was long and grotesque; a primitive ritual to welcome the return of the warmth and life. Warriors as well as women and children, craving the fresh, bloody, half-raw buffalo meat they had done without during the long winter, gorged themselves, stuffing hunks, slabs, strips and pieces of the savory flesh into their mouths. They crammed the food in until they were sick. Then they ate more. They danced and sang and crowed and boasted around the fires.

Three days later the Indians moved to a more permanent camp for the summer months, a little further east on the Arkansas. There the warriors prepared to take the warpath.

The mountain man, though, was making ready for his trip into Santa Fe.

Thunder Blanket joined Zack by the fire one evening. Zack grunted a greeting as he continued to hone his knife. "My brother does not plan to ride against the enemy this year?" asked the Indian.

"Naw," said Zack. "I ain't got no hankerin' to raise hair this year. 'Sides, I wanna git back to Santy Fe an' sell my furs. I bin too long hyar already. If it hadn't of bin fer the long winter, the hunt would've bin over a long time ago, an' I could've bin back in Santy Fe by now. If'n I kin git outta hyar afore the war parties start roamin' 'round, mebbe I kin git down into Spanish territory 'thout worryin' 'bout losing my furs. Or my hair."

"Has my brother grown afraid of the Kiowas?" demanded Thunder Blanket.

"Hell, no," snapped Zack. "I ain't skeered of no Kioways, nor Comanches or Osages or Pawnees or 'Paches neither. But it's almost June, an' I wanna git back to Santy Fe afore the price of plews goes down. 'Sides, I got me a friend I'm supposed to meet thar."

"The Dog Soldiers will be disappointed that Enemy of Kiowas will not ride with them this year."

"Wall, now, I know that, or I wouldn't say so," said Zack. "But it's too damned late in the season fer me to start ridin' 'round, lookin' fer a fight. If'n I'd got back two, three weeks ago, an' the hunt was over, I would've bin glad to go out an' sculp some Kioways. But not now."

"I understand," said the Indian. "When will you leave?"

"Day after tomorrow, less'n we git some poor weather."

That night he offered another disappointment. "You will take me into the settlements now that I am carrying your son?" asked She-Who-is-Wind-in-the-Morning after they had climbed into their sleeping robes.

Zack had often wondered whether the baby would be a boy or a girl, but Windy seemed sure that it would be a son. Uncomfortable now, he answered, "Naw. Ye know I nary take ye down to Santy Fe. Carryin' my chile ain't gonna make no difference."

She rolled over, turning her back, now cold, toward him. Zack tugged at her, trying to get her to face him again. But she was immovable. "C'mon, Windy," he moaned. "Don't be actin' this way now."

She shrugged her shoulder away from him. "Then why will you not take me into the land of the Spanish people? Are you ashamed of your wife and the child I will bear?" she demanded.

"Now, don't say that. Ye know it ain't true." He finally pulled her around to face him, but her face remained hard and stern. "Ye'll be better off," he continued, "bein' hyar with your friends than ye would down in Santy Fe. Ye wouldn't want ary of them Spanish wimmin helpin' ye out, should the baby come whilst we was thar, now would ye?"

Reluctantly she shook her head. "Wall, then," he said, "ye'll be better off hyar. 'Sides, Santy Fe ain't no fittin' place fer no proper woman and new born chile. It jist ain't right takin' ye down thar. I tole ye that afore."

He paused to collect his thoughts and then continued, "It'd be even worse if'n ye started to have the baby whilst we was on the trail. I wouldn't be of no help to ye."

She relaxed a little, and he pulled her closer. "But I want to be with my man," she said. "Not here alone."

"Ye ain't gonna be alone. Ye got yore whole family hyar, includin' yore sister. Ye got plenty of meat and a heap of buffler and deer skins gotta be worked. Ye got plenty of work to keep ye busy whilst I'm gone.

An' ye got all the wimmin in the village to help ye when the baby comes.'' He patted her bulging belly softly.

"But you will be gone so long," she whispered.

"Naw, I won't be gone more'n two moons at the most."

"You will not be here to see your son born, then."

"When ye 'spect 'im?" he asked, a little worried.

"Near the end of the Moon-When-the-Cherries-are-Ripe."

He stroked his beard. "Late July. Wall, mebbe he'll wait a leetle, an' I kin be back afore he arrives. I should be back by the beginnin' of August. Mid-month at the latest."

"But wouldn't you like to be here when your son is born?"

"Wall, it'd be nice now, or I wouldn't say so. But what kin I do anyway? That's wimmin's work, an' ye wouldn't let me nowhars near anyways, so's it don't make no difference."

They argued some more, but the woman finally relented and gave in to his wishes. She would pack well for him, he knew, even though she disliked to see him leave. But it was not her place to argue. This was man's business.

And she did pack carefully, distributing the packs of beaver, fox, wolf and other pelts evenly on the pack horses. His possible sack was prepared just the way he liked it, each item in its place, ready at hand when he would need it. Wind-in-the-Morning grumbled constantly while making the preparations, but she made sure he had enough food and other supplies. Yes, despite her anger, she was his woman and would care for him the best she knew how.

He mounted the big appaloosa and leaned over to touch her cheek. "I'll be back afore ye know it," he said. "Ye jist take keer of yoreself and the baby till I git back. Don't ye be doin' too much heavy work, ye understand? Git yore sister to help ye."

She nodded and lightly touched his hand. She knew he would be back, but it would seem like an eternity until he returned and she would miss him terribly. Already the feeling of loss was rising up to clutch at her throat.

He straightened up and rode out of the village, the string of pack horses kicking up dust behind him. He turned only once to look back at the village, but he could not see Windy. He knew she would already be back inside the lodge, working, preparing for the winter trip to the mountains.

By early afternoon he had covered nearly eight miles. Ahead, he could see a large cloud of dust over the horizon, blowing wistfully in the light breeze. He pulled the horse to a stop. "This could mean trouble, boy," he said, talking to the horse as he usually did when he was alone.

He broke the horse into a trot, angling off toward the top of a bluff to the west. Before he reached the crest of the bluff, he stopped the horses. Letting them crop the short bunch grass near a tree, he took his rifle and crawled the rest of the way to the summit.

Carefully he poked his head above the ridge and swore, "Damn. Kioways." About half a mile away rode a war party of fifty painted Kiowa warriors. He knew they would have scouts out, and he wondered where they were, the slightest twinge of alarm flickering through him. He crawled back down the grassy hill to where the horses were grazing complacently, and found one of the scouts.

The Kiowa, hideously painted, most of his body covered in white flecked with black spots, was gathering up the reins of the pack horses. Stealthily Zack

141

crept closer and closer to the unsuspecting Kiowa. He hoped the horses would not betray his presence. If they did, he would have to shoot the Indian, and that would alert the others in the war party.

He was only five feet away now. Silently he slid the iron-headed tomahawk out of his belt. As he raised his arm to swing, the Indian turned around. Before he could scream, Zack leaped, tomahawk flashing in the sunlight. The fine blade of the hatchet cleaved the warrior's face. The Indian fell, making only a soft grunting noise as he did so.

An arrow struck the ground near Zack's feet as he wrenched the tomahawk free. "Damn, another one," he muttered. He dove and rolled behind the trunk of a cottonwood. Another arrow struck the place where he had stood. Cautiously he poked his head out around the tree and looked for the enemy. He crouched, almost unblinking, waiting for the Kiowa warrior to show himself. "Show yoreself, ye son of a bitch," he mumbled softly to himself. Zack fervently hoped the Indian had not slipped away to warn the war party. He counted on the brave's desire to count coup to keep him from fleeing toward help.

An arrow struck the tree inches above Zack's head with a soft thunk. Zack instinctively flinched away from it, and another struck close to it. Zack was ready for the second one, and he remained steady. He saw the feathered, painted brave, his face a frightful mask of red and yellow. Even at this distance he looked devilish. As the Indian quickly ducked behind the crest of the ridge, Zack stood and ran for the shelter of another tree.

Behind the woody shelter Zack breathed deep, trying to calm himself after the short, frantic run. He checked the priming on his big rifle and sighted at the spot where he had last seen the Indian. Patiently he waited, sweat trickling down his forehead, knowing there was little he could but wait for the warrior to show himself. He doubted he could make it up the hill unseen. He would, he knew, have to shoot the Indian and then try to outrun the alerted war party.

The time seemed interminable in the heat of the June afternoon, but Zack moved only once, to wipe off the sweat that dribbled down his face and into his eyes. "C'mon, ye coward," he said inwardly, "show yoreself. That war party's gittin' closer all the time."

But still he waited, outwardly unmoving, muscles tense. He let out a soft gush of breath as he saw a slight movement on the crest of the hill only a few feet from where he had last seen the Kiowa. Zack steadied the rifle. The Indian, counting on fear and surprise, leaped up and let fly an arrow at the tree where Zack had been. With snake-like speed he notched and drew another arrow.

The sound of the Hawken echoed off the low hill and fled across the prairie. The Kiowa toppled forward, a bullet in the brain, the bow and arrow slipping harmlessly from his nerveless fingers. He tumbled and rolled, lifeless, down the incline.

Zack jumped up and raced for the horses. He grabbed the lines holding the pack horses and flung himself up on the appaloosa. "Wall, boy," he said. "That's shore torn it. We'd best be leavin'. We ain't even got time to sculp the varmints."

He could hear the shouts of the warriors, closer now, calling for the two dead scouts. He knew he had precious little time. Once he rounded the bluff, he would be in sight of the angry war party.

"C'mon, boy," he yelled to the horse. "Run!" They sped off across the land. He kept the slight bluff between him and the Kiowas as long as possible. But eventually he had to come within their sight. As he did, the warriors screeched and raced after him. It was plain, now, to the Kiowas, what the shot had been and why there was no response by the two scouts.

Zack looked hurriedly over his shoulder. "Damn," he shouted, they's closer'n I thought. I'll nary make it with these pack horses." One more glance behind him at the charging warriors, gaining quickly, convinced him. He would have to leave the loaded pack animals behind.

"Damn ye, ye heathens," he shouted uselessly back at the Kiowas. "I'll git ye fer this." He dropped the reins holding the pack animals and, taking off his hat, he swatted the stallion and said to it, "C'mon, boy. Run fer yore life."

The big spotted horse heeded the call of his master. Ears flattened out and nostrils flared, the animal thundered along, leg muscles stretching, pulling, pushing. Air pumped in and out of the massive chest as sweat foamed on his flanks. Seemingly without effort, the appaloosa reached within himself for the endurance he had and raced, pounding, across the grassy land.

Zack again looked back and saw the war party falling behind. "Good boy," he shouted at the horse. "Keep goin'. Run, boy, run. We'll be home soon."

The horse ran its heart out, hooves flying. His great head rose and fell rhythmically in tune to the thudding hooves. Zack and the horse raced straight for the village. Without the zigzagging course he would normally take, it would alert the Cheyennes that there was some danger.

The horse herders saw him first, and they knew something was wrong. As the white man and the dotted horse got closer, people within the village watched intently, anxious to learn of the danger. On the outskirts of the village, Zack bellowed, "Kiowas! Kiowa war party comin'!"

The village erupted. There were shouts and a few

war cries, as the women gathered up children and ran for cover. Warriors quickly grabbed their weapons and their favorite war ponies. All seemed confusion, but within minutes clan chiefs and recognized war leaders organized the shouting warriors.

Zack jammed the horse to a stop in front of his lodge. She-Who-is-Wind-in-the-Morning was already saddling another horse for him. Almost immediately she was done. Zack handed her the reins to the appaloosa and said, "Rub 'im down good, but keep 'im saddled. He's the best warhorse in the village an' I may want 'im agin afore the day's over."

She nodded and hurriedly led the big horse away. The stallion plodded along, blowing and sucking wind through the widely flared nostrils, gulping huge amounts of air into the large, broad chest.

Zack kicked the war pony, one of the many horses owned by Hawk Wind, into motion. He joined Hawk Wind and Thunder Blanket at the former's lodge, where the Dog Soldiers were organizing.

"You have returned, my brother," said Thunder Blanket. "That is good."

"I could not leave my brothers to the mercy of the yellow Kioways," answered Zack.

Hawk Wind held up his hand, and the small band of warriors grew quiet in the midst of the shouting, noisy village. "Brothers," he said in Cheyenne, "we are to be the first to attack the enemy before they can reach our village. Once we have met the enemy and the other warriors have joined the battle, we are to leave the fight and return here to the village to protect the women and children."

There were shouts and war cries. The Dog Soldiers brandished bows, lances and the few rifles they had. The ponies, feeling the excitement, began to snuffle and snort, anxious to be gone.

Hawk Wind shrieked his war cry, one piercing,

ululating scream that rose above the noise in the village. Then he shouted, "Brothers, we ride!" He wheeled his horse and raced out of the village, the others close behind.

They found the Kiowas two miles from the village. The Kiowas had stopped briefly to rest their horses after the long run. Without slackening speed and without warning, the Cheyennes charged into the midst of the enemy. The fury and speed of the Dog Soldiers took the Kiowas by surprise. A number of them fell immediately. The force of the attack carried the Cheyennes through the ranks of the Kiowa war party. But now the Kiowas were ready for them.

Zack and Thunder Blanket pulled their horses up together and turned back toward the enemy war party. "I shore hope the other warriors git hyar soon." said Zack. "Thar's certainly a heap of them thar Kioways."

"Are you afraid to die on such a fine day?" asked the Indian.

"Naw, I ain't skeered of dyin'. I jist ain't riddy fer it yet. I aim to keep my hair fer a while."

Thunder Blanket just nodded. War was serious business to the Indian. The two charged back into the fury of the battle. The noise was deafening—war cries, shouted insults, wounded men shrieking in pain and fear and horses screaming from the wounds they received. Dust choked men and animals, clogging their mouths and nostrils. Eyes teared in the cloying cloud.

Zack and Thunder Blanket slashed and hacked their way, with tomahawk and lance, through the throng. Already five Dog Soldiers, hopelessly outnumbered, were down. Zack reached down and helped a wounded Cheyenne fling himself across the war pony's saddle. With a burst of savagery, Zack forced his way through the clinging knot of Kiowa warriors and then gasped in the fresh air.

He saw Thunder Blanket, slightly injured, off to one side with another wounded Cheyenne sitting astride the horse with him. A small trickle of blood ran down the white-painted arm of Thunder Blanket. The other Cheyenne warriors were now streaming into the battle, their savage cries mingling with the cacophony.

The white man and his red companion looked for the lance that was used as the Dog Soldiers' battle standard. It was carried by Hawk Wind. They finally spotted it in the thick of the fighting, low to the ground. Zack flung the wounded warrior off his horse and shouted to another Dog Soldier, ''Git 'im back to the village an' take the rest of our people with ye. Stay in the village like ye're supposed to. The wimmin an' children need ye.''

The Dog Soldier nodded, and Zack plunged back into the fighting. Thunder Blanket joined him, aware too that Hawk Wind was down. With even more ferociousness than they had shown earier, they fought their way back to Hawk Wind. The old warrior was hurt, an arrow imbedded in the fleshy part of one thigh. But the big Indian had fought so valiantly that none of the Kiowas could reach him. Though the Kiowas pressed their attack, they also regarded him with awe. Standing there, next to his dead horse, his courage inspired feelings of hate and fear in the attacking Kiowas.

The white Cheyenne and his red brother broke through the small circle of warriors surrounding the wounded Hawk Wind. ''Ye git 'im on yore horse an' git outta hyar whilst I protect ye both,'' Zack bellowed above the din.

Thunder Blanket did not argue. With outstretched hand he pulled his father onto the horse behind him. Slashing at a Kiowa warrior with his lance, he directed a shout of derision at his enemies, turned his horse and plunged through the milling mob, racing for freedom.

Zack followed more slowly, swinging the deadly tomahawk with wild abandon, shouting until he was hoarse. The small, sturdy war pony remained stolid amidst the noise and confusion, guided only by Zack's knees. Like the man astride him, the horse showed no fear.

Some of the Kiowas recognized Zack from their earlier battles and charged to take him. "This's it," Zack said to himself. But he continued to fight furiously. Before the Kiowas could reach him, Zack was surrounded by bloodthirsty Cheyennes.

"Leave here!" commanded one of the war leaders. "Return to the village with the others."

Zack nodded, plunging ahead. He brained another Kiowa warrior with the tomahawk as he surged through the line of friendly warriors. He finally broke all the way through to freedom. With a deep breath of clean fresh air, Zack and the weary pony hastened for the village.

In the village, he flung himself off the pony and turned it over to a boy who had stayed to watch some of the war horses. The boy pointed to the appaloosa, standing near a tree, saddled and ready. Zack nodded his thanks. "Take good keer of this pony," he said. "He has served us well." He ran toward the stallion and jumped on. The appaloosa, well rested, snorted once and instantly obeyed his master's command to join the others.

But the village was in no danger. The other warriors fought well and scattered the Kiowas, who fled on foot and horseback to escape the terrible horde that had descended upon them. Some of the more wild Cheyennes raced after them. But most of the warriors, sated now, the bloodlust slackening, rode happily back to the village, brandishing bloody scalps and other grisly mementos of the battle. Zack had watched some of the mutilations, but did not take part in them. Except for a few scalps, he could not bring himself to maim the corpses. Though the Kiowas were the enemy, Zack could not mar their life in the spirit world.

The feasting and dancing began. But the mourning also began. Women who had lost husbands, fathers, sons or brothers hacked their hair short and slashed their arms and legs with knifes. They tore their faces with their fingernails, and chopped off one or two joints from their fingers. As they keened a high wail, never ceasing, they spread ashes over their heads and shoulders.

Zack at first took no part in the celebrations. Although he was happy about the outcome of the battle, he was still angry. "Damned Kioways," he said to Wind-in-the-Morning. "They got everthang I had; traps, pelts, everthang."

Before dusk settled, a small group of young men who had chased the Kiowas rode victoriously back into the village amid much shouting and yelling. Inside his tepee, Zack heard the commotion and poked his head through the skin door to see what all the noise was about.

One of the warriors saw him and called, "My brother, Enemy-of-Kiowas, come welcome me. I have something of yours."

Zack recognized the warrior as a lad of not more than seventeen years. His name was Once Ran. Zack stepped out of the tepee and stopped in amazement. There stood his whole pack train, intact.

"Wall, I'll be damned," he said. He ran over and began looking through the packs. "Ye found all of 'em." A smile spread on his face. "Whar'd ye find 'em, boy? The Kioways had 'em stole from me right good and proper."

The young man, who had just returned from only

his second war party, beamed. He hopped off his pony and strutted proudly about, chest puffed out, head held high. "I, Once Ran," he said, "followed our enemy, the Kiowa, and fought bravely against the ones who held the possessions of my friend, Enemy-of-Kiowas. After a fierce battle, I took back what belonged to my friend, that which had been stolen, and returned it."

Zack almost laughed. Until now, he had hardly known the boy. But that would change. "Wall, ye shore are somethin', boy, or I wouldn't say so," shouted Zack. "I'll repay ye handsomely someday, boy. I most shorely will." He laughed happily, slapping the youth on the back. The young man, still beaming, handed over the lines to the horses and jumped back on his own mount. He rode around camp whooping and boasting of his great deeds.

Zack joined the celebrating, which seemed endless; the hours of dancing and singing, and of telling stories. Zack was anxious to be off, but he would not offend his friends by leaving before the celebration had run its course. And finally, as it must, the drums and rattles stopped and the voices were still.

The next day, Zack told Wind-in-the-Morning, "I'd best be leavin' in the mornin'. I bin hyar too long already."

The following day he once again took the rope leading his pack horses and turned the appaloosa toward the south. As he neared the outskirts of the village, he saw Once Ran. The young Indian, through fierce pride, had decided to keep the name given him as a youth after he had once ran away from a wild horse. Many had urged him to change his name, now that he was a warrior and had counted coup. But he would not.

"Ho, Once Ran," shouted Zack. "How is my friend?"

"I am well," said the new warrior, still proud as

150

a peacock. Zack noticed that the young man who, only two days ago, had been a horse guard, was holding himself straighter. He also wore the painted feathers he had earned in battle. Three scalps that he had taken dangled from the coup stick he would not relinquish. The grim trophies fluttered lightly in the breeze.

The young man sat, waiting, by some bushes near the path leading down to the river bank. "What're ye doin' out hyar, boy?" asked Zack, who already knew the answer.

"I am just waiting," said the Indian, suddenly shy.

Zack grinned. "What's 'er name?"

The Indian looked up sharply and then grinned himself. "Young Willow Woman."

"Ye've made a fine choice thar, my friend. She's a fine woman and'll make ye a good wife."

"I think so. If she will have me."

"She'll have ye, less'n she's loco. Ye're a fine figger of a man as well as a great warrior. She could do no better."

"Thank you," said Once Ran shyly but with dignity.

"Wall, boy," said Zack, tugging at his horse. "Good luck to ye. I'll be back by fall. An' I ain't fergot what ye did fer me neither." He turned the horse toward the south and rode off at an easy trot.

Mose was already near broke when Zack rode into Santa Fe. "Whar'n hell ye bin?" he shouted, half drunk, leaning on a young Mexican woman. "I thought ye was gone under, fer sartin. We done already celebrated yore funeral."

Zack just grinned and slapped his friend on the back. "C'mon ye weak-kneed ole bandit. I'll buy ye a drink."

The spree, at least for Zack, was short but furious.

He had seemed always trying to catch up to Mose, who had almost a month's head start on him. But sooner than he would have liked, it was over. It was time for them to leave. In early August, they rode out of town, heads aching, stomachs turning. Mose's throbbing head came not only from a royal hangover but also from being hit with an empty whiskey jug.

It had been early in the evening before. Zack and Mose already had nearly their fill of the fiery *aguardiente* and were noisily playing monte in the saloon, when some greenhorn trader called Mose a cheat.

The room suddenly became deadly quiet. The young fool, with more than his share of whiskey under his belt, tried to brazen it out. As his hand flew toward the big pistol in his belt, Mose's knife flashed out and flicked across the youth's chest laying open a superficial wound. A trickle of blood oozed out, and the young man's hand stopped in midair. He looked down at the thin ribbon of red on his chest.

"Watch who ye're callin' a cheat, boy," snapped Mose.

An old trapper known only as Dufrain shouted, "Ye cain't do dat to my frain, *mon ami*."

As Mose turned to look at the old French Canadian, who was not well liked by most beaver men, Dufrain swung a heavy clay jug. It caught Mose square on the side of the head, but it failed to knock him out. It was a mistake Dufrain would live to regret. Mose's knife hand flicked out again with blinding speed, and Dufrain looked sadly down at the gaping hole in his stomach.

The room seemed to explode; a wild-swinging haphazard free-for-all broke out. Men swung at other men with fists, jugs and table legs. A few knives were pulled. But it ended as quickly as it had begun, the men out of breath and strength, slumped on chairs or sprawled on the dirt floor.

Mose's head pounded after that little spree, but he was in better shape than Dufrain. The French Canadian did not die, but he missed the trapping season, and he was never the same again.

On the trail, Zack drove a herd of ten fine appaloosa horses he had bought from a trader in Santa Fe, who had traded directly with the Nez Perces for them.

"What're ye gonna do with all them horses?" Mose asked Zack when he bought them.

"Give 'em to a friend," Zack answered. He told Mose what Once Ran had done for him.

"That's a mighty generous gift," Mose commented.

They split up, and Zack hurriedly headed toward the Cheyenne village, fearful of attack. But he went unmolested, a fact he was grateful for. He had been unable to find anyone in either Santa Fe or Taos who would ride with him to help watch the herd. The Spanish youths had all been afraid of the trek across the land roamed by hostile Comanches, Kiowas and even some occasional Apaches. So he herded the horses himself.

He rode into the Cheyenne camp late one afternoon, accompanied by a group of yelling warriors who had ridden out to meet him. They joked and kidded him on the way in about the horses. The rumors were rampant: Enemy of Kiowas was going to buy a new wife.

But he just smiled and rode ahead. He went directly to his lodge. Any other time he would have gone either to say welcome to Strong Horse, or to Once Ran's lodge. But this year he was a new father and had not yet seen the child. The young warriors who had ridden in with him, regaled him about the child. Their ribald humor had him grinning all the way in.

He threw down the reins in front of the lodge and rushed inside, almost knocking the tepee down. Inside, he heard a screech that he knew could only have come from She-Who-is-Wind-in-the-Morning. He waited until his eyes adjusted to the darkness.

Then he saw her, sitting in the dim tepee, happily holding a small, blanket-wrapped bundle. He heard the joyful gurgling of an infant.

He went to her and knelt. "Windy," he said. She held up the bundle, and he parted the blanket. There she was, a fat little baby, kicking and fussing happily. "It's so tiny," he said stupidly.

"You are not unhappy?" she asked. He could hear fear in her soft voice.

"Unhappy?" he laughed. "Why'n hell should I be unhappy? I'm a new papa."

"But it is not the son which I had promised."

"I don't keer," he said, contented. "It's a fine baby, an' she'll grow up to be jist like her mama, a fine wife fer some brave warrior and great hunter. Don't ye fret 'bout it."

"Then you are really happy?"

He stroked her cheek and forehead. "Shore, 'cept fer one thing."

"What is that?"

"Are ye gonna be able to head up into the mountains with me this year? I mean, mebbe it'd be better if'n ye stay hyar with the baby till next winter."

"That will not be needed," she said indignantly. "There is no need to leave me behind. I will go when you go. The baby will not slow me down."

"Bueno," he said, and left after playing with the baby for a few minutes.

Then he rode to the lodge of Once Ran. He had given his pack horses over to someone to be taken care of, and he now held only the rope of the lead appaloosa. The rest of the herd was tied loosely behind so they could not run.

Most of the tribe had gathered around by now, waiting, curious about what was going on. They whispered and giggled and pointed, not knowing what this could be. The commotion drew Once Ran's mother partially out of the tepee. To her Zack said, "Mother, it'd please me if'n ye would call out yore son, He-Who-Once-Ran."

She ducked her head inside, and Zack could hear her whispering in Cheyenne. He knew she was telling the youth to prepare himself properly, though quickly, to dress well to meet the white man who beckoned.

Zack and the rest of the tribe waited patiently until the tepee cover opened. Once Ran stepped out, dressed in his simple finery. With decorum, he held the bright blanket close around him. A slight breeze wafted gently through his long hair and fluttered the eagle and hawk feathers adorning his braids. Zack was glad to see the Indian taking his new role seriously.

"I tole ye I'd not fergit what ye did fer me agin the Kioways, my friend. That someday I'd repay ye?"

The Indian nodded solemnly, and Zack continued. "Wall, boy, I figgered a fine young warrior like ye'd go far, given half the chance. So's I'm givin' ye that chance."

Zack climbed down off his horse and took the two strides that brought him face to face with Once Ran. "I ain't much at makin' speeches, so I won't. All's I wanna do is give ye these hyar horses."

He handed the rope out to Once Ran. The young Indian stood in wonder, unable to reach for the rope. Finally Zack took Once Ran's hand, opened it, placed the rope inside and then closed the fist back over it. "Wall, take it boy, they're yores," he said in exasperation.

The Indian still stood rooted, tears of joy streaming down his face. The other members of the tribe stood around and oohed and aahed over the magnificent gift.

"Wall, don't jist stand thar, boy," said Zack. "Go look at 'em."

The young man slowly, almost woodenly, dropped his blanket to the ground and walked toward the horses. As he began to inspect them, he became more animated. He tried to remain stolid, but could not, alternately crying with joy and laughing. He began to strut and shout, walking around the horses. The crowd added its noisy approbation. They murmured among themselves about Zack's generosity and shouted encouragement and advice to the young warrior.

Once Ran still looked over his new-found wealth and Zack sidled up to him. In a low voice he said, "I see ye're still livin' in the lodge of yore father. I guess ye ain't took a woman yet."

"Young Willow Woman will not have me if I cannot give her father something in return. Something to show my good intentions. She has many other suitors who are richer than I."

"But now ye're rich," said Zack. "Ye have war honors an' now ye got yore own horse herd."

The young man's face, which had darkened at the talk of the woman he desired, brightened. "You are right, my friend. I am now rich. And you have made me so."

"Ye may not want it," Zack said seriously, "but I'm gonna give ye some advice anyway." Zack stepped closer to the young brave, so they would not be overheard. "Her father's over thar an' he know's ye got these horses. I figger he'll try'n git 'em all from ye, if'n he kin. So don't give 'im more'n a few fer his daughter."

Once Ran turned angry. "But she is worth all of these horses and more."

"I know that, but ye don't need to give the ole man all the horses fer his daughter. Jist offer a few. If'n

156

he demands more, tell 'im ye'll take ole Buffler Tail's daughter fer a wife. That'll change 'is mind fer 'im.''

The young man still looked dubious. "Look, boy,'' said Zack. "Ye're a fine warrior and a good hunter. A man couldn't ask fer more'n that in a husband fer 'is daughter. Willow Tree Woman wants ye bad, an' she'll annoy her pa into it. So don't give away all yore riches afore ye even git married.''

The young Indian looked at Zack and grinned. "You may be right, brother. I will do as you say.'' With most of the other people following him, Once Ran led the horses away.

Zack went to say his welcome to Strong Horse who was accompanied, as usual when greeting Zack, by Hawk Wind, Thunder Blanket and a few other warriors. When they had smoked the pipe of welcome, Strong Horse said to him, "My son, that was a good thing you have done.''

Zack nodded. "It were worth it. That young buck saved all the pelts I took all winter gittin'. 'Sides, he's gonna make a right fine war chief one day, an' I figgered I'd give 'im a helpin' hand.'' He chuckled softly. "Hell, he wanted that woman fer a wife real bad, an' with no horses, it was gonna be mighty tough to git her. This way he kin git her as a wife an' then he kin put his mind back whar it belongs, 'stead of moonin' over that squaw all the time.''

The other warriors also laughed softly, nodding. "Yes,'' said Thunder Blanket. "He should be happy now.''

They talked some more before Zack returned to his own lodge. Since the weather was warm, Wind-in-the-Morning had a fire going outside the teepee. The sides of the lodge were raised, rolled up, allowing the fresh breeze to blow through it, cleansing and refreshing the interior.

Windy sat, her fingers busy, repairing one of his

shirts. She had already taken the appaloosa out to pasture and placed Zack's belongings inside the tepee.

Zack sat cross-legged by the fire, and Windy brought him some food. He relaxed and ate, talking quietly with the woman, whose fingers worked busily with awl and sinew. Later, Once Ran came to visit. He sat beside Zack and was also fed. When they had finished, Zack pulled out his pipe. Lighting it, he asked, "What kin I do fer ye, boy?"

"I have come to tell my friend, Enemy-of-Kiowas, that Once Ran is soon to take Willow Tree Woman as his wife."

Zack laughed and clapped the Indian on the shoulder. "Ye didn't waste much time, did ye, boy?" he joked.

The young man relaxed a little and smiled.

"How many horses did it take?" asked Zack, who rocked back and forth in silent glee.

The Indian grinned even more broadly. "Only three. You were right, my friend, the old thief wanted all the horses, so I told him I'd take the daughter of Buffalo Tail as my wife."

Zack broke into laughter. "Ye did fine, boy. Ye shore did. That's really showin' 'im now, or I wouldn't say so."

Once Ran was also laughing harder now. "He looked like some bad spirits had entered his body, making him sick. Then he said he would take only five of the horses. The best ones."

"What'd ye tell 'im then?" asked Zack, still laughing.

"I told him I would not offer more than one horse. Of course, I said to him, it would be the best horse. He screeched and hollered that everyone would think badly of him because his daughter was gotten so cheaply and he could not do such a thing to his daughter. Finally we compromised on three."

"Why, ye ole horse trader. I didn't think ye had it in ye to stick it to the ole man thataway. I'm right proud of ye, boy."

The Indian blushed, then grinned. "I only hope that I have not insulted Willow Tree Woman by my offer."

"Hell, boy. Don't werry 'bout it. She's gittin' the best young warrior in the village. She ain't gonna do no complainin'. 'Sides, she an' her ole man knows ye're gonna have a large horse herd someday, an' he kin approach ye then fer some more horses. Naw, I wouldn't werry none, was I ye."

"I think you are right again, my friend," said Once Ran. "Well," he said, standing, "I must go now. There is much to do. I just wanted my friend, Enemy-of-Kiowas, to be the first to know that Once Ran is soon to take a wife."

"Why, thankee, Once Ran. That's right nice of ye to think of me at sich a time."

The young man nodded, still smiling, and walked swiftly off.

"It is good that such a young man has found a fine young woman to be his," said Wind-in-the-Morning. She had been silent when the men talked. It was man's business.

"He shore is lucky," said Zack. "He's got himself a right fine woman. And," he chuckled again, "he still gits to keep most of the horses fer a start. He'll go far."

The fall hunt was again successful, and Zack and Windy, who carried the baby in a cradleboard dangling from the saddle, were off to the mountains again. But this time they left much earlier. They rode slower this year, but hurried still, not wanting to get caught in the snows with the child along.

Windy had named the baby She-Who-Came-When-the-Mist-Was-Rising. Zack had tried valiantly, though vainly, to pronounce the gutteral Cheyenne words that were his daughter's name. But it was no use. He settled on Rising Mist or Misty.

The years went on the same way for Zack, Windy and the daughter, Misty. After every winter, some worse than others, the three would ride with laden pack horses into the village of the Cheyennes. There Zack usually took part in the spring hunt and, more often than not, in the raids against the Kiowas, Pawnees or Osages that followed.

Occasionally they arrived in the village late, after having stopped off at the annual June rendezvous on the Green. But Zack, who usually had quite a spree there, was too mountainwise to sell more than a few pelts to the traders, knowing he could get more goods for his pelts in the Spanish towns.

In early summer, he would head southwest from the Cheyenne camp toward Santa Fe. Sometimes he met Mose on the trail, and they would ride into the Spanish town together in high style. If they missed each other on the trail, they would find each other in Santa Fe, usually with the earliest arrival half full of Taos Lightning.

The two half-wild mountain men spent most of the summer getting drunk, gambling, dancing, brawling, yarning and more often than not, making love to the pretty young Spanish girls that were so plentiful. They saw nothing at all wrong with it; it was accepted, and they knew that their Indian women could take an Indian husband while they were gone. Mose had lost more than one squaw that way.

They lived high in the Spanish settlements, eating the best food and gambling their money away like it was their last chance to do so. They spent nearly all the money they made in a trapping season on high times and finery for themselves, the laughing Mexican girls and for the women they had left behind.

Sometime in August, usually regulated by how soon their money ran out, they rode out of Santa Fe. They were hungover and aching, but they left in high style, guns blazing and voices yelling, their pack horses clumping behind, loaded with supplies, mostly gotten on credit.

They split up somewhere along the Apishapa River or the northern reaches of the Rio Grande. Zack headed slightly northeast toward the area between the Arkansas River and the South Fork of the Republican River. There he found the many small subdivisions of the Southern Cheyenne nation that came together to form one large village for the hunt and to make war.

Mose headed almost directly west and then northward, heading straight up into the heart of the mountains, up past Roaring Fork and past Bayou Salade, far up toward the Snake River and, often, beyond.

It was later that Zack made the long trip into the mountains. But first he would stop in the village, located near many of the smaller streams that would play out quickly in the blazing heat of the summer sun. Sometimes, if the spring had come early and the stream had dried up, the villagers would congregate on the main rivers themselves.

He would ride in, happy to be back. There would be feasting and celebrating and boasting and gambling and horse racing. And then there was the excitement of the hunt and the fearful exhilaration of war. It was, thought Zack, a fine way to live.

He would go with his Indian companions on the fall hunt, securing a large supply of meat and furs for the winter ahead. He settled into the camp life of the Cheyennes while Wind-in-the-Morning prepared the hides and jerky and pemmican and clothes and moccasins and the numerous other items they would need.

Working beside her was Zack. Traps needed repairing and knives needed honing. Horses had to be strong and well and his guns needed cleaning and oiling. Trade items had to be packed just so, and a dozen other things needed doing. Zack often thought that all the chores would never be finished. The mountain man chaffed at the numerous little details that kept them in the village day after day. But the work was soon enough done, and they would ride out.

It was usually near the middle of September when they set out, though they tried to leave earlier. Zack, Windy and Misty headed northwest into the Rockies, following the North Platte River, up past Medicine Bow River and across the Sweetwater and the Popo Agie. If the beaver were played-out there, they'd head further north, high into the Bighorn Country. More than once they had turned west instead of north, working their way into what would become Idaho, wintering near the Snake River or the Bruneau River, or a dozen other places that were rich with beaver.

The winters blurred together for Zack. Some were better than others, and sometimes he trapped more than at other times. But they all flowed together.

Sometime in May, depending on when the weather broke, the three would head southeastward back toward Cheyenne country. Along the way they tried to avoid the Utes and some of the other warlike Indians. They would cross the Green and the Bitter Creek; then eastward past the Uncompahgre and over the Continental Divide, where the waters of America were split into those flowing east and those running west. Then it would be down the course of the muddy Arkansas to the village.

On the trip they would stop and trade with the

Arapahoes, allies of the Cheyennes or the Shoshonis. Before leaving, they would also trade with the Nez Perces up north and the shy Paiutes.

CHAPTER 8

A hawk circled high in the cloudless blue sky, waking Zack from his reverie. "It's bin a right long time, it has," he said to himself. As he urged the horse gently toward the village below, he thought aloud, "I hope Misty likes the presents I brung her."

The girl would be five years old now, her birthday having fallen two weeks previously. She was a happy child, and Zack loved having her around. He played with her endlessly during the long nights in the trapping shack in mountains. He laughed at the thought of the first night he had seen the baby and his botched attempts to pronounce the child's name.

The girl would grow to be a little taller than her mother, Zack thought. But she would be broader—she had taken after his short, stocky build as well as that of her wide-bottomed mother. Her color was a little lighter than her mother's, but not much. With the long, straight, pitch-black hair and almond brown eyes, she was pure Indian.

"Yep," said Zack to himself, "it's gonna be good to see both of 'em agin." He thought again on how inconsiderate of him it had been all these years not to bring either of them into Santa Fe on his annual trips.

"Shore," he said aloud, urging the appaloosa into a trot. "This year I'll do it. I'll bring 'em both into

Santy Fe an' show 'em off." He yelled at the top of his lungs into the emptiness, "Ye hear me, Windy? I'm gonna take ye both to Santy Fe." Laughing at himself he said more softly, "C'mon thar horse, lit's git a move on. We're gonna see Windy and Misty."

He laughed even harder when he saw the young riders coming out to meet him. They had heard his yelling, and while they did not know what he had said because of the noise in the village, they did know he was coming.

The youthful riders escorted him into the village, shouting friendly insults and joking with each other. Traps clanking, he rode into the village and handed over the pack horses to be cared for, before trotting on the appaloosa in the direction of Strong Horse's tepee, where he would smoke the pipe of welcome.

One of the horsemen who had ridden out to greet Zack was Once Ran. He, too, sat in the lodge of Strong Horse, smoking the pipe. He was now a fast friend of Zack's and was already a member of the Dog Soldiers. His feats in battle were becoming legend.

After smoking the pipe, Zack headed for his own lodge. Windy sat outside, as usual, working, fingers flashing over the beading she was using to decorate a new pair of moccasins for the fast-growing child. Misty, playing nearby, laughed with happiness when she saw her father. He dropped off the horse and grabbed the child and swung her high in the air. Although she spoke mostly the language of her mother, she was fast learning English, in the argot Zack spoke. She happily gurgled her welcome.

While Zack played with Misty, the child's mother led the appaloosa off to pasture, unsaddling and rubbing the horse down before turning it loose to graze. She returned to the tepee and her work, smiling as she watched her man and their child playing and rolling in the dust, laughing and noisily carrying on. Indian parents loved their children deeply and spoiled them. Children were not spanked, but they learned their manners well. Zack followed the Indian way. There was nothing he would not do for the child.

At last he stopped playing with the child, sending her off with a light smack on her pudgy little behind. He sat near the fire, and Wind-in-the-Morning filled a bowl with steaming meat and handed it to him. He ate ravenously, not realizing his hunger until now, and asked for more. While he ate the second bowl, more slowly, the woman told him the news of the village. "Yes," she said, "there was a raid. On the Pawnees. One Cheyenne was killed and two hurt." The buffalo had been plentiful, and there had been little trouble.

As he filled and lighted his pipe, he saw a woman approaching. "Yore sister's comin'," he said.

"Yes, she has visited with me often while you were gone."

"Ain't she got herself a husband yet?"

"No, not yet. She has many fine warriors playing the love flute for her," said Windy proudly. "But she has not yet spoken."

"Ain't Hawk Wind made a choice fer her? She must be close on seventeen-year-old by now."

"Yes, she has seen seventeen summers, but my father has not made a choice for her. Hawk Wind is a powerful man and can wait until a pleasing offer is made. It has not."

"Well, he'd best make a decision soon, or she ain't gonna be able to find herself a husband. She ain't gittin ary younger."

"Why do you not take her for a wife?" asked Wind-in-the-Morning quietly. "She would make a fine second wife for such a great hunter and warrior."

"Ye're crazy," exploded Zack. Although the practice of taking multiple wives was not all that common

166

among the Cheyennes, it was practiced by the chiefs and warriors who were able to support more than one wife.

But Zack, though he had enough wealth and often enough work to keep more than one wife busy, could not accept the practice for himself. He did know that warriors who took more than one wife often married sisters.

"Is that why she ain't took a husband yit?" he asked.

"Yes," said Wind-in-the-Morning shyly. "She would like to be your wife."

"An' how d'ye feel 'bout it?"

Wind-in-the-Morning looked down. Softly she said, "With the child I now have more work. Because you are a great hunter I often have more hides and meat than I can care for properly. That is why so often after the big hunt I have asked my sister for her help."

Zack would never know it, but Wind-in-the-Morning wanted him all to herself. But she realized that the need for another wife might become apparent to him. If it did, she wanted some say in who was chosen. Rain Cloud Woman would make a good second wife for Zack, if that became necessary.

"Hell, I got enough on my hands with ye. I doubt if'n I kin handle another 'un."

"Maybe you will change your mind?"

"I misdoubt it."

Rain Cloud Woman paused only briefly at their fire before moving on. And the subject of a second wife was dropped while plans for the hunt were made.

A week after Zack arrived, the decision about the hunt was made. Zack was casting lead balls for the rifle in front of his tepee when the crier came along shouting, "The hunt begins in two days. The women and children will stay behind."

Zack finished and put away the mold. He called to

167

Wind-in-the-Morning, working nearby, "I'm goin' over to see yore brother. I'll be back after a while."

The woman grunted an affirmative and continued working as he strolled over to Thunder Blanket's lodge. He found the warrior outside, methodically smoothing an arrow shaft. With him was Once Ran.

"I jist heard the crier," said Zack.

"Yes, the hunt begins soon," said Thunder Blanket.

"The buffler bin seen yit?"

"Yes," answered Once Ran. "The other scouts and I spotted them not more than fifteen miles from here. To the north. They will be within ten miles by the second sun."

"So ye figger to leave the village hyar, ride out fer the meat an' then come back an' git the wimmin?"

"Yes," said Thunder Blanket. "It is hard to move the village, and so the women, children and old ones will stay behind. They can get there quickly enough when the killing is done."

They were silent for a few minutes before Thunder Blanket said, "I was soon to come and see you, brother. Again we must watch the people carefully so no one endangers the hunt by frightening away the buffalo."

"I'm riddy," said Zack. "But I wondered. If'n ye're so werried 'bout some young buck scarin' off the herd, then why do ye run the buffler, 'stid of shootin' 'em from a stand?"

"For many reasons," said Thunder Blanket. "Our arrows are not so effective as your rifle at long range. So, we must be closer to the animals. If we get close enough to shoot them from one position, they will only stampede anyway. By charging the way we do, we keep some control over when they run and in what direction."

"Sounds reasonable."

The Indian put down the unfinished shaft and picked up another. As always, he spoke in Cheyenne. "You have also seen that we station some hunters further down?" Zack nodded and he continued, "The buffalo are directed to run toward them."

"I knew that much."

"Well, it comes from the ancient times. Before the Cheyennes had horses. The men would hunt on foot. Some would hide behind rocks or bushes or in tall grass. Others would frighten the buffalo, forcing them to run toward where the other hunters were hidden. There the hunters could kill the buffalo with lance or arrow."

"Don't sound none too easy to me," snorted Zack.

"It was not. Those were hard times for the people."

Two days later, the long column of warriors rode out, most of them stripped to breechcloth and moccasins. With few exceptions, the men rode one horse and led their favorite buffalo pony. Zack was mounted on a sturdy, wiry mustang. His appaloosa was led by one of the young boys accompanying the party.

Zack, with Thunder Blanket, Hawk Wind, Once Ran and other Dog Soldiers, policed the slow-moving column, insuring that none of the young men rode out and jeopardized the hunt. By midday the long line of warriors spotted the herd. Silently they massed a safe distance from the bison. They began to fan out in a semi-circle after mounting their buffalo ponies. The other horses were left behind.

Gradually the horsemen edged closer and closer, taking care not to disturb the tremendous herd of grazing buffalo. As they closed in, the hunters withdrew handfuls of arrows in preparation. Zack filled his mouth with lead balls for the Hawken. The appaloosa waited patiently, anxiously, shuffling his hooves and champing at the bit.

The hunters were less than a hundred yards away when the herd started growing uneasy. The men waited. When the buffalo had quieted, the men edged a little closer. The signal, one shattering scream, was given, and with whoops the men raced off. The buffalo stood stupidly for a few precious seconds, stunned by the unexpected noise and flash of color. Then they turned and ran ponderously, gaining speed, thudding heavily across the open spaces, the hunters in pursuit.

Zack again felt the exhilaration of the ride and the hunt as the wind sliced through his hair, hanging loosely underneath the old buffalo cap. The horse flowed effortlessly over the terrain, needing no urging, picking out the fattest cows. Only once did Zack direct the horse, turning it toward a shaggy, lumbering, half-blind old bull.

The kill was over quickly, it seemed, and the hunters began to regroup where they had started. But the noise of countless thousands of buffalo continued to roll over the grassland, reverberating back from the mountains to the west.

Then, suddenly, the world was silent, the buffalo far to the north now and beyond the hearing of the men. But as quickly as the silence descended, another sound, heard in the distance, shattered the new-found stillness.

"My gawd," said Zack to Thunder Blanket. "It sounds like the village is bein' attacked."

From far away they heard a few gunshots and what sounded like the screams of hurt people and the war whoops of an attacking party of warriors. But the distance was great and the sounds faint.

Their shock was momentary. With a scream that split the almost dead air of the prairie, Once Ran leaped on a fresh horse. Beating the animal ruthlessly, he took off at a dead run, heading for the village. The other warriors were close behind, most remounting on the run.

Zack swore under his breath, as fear clenched him, and kicked the appaloosa into a run. This was danger, and he wanted the big spotted horse under him. He had been one of the earliest hunters back to the starting point, so the stallion was rested. The powerful horse raced over the broken ground, legs stretching as never before, as if he had not sped carelessly after the buffalo only a short time before. Zack flattened himself on the horse's neck, knowing the animal needed no urging. The appaloosa realized, through something unspoken, that the ride was urgent.

When still a mile away from the village, Zack heard the screams of the people over the sound of the rushing horse. He could see the black, oily smoke curling into the air to hang like a pall, the slight breeze not enough to push it away.

Zack was far ahead of the others with Once Ran close beside him. The Indian screamed, "No!" It was a cry that ripped through his throat and out to tear through the wind of the speeding horses. Zack looked over at the young Indian, shivers rippling down his back at the eerie sound. The young Indian was crying in grief already, the tears streaming down his cheeks, whipped away in the wind of the speeding horse. His face was etched with pain.

They topped the slight rise above the village, and the screams grew louder. The smoke hung gloomily over the devastated village as if trying to hide it from sight. Flames licked relentlessly at the skeletons of tepees. The stench of burned flesh, human and animal, was nauseating.

Zack pounded into the village, the streaking hooves of the horse barely missing many of the dead, wounded and dazed who littered the ground. He slammed the horse to a stop where his lodge had once stood. Only a pile of smouldering ashes and a few stark tepee poles were left, standing nakedly against the pallid sky.

With dread, he dismounted, unaware of the other grief-stricken hunters swarming around; unaware of the screams of the wounded and those already mourning, grieving over the dead.

He dropped the reins of the horse, which stood blowing heavily. Stiffly he walked to where the inside of his home had been. It was a shambles, the few items left untouched by the fire scattered about. But his woman and child were not there. His hopes began to rise as he walked toward a small arroyo that ran behind the tepee. He knew Wind-in-the-Morning would have grabbed Misty and run for it when the camp was attacked.

He found them there. Wind-in-the-Morning had tried to protect the child by using her own body as a shield. But it had been in vain. The long war lance had pierced the mother and continued on through the smaller, more fragile one. Zack stumbled into the arroyo, not feeling the tears fall down his cheeks.

He reached the bodies and, in rage and grief, wrenched the deadly shaft from them. He cuddled them to his chest as best he could, tears flowing unchecked, sobs racking him. Almost silently he shook, whispering only, "No, no," over and over.

Hawk Wind found him there two hours later, still frozen in the same position, rocking back and forth, moaning in his sorrow. Gently, Hawk Wind placed his hand on Zack's shoulder and tugged softly, trying to get him to rise. But Zack shrugged off the hand.

The Indian grasped him more firmly. "Come, my son," he whispered. "Leave them for now."

"But she is my wife," sobbed Zack.

"She is my daughter," said Hawk Wind gently, dignity masking his own sorrow.

Zack nodded numbly and stood shakily. "We must eat," said Hawk Wind. "Life must go on, and though we mourn, there are the living that need us. We must care for them."

Stiffly, Zack touched the bodies one more time and then let Hawk Wind lead him away. Outside the village there was a cook fire with fresh buffalo meat roasting. Zack ate automatically, not tasting the sizzling, half-raw ribs, heedless of the hot juice that slid down his chin and onto the front of his shirt.

The young warrior Once Ran, shocked and dull, eyes clouded in pain and grief, squatted next to Zack. He, too, ate without savoring. Now and again, tears would squeeze out from under his eyelids and seep down his face to mingle with the grease of the meat.

The wail of the women who had survived, and that of many of the men, could be heard loudly back in the charred village, as the living mourned the dead.

Once Ran stared into the fire. "I will kill all the Kiowas for this," he hissed with clenched teeth. "None will be left."

"No," said Zack.

"Why not?" demanded the young warrior. "Is Enemy-of-Kiowas now afraid of them?"

Zack's face turned rock-hard, lines of grief etched on it. "Ye know better'n that, boy. I ain't skeered of nobody. But it warn't Kiowas what done it. It was Comanches."

Thunder Blanket and Hawk Wind, who had been seated at the fire with them, nodded to each other. They had known it was not the work of the Kiowas. "Your grief may be deep," said Hawk Wind. "But like a seasoned warrior, you have noticed many things."

"Comanches?" asked Once Ran in dull amazement.

"Shore," answered Zack. "Them markin's was as clear as day. I don't know why they did it. It ain't like

173

the Comanches to attack a village full of wimmin and ole men, but it was them all right, or I wouldn't say so.''

Zack stood up. With trembling lower lip, he said, ''Guess I'd best go see to my family now.''

The mourning went on for days. Thirty-five women, seventeen children and six old men had been killed in the raid. Many more were wounded, and some of those would die within the next few weeks. Hawk Wind and Thunder Blanket had been luckier than some others. Both of Thunder Blanket's wives survived, one being wounded slightly. Hawk Wind lost only his one daughter, She-Who-is-Wind-in-the-Morning, and a granddaughter, She-Who-Came-When-the-Mist-was-Rising.

And so the mourning continued, the wails drifting off across the plains, flooding the emptiness with an eerie intonation. The burial scaffolds were many, and the horses were killed by the dozens to help the dead Cheyennes on their journey. Offerings and presents were made to the spirits, and many items were laid on the scaffolds with the dead to make their trip easier and more comfortable. Many members of the tribe who had lost relatives destroyed their lodges and virtually everything they owned. Life for them would start anew.

Zack placed numerous items on the death scaffold of Wind-in-the-Morning and Rising Mist. He had dressed them in their finest clothing, baby-soft buckskin dresses, so tanned they were almost white, beaded and fringed. And finely decorated moccasins. Carefully he braided their hair.

He destroyed all the possessions they had together, keeping only his horse herd, less a big mare and a small pony he had given to the dead for their journey, his traps and his gun.

He said his own kind of prayers over the two

bodies—part Christian invocations vaguely remembered from childhood, and part Indian, prayers to the Great Spirit, asking that his wife and child be watched and protected.

But then it was over. The dead had been mourned, and the living could do no more than go on living. The Cheyenne people were to move, never again to make a village here on the wide bend of the Big Sandy Creek.

As the Indians packed their meager belongings in preparation for the move, Zack also packed his few possessions. He was tying down his possible sack when Once Ran strode purposefully up. "I am going after the Comanches," he said, spitting the last word out as if it were poison. "I would like you, my friend, to go with me on the war trail against the enemy."

Zack stood up and put the possible sack on the saddle horn. He turned to face the young Indian, noticing that Hawk Wind and Thunder Blanket stood a discreet distance away, watching them.

"Winter's almost hyar," said Zack, "an' I'm headin' up to the mountains. I got me some trappin' to do. Jist like always. They's gone now, but the beaver's still thar."

"I did not know Enemy-of-Kiowas was afraid of the lowly Comanches," sneered Once Ran. "But it seems he has grown soft."

"If I didn't know ye was grievin', boy, I'd stick my knife in yore gullet fer sayin' them words. I'll lit it pass this time. But don't ye never say ary a thang like that to me agin, or I'll cut yore heart out."

"Then why will you not ride with me against the Comanches?" demanded the Indian, eyes glittering like black diamonds.

"'Cause thar ain't no point to it, far's I kin see. They's daid, an' killin' one Comanch' or a hundred

Comanches ain't ever gonna bring 'em back. 'Sides, like I tole ye, the snow'll be hyar soon. It's too late to go lookin' fer no Comanches. Ye best wait till spring, when ye've cooled off some."

"But their spirits will be uneasy if their murders are not avenged," shouted Once Ran vehemently, lower lip quavering.

Zack looked weary, and the light in his eyes seemed to fade. "I don't believe that, boy, an' neither should ye. It's a good way to git yoreself kilt."

"I am not afraid to die," said the warrior. He drew himself up straighter to show his fearlessness and bravery.

"I ain't either," said Zack, looking the young man in the eye. "But I ain't hankerin' to git myself kilt over nothin'. Committin' suicide ain't whar my stick floats, boy."

Once Ran stalked angrily away. Zack, one arm on his horse, watched him leave. Hawk Wind walked up. Zack looked at him and said, "I suppose ye're gonna tell me he's right and I should go with 'im."

"No, my friend. You must go your own way in this matter. It is not for me to say what is right. You must decide on it in your own way. But I did not know you were not moving on with the people, that you are going off to the mountains alone."

"Wall," said Zack slowly, "I were gonna tell ye what I was doin' jist afore I left. Thar's nothin' fer me hyar ary more, ole friend, an' I was thinkin' it's better if'n I jist left out."

"If that is the way you feel it must be, then you must go. But there will always be a welcome for you in the lodge of Hawk Wind and many others."

"Why, thankee, Hawk Wind. But I misdoubt I'll be back this way agin." He looked toward the many burial scaffolds. "It's too painful." He swung up on

176

the appaloosa and looked down at his friend. He reached out for his hand.

"You will be back some day," said Hawk Wind as he took the proffered hand, the gesture strange to the Indian.

"Ye may be right." With a last look around, Zack settled the battered old cap more firmly on his head and urged the horse forward, trotting out of the area without looking back.

He headed into the mountains, going higher and farther than he ever had before. There were some streams he had heard about, that were teeming with beaver. Some he had seen before, but for others it was his first time.

So he followed the tales of the streams and beaver, reaching high into the Rockies. He drifted through the Bighorn Mountains and the Wind River Range and up toward the Snake River and up into the Tetons. He rode fearlessly, as if challenging the hostile Indians or the even more hostile Mother Nature.

He did not winter in a camp that year. He kept on the move, stopping only when the weather forced him to. He spent a few days in one place, trapping, before moving on again. He was caught in howling blizzards and fought his way through snow-choked passes. Occasionally he saw other trappers or parties of trappers. But mostly he avoided them.

Once in a while, though, hungry for some news or companionship, he rode into one of the trappers' camps to spend a day or two gambling, drinking and yarning with them.

But mostly he kept to himself, always on the move, trying to forget the hurt and sorrow that ran deep within him, clutching his insides, eating at him. Only once did he stop for more than a day or two with a trapper he found. He had spotted a small trapper's cabin near the Raft River. Slowly he rode toward it. And then he recognized the lightly-bearded, long-haired trapper.

"Mose!" he yelled, breaking the horse into a trot, his pack train, laden with furs, clomping behind.

The tall muscular trapper reached for the rifle lying nearby and yelled to someone in the ramshackle cabin. Then he realized who the rider was. "Zack!" he shouted and ran toward his old friend.

Zack jumped off the horse, and Mose ran into him, knocking them both to the ground. They wrestled around on the snow-covered ground before getting up and brushing themselves off.

Mose looked around, still excited. "But whar's yore squaw? An' yore young'un?" he asked. "Ye ain't left 'em behind this year, have ye?"

The excitement and happiness fell from Zack's face. Sadly, he said, "They're daid, Mose. Rubbed out."

Mose was shocked. "Ye ain't tellin' me true now, are ye Zack? Ye must not. It cain't be. Ye really had a fallin' out with her an' left the two of 'em back in the village, ain't ye?" He blinked rapidly in disbelief.

But he could tell by Zack's pale face and tight mouth that it was the truth. "It's true," said Zack. "They was rubbed out."

"How?" asked Mose. But Zack looked disconsolate, and so Mose said, "C'mon, amigo." He put his arm around his friend's shoulder, and the two of them walked toward the little cabin. "Hey, Horse," he bellowed.

A young, dark-skinned Indian woman poked her head out the door of the rude shack. To Zack, Mose said, "Ye 'member Horse Hair Woman, don't ye, amigo?"

Zack nodded glumly. To the woman, Mose said, "Git some food fer my friend hyar, an' then take keer of his horses."

The woman nodded and scurried inside. When Mose and Zack entered, there was a steaming bowl of stew on the crude table hacked out of a tree stump. "Siddown, boy, an' eat," ordered Mose. "Ye'll purely like it. Ain't no woman kin make stew better'n old Horse."

Mose sat back quietly puffing on a pipe, while Zack ate the warming stew, throwing off the chill and gloom of the mountain winter. He had another bowl. Before he had finished his second bowl, Horse Hair Woman returned with his possible sack. He nodded gratefully.

When he finished eating, he dug in his possible sack for his old pipe. He sat back and lighted it, while Mose did the same again. Zack looked at the woman. "That was right fine stew. Thankee."

The woman blushed in embarrassment and Mose said, "See. I tole ye."

Zack nodded. "Whar's she git sich a name anyhow?"

"Best I kin understand it, when she was born her ma put her in a cradleboard decorated with a lot of horse hair. So thet's what they named her."

"Cain't ye call 'er somethin' better'n Horse? She's a purty leetle squaw and seems right capable, so it seems a shame to call 'er sich a thing."

"What'd ye rather I call 'er? Hairy?" They both laughed.

"Wall, now, I guess ye're right, amigo. That shorely wouldn't be ary better, would it?"

The laughter ran out, and Mose asked softly, "What happened?"

"Comanches raided the village whilst we was off gittin' meat. Warn't nobody left in the village 'cept wimmin an' kids an' a few ole men. We was only ten mile away, but we couldn't hear nothin' cause of the buffler runnin'. When I got back I found her an' the baby, dead from a Comanch' lance in an arroyo behind our lodge. They burnt the lodge down too.''

Mose sat back, puffing on his pipe. "I jist cain't believe it. It ain't right. When did it happen?''

"Whilst we was on the fall hunt.'' He looked weary and said, ''Mose, we was only ten mile away when it happened. But we couldn't hear a thang. It warn't till we was done with the huntin' that we heard the noise. By the time we got back, it was too late. Only ten mile, Mose.''

"That's damp powder, fer shore,'' said Mose, shaking his head. They sat quietly for a while, puffing their pipes, thinking their own thoughts. Finally Mose broke the silence. ''Did ye go out after 'em?''

"Naw.'' said Zack. ''Winter was comin' on.''

"But ye are goin' after 'em soon's good weather comes along, now, ain't ye, amigo?''

"I hadn't thought to do so,'' said Zack softly.

"Wall, why not?'' exploded Mose. ''Ye cain't lit them devils git away with somethin' like that. It ain't good fer ye, an' it ain't good fer the Shyans. Ye lit them Comanches git away with it this time, they'll be back ever year.''

Zack looked pained. ''But what good's it gonna do?'' he wailed. ''It ain't gonna bring 'em back. They're gone, Mose. Gone under.'' Zack wept openly, something he hadn't done since he left the Cheyenne village.

Mose's hand smacked the crude wooden table with a sound like a gunshot. Zack jumped at the sharp report. ''What in hell's wrong with ye, boy?'' shouted Mose. ''I ain't ever seed ye like this afore.''

"What d'ye want me to do?'' Zack moaned. He had never seen Mose so mad. The usually calm, quiet Mose seemed to seethe with anger.

"Go out an' git them devils,'' snapped Mose. ''It

mightn't bring yore woman and chile back, but ye kin sculp them Comanches an' let yore family join their ancestors. Ye kin free their spirits. Were they cut up?''

"Some," admitted Zack.

"Then ye gotta go git them Comanches. Ye know's well's I do that if the dead been mutilated, ye gotta avenge 'em afore their spirits kin be free."

"Maybe ye're right," said Zack, unconvinced.

Mose grabbed Zack by the front of his buckskin shirt, yanking him up. "Ye know I'm right," he said roughly. "Onct ye free their spirits, ye kin git rid of this guilt and git back to livin' like ye're supposed to. It'd make ye feel a heap better, an' ye know it."

Zack stood there dully. In disgust, Mose let him sink back onto the wooden bench. He looked at his friend and sadly shook his head. He turned and walked across the room, picking up a large earthen jug that sat in the corner. He picked up two battered tin cups and returned to the table.

Zack hardly moved as Mose poured the liquid into the two cups. "Hyar," he said. "This'll put some life back in ye, amigo. Drink it."

Zack took the cup and, without looking, poured it down his throat. The liquor hit him, and he choked. Through a constricted throat he managed to squeak, "What'n hell's that?"

Mose laughed at the expression on Zack's face. "Wall, now, that's pure Taos Lightnin', or I wouldn't say so. Made it myself. Right hyar."

Zack reached out and grabbed the jug. He sniffed suspiciously at the opening. "Ye didn't put no tobacco in hyar, did ye? That'd give it a kick."

Mose laughed some more and took back the jug. He poured Zack another drink and took a good-sized one of his own. "Naw, I wouldn't put no 'bacca in my own stuff now, would I? But it did need a leetle spicin' up after I made it, so's I put in a pinch or two of chilli powder.''

"A pinch'r two?" wheezed Zack. Gingerly he took a sip. His eyes winced involuntarily. "Ye ain't tellin' me true, amigo. Ye must've put in a whole sackful.''

Mose grinned. "Ain't ye man enough to take it?"

"I'll outdrink ye, ye old horse thief. If ye've got the guts to sit an' drink with a real mountain man.''

Mose threw back his head and laughed. He settled himself in across the table from Zack and plunked the jug down squarely between them. He raised his cup and said, "Hyar's to ye, ole hoss.''

The woman entered the room with a load of firewood and shook her head. She knew it would be a long night for the two trappers and that they would both be roaring drunk before they were through. She shrugged and went about her chores, ignoring them. In the morning, she found both of them snoring, heads slumped on the table. She began to prepare breakfast, banging the few iron pots and kettles around to show her displeasure.

It worked. Mose groggily raised his head. "Be quiet, woman!" he bellowed, holding his aching head in both hands. But the shout woke Zack, who raised bloodshot, bleary eyes to look at his friend.

"Damn," he muttered, and laid his head back down. Mose did the same.

CHAPTER 9

Zack rode out three days later, glad he had stopped, but no longer wanting company. It was a frigid, blustery day, with signs of snow appearing over the ridge of the mountains. Mose had tried to persuade him to say for a while longer.

"Ye're crazy leavin' on a day like this," Mose warned. "Why, there'll be more'n a foot of snow afore it's bin snowin' an hour."

"I'll be holed up afore it gits too deep," said Zack. "I gotta git movin', Mose, else I'll nary take enough beaver to make a season."

"Wall, now," said Mose. "If that's whar yore stick floats, I ain't gonna stop ye. Ye still wanna meet down to Santy Fe come spring?"

"Wall, shore now. Ain't no reason not to, far's I kin see. See ye then." He wheeled the horse and, leading the string of pack horses, slowly walked away from the shack. As he rode, his mind wandered over the past three days.

When they had recovered from their one-night spree, Mose had again tried to talk to Zack about going against the Comanches. But Zack steadfastly refused to do it. Mose finally gave up, almost in disgust, Zack thought.

"Wall, amigo, I guess I kin see why ye got the fear of the Comanches in ye," Mose had said. "After

183

seein' yore woman an' chile kilt thataway.''

"I ain't skeered of no Comanches, nor ary other Injuns,'' Zack countered vehemently. "I jist cain't see no purpose to goin' agin 'em. They's too many of 'em, an' I cain't kill 'em all.''

"But what about the spirits of yore family?'' asked Mose.

"Ye ain't tellin' me ye believe in sich foolishness now, do ye, Mose?''

"Wall now, I ain't sayin' I do, an' I ain't sayin' I don't. I'm jist sayin' it might be a leetle smarter to pay attention to sich things.''

"Waugh,'' spit out Zack. "Ye're as bad's the Shyans.''

"Wall now, all's I know is that, was it me whose woman an' chile got kilt, I'd be out lookin' fer them devils soon's I could git myself a horse.''

"Yep. An' most likely git yoreself kilt, too.''

It remained a sore spot between them and was the main reason why Zack wanted to head away from the small, cramped cabin as fast as he could. But as he rode, he wondered if Mose might be right in his thinking.

He remembered his resolve to take She-Who-is-Wind-in-the-Morning and their daughter back to Santa Fe with him this year. It was then, he now realized, that he finally freed himself of the last cloying bonds of his youth. He looked at the sky with a practiced eye. "Damn,'' he said aloud. "The snow'll be hyar in less'n an hour.'' He hurried the horses along, looking for a cave or grove of trees he could use for shelter.

Before long he found what he was looking for, and he lost his earlier thoughts in the necessities of making camp. It was already snowing heavily, the thick, wet flakes falling silently with no wind to blow them. Zack gathered firewood and enough feed for the horses and then settled in, glad there was no wind. The mountain wind could drive the temperature down to dangerous levels. He had lived through that type of winter night before and knew he would do so again. But he did not relish the thought.

As he slowly chomped on some jerky he had warmed over the fire, his thoughts went back to Mose and his dead wife. "Mebbe the Shyan way is better this time. Mebbe Mose is right," he murmured into the sputtering flames.

But he made no decision. It was easier for him not to. He stayed in the tree-covered shelter until the snow drifted to a stop two days later. He dug a path out of the grove and, with snowshoes firmly strapped on, tramped a path out for the horses. The sun was high and brittle, throwing little warmth.

He traveled as he had before: always on the move, rarely stopping more than a day or two unless the weather, always unpredictable, kept him longer. He trapped as he went, gathering pelt after pelt, curing them himself. With each one he gathered, the painful memory of Windy gripped him.

He avoided company, red and white, going his own lonely way through the mountains. He ate little, not seeming to care. He thinned and gaunted down in the cold air of the Rocky Mountain chains through which he moved.

But finally the weather began to break, and he knew it was time to head back down out of the mountains, out across the flatlands and into the Spanish town of Santa Fe. This time, though, he did not head out of the mountains into the country of the Cheyennes. He skirted the Utes and then came into the land of the pueblos, following the ragged course of the upper Rio Grande.

For the first time since he could remember, he rode

sedately into Santa Fe instead of roaring in, finery on and guns blasting. This time he also rode in early, near the beginning of May. He was gaunted down, and sad eyes peered out from his bearded, grimy face.

Nothing could be kept a secret in the mountains for long. The trappers already in Santa Fe had heard of the Comanche attack on the Cheyenne village and had spread the word. They knew Zack was suffering and left him alone for the most part.

Mose rode into town a week later in high style. He had figured Zack would drift down early and so had rode on in early himself. With the help of some rum, fine brandy and Mose's own Taos Lightning, the men helped Zack out of his shell. They danced and drank and gambled and whored. And they fought two hardy brawls. But it was not the same, and both knew it.

In late May Zack made his decision. He sought out Mose, finding him in one of the saloons, playing monte.

"Hyar now, amigo," Mose shouted as Zack walked in the door. "Hyar's a game of monte ye cain't beat."

Zack cracked a small smile. "I ain't got no time fer monte. I'm leavin' out."

It got quiet in the saloon. "When?" asked Mose.

"Soon's I git my string together an' possible sack filled."

"Whar away, amigo?"

"Toward the Republican River, I reckon. Past the Smokey Hill. Mebbe the Arkansas."

"Shyan country?" Mose put down his cards.

Zack nodded. "I done made up my mind. Ye was right. I gotta go back."

"Ye goin' after the Comanches?"

"Wall now, I reckon I jist might."

Mose jumped up and war-whooped around the table. "I'll be ready to leave when ye are, amigo," he said joyfully.

186

"Naw ye ain't," said Zack quietly. "Ye ain't goin' with me. I gotta do this alone."

"Ye're loco. Shore I'm goin' with ye. Me an' ye'll take on the whole Comanche nation." He had stopped his whooping and dancing around the table.

"It ain't yore fight, Mose."

"Why shore it is. . ." started Mose, but Zack stopped him.

"Naw it ain't. Ye got other werries."

"Are ye sartin?"

"Shore."

"Wall now," said Mose, not letting the bad news affect him overly long. "Then the least I kin do is help ye git yore string together."

Mose cleared away his money from the table. "Sorry, boys," he said cheerfully. "But I got work to do."

The two walked out of the saloon and headed toward the corral where Zack kept his horses. He told the young stable boy to get the pack animals ready and the appaloosa saddled. They headed for the trading post where he bought lead and powder and trade items and flour and coffee and sugar and some hardtack. And a few gallons of whiskey.

They carried the supplies back to the adobe hotel where Zack was staying. As Zack began to arrange the items and fill his possible sack with personals, Mose said, "I'll be right back, amigo. Thar's somethin' I gotta do afore ye leave."

Zack nodded, and Mose left. He returned in a few minutes and said, "C'mon, Zack, I got somethin' to show ye."

Puzzled, Zack followed Mose out of the small room, not knowing what to expect. Mose suddenly pushed him into a room where a tub of steaming hot water sat. "Shuck down, an' git in," Mose said. "Ye're leavin' this town in style."

Zack started to protest, but Mose cut him off. "Jist shuck down an' git in thar, or I'll throw ye in the way ye are. It took the boy a lotta effort to fill that tub."

Zack gave in. He grinned and stepped out of the crusty, blood- and grease-stained buckskins. He wrinkled his nose. "Phew," he said, "I am startin' to smell purty high, ain't I?"

"Startin'?" snorted Mose. "Ain't ye ary wondered why no one in town wants to spend much time with ye? Ye're worse'n a herd of buffler all by yoreself."

They both laughed, and Zack gingerly stepped into the tub, wincing at the hot water. "Ye shore this's necessary?"

Zack laughed at himself while Mose went to answer the door. In walked a barber. Mose said, "This hyar coon's gonna trim yore beard a mite, whilst I go out an' git ye some proper finery to wear on yore way outta hyar. So's ye jist set back an' enjoy it all."

When Mose returned, the barber was gone and Zack was getting out of the old wooden tub. "This suit yore fancy?" Mose asked, holding out a beautifully soft, almost white buckskin shirt, exquisitely embroidered with beads, painted porcupine quills and small shiny bits of metal that dangled and glittered.

"Wall now, it shorely does," said Zack, drying himself off. "That's shore some fine shirt now, or I wouldn't say so. Whar'd ye git it?"

"Horse did it. Fer ye. An' thar's a pair of buckskin pants to go with it. I got ye moccasins, too, so's ye'll be decked out proper when ye leave."

"Why that's mighty nice of ye, amigo," said Zack. He finished drying off and donned the new outfit. "Yore woman shore does fine work, Mose. This's a right nice getup hyar."

They walked back to the tiny, dingy room where Zack pulled an old, highly colored scarf out of his possible sack. He tied it around his throat and then reached far into the recesses of the sack to pull out his favorite buffalo-fur cap, now dull and slick with age. He plopped the hat on his freshly washed hair and said, "Wall now, amigo, what d'ye think?"

"Ye shore are a fine sight," grinned Mose, "or I wouldn't say so. Yep. A fine sight."

They grinned at each other, remembering the old days when they had celebrated in high style. Then Zack grew serious. "Like I said afore, over to the saloon, Mose. I think mebbe ye're right. That's why I'm goin' back."

Mose just nodded and said, "Ye best git a move on. It ain't gonna be light out ferever."

Zack finished filling his sack, and they lugged all the supplies back to the corral, where Zack could pack all of them on one of the pack horses. There wasn't much. Zack stuffed his pistols in his belt and climbed on the appaloosa. Mose handed him the old Hawken. Zack looked down at his friend. "Wall, amigo," he said. "We shore had us some fines sprees now, didn't we?"

"We shore did, amigo."

"I don't know's if I'll be comin' back through this way agin, if'n I go agin the Comanches."

Mose nodded. "Wall now, amigo. I know that. But then, all of us take them chances ever time we set out fer the mountains. Cain't 'spect to live ferever now, can ye?"

Zack grinned. "Naw, reckon not." He sat straighter now on the horse, almost back to his old self. "But I ain't got no likin' fer the idee of bein' rubbed out by no Comanche war lance. I ain't much taken to the idee of losin' my hair to no Comanche buck either."

"Ain't aryone I ever heered of wantin' to go under thataway. But it's part of bein' a mountain man now, ain't it?"

"Wall now, that's true. But I jist wanted ye to know

ye bin like kin to me." He started to say more but faltered.

"Save yore sentiment fer the Comanches. I know how ye feel, amigo, an' thar ain't no good in ye sayin' it. Ye jist git out thar an' do what ye gotta do, an' I'll see ye back hyar next spring or else somewhar in the mountains this winter. Jist 'member, if'n ye need anythin', ye kin always find me."

"I'll remember," said Zack, suddenly wanting to be off. "Wall, now, amigo, ye jist take keer of yoreself. I don't wanna go off fightin' no Comanches only to come back an' hear ye was rubbed out by some Ute with a hankerin' fer hair."

"Ye watch yore hair, too, amigo," said Mose, chuckling. "Ye got more to werry 'bout then I do. I ain't the one goin' out searchin' fer Comanches."

Zack nodded, abruptly pulled the horse around and kicked it gently into motion. Then he remembered his finery. Zack stopped the horse and looked back toward Mose who was still watching him. He grinned and raised his rifle in salute. Then he bellowed at the top of his lungs and fired off the heavy rifle. The sounds woke the sleepy village. Children began to cry and dogs began to bark and howl. With a full-throated laugh, Zack spurred the horse forward at a gallop, people and dogs jumping out of the way of the pounding horse. Halfway through town, he fired off one of his pistols and bellowed again.

Then he was out of the town and slowed his pace. He raised his head and laughed at the sky. He felt fine. He was whole again. "Look out, Comanches. Zack's comin' fer ye," he shouted.

He made good time, not idling along the way. He was in a hurry now and traveling light. The time for him went fast. He also rode fearlessly, cutting directly across the plains through the heart of Comanche and

Kiowa country, the straightest route to the land of the Cheyennes. He found the village near the juncture of Bear Creek and the Arkansas River. He rode into it amid the shouts of wonder and welcome. Without stopping or returning the salutations, he rode right to the lodge of Strong Horse.

"Father," he said to the old Indian who had come to stand outside his tepee to wait for Zack. The mountain man had drawn a crowd. Everyone waited to see what he had come to do. He was uneasy with all the attention, but said, "I ain't quite shore how to say this, but I'd like ye to be my sponsor fer the Sun Dance."

"You wish to endure the pain?" asked the chief.

"I·do."

"Why?" asked the Indian.

With emotion, Zack lapsed back into his own language. "Because I need the strength it will give me to go to war agin the Comanches; to avenge the death of my wife an' chile so their spirits may be free."

Strong Horse's impassive face almost broke into a grin. He was happy at the news, but this was not the time or place for smiling. "It is good," he said, once again stern. "I will do it."

Zack had arrived barely in time. From others he heard that the holy tree was to be cut and brought into the village on the next day. He had not known when they would have the Sun Dance. It could come at any time during the summer. But now he would have just enough time to purify himself and prepare for the ceremony.

Strong Horse re-entered his lodge, and Zack jumped off the horse and walked with Thunder Blanket to the Indian's tepee. They were joined on the walk by the still-reckless Once Ran.

"It is good that my friend, Enemy-of-Kiowas, has

191

come back to follow the ways of the Cheyenne."

Zack only grunted and the Indian continued. "I knew in my heart you were not afraid of the Comanches and that you would return to ride with me on the warpath against those killers of women."

Zack continued to ignore the young Indian, who finally stalked away.

"He has spoken of nothing but going on the war path against the Comanches for many moons now," said Thunder Blanket. "His blood runs hot, and he is full of talk of revenge. Winter and the hunt have kept him in the village. But now that the hot weather is almost gone and the hunt is long over, he is impatient."

"He does seem a mite feisty, don't he?"

"Yes. He hungers for the hair of the Comanche. We must soon go on the warpath into Comanche country to let him have his revenge. If we do not send a war party with him, he may be foolish enough to go himself."

"That wouldn't be ary good now, would it?"

"No. The People cannot lose such a warrior."

"Ye plannin' on goin' on the warpath with 'im?"

"Yes. I, too, am filled with thoughts of revenge. Or have you forgotten it was my sister that was killed?"

Zack gave the Indian a black look. "Naw, I ain't fergot who it were that got kilt," he said slowly.

"Will you join us on the warpath?" asked Thunder Blanket.

"That's why I'm hyar."

"It is good."

They entered the lodge. The Indian's youngest wife gave them roasted buffalo ribs. "Eat well, my friend," said Thunder Blanket. "It is all you may have for some time." Zack nodded.

192

They ate silently, Zack already thinking of the ordeal he was soon to go through.

The next morning Zack and some of the other young warriors of the village were led toward the sweat lodge. He sat inside the dim interior, immersed in his own thoughts as he smoked the pipe as required and squinted at the swirling, stifling clouds of smoke. Periodically the flap would open and a young Indian would toss in some heated rocks and pour water on them, freshening the steam.

The time in the small, foggy sweat lodge seemed interminable, but Zack stoically accepted it. When it was over, he was led to the river where, naked, he plunged into the cold water. The shock of it brought him out of his fog. Then he was led back to the lodge of Strong Horse. There he slept.

The next day the sacred pole was in place, with the thongs of rawhide that would be attached to the skewers through the flesh. The rawhide thongs blew lazily in the air. He fasted all that day and the next.

The following morning, he was painted by Strong Horse in a way he did not understand. He knew all the symbols the chief used meant something, but he knew not what. Hunger gnawed at him, and he found he did not care what the symbols meant. After he was painted, he was dressed in a skirt of beaded cloth. A wreath of sage was placed on his head and he was given a ring of sage to hold in each hand as he danced.

After he was led to the sacred circle, Thunder Blanket placed an eagle-bone whistle in his mouth. The whistle hung around his neck on a rawhide thong. He began to dance, blowing the eagle-bone whistle. He would play his tune on it all day, a monotonous, hypnotic melody that became a part of his being. The dance wore on and on. Then he knew it was time to have his flesh pierced.

Strong Horse, experienced in such matters, came up to him. The old Indian gently laid Zack down on the earth and then grasped the skin above Zack's left breast between his fingers. With a sharp knife, he made a quick incision. Zack gasped an involuntary intake of breath, but made no other sound. Before the wound could close, Strong Horse thrust a wooden skewer, pointed on each end through the opening.

He followed the same procedure with the other breast. This time Zack made no sound. When the skewers were in place, Zack was pulled to his feet. As he stood, Strong Horse attached the rawhide thongs to the ends of the skewers.

Zack, with fire in his chest, turned his mind inward, listening, becoming absorbed by the hypnotic beat of the skin and log drums. The throbbing, combined with the incessant sound of the rattles, drove him closer to a trance. He sucked air and blew it out through the eagle-bone whistle, creating his own abstract music.

He continued, hour after hour. Shuffling slowly, whistling, straining. Time had no meaning for him. His feet shuffled to the various beats and rhythms. Back and forth. Back and forth. The whistle sounded louder and louder in his ears. Each time he danced back, he gave a jerk and drew back on the wooden pegs through his chest.

The pain became non-existent. There was only the drums, and the rattles, and the whistling, a shrill trilling. There was only the straining in his chest and the now soothing music.

He stood on the top of a high hill, a tall promontory facing the east. The sun was yet low, only recently risen. He saw a buffalo far down on the plains below him. Although he was far away, he could see that the buffalo had his own features. He watched in wonder

194

as a band of Indians whom he recognized as Comanches charged the old bull. The bull bravely faced the attacking warriors, who flung at him all they could, their lances and arrows falling like rain all around the bull, but not touching him. The warriors charged again and again, but still the bull held his ground, not moving an inch. A long piece of cloth that Zack had not seen before wound around the bull and was attached to the ground.

Finally the warriors had no more weapons left, and the bull charged, goring horses and trampling fallen riders. The long strip of cloth grew longer and longer, stretching to let the bull attack. But it remained pegged to the ground.

The Indians seemed frozen to where they sat, unable to move out of the way of the charging bull. Lightning crackled between the bison's horns. The bull also grew larger and larger, dwarfing the warriors. Finally the bull floated up to the sky and was gone, leaving only the bodies of the Indians who had attacked him scattered on the ground.

Zack awoke in a dim tepee with Thunder Blanket and Strong Horse looking over him. He tried to talk, but couldn't. Thunder Blanket gently raised his head, and Strong Horse poured some water on his lips. Zack's mouth opened to lap up some of the water, and more was poured easily down his throat. He choked and sputtered, but did better with the next swallow.

"Whar am I?" he managed to croak.

"In my lodge," said Thunder Blanket.

"What happened?"

"We do not know. Perhaps you had a vision. You were dancing the Sun Dance, and then you broke free of the thongs. You seemed to not be yourself, and we thought you were having a vision. When we thought it was over, we brought you here."

Zack beckoned for more water. After he had sipped

a little, he said, "Wall now, I shore did have a vision." He struggled to sit up, and Thunder Blanket helped him. "I guess I should tell ye 'bout my vision."

"Not now," said Thunder Blanket. The Indian's wife handed Zack a bowl of thin, watery stew. With Zack's head propped up, the Indian began to feed the white man with a horn spoon. "This will not fill you up," he told Zack, "but it will give you nourishment. You could not hold anything heavier now."

Zack did not complain but ate the thin soup eagerly. "It's good," he said between mouthfuls.

His chest healed rapidly. It was only a few days before he had enough strength to get up and walk around the village. But when he did, he was looked upon with more respect. When he was completely healed, he went to see the medicine man, Grass Grows, to tell the old man his vision and to learn its meaning. After smoking a pipe and giving the old Indian his payment, two small bags of tobacco and a Green River knife, Zack told him of his vision.

The old man listened patiently and was silent for several minutes after Zack had finished. Finally he said, "It is so. You are the buffalo and the warriors are your new enemy, the Comanches. From now on you will be known as Bull-Who-Stands-and-Fights."

"That still don't explain the vision," said Zack.

"It is simple," said the old man. "Yes, you are the buffalo in your vision and the Comanches are your enemy. You will go out and fight the enemy, and will do so fearlessly, even to standing there and facing their charges. But you will not be hurt if you carry your medicine with you."

"What's my medicine?" asked Zack.

"I will make a sacred bundle for you. A new one to replace the one I gave you many winters ago. One that you will carry into battle. Then you will not be harmed."

"When'll it be ready?" asked Zack. "It won't be long afore a war party'll be formed."

"These things take time," Grass Grows told him. "You must be patient. But I will tell you that it will be ready before you leave to go into battle."

At a council meeting that night, Zack told the assembled warriors of Grass Grows' interpretation of his vision.

"It is good," said Once Ran. He leaped up. "Now is the time to go to battle. We have fresh meat in the camp, and the winter is yet far away. Now is the time for battle."

Several other young warriors joined him in his call for war, but they became silent when Thunder Blanket shouted, "We will go to war when the time is right."

The young warriors scowled but did not press the point. They knew they would be unable to influence the older, wiser warriors.

Zack did not know how he knew, but a week after he learned of the meaning of his vision, he knew the time was right for a war party to be formed. He asked for another council and the warriors met that night.

He was to speak that night and knew he must be eloquent. But he was nervous. For the same unfathomable reason that he knew the time was right for forming a war party, he knew he would be the one to lead it.

He rose to speak. "Brothers," he started. "It was a winter ago that the hated enemy, the Comanches, attacked our village, untended because of the hunt. Since then we have waited for the opportunity for revenge."

Some of the younger warriors shouted, and Zack, dressed in leggings and breechcloth, a blanket held around him, waited patiently for silence. It was not long in coming.

"Through fasting and dancing, I have had a vision.

It was explained to me by Grass Grows, and I have told it to you. You know that we cannot be defeated."

Some of the warriors broke into war whoops, and again Zack waited stolidly for quiet. When it came, he said, "There was one point in the dream that was not explained to me and was not clear until now."

Complete silence settled in. Zack looked at the old medicine man, who nodded at him gravely.

He continued: "I did not know why the bull was a solitary one facing the enemy. But now it is clear. The spirits wish me to fight the Comanches in their own way. I will be as one of their warriors in the Society of the Ten Bravest. I, Bull-Who-Stands-and-Fights, will stake myself down with a sash of black elkskin in the face of the enemy."

The tepee burst into heated arguments among the warriors. In the face of it, Zack sat, his face set. The arguments continued, some of the warriors not believing, others wanting to join Zack in his personal battle. Among those was Once Ran, who shouted louder and more often than the others.

Finally Strong Horse rose, and the rest of the warriors fell quiet. "Brothers," said the old warrior. "Our cousin, Bull-Who-Stands-and-Fights, has spoken of his vision. He must follow his vision, and we, too, must obey what he has seen. Bull-Who-Stands-and-Fights should lead this war party against the enemy. He has earned that right. He should lead the war party, and those who are brave enough should follow him. He should also fight in the way the spirits have indicated. To do less is to invite defeat. I have spoken."

Although his word was not law, most of the warriors were not of a mind to go against the wishes of the principal chief of the village. A few young men clamored for attention, but they went unheeded.

Zack again stood. He started to speak, but before

he could, Grass Grows handed him a small pouch. "Your medicine," he said.

Zack carefully tied the thong around his neck after dropping the blanket. He adjusted the small bag, filled with he knew not what, so that it rested under his left arm. He retrieved his blanket. Then he spoke. "Brothers, tomorrow I prepare a sash of blackened elkskin. The day after, I go in search of the Comanches. Those who are afraid may stay behind. But those who are true Cheyenne warriors should come behind me. We will be successful in this battle. I have spoken."

The council broke up, and most of the warriors spoke to Zack, telling him they would follow him in his war against the Comanches.

CHAPTER 10

Once again Zack sat in the gloom and steam of the sweat lodge. With him were Once Ran, Thunder Blanket and Hawk Wind. Following the council meeting the night before, Zack had fasted. In the morning, still fasting, he pieced together some strips of elkskin, forming a sash. This he painted black and left in the sun to dry.

The elkskin sash had a loop at one end, which he would wear over his right shoulder, under his left arm. The rest of the length of the sash would be staked down to the ground at its end. After making his sash, Zack had prayed to the spirits, seeking success in his venture. Then he had entered the sweat lodge.

But now he had been there long enough. With a last passing around of the pipe, Zack and the others stepped into the brilliant, brittle glare of the sunlight. Quickly, but with dignity, the naked men walked the steps to the stream and plunged in.

When they walked from the water, Thunder Blanket said to Zack, "Will you eat at my fire?"

Zack nodded agreement. He had fasted and had been purified. Now he was pure and could eat. But there were rules he must obey, rules handed down to him from the spirits through Grass Grows. He must eat only of the buffalo, one freshly killed. He must not eat at his own fire. And he must eat without utensils, using only his bare hands and teeth to devour the rich, red meat. Not to follow these rules would jeopardize not only his own life but also the lives of those who followed him.

The two men sat outside Thunder Blanket's tepee in the warm sun. They were joined there by some of the other Dog Soldiers, warriors who would follow Zack into battle against the Comanches.

They ate in silence the roasted buffalo ribs that Thunder Blanket's young wife passed around. When they had eaten their fill, a pipe was passed around. As they smoked, Thunder Blanket asked Zack, "You have not changed your mind?"

"What?" snorted Zack. "About the battle?"

Thunder Blanket nodded, and Zack said, "Hell, no. I aim to git me as many of them damn Comanches as I kin afore I go under."

"So you think you will be killed?" asked Once Ran.

"Hell, boy, I'm gonna be out thar in front of all of ye, facin' them Injuns all by myself. I don't 'magine the Comanches're gonna leave me be fer long."

"I will be there to save my friend," said Once Ran simply. The other Indians nodded agreement.

"Hell," spat Zack. "By the time ye git thar, I'll be rubbed out fer shore. But I'll take the hair off'n more'n one of them Comanches afore they git me, or I wouldn't say so."

"Then you are not afraid to die?" questioned Thunder Blanket.

"Naw, I ain't skeered." Zack took a few puffs on his own pipe before continuing. "I cain't rightfully say I'm taken with the idee of gittin' rubbed out by anyone, least of all the Comanches. But I cain't say's I'm skeered either."

"That is good," said Thunder Blanket. "You will do well in the battle, and the men will not be afraid to follow you."

"Well, I jist don't want none of ye takin' any damn fool chances to try'n save my hair. Ain't no use fer ary of ye to git yoreselves kilt on my account. Ye all got families to werry 'bout. Ye all jist 'member that."

By now the sun was dropping lower in the western sky. The men picked themselves up and, with words of good wishes, moved off toward their own lodges, leaving only Zack and Thunder Blanket.

"I best be gittin' on toward my own lodge, so ye kin git some robe time," said Zack. "We'll be gittin' an early start."

"You will leave soon enough," said the Indian. "But first I would spend a little while longer with my brother."

"Afeared it may be the last time ye'll git to see me alive, sittin' 'cross the fire from ye?"

Thunder Blanket smiled wanly. "That well may be, my friend."

They sat silently, thinking their own thoughts. Finally Zack lighted a last pipe, and they smoked together. When it was done, Zack stood. Thunder Blanket looked up at the white man.

"Well, my friend," said the Indian, "the time before the battle grows short."

Zack stood, a thoughtful look on his face. "It shore does," he said finally. They looked unblinkingly at each other for a short time before Zack turned and walked toward his tepee.

As he rolled himself into the sleeping robes, Zack said in a low voice, "Wall, ole Windy, I don't rightly know whar ye are now, but purty soon ye an' our chile'll be with the Great Spirit." He thought for a minute and then added, "An' I jist might be thar along

202

with ye. But I'll shore as hell take some Comanches with me.''

He settled himself more comfortably into the soft, heavy buffalo robes and was almost instantly asleep.

He awoke with the noise of the village: the yelling children, the barking dogs, the snorting horses. There was another sound too—the loud strutting of the warriors. The previous night had been unusually quiet for an Indian village whose warriors were about to embark on the warpath. But that unusual silence was gone now, the warriors swaggering around the village boasting of their past deeds and telling the village what they would do to any of the yellow Comanches that fell into their hands.

Zack himself had felt the quietness of the previous night, but now, listening to the sounds of an active Indian village, he smiled. ''It's a fine day,'' he said aloud.

Still smiling, he got up and stepped out of the tepee, squinting in the glare of the early morning sun. Some of the braves were already trying to gather support for a war dance they would hold before leaving. Others hurriedly finished their morning meal and began preparing themselves for the battle. Stray face hairs, unsightly and unmanly, were plucked with tweezers made of bone. The warriors' long, flowing hair was carefully parted, braided and wrapped in otter fur. The hair part was carefully painted, as were eyes, cheeks, chins, foreheads, chests, arms and legs. Even the horses were painted.

The women, too, were busy. Carefully, they helped their men prepare, putting the finishing touches on their breechcloths and helping to decorate the horses.

Thunder Blanket strode up as Zack watched the activity. ''Have you eaten?'' asked the Indian.

''Naw, not yit. I jist woke up.''

"Then come."

Zack followed his friend to his lodge where one of Thunder Blanket's three wives handed him a slab of freshly roasted buffalo ribs. Zack knew he had little time left, so he ate quickly, only half tasting the succulent meat. After his meal he plunged into the river to rid himself of the grease and the final remnants of sleep. As he splashed in the water, he heard the drums beginning. "Hell, I ain't got much time to git ready," he mumbled to himself as he climbed out of the river and trotted, still naked, to his tepee.

Inside, he combed his hair with a comb made of porcupine quills. Then he put on his best pair of buckskin pants and breechcloth. The pants were pale tan, with long fringe running down the length of the outside seam. He picked up his buckskin shirt and started to pull it over his head. But he stopped and threw the shirt aside. "Hell, I don't need that damn thing."

He stepped into his moccasins, finely beaded and decorated with tiny bits of metal. Each one had a small bell tied to it and tinkled gently as he walked. Then he put on his old buffalo cap, the one with the feather sticking out of one side.

Grabbing some of his other things, he walked outside where he could see better. Waiting for him were Thunder Blanket and Once Ran. "Here," said Once Ran, handing him two pots of color. "Paint yourself."

He felt foolish. He knew the war party would not meet the enemy for some time. Once out of the village they would fall into the routine of travel. Their paint and their medicine would have to be refreshed before the battle. He began to wonder if he hadn't gone too far this time. He started to protest, but then thought better of it. He dropped the things he was carrying and took the small pots of paint. Sitting cross-legged on the ground, he began to apply the paint under the watchful eyes of the two warriors.

He stroked the paint—red and black—on in fine, even strokes. He thought he was putting it on randomly, but he soon realized there was a pattern to his movements. "Guess my spirits are helpin' me with this, too," he thought.

The two Indians grunted their approval as Zack spread on the color: black rings around the eyes, down across the nose and upwards from the eyebrows, slanting outwards. The paint gave him the look of a buffalo. He painted other designs of power in the red and black on his chest and down his arms.

When he was finished, he wiped his hands on a piece of buckskin scrap. The Indians nodded.

Done with his paint, Zack looked to his weapons. He carefully, though quickly, cleaned the long Hawken he called Thunder. He checked the mechanism to be sure it was operating properly. He did the same with both pistols. He checked the powder horn to make sure it was full and looked to be sure he had enough rifle balls in the pouch he would sling over his shoulder.

The close-fighting weapons were seen to next. He checked the keenness of the tomahawk's blade and made sure the head of the instrument was on tightly. With his knife, he cut the old thong from the handle and in its place tied a new piece of rawhide strip. This he would loop over his wrist so the tomahawk could not be yanked from him.

He sharpened the big, mean-looking Green River knife that was his constant companion. He honed it slowly and carefully, heedless of the time he used. Finished, he slipped it back into the hardened leather case that hung from his belt.

Thunder Blanket, who with Once Ran sat quietly and patiently throughout the preparations, said, "Come. It is time for dancing."

Zack nodded and stood. Together the three walked

toward the ring of dancing warriors, surrounded by a larger ring of watching, singing women. As they drew closer, the drumming seemed to invade their blood, making their hearts begin to beat in time with them.

Zack could feel his feet and body begin to be taken over by the incessant throbbing of the drumming; the hypnotic thumping forcing him to dance, to shuffle his body back and forth, slowly, then faster, and back again slowly. The circle of women parted to let them through, and they danced into the circle.

As they danced, Zack found a rattle and an eagle-bone whistle thrust into his hands. Blindly he took them, shaking the rattle without effort in time to the drumming. He jammed the whistle in his mouth and, like a sleepwalker, began blowing an almost tuneless trill, all the while gliding in a circle with the other warriors, around and around the post that, for now, was the enemy.

The dancing grew more frenzied, and war whoops began to pierce the air. The warriors attacked the post, imitating what they would do to the Comanches when the battle was joined. The shrieks and screams grew more numerous and more persistent. Louder and louder they rang, the women adding their voices to the cacophony.

Zack's feet flashed, increasing the tempo of their stomping. The tiny bells on his moccasined feet jangled continuously. He, too, shrieked and shouted. Angrily and with passion, he repeatedly attacked the pole, slashing and jabbing with a long stick someone had handed him. Suddenly the drums stopped, and Zack knew it was up to him. The warriors stopped a few beats after the drum and, breathing heavily, waited.

Zack took a minute to reorient himself. The camp was quiet now, except for an occasional dog bark or whimpering child. Zack threw down the stick. Throwing a fist into the air, he shouted in Cheyenne, "We go!"

The frenzied shouting began again as warriors hollered and yelled on their way to their mounts. Zack broke and ran for his tepee. There, to his surprise, he found Rain Cloud Woman, his dead wife's sister. Quietly and with pride she waited, holding the reins of the big appaloosa, saddled and ready to go. She also held the reins of two other horses Zack could trust.

Without knowing what to say, he nodded to her and accepted the reins to the stallion. With an easy, fluid motion, he leaped on. Rain Cloud Woman dropped the reins of the other horses so she could stoop to get his weapons. Almost with reverence she handed him his pistols, which he stuck in his belt.

The woman then handed him the elkskin sash, carefully folded and wrapped in buckskin to protect it. He tied the bundle to his saddle. The bullet pouch and powder horn followed. These he slung over his shoulder, and he was almost ready. He took the Hawken that she handed to him, and then she handed him the reins of the two extra horses.

Sitting atop the appaloosa, he looked down at the woman. "Gawd," he thought, "she shore does look like her sister." She was a little shorter and a little thinner, but there was no mistaking that she was the sister of She-Who-Was-Wind-in-the-Morning.

Aloud he said, "I thank ye fer doin' this, Rain Cloud Woman. It's mighty nice of ye."

She blushed with pride at his words and lowered her head. Knowing he was still watching her, she looked up at him again.

"I must be goin' now," he said.

She nodded silently. As he turned the horse to start

riding toward the waiting war party, she said to him in Cheyenne, "Fight bravely, but use care."

He faced her again. "I will."

"I would like you to return," she said, averting her eyes.

He walked the horse closer to her and reached down. Cupping her chin, he raised her face to look at him. "I will try, Rainy. I will try. But I'm doin' this fer yore sister, who was my wife."

The woman nodded. She reached up to take his hand. Pressing it to her cheek, she said, "You must go now. The others are waiting."

He nodded once and rode off, afraid to look back, trying not to think of the desirable young woman, the sister of his dead wife, waiting there for him. It would be too confusing, he knew, to add that to his life now.

At the edge of the village, the other warriors waited for him. He turned the two extra horses over to the boy who was to watch the horses. He looked over the expectant braves for a few seconds and then, without a word, turned his horse and spurred it at a fast trot across the plains.

The pace slowed within minutes, and the warriors trotted patiently over the long stretch of emptiness. Thunder Blanket rode up alongside Zack, who asked, "How long ye think it'll be afore we find the Comanches?"

Thunder Blanket shrugged. "I do not know. They may be close."

"But ye don't think so, do ye?"

"No."

"Why?"

"Because the Comanches are not fools, regardless of what some here may think of them. They know we might seek revenge on them and will probably stay in the heart of their own country."

"That makes sense, I reckon," said Zack. "How fur d'ye think we'll have to ride then?"

"Four suns. Maybe five. Long days. With only the warriors, we can ride fast and hard."

"That long, eh? D'ye think them young bucks'll stick with it that long on the trail?"

"Yes. They are bent on revenge and will stay on the trail as long as necessary." He looked sideways at Zack. "Do you have the patience to stay on the trail that long?" he asked.

Zack looked venomously at Thunder Blanket. "Ye should know better'n to ask somethin' like that. Don't do it again." He started to ride away from Thunder Blanket, but the Indian's hand stopped him.

"Many of them," said the Indian, nodding his head in the direction of the war party, "have as much reason as you to keep on the trail."

"Naw, they don't," Zack started to say. But he caught himself. "Ye're right, of course," he said, hanging his head. "I am sorry."

They rode along in silence.

But it took a week of hard riding before Cheyenne scouts brought word to the party that a Comanche village had been spotted a few miles ahead.

Zack, leading the war party and knowing the Comanches would see them shortly, called a halt to the travel. He ordered the warriors to make camp. It was late afternoon, and they would wait until the morning to fight the enemy. One more night, they knew, would make little difference. And they would need the rest after the long days on the trail.

As the camp was made, the Cheyennes saw two mounted Comanches watching them from afar. With almost a hundred warriors in the war party, the Cheyennes had little fear of an attack. But a few of the younger braves wanted to ride out and fight the two who watched. But Zack, older and wiser, impressed upon them the importance of waiting. The spirits, he told them, would not be kind, if they attacked too soon.

So the Cheyennes just watched the two warriors, who watched them.

The small camp was made quickly and guards were posted. Although they were unafraid, they took no chances. The Cheyennes camped at fires in small groups, each following their own way, either gambling or praying to the spirits. Zack's fire served Once Ran, Hawk Wind, Thunder Blanket and himself. They sat eating fresh buffalo, shot that day, which they sizzled briefly over the small fire. "Wall, now," said Zack, "I guess tomorrow is the day. Or do ye think they'll turn tail and run?"

"Then we will follow them," said Once Ran heatedly. "I will not give up now."

Thunder Blanket said softly, "They will not run. They have nowhere to go. They know we could catch them easily on the trail. They must bring along their old and their women and their children, as well as all the supplies of the village. No, they will not run. They will prefer to face us on their own ground where they can be prepared."

"Then ye think we'll have to attack the village?" asked Zack.

"No," answered Hawk Wind between bites of roasted tongue. "They will be waiting for us outside the village. On the prairie. They will not let us get near the village, if they can stop us. They will want to protect their women and children."

Zack grunted, "Good. I ain't too taken with the idee of attackin' a bunch of wimmin an' kids." He chewed briefly and then asked, "D'ye think it's the same bunch what attacked our village?"

"Does it make a difference?" snapped Once Ran. "Are not all the Comanches our enemy?"

"Naw, I guess it don't matter none. I'll still kill all of 'em I kin. I were jist wonderin'."

Finished with the small meal, Zack lit his well-worn pipe. He puffed quietly for a few minutes, watching the day grow older, the lengthening shadows creeping up. Abruptly he stood, knocking the ashes from the pipe. "I'm goin' out a leetle ways an' see if'n I kin find the right place."

Without thinking, Once Ran asked, "Right place for what?"

Zack looked at him hard for a few seconds before stalking away. He was joined by Thunder Blanket who said nothing, but walked quietly alongside. They mounted up and rode out of camp. About three miles from the camp, they spotted a small, stunted tree, its bare branches sticking forlornly into the late afternoon sky. The tree stood on a slight rise, giving it a good view and a commanding position.

Zack jogged his horse up to it and surveyed the land before him. "This's the spot," he said softly to Thunder Blanket. "This's whar I will stand."

Thunder Blanket nodded approvingly. "It is a good place. Your back is protected, and you are high enough to watch the enemy come at you."

Zack dismounted and inspected the land ahead of him from this position. He could still see for miles out on the prairie, including the tepees of the Comanches, tiny at this distance. He knew none of the enemy could sneak up to attack him. With his back protected to some extent by the little tree, they would have to come at him from the front.

Once again mounted, Zack and Thunder Blanket rode silently back toward the camp. Darkness was falling rapidly and there was a definite chill in the air.

A brittle wind whistled through the tall grass. "Won't be all that long afore winter's hyar," he said to the Indian. "Glad I brung that big buffler robe fer slee-pin'."

"Yes," chuckled Thunder Blanket. "It will not be long before the snows come." A look of anxiety crossed his face.

"What's the matter, amigo?" asked Zack. "Skeered?"

"No, my brother, it is not fear of the enemy. It is just that I have realized we must still go on the fall hunt, and time is growing short. We spent too many days on the Sun Dance and preparing for the battle. Last winter was long, and the spring hunt was late. And already the days grow shorter. We must return quickly to the village when we are finished here."

They were at the camp now and handed over their horses to the young men. "I guess ye're right," said Zack. "It's already late August. The hunt should soon be over, or winter'll be hyar afore we kin git enough meat. An' it looks like an early an' long winter agin this year." He paused before saying, "But I may not be with ye on this hunt, old friend, or ary other one ye might make."

The Indian nodded silently into the darkness lit only by the flickering fires of the Cheyennes. They rejoined the other two Indians at their fire, and Zack lighted his pipe. "Wall," he said, "we found the spot. Guess I'll jist have this hyar one last pipe afore gittin' some robe time."

The others said nothing.

Finished with his pipe, Zack spread out the large, fur-heavy buffalo robes he used for sleeping and made himself comfortable. He smiled when he thought it might be his last night on earth. But he was instantly asleep and did not dream.

He was one of the first men up in the morning, the chill still thick, and the inky blackness that preceded the dawn lying over the camp. But far to the east he could see the first glimmer of the pink rays of the sun splitting the sky. He stood, grunting his displeasure at the chill, almost regretting having left the warmth and comfort of the heavy robe. Stretching, he quietly built up the fire, rubbing his hands at the welcome heat of it.

He grabbed some meat with his hands and hung it over the fire to roast, noticing the first stirrings of life in the small camp. Thunder Blanket was awake and ready to join him. Some of the other warriors had risen and were building up their fires.

Silently, Zack took most of the cooked meat and handed it to Thunder Blanket, who nodded his thanks. Zack threw more of the meat over the fire to roast. By the time it was ready, the sun could be seen a little in the east, and the other two men at Zack's fire had risen. Once Ran went to the brook and returned with a small pot of water. He passed it around, each man drinking his fill of the cold, clear water.

The warriors passed around a pipe after the meal. By the time they finished, the sun was bright, although its heat would not reach them yet for some time.

"Wall," said Zack. "Guess it's 'bout time to git ready."

He went a few feet away from the others and made a small offering of meat and tobacco to the spirits. Then he repainted his face, arms and shoulders, freshening the color that had worn off in the heat and dust of the week-long ride.

Finished, he walked back to the fire and waited patiently for the others in the war party to ready themselves. Some of the younger warriors, late to rise, hurried their prayers and applications of paint.

But then they were ready. Solemnly Zack walked to the makeshift rope corral and mounted the big appaloosa that was saddled and ready for him. The other men did likewise, and they rode, strangely quiet, out onto the plains.

Far away, small specks appeared, finally showing themselves to be Comanche warriors, fully painted and decorated for war. As they got closer, Zack said to the noted warriors who rode in front with him, "Impressive, ain't they?"

He continued riding, the warriors following quietly and proudly behind, spread out only a little.

The war party halted some distance from the small gnarled tree. They could plainly see the Comanches now, less than half a mile away. Zack and the others waited for them to approach. When the Comanches were close enough to be able to distinguish individual warriors, they too halted. A few Comanches rode out a little further to taunt the Cheyennes. Some of the Cheyennes indicated their willingness to start the battle.

With a sharp word, Zack checked the impetuous young warriors. Then he said to them, "Jist calm down, boys. Ye'll git yore chance to kill some Comanches. Jist don't lit 'em rile ye an' git ye to make mistakes."

Zack sat and surveyed the enemy. Suddenly he started; his face grew hard and cold creases appeared on forehead and chin. A vein throbbed in his temple as he grated his teeth.

"What is wrong, my brother?" asked Thunder Blanket.

In a raspy voice, Zack said, "Thar's the son of a bitch what kilt my wife and chile."

An uneasy murmur ran through the Cheyennes. "Which one?" asked Once Ran excitedly.

"The big bastard out front," grated Zack, still scowling. "The one with the big bonnet, sittin' on the roan."

"How can you tell?" asked Hawk Wind.

"By the lance. It's got the same markin's as the one that kilt Windy and the baby."

"Are you sure?" asked the older Indian.

"Course I'm shore. D'ye think I'd fergit somethin' like that?"

"No," answered Hawk Wind. "You would remember."

"I want ye to pass the word," said Zack. "That big bastard's mine. Ary one of these other bucks goes after 'im, an' I'll slit their throats. Ye tell 'em."

Hawk Wind called back in Cheyenne and told the others what Zack had said. Suddenly he swung around and said to Zack, "Yes, I remember him now. He is a well-known Comanche warrior, fearless and strong. His name is Iron Lance."

"I've heard of him," said Zack. "He's got quite a name fer hisself further south." He sat thoughtfully for a few seconds and then said, "Wall, he don't skeer me none. He's raided his last village of wimmin an' kids."

Zack started to walk the horse slowly away from the warriors, but he was stopped by Hawk Wind's hand. The older Indian looked gravely at Zack as he held out his long, iron-tipped lance, emblazoned with bright red paint and feathers. "Here," he said to the white man. "Take this lance. You will use it well against our enemy."

Zack cradled the big Hawken across his left arm, holding the barrel in the crook of his left arm, balancing it. He grasped the lance. "Thankee," he said. "I hope I kin use it with honor and not disappoint ye."

215

"You will not," said Hawk Wind.

Zack, using just his knees to guide the horse, walked it out toward the tree. When he got there, he dismounted and tied the big appaloosa to it. "Wall, boy," he said, "ye may jist git yoreself kilt standin' hyar with me, but if'n I go under, I want ye along fer the ride to the spirit world."

The horse snorted and stamped a foot but began to crop at the grass as if understanding what was required of him and accepting it. Zack stabbed the lance into the ground and leaned the rifle against the tree. Deliberately he took the black elkskin sash from its wrappings and, stepping out from the meager shade thrown by the bare tree, carefully put it on. He wanted the Comanches to see him draping it over his shoulder.

The action caused a stir of excitement and consternation among the Comanches, who howled and shouted at the white man.

Zack stepped back toward the tree, the long sash dragging behind him. With deliberation, he pegged down the end of the sash with a large wooden stake he hammered through it deep into the soft earth. Here he would stay until rescued by the Dog Soldiers. Or until he died.

He left the rifle leaning against the tree, within reach, and tore the lance from the earth. He stepped out as far as the sash would permit. All was now silent across the prairie, except for the occasional snort or shuffle of the horses and the never-ceasing wind, only a breeze on this now hot August day.

Defiantly Zack faced the Comanches. He shouted, his voice shattering the stillness. "Iron Lance!" The noise faded away quickly in the emptiness, but the warrior named moved a few feet out from the others with him. Zack smiled wickedly and again shouted. "Whyn't ye come'n git me, Iron Lance? I'm waitin' fer ye."

Once more the voice faded rapidly. Iron Lance had not moved further. Zack bellowed, wanting to make sure all the Indians heard him. "Are ye skeered, Iron Lance? Mebbe ye'd like it better if'n it was jist a bunch of wimmin an' kids hyar."

Again nothing happened, so Zack shouted, "I didn't know the Comanches had sich a woman leadin' 'em. I thought they was brave warriors. Guess I was wrong. Yore leader, Iron Lance, ain't much of a warrior, less'n he's attackin' a village with no real men to protect it."

Finally he got a reaction. Some of the younger Comanches started to ride out to attack. But they were stopped by a sharp command by Iron Lance.

Zack again shouted, his voice whipping away across the plains. "Hey, Iron Lance. Whyn't ye lit them young bucks come out hyar an' git me? That'll save yore cowardly hide. Ye don't even have to face me, if'n ye're skeered."

There was more consternation among the Comanches. Some of the warriors taunted Iron Lance. The Indian walked his horse away from the war party, stopping twenty-five yards from Zack.

"Ye jist gonna stand thar all day, ye chicken-hearted savage?" yelled Zack.

The Indian sat up straighter on his horse, the feathered war bonnet flowing down his back, across the horse's rump and onto the ground. Without warning, he yelled his war cry and savagely kicked his horse into a run, charging down on Zack, a long lance held tightly in his right hand.

Iron Lance thrust the wicked-looking spear at Zack but missed as the white man ducked out of the way. The Indian pulled his horse up around the tree and attacked again. Once more he plunged the lance at his target. But Zack blocked the probing weapon with his own lance. As the Comanche circled the tree, Zack

217

yelled at him, "What's the matter, Iron Lance? Cain't ye stab nothin' but wimmin an' children hidin' on the ground?"

The Comanche rested his horse for a few seconds and then returned to the siege. As he closed in on Zack, he threw the lance. The long, heavy spear slid through Zack's leggings on the outside near the thigh, slicing the flesh slightly. The force of the blow knocked Zack to the ground.

Zack stood up and pulled the lance from the ground where it had imbedded itself after ripping through him. "Hey, Iron Lance," he shouted. "Ye fergot somethin'."

Zack looked down at the leg to assess the damage. A bit of blood welled up out of the shallow wound. Zack gave it no further thought.

The Comanche again pulled his horse up, facing Zack. He pulled out a war club from his waistband. The weapon was lethal-looking: a heavy, large, smooth stone, slightly pointed at each end, secured to a two-foot-long shaft. Wrappings of rawhide thong, which had dried firmly, bonded the head to the shaft.

Zack, watching the enemy, shifted his weight to the balls of his feet, preparing himself. The Indian charged, riding almost directly at the stationary Zack. Iron Lance swung the wicked weapon with all his force as the horse almost ran over the white man. But Zack had been ready and fell out of the way of both the charging horse and the powerfully swung war club. He bounced back to his feet, only to see the Comanche attack again without waiting, jerking the horse brutally around. Zack hurriedly stepped over a few paces so the tree trunk was directly at his back, forcing Iron Lance to ride wide, not allowing him to run Zack over with the horse.

Again the fiercely painted warrior swung the heavy-headed war club, hoping to crush Zack's head. But again Zack was ready and dropped low to the ground, the stone whistling close past his shoulders.

The Indian trotted to a halt again, letting the blowing roan catch its breath. Zack, brushing the dirt from his leggings and bare back, watched the Comanche. Sweat streaked his face and chest, mingling with the paint. "I'm through foolin' with ye, Iron Lance," he shouted. "Now I'm gonna kill ye. Come an' meet yore maker."

Iron Lance's war cry ripped through the stillness, raising the hairs on Zack's neck. The whole world, except for the charging Indian seemed to shrink for Zack. He watched Iron Lance, conscious of seeing him vividly, larger than life itself; the foam and sweat flying off the running horse and the almost unnatural sounds coming from the mouth of the Indian seemed to still time for him. The deadly club, swinging lightly in the Indian's right hand, moved in slow motion for him.

Iron Lance swept closer and closer, still shrieking. Zack suddenly stood up straight from the crouch he had taken. He hefted the long, sharp lance. When the Comanche was only a few yards away, Zack drew the lance back over his shoulder and threw it, the muscles in his back, arm and shoulder tensing with the tremendous effort.

The iron-shod spear tore through the chest of Iron Lance, the point coming through to stick two feet out his back. The shock of the wound brought an instantaneous grimace of pain, as Iron Lance toppled from the roan, falling almost at Zack's feet.

Zack shouted his own war whoop, happy now, feeling as though a great weight had been lifted from him. With another shout, he pulled out his Green River and sliced off the scalp of the dead Indian. He held the grisly trophy over his head, screaming his joy. He danced a little victory dance over the fallen enemy. He was tempted to mutilate the corpse further, in retribution for the death of his wife and child. But he could not bring himself to do it. Instead, he laughed aloud, the sound racing hollowly over the empty spaces.

Zack taunted the Comanches now: "C'mon, ye heathens," he shouted. "Come'n git me. Are ye skeered?"

He danced and whooped some more, holding the scalp high above him.

Across the prairie came the sound of almost one hundred Cheyenne warriors taunting and berating the Comanches who sat in shock at the loss of one of their most revered leaders. The voices thundered across the emptiness, rolling away, filling the blue sky.

A mourning wail from the Comanches joined the cacophony, but just as quickly faded away.

CHAPTER 11

Silence suddenly reigned on the prairie. The sounds of the jubilant Cheyennes and the mourning of the Comanches drifted away, until only the wind could be heard. The roan of the dead Iron Lance walked slowly, aimlessly around, munching the short-cropped grass, turning brown now in the late summer.

In the silence and the lull, Zack rolled the body of the dead warrior out of the way, giving himself room to maneuver. Before moving it, though, he pulled the lance, now bright with blood, from the corpse. He stuck it into the ground near him and picked up the rifle. Then he waited.

The Comanches were now talking among themselves, arguing and gesticulating wildly. Zack could understand little of the Comanche tongue, but from what he could hear of the shouting, angry voices, he knew that some of them, mostly the younger warriors, wanted to attack. The others wanted to ride away to mourn the loss of Iron Lance.

The shouting dwindled and Zack knew a decision had been made. Another war-bonneted chief rode to the front. He faced the Cheyennes and, voicing his war cry, led the attack. The Cheyennes, too, screamed their cries of war and charged, let by Thunder Blanket, Hawk Wind and the irrepressible Once Ran.

The noise was deafening, the bellowing warriors and the thunderous rush of many horses. Soon there were the screams of pain from both man and horse.

But Zack could no longer hear the individual noises. They all ran together, blurring in his ears and he blotted them out as best he could.

Two young warriors split off from the main group of Comanches and raced toward Zack. One raised his bow and let fly an arrow. The stone-tipped projectile sliced through the flesh of Zack's ribs on his side. Blood slowly oozed out of the wound, running down to stain the grass.

The Indian was preparing another shaft. "Why, ye son of a bitch," Zack shouted. He raised the Hawken and fired. The ball caught the brave in the chest, smashing him off the horse and onto the ground, dead.

Zack threw down the rifle and was reaching for a pistol when the second warrior threw his lance. The iron tip of the weapon pierced Zack's right thigh, knocking him to the ground. From his position in the dirt, he managed to yank out one of his pistols.

The young Indian had pulled his pony to a sharp halt and jumped off, fixing to finish Zack off with his knife; to count first coup on this crazy, brave white man. He was unprepared for the blast of the pistol that caught him in the face as he bent toward his intended victim.

Zack pushed the dead body off his feet and struggled to rise. Upright, he wrenched the shaft of the lance, pulling it from his flesh, gasping as the point ripped through the muscle. An arrow twanged past his head and thudded into the tree behind him. Looking up, he saw three more Comanches riding toward him.

"Damn," he swore. He yanked the other pistol from his belt and fired hastily, wounding one of the Indians, who screeched and toppled off his horse. Zack threw the lance he had yanked from his leg, catching another of the charging braves in the stomach.

He threw himself down and to the side as the third warrior thundered past, swinging an iron-headed tomahawk. He struggled back to his feet, turning as quickly as he could, hobbling. The young Comanche was already rushing toward him again. He grabbed the other lance, the one given him by Hawk Wind, and thrust it mightily at the Indian, as the Comanche viciously swung the tomahawk once more. The point of the lance caught the Indian in the leg and unhorsed him. The collision yanked the lance from Zack's grasp.

Both men, hobbling and bleeding from a leg, turned to face each other on foot. The Indian had kept his grip on the tomahawk, and Zack jerked his own finely-honed hatchet from his belt. The Comanche advanced warily, lightly swinging the tomahawk back and forth in front of him.

Suddenly the Indian leaped at Zack, thrusting off his unharmed leg. He swung wildly at the white man, hoping to take him by force as well as surprise. Zack fell to the side, crazily swinging his own tomahawk. The metal blade ripped through the young Indian's stomach. The Comanche fell heavily, grunting, not yet dead.

Zack once more labored to his feet, swearing, "Damn laig." He limped over to where the lance had fallen, still not reaching the length of the sash which had stayed pegged to the ground.

As he pushed the lance unfeelingly through the body of the Indian, he felt the shock of an arrow as it entered his back, low and toward the left side. He grunted in pain, only his grip on the lance keeping him from falling. He yanked the weapon out of the dead warrior and turned to face his newest foe.

The Comanche, one side covered hideously in white

paint, had pulled up his horse and was notching another arrow. Zack limped toward the tree, leaning on it after retrieving one of his pistols. The tree would give him some cover, he knew. He hurriedly loaded the pistol, spilling powder as he did. He kept a wary eye on the Comanche, ducking when the Indian released the arrow. The projectile clunked harmlessly into the tree's trunk, and the Indian began notching another.

But Zack had his own weapon loaded. "Ye've had yore chance," he bellowed. Leaning heavily against the tree to steady himself, he fired.

The Indian looked up in surprise as the ball smashed into his chest. Blood spurted, but he tried for one last shot with the bow. But the arrow fell weakly on the grass as the warrior slumped to the ground.

Calm descended over Zack, the Comanches seemingly forgetting about him in the heat of their battle with the Cheyennes. The prairie was littered with fallen men and horses, most of them Comanche. The Cheyennes fought like demons, bloodthirstily seeking revenge for the loved ones they had lost a year before. They were spurred on by Zack's bravery and recklessness.

Zack looked down at the arrowhead sticking a few inches out of his stomach. He leaned back against the tree, sucking in his breath as he pushed the shaft, slippery with blood, through his body. When the arrowhead stuck out far enough for him to grasp the shaft, he broke off the point, grunting in pain, sweat beading on his forehead.

That done, he painfully reached behind him and grabbed the feathered part of the shaft. Bracing himself, he yanked the last of the arrow out. The action left him weak and dizzy, but he pulled himself up straighter, breathing deeply.

With a quick look to make sure no more of the

Comanches were approaching, he sliced off a piece of his leggings and tied it around his middle, hoping to staunch the flow of blood. Sweat covered him, and pain almost glazed his eyes. He glanced over at the big appaloosa. The horse had reacted nervously to the activity around him, but now that it was quiet near him, the horse was again complacently chomping grass.

Zack looked over and saw the battle had lost some of its ferocity. Groups of warriors were engaging other small groups of warriors. With sweat-soaked, bloody hands, Zack loaded his weapons.

He remained leaning against the tree, still weak from the loss of blood and the shock of his wounds. He thought the end would come soon when he saw six Comanches break off and begin riding hastily toward him. ''Guess they saw their brothers didn't do too well agin me,'' he said aloud.

With a deep sigh, Zack pushed himself away from the tree, ready to meet the enemy. He felt he would die but wanted to make as good a show for himself as he could before he was killed.

Under his breath he muttered, ''C'mon, ye bastards. I ain't daid yit, an' I'll take a couple more of ye with me afore I go under.''

In the distance he could still see the battle and thought he saw a group of Cheyennes racing recklessly after the Comanches who were drawing near to him. But he couldn't be sure. The Comanches were closing in on him and demanded all his attention.

While still some distance away, Zack raised the Hawken and fired. The shot killed the full-bonneted warrior in the lead. The others did not slacken their pace, and Zack realized with sudden dread that more Comanches were also headed his way.

''Damn,'' he mumbled. ''Guess they figger if they

kin wipe me out, the Shyans'll leave off the fight.''

He fired one of his pistols, badly wounding another of the attackers. But the others were drawing closer now and he hastily fired his other pistol, killing another warrior with a shot he knew had been guided only by luck.

He felt an arrow pierce his already wounded leg while another flew by him. Leaving the arrow in his leg, he shouted, ''C'mon, ye bastards! C'mon. I'll show ye how to fight.''

He swung his lance wildly in an arc as the rushing Indians swept around him, not close enough to touch him with their war clubs. They circled around the tree and one of them notched another arrow. The rest charged again, war clubs in hand.

Zack tried to dodge the arrow as it left the bow, but his wounds slowed him down and he was unable to move quickly. The arrow jolted into his left shoulder, just above the breast. He felt himself falling.

He tried to rise, moaning through a haze of pain, his breath rasping in his throat. But he managed only to get to one knee. He glanced up and saw, through a falling curtain of black, two warclub-wielding warriors bearing down on him. No strength left, he collapsed, falling flat, as the Comanches swept past, their clubs missing his head by inches.

He lay in the grass and dirt, not having the power to get up. ''Wall,'' he said aloud, gritting his teeth, ''guess this is it, old Zack. Ye're finally gonna git rubbed out after all these years.''

He drew a long, ragged breath that seemed to set all his wounds to hurting. ''Damn,'' he said. He managed to raise his head a few inches and look around. Seeing the dead Comanches littering the area, he smiled, then grimaced in pain. He tried, almost successfully, to smile again. Once more he talked to himself. ''Wall, ole Standing Bull, ye shore made 'em come now, or I wouldn't say so. Windy'll be right proud of ye when ye git to meet her agin.''

His head plopped down again, and he struggled just to get air into his lungs. The sound of the battle faded into nothingness, and the sky grew gray and dim. He heard the soft shuffling of an approaching Indian, and knew he was about to die. But he lost consciousness before the warrior reached him, sliding gratefully down into the darkness of not knowing or caring.

He smelled fresh buffalo meat—humps and ribs—roasting over a fire, the fat dripping into the flames, searing the outside of the meat. His mouth watered. Then he remembered the battle.

"It's jist like the Shyans always said," he thought. The spirit world is jist like the real world. Mebbe I really will git to spend an eternity with Windy and Misty.''

He cracked his eyes open and in the dimness saw a woman bending over the fire, tending the meat cooking there. "Windy," he called softly. But she did not answer, or even acknowledge his presence. He tried calling out to her again, but he could feel the blackness sweeping down over him.

He awoke again to the smell of roasting meat. But this time there were low voices mumbling in the background. He opened his eyes and realized he was in a tepee. "It really does seem jist like life afore," he mumbled.

He tried to sit up but cried out in pain. The figures sitting around the fire started at the noise, wavering before his eyes. As they turned to look at him, he recognized Thunder Blanket, Hawk Wind and Rain Cloud Woman. With a flash, it dawned on him as the surprised Indians approached that he was not dead at all, but was lying in the lodge of Hawk Wind back in the village on the Arkansas River.

The Indians knelt by him. An old woman entered

227

the tepee and came near. She started to stroke his forehead with a cool, wet cloth. He recognized Woman-Who-Walks-Softly, one of Hawk Wind's wives.

The woman brought the cloth to his mouth and squeezed some droplets of water onto his lips. He parted them and licked the liquid into his mouth. The effort tired him, and he relaxed briefly before the woman, who had left, returned. She poured some water into his mouth. He gagged and sputtered, but swallowed some of the water. With a mighty effort, he managed to croak, "Whar am I? What happened?"

Hawk Wind answered. "You are in my lodge, my son. In the village. But you must rest some more now. We will explain all to you later."

Zack tried to nod, but couldn't. Instead he whispered, "It is good."

He closed his eyes and drifted back into unconsciousness, not knowing about the group of people who had gathered outside. Or about Grass Grows, the medicine man, who had entered to make his medicine to heal the wounded man.

Many times Zack woke up for brief periods. He took a little water and occasionally the broth of elk or buffalo stew. Then he lapsed back into unconsciousness.

But one day he awoke, knowing for the first time that he would be all right. Old Yellow Woman, Hawk Wind's oldest wife, came to kneel by his side. Somehow, she, too, knew Zack would now be all right. Carrying a bowl of steaming stew in her hand, her wrinkled face split into a wide grin, showing her toothless gums, as she indicated she would feed him.

He could only manage a weak, lopsided smile. The old woman, looking older even than her years, propped his head up and began to gently spoon-feed him. He swallowed eagerly and hungrily, sometimes too much. Once he choked, trying too hard to get the soupy liquid into his mouth.

"Slow down," Yellow Woman said in Cheyenne. "There is enough. It will not go away."

He nodded and indicated he wanted more.

The next day, when the old woman came to feed him, he demanded some meat in the broth. "Come, now, mother," he said weakly, "gimme somethin' I kin sink my teeth into."

She chuckled softly and went to the stew pot that always simmered over the fire and fished out some small hunks of dried elk and buffalo meat. She returned to where he rested and again gently began to feed him.

Soon, some of his friends braved the fierce wind and bitter cold, as well as the drifting snow that already covered the land, to visit. The old woman helped him sit up a little and then left. He sat there only a short while talking to them, hungering for conversation. But his strength was slight, and he tired easily. They left him alone before too much time had passed, and he asked Yellow Woman, who had returned, for more of the nourishing stew.

When he had again been fed, he allowed himself to drift back into sleep. The next day he awoke feeling stronger, and he ate more of the thick stew, chunks of meat now floating through the soup. He could taste and savor the corn that thickened it and the grease that gave it body. Each day he grew a little stronger and healthier, hungrily wolfing down larger and larger quantities of food. In a few weeks he was eating roasted meat, some of it freshly killed just for him, despite the bitterness of the winter.

He stayed inside the tepee all that winter, keeping close to the small fire that burned almost constantly as the wind howled, blowing snow viciously around the small camp. Each day his few close friends would drop by, sometimes for a quiet pipe, but mostly to talk. Gradually, as Zack gained in strength, the others—Hawk Wind, Thunder Blanket, Once Ran and, rarely, old Strong Horse—would stay longer. Zack was able to sit up for longer periods and, finally, he forced himself to stand, wincing at the still-fresh scars, as he moaned slightly with the pain and the unaccustomed exercise.

It was during these talks that he learned how he had been brought to the lodge of Hawk Wind.

After he had fallen, the two Comanches dismounted, aiming to scalp the still-living, fierce white warrior. But Zack had been right when he thought he had seen some Cheyennes coming. Once Ran and Thunder Blanket were the Cheyennes riding urgently toward the stunted little tree. They had seen Zack fall and feared he was already dead. But they would not allow the scalp of their friend to be taken. His spirit would not be left to wander aimlessly.

Once Ran quirted his pony, getting every ounce of speed out of the trusted mount. One Comanche already had Zack's long brown hair in one hand and his scalping knife in the other when Once Ran launched an arrow. The shaft caught the unsuspecting Comanche in the throat. He gurgled and choked on his own blood, his scream of pain smothered. He crumpled across the prone figure of Zack.

The other Comanche turned just in time to take Once Ran's war club full in the face. But the rushing horse swept Once Ran past the little tree. He turned his gasping mount around to see three more Comanches swarming toward Zack and Thunder Blanket. With a bloodcurdling scream, he dashed back. His ferocity was awesome. He was swept with rage. Viciously, his eyes lit with the fires of anger, he swung his club.

Two of the Comanches died under his savage onslaught. The third Comanche turned tail and headed for the safety of the rest of his warriors. But he never made it. The long lance of Thunder Blanket crashed through the Comanche's back, flinging him off the horse into a pile on the ground.

Once Ran leaped off his horse at Zack's side. "Keep a watchful eye toward our enemy," he shouted to Thunder Blanket. "I will help our brother."

Thunder Blanket nodded, dismounted and gathered up Zack's weapons. Once Ran gently picked up Zack in his arms and laid him as softly as he could across the big appaloosa's saddle. He left the horse there, turning and drawing his knife.

"Why the knife?" asked Thunder Blanket, now remounted.

"The scalps of the Comanches will fly from the lodgepole of our brother."

"It is good. But be quick."

But speed was no longer necessary. The Comanches were fleeing helter-skelter across the prairie, howling Cheyenne braves chasing after them.

Once Ran mounted and gathered up the appaloosa's reins behind him. They rode off, secure in knowing the Cheyennes were the victors and would protect them.

The day after his first tentative steps, Zack's friends came to the lodge as usual. As the Indians entered the tent, Zack could see the snow swirling and blowing outside. All morning he had heard the wind whistling through the skin walls of the tepee, but he hadn't realized quite how bad the weather was until he looked through the opening when his friends entered.

As they sat around the pitiful little fire he swore,

231

"Damn winter."

"It is no worse than the winter before," said Once Ran. "Or the winter before."

"Wall, now, I know that," Zack snorted. "But *ye* kin git outside fer a while to stretch yore laigs. All that damned snow is keepin' me penned up in hyar. Ole Yellow Woman ain't gonna let me outta this lodge till spring."

The others laughed. "You will be out soon enough, my friend," said Thunder Blanket. "If you were well, you would be in the mountains now, complaining about the cold and snow up there too."

Zack grunted, not convinced. "Wall, now, I guess ye're right. But I still don't like it. Nosiree."

The talk drifted off into other areas, and soon the men were gambling small articles on a round of the Indian hand game, shouting and hollering over their losses, crowing over their wins.

The winter dragged slowly on. Zack chafed at his confinement. The scars slowly healed, and his strength and vitality returned. Old Yellow Woman continued to wait on him but, on occasion, it was Rain Cloud Woman who served him. In doing so, she remained shy and quiet, averting her eyes most of the time. But Zack sometimes caught her gazing at him when he looked up suddenly.

The days soon began to grow a little longer, and the wind blew a little warmer each day. "Spring's comin'," said Zack to the old woman one day. "It won't be long now."

And it wasn't. One morning Zack awoke to feel the air a little warmer than it had been. He put on his breechcloth and slipped on his worn moccasins. He ignored the high-pitched scolding of Yellow Woman.

After taking a deep breath, he pushed aside the flap of the tepee and stepped into the pre-dawn chill.

EPILOGUE

Zack spent the spring with the Cheyennes, taking only a small part in the spring hunt. But he hunted on his own the rest of the time, piling up hides and supplying some of the needier families in the village with meat. He worked himself hard, rebuilding the lost strength and the skills that had faded slightly during his recovery. He spent many hours riding the prairies alone, increasing his tracking abilities and his stamina. By June, he thought himself back to his former self and was anxious to be on the move. He felt he had been with the Cheyennes long enough and wanted to get away: to see and talk to other trappers, to hear the news of the mountains.

Zack joined Thunder Blanket at the fire one night and, after smoking a pipe in quiet, said, "I'll be leavin' hyar in the next day or so."

"Why are you leaving?"

"Wall, now," said Zack thoughtfully. "I'm gittin' itchy. I gotta be movin' on. I bin in one spot fer too long now."

"Where will you go?"

"Back to Santy Fe fer a spell. I want to see my old friend, Mose. It'd be nice to hear some news of the other trappers, too. 'Sides, I wanna git me some supplies fer winter. I'm aimin' to git back up into the mountains agin, come cold weather."

"It sounds like you miss it," commented Thunder Blanket.

"I purely do now, or I wouldn't say so. I bin away from them beaver fer too long now. Mebbe ye cain't understand it, but the pull of the mountains and the beaver is strong. It's almost like the hunt ever' year. Ye don't go on the hunt like ye do jist cause ye need meat now, do ye?"

"No," answered the Indian carefully. He gazed into the distance, as if seeing himself on the hunt. "No, there is more to the hunt than the need for meat. It is life. The excitement is great, like going on the warpath against our old enemies."

"That's right," said Zack. "Thar's a pull thar. Mebbe in different ways. But the pull is jist as strong."

"I understand, my friend. You must go, and no one here will try to stop you." He paused briefly before asking, "Will you ever return?"

"Wall, shore now. I don't rightly know when, but I'll be back one of these days. I ain't leavin' hyar ferever, ye know. Jist to git away fer a while, back up into the mountains to do some trappin' is all."

"It is good," said Thunder Blanket.

Zack left two days later, three horses loaded with buffalo, elk and wolf hides strung out behind him. He had accomplished much in a little time and would have enough for the next year's stake.

Two weeks later he rode into Santa Fe in high style. He was dressed in the finest buckskin shirt and pants that Yellow Woman and Rain Cloud Woman could make. His moccasins glimmered with tiny bells and bits of metal. He charged into town whooping and hollering, firing off his pistols and the big Hawken, the three pack horses, gifts from Once Ran, lumbering behind the appaloosa.

As he roared into town, he heard shouts from some

of the other trappers who were there. "Hey!" shouted one, "Thar's ole Zack hisself. Come back from the dead."

"Hey thar, Zack. How ye bin?" yelled another.

"Whar ye bin, ole coon?" bellowed still another.

He heard the shouts in passing, the horse enjoying the run as much as the man. He drew the horse up short in a choking cloud of dust in front of the adobe saloon.

"Wall, now," he bellowed. "I'm hyar. I'm Zachariah Dobson an' I'm aimin' to git me a drink afore I go trade in my furs. I also aim to find my furs right hyar when I git back out. I'm half mountain lion an' half buffler bull, an' I'll belly shoot any manjack of ye that touches my pelts whilst I'm in yonder doin' somethin' 'bout this prodigious thirst of mine."

He dismounted, leaving the heavily-breathing horses outside, untied. He pushed his way through the doors of the saloon and shouted, "Ho, amigo. Git me a glass of the best Taos Lightnin' ye got."

He strutted up to the bar, where the bartender hastily slopped some whiskey from a jug into a cheap china cup. Zack grabbed it and swallowed almost half of it in one gulp. The potent whiskey made his eyes water, and he almost choked. "My, that's good," he managed to squawk. He finished the rest of the liquor and said, "Gimme another."

When he finished the second drink, he walked outside into the biting glare of the sun and stopped in his tracks. The appaloosa and the three pack horses were gone. Some trappers stood around snickering.

"Whar'n hell's my horses and my pelts?" he bellowed.

Some of the trappers were laughing openly now, while others still tried to contain their mirth. "Lose somethin'?" asked one.

"Ye're gonna lose yore hair, if'n ye don't help me find my property," said Zack angrily.

But the others continued to laugh. Then it dawned on him. He hadn't seen Mose when he rode in, and Mose was sure to be here this time of year.

"Mose!" he shouted. "Mose Smithfield! Ye best git yore ornry hide back hyar with my horses and my plews, or I'll have yore scalp."

Mose stepped out from behind the corner of one of the adobe buildings. He waved at Zack. "Lookin' fer me?" he asked.

"Ye old horse thief," shouted Zack. "Ye don't gimme back my pelts an' my horses, I'll see ye dead." But he was grinning now.

Mose stepped a little further away from the building, and Zack could see he held the reins of a horse. As Mose walked out into the sunlight, he was followed by the appaloosa and the three pack horses. "These what ye're lookin' fer?" Mose asked innocently.

Zack laughed and walked toward his friend. He clapped Mose on the shoulder and said, "Ye bastard I oughtta cut yore heart out and feed it to the coyotes fer this. But it's shore some good to see ye now, or I wouldn't say so."

Mose laughed. "Ye git rid of these pelts an' I'll buy ye a drink, ye ole coon."

"What? Only one drink?" demanded Zack. "I ain't seed ye in a fair piece, an' all ye're gonna do is buy me one drink?"

"Well, now," said Mose. "Ye've shore gotten greedy since I last seed ye, or I wouldn't say so. But jist to be neighborly, I'll not only buy ye a drink, I'll buy ye dinner too."

"Well that's right generous of ye. Let's go."

They enjoyed themselves the way they had in the old days, drinking, gambling, dancing and whoring Half drunkenly, Zack told Mose the story of his figh

236

with the Comanches.

"I thought ye'd gone under fer shore after I didn't see ye at the beginnin' of summer," Mose said.

"Wall, now, I almost was, or I wouldn't say so," said Zack. "It was damp powder fer sartin now."

So they drank to Zack's good fortune, and past dangers were lost in present pleasures. Autumn was fast approaching. One afternoon Mose blearily asked, "Ye aimin' to head fer the mountains this year, Zack?"

"Wall, now, I shore am. Why?"

"The season's almost hyar already an' I figger to be leavin' hyar right soon. I wanna git up in the hills afore the real cold sets in."

"When ye leavin'?"

"Two, three days, I reckon. Ain't no hurry."

"Wall, now, I guess I'll jist ride along with ye fer a piece. If'n ye don't mind, of course."

"Suits me. Ye gonna head straight up to the mountains this year?"

"I reckon. Why d'ye ask?"

"Thought ye might be headin' toward the Smoky Hill first."

"What fer? I ain't got nothin' to go back thar fer."

"Jist askin'," said Mose. "Don't git so riled up."

Three days later they were packed and ready to go. They were sickeningly hungover, but left in fine style, shooting, yelling and fancily dressed.

A few days out of Santa Fe, Zack suddenly asked Mose, "Whar'd ye leave Horse?"

"Took her back to her village. She was gittin' lonely fer her own folks. Why?"

But Zack was thinking and did not answer. Later that night, as they were making camp for the night, Zack said, "I think I'll be goin' my own way hyar soon."

Mose looked up. "Shore, amigo," he said. "If

that's whar yore stick floats. Whar ye headin'?''

Zack hesitated before answering. "Toward the Arkansas or mebbe the Smoky HIll.''

Mose grinned. "Got yore eye on another one of them Shyan squaws?''

Zack's face darkened wtih anger. But then he relaxed and also grinned. "Mebbe,'' he said. "Mebbe.''

They split up, and Zack rode with haste toward where the Cheyenne village would be at this time of year. Now that he had decided, he was in a hurry and he rode long hours with little rest.

Then he spotted the village, further south this year than he had expected. He was, as usual, spotted. A number of young men raced their ponies out onto the prairie to greet him, frolicking their horses around, showing off their growing skills of horsemanship.

He rode into the village and headed toward the lodge of Hawk Wind after making his welcome to Strong Horse. He handed the horses over to Yellow Woman.

"It is good that you have returned," said Hawk Wind.

"Wall, now, it shore is some good to be back, or I wouldn't say so," said Zack.

They sat at the small fire outside the tepee and smoked in silence. They were joined by Once Ran and Thunder Blanket. When they had finished the pipe, Hawk Wind said, "Something is troubling you, my son. What is it?''

Zack looked around the circle of dark Indian faces, looking at the men with whom he had fought, lived and eaten. He looked at Hawk Wind last and said to him, "Father, I'd like to marry yore daughter, Rain Cloud Woman.''

"This is good," said the older man, a smile creasing his face. "But why do you seem sad?''

"'Cause I cain't help but remember what happened

238

to yore other daughter, my wife, She-Who-Was-Wind-in-the-Morning.''

''But what has that to do with your asking me to marry my other daughter?''

''I'm afraid it might happen agin.''

''We all must come to an end sometime, my son,'' said the Indian. ''It is the way of life.''

Zack thought about it silently. He again surveyed the faces around him. Although serious, they had grins hinting around their mouths.

Before Zack could speak, Once Ran, always impetuous, broke the silence. ''My wife, too, was killed in the attack by the Comanches,'' he said. ''But I have taken a new woman. The sister of Willow Tree Woman.''

Zack nodded and suddenly broke into a grin. ''She as feisty as the first one?'' he asked.

The Indian laughed, nodding.

''Wall, now,'' said Zack. ''If'n Once Ran kin marry his ole wife's sister 'thout worryin' 'bout it, then I guess I kin too.''

The Indians laughed and joked with Zack, their comments ribald. When they had settled down a little, Zack asked Hawk Wind, ''Then, ye don't mind?''

''My daughter will get a fine husband,'' said Hawk Wind. ''A fine warrior and hunter.''

''And I will git a fine wife,'' said Zack.

With the serious business over with, the talk turned to the fall hunt, which had recently been held. And Zack related his experiences in Santa Fe and on the trail. It was late when the men turned into their robes for sleep. But by then the news of the impending marriage had trickled through the village, started by Yellow Woman, who was as nosy as she was old.

The ceremony did not take long. The woman, knowing the ways of the mountain man, was ready to leave her family and to move on. Three days after Zack had ridden into the Cheyenne village, he rode out again, mounted on the big appaloosa. His woman, riding a pinto mare, followed along, holding the reins of the three pack horses they had.

"The cold months will be here soon," said the woman as they rode along.

"They shore will," said Zack. He looked back at the woman and smiled. Rain Cloud Woman smiled back at him. Zack whistled a happy, nameless tune as they rode across the wide open spaces, heading toward the snow-capped mountains they could see to the west.

"Yep," he thought, "another winter's comin'."

MEDICINE WAGON

Chapter 1

Her bright red hair flashed in the sun, the strands glinting sometimes gold as she twirled and spun. Her legs stepped high, keeping time with the music, and her skirts swirled.

The men standing on the dusty street watched appreciatively, hands and large-brimmed Stetsons shading their eyes from the bright, brittle sunshine. Dressed in faded denims and worn woolen shirts, they were a scruffy lot; mostly dirty, unshaven. Their womenfolk, wearing torn and dingy calico, looked on in contempt. A few were openly scornful as the dancing figure showed occasional glimpses of shapely calf covered by thin black stocking.

"Higher!" one of the men shouted, as the woman performed a daring pirouette that flipped the bottom of her long, satin dress almost to her knee.

"Go ahead, Lila," said the stunted little man playing a squeezebox behind her. Nearby, a tall, thin man, only half visible in deep shadow, sawed at a fiddle.

Lila O'Shaughnessy smiled at the man in the crowd, showing her perfect, white teeth. Then she spun, without missing a beat, and stuck out her tongue at the midget playing the accordion. She twirled again, smiling, to face the good-natured leers and catcalls of the wornout farmers, townsmen and cowboys.

A shot rang out, splitting the still afternoon air. Lila stopped in midstep. The music screeched to a halt. Fear flickered in Lila's clear green eyes. The men, too, were startled. Some reached for the six-shooters strapped to their hips. Others moved quickly to get the women and children to safety.

"All right!" a voice boomed. Everyone stopped. "Let's git a move on here. Break it up. The fun's over, boys."

"Aw, Sheriff," said one of the men. "What'd you go and do that fer? She was jist gittin' warmed up."

"Yeah," chorused the other men, some of them growing surly.

"Now you boys jist go on home to your wives and families. You ain't got no business here. Now git."

The men grumbled, only a few moving off. "Go on. Git!" bellowed the sheriff. "Before I run the lot of you in." He holstered the big .45-caliber Colt, as the men began to drift off. The sheriff was a big man, a powerfully built former blacksmith, and few men in the sleepy Nebraska town would face up to him.

He turned to look at the striking redhaired woman, and tipped his hat. "Sorry, ma'am. But I'm gonna have to ask you and your friends here to leave."

Lila wiped the perspiration from her high white forehead with the back of her hand. "Right now?"

"I think it'd be best, ma'am."

Lila nodded and her shoulders slumped. The sheriff took off his hat and held it stiffly in his hands. He felt he had to explain to her. "It ain't that you're doin' anything wrong," he said. "It's jist that this here's a small, kind of an out-of-the-way place. Folks 'round here ain't like them in big cities like Dodge or Omaha. And there's them that don't want folks like you 'round."

6

"Didn't seem that way to me," snorted the little man holding the accordion. His short, stumpy legs were spread wide. Looking at him, the sheriff took in the sneering, weathered face. The midget wore greasy denims and a battered black hat. His barrel chest was covered by a buckskin Indian shirt and his feet were stuffed into torn, tiny, finely beaded moccasins.

The sheriff moved his eyes past the midget, toward the massive block of a wagon behind him. The billowing white canvas was torn in a few places, but the gold, filigreed letters on its broad side gleamed in the sun: DR. MCGILL'S TRAVELING MEDICINE SHOW.

"Think you're purty big, don't you, Sheriff?" retorted the little man. He started to say something else, but was stopped when another voice said sharply, "That's enough, Zeus."

The tall thin man stepped out from the shadow thrown by the giant wagon. He placed his fiddle and bow on the wagon seat.

"Who're you?" the sheriff asked.

"Doctor Winthrop McGill, at your service." He bowed slightly from the waist. "My little friend meant no harm."

The sheriff nodded while examining the stranger. McGill was wearing what had once been a fine suit—heavy black trousers, frilled white shirt, string tie, a vest of dusty black, and black frock coat. The clothes were frayed now, and worn. The boots, of good leather, were scuffed and cracked.

The sheriff could see, though, that McGill was educated and cultured. He was in his mid-forties and needed a shave, but his hair was neatly combed and his clear blue eyes stared calmly back at the lawman. He seemed a little sad.

Plopping the hat back on his head, the sheriff

7

said, "Well, you folks best be movin' on. There's still plenty of daylight left. You can more'n likely make it to Forked Creek by dark."

"We'll leave directly," McGill said.

The sheriff nodded. Pulling a long, thin cigar from his shirt pocket, he lighted it. Giving the three one last, hard look, he spun on his heel and walked quickly away.

"Why'd you let him git away with that?" Zeus snapped. "He can't run us outta town."

Patiently looking at his small friend, McGill said, "Yes he can." He smiled a sad little smile. "It's not the first time and I think you know it won't be the last. Now you and Lila pack up the wagon. I'll hitch up the horses."

He smiled quietly at Lila and moved off.

Chapter 2

The rattletrap old wagon pulled up in front of the ramshackle sod and wood farmhouse. The wind gently blew through the tattered canvas of the old Conestoga.

"Hello, the house!" shouted the somberly clad driver. "Anyone to home?" McGill sat silent, tired, waiting for a response. On the seat with him was Lila, nicely dressed, looking beautiful. The midget sat between them.

"Hello, the house!" McGill called again.

The door of the house opened a bit and someone eyed them warily from within.

"Howdy," McGill said. "My name is Doctor Winthrop McGill. And, as you can see from my wagon, I am a traveling medicine salesman. I

8

wondered if we might be able to stay the night on your land. We've been traveling for quite a spell now, and sure could use a place to bed down."

The door opened wider and a large, heavily bearded man stepped out onto what passed for a porch. The old wooden boards creaked, and the slanted plank roof looked ready to fall.

"What say yore name was?" the man called.

"Doctor Winthrop McGill. This is Lila and Zeus."

The man stepped a little farther out onto the porch, shading his eyes against the late afternoon sun. He silently surveyed the weathered old wagon. Other faded lettering proclaimed that McGill, Lila and Zeus sold elixirs, potions and other medicines. They also danced, sang and played music to entertain. In addition to the normal accoutrements of traveling by wagon—tool kit, canvas water bags and more—there hung many odd and interesting gadgets from the wagon.

The bearded man stepped forward, followed by his family. "Light and tie, Doctor. My name is Jonathan Whitlock." He began walking down the three porch steps as his family moved out into the open. "We don't git many strangers 'round here, so we're a mite careful when someone does come along."

"Perfectly understandable, sir," McGill said. "Might we water our horses and spend the night here in the fields?"

A small, slightly worn-looking woman stepped down off the porch to join the man.

"This is my wife, Emma, Doctor McGill," Jonathan said.

McGill doffed his hat. "Pleased to meet you, ma'am."

"The pleasure is mine, Doctor." She looked up

9

at the other people on the wagon. "You all look mighty tired to me. Set yourselves down here. You, your wife and son are more'n welcome to join us at dinner."

Zeus bristled at the reference. Angrily, he said, "Why you—"

McGill clamped his hand over Zeus's mouth. He and Lila valiantly tried to hold back their laughter. "Zeus is not our son, Mrs. Whitlock. He's one of the little people. A midget."

"Oh, my dear," Emma mumbled. "I'm sorry. I really am. I didn't mean . . ."

"Oh yes you did," Zeus snapped. McGill regretted having removed his hand.

"It's quite all right, Mrs. Whitlock. You just didn't know. An understandable error. No harm done, was there, Zeus?"

The midget looked balefully at the older man. He opened his mouth, intending to tell the woman what he thought of her, but stopped when he saw the look of warning on McGill's face.

"Be polite to these nice folks now, Zeus," McGill said.

Still angry, Zeus said, "Yes, ma'am. It's all right."

Embarrassed, Emma Whitlock told the newcomers, "Let me introduce my family." As she named them, they stepped off the porch into the waning afternoon light. "My two sons, Charles and Joshua; my daughters, Martha and Rebecca; and my husband's mother, Elizabeth."

McGill, Lila and a sullen Zeus nodded their greetings.

"Our invitation still stands, Doctor McGill. You and your—the others are welcome to dinner and to spend the night anywhere you can find room."

"Why that's right nice of you, Mrs. Whitlock.

We'd be more than happy to share your table and your hospitality."

"It's the least she can do after that insult," Zeus said in a barely audible whisper.

"Mind your manners, you little pipsqueak, or I'll have Winthrop make you clean up after the horses," Lila said in the same tone.

McGill, with shopworn dignity, slowly climbed down off the wagon and brushed the long frock coat he habitually wore. Setting his battered silk top hat more firmly onto his head, he reached up to help Lila down.

Dropping her lightly to her feet, McGill again reached up, this time to help the midget. Zeus still stared sullenly at him. Grasping the little man under the arms, McGill cheerfully and quietly said, "Any more nonsense from you, my little friend, and I'll drop you right here."

Without another word, McGill placed the small man on the ground. He walked over and shook hands with Jonathan.

The Whitlock women gathered around Lila, commenting excitedly on her fancy clothes, touching the satiny cloth and lace trimmings. "They're really very old," Lila told them, "and not very pretty."

"But they are," argued Rebecca, the youngest Whitlock child. "We ain't got nothin' so purty." She reached out to touch a grimy finger to Lila's shining red hair and flawless cheeks. "She shore is beautiful, ain't she, Ma?" Rebecca said.

Her mother nodded, smiling a little sadly.

Lila realized with a shock that her faded finery was, indeed, quite gaudily beautiful compared to the bland, plain frocks of the Whitlock women. She felt ashamed looking at the patched, faded dresses of her hostesses.

"Charles. Joshua," Jonathan yelled over the noise of the gossiping women, "tend to Doctor McGill's horses and wagon. Make sure the horses're well fed and watered."

"Yes, sir," chorused the two well-muscled young men.

"And don't dally none. Supper'll be on the table soon and we don't want you holdin' things up."

As the two youths hurried off on their chores, Jonathan turned to McGill. "Well, Doctor, c'mon into the house. It ain't much by yore standards, I'm shore, but we call it home."

"Well, sir," McGill answered in polite, sincere tones. "I'm sure that whatever it lacks in refined furnishings, it more than makes up for in hospitality. And after so many months on the trail in that old wagon, cooking over an open fire, it'll be downright pleasurable to have a home-cooked meal for a change."

"Prob'ly looks like a pig sty," Zeus snarled. Lila gave him a withering glance of warning, and Zeus clamped his lips shut.

Still talking jovially, they all walked up the few steps and into the house.

Chapter 3

"Martha. Rebecca," Emma ordered. "Bring all the chairs. Gather them 'round the table for our guests."

The chairs were gathered quickly and Emma told McGill, "Please, Doctor, sit. All of you." She bustled about, preparing the meal.

"I hope you all don't mind what we have to offer. We ain't got much. Martha, go'n fetch some wood for the fire."

Martha opened her mouth to protest, but her mother said, "Don't back talk me, girl. Just git." Emma turned to McGill and said, "I hope we don't forget our manners, neither, Doctor. We don't git many visitors, 'specially someone as distinguished as you."

"You needn't worry, Mrs. Whitlock. You have a fine home and a lovely family. It's been quite some time since we were treated so well."

"The home ain't much, but the girls are certainly nice," Zeus said almost under his breath. "I may get to like it here."

Lila, sitting next to him at the long scarred wooden table standing in the center of the large main room of the simple house, said, "Pipe down, you fool. You want to get us thrown outta here? This is the first decent meal and place to stay we've had in months. You keep openin' your big mouth and they're likely to toss the bunch of us out."

"Yes, ma'am," Zeus said sarcastically.

"You get us thrown outta here before I've had a good meal and some sleep, and I'll tie you behind the wagon before we leave and let you walk awhile. Now hush up. And be polite."

As the Whitlock women bustled around the house, Jonathan grabbed a large earthen jug from above the mantel piece and carried it to the table. As he did, McGill noticed the rifle, shotgun and a few large-bore pistols hanging from nails above the fireplace. The guns were old, but they looked to be in excellent condition.

"Care for a small taste of corn, Doctor?" Jonathan asked as he plopped down in a chair near McGill. The doctor nodded and Whitlock poured them each a small cupful. "It ain't as good as store

13

bought likker, or imported, but it's got a good kick to it."

"I'm sure it does," McGill said, eyeing the jug.

"Hey, what about me?" Zeus shouted from across the table. He sat licking his lips. "Don't I git any?"

Jonathan laughed. "Sorry, Zeus. Yore so small I just kinda forgot you was full growed." McGill joined in the laughter, but the midget did not. "Shore you kin have some, Zeus. Emma, fetch me 'nother cup for Zeus here."

As Emma placed the cup on the table, the door opened and Martha walked in carrying the firewood. Charles and Joshua followed her. The young woman, small and pale, went to the stove and began helping her mother and sister. She seemed to struggle to catch her breath.

The two young men hung their hats on a peg by the door and sat down at the table. "How's 'bout a taste o' that for us, Pa?" Charles said.

The oldest, Charles, was in his late teens, tall and strong built. Unable, yet, to grow a full beard, his square, determined jaw jutted out. Big, work-hardened hands rested comfortably on the table.

Jonathan looked at his wife. "Well, Ma, think the boys kin stand a little snort?"

She looked doubtful, but said, "Sure, Jonathan. I guess so. They's growed and it is kind of a special occasion."

"Git yoreselves some cups then, boys, and be quick about it. Doctor McGill's waitin' here for his drink."

"Yes, sir, Pa," Charles said. He hurried to get some of the cracked crockery cups that were the family's only drinking vessels.

When they were filled, Jonathan raised his glass in a toast. "To a good family and to good

14

friends."

The others echoed the toast and gulped down their drinks. They almost choked on the potent liquor. The first one to break the silence was Zeus. "How's 'bout another one? That was just 'bout enough to wet my lips."

"Stout little feller, ain't you?" Whitlock laughed. "Shore you kin have another." Jonathan filled their glasses again and they sipped.

"What brings you to these parts, Doctor?"

"He's runnin' from the law," Zeus chuckled.

McGill shot him a black look. Turning to Whitlock, he said, "My friend's jokes are not very humorous." He paused for a sip of liquor. "We travel the countryside," he said, "selling our potions and entertaining townfolk. We sing, we dance, we play musical instruments. We sell gadgets and items of all sorts."

McGill was warming now, with the liquor and the thought of some possible sales. He launched into his sales pitch. "Not only do we have the best medicine this side of the Mississippi River, but we have the finest line of newfangled inventions, contraptions and other sundry wares. We have items for the men, and items for the women, and items for the young 'uns. No one is left out when they come to Doctor Winthrop McGill. Our merchandise comes from the finest stores in St. Louis, New Orleans and even from New York. We do not skimp when it comes to quality."

He indicated that Jonathan should refill his glass. When it was done, he continued, "We carry a full line of medicinals, herbs and potions. We also have a full range of musical instruments including fiddles, banjoes, mouth organs and accordions. If you are a reader, I also have books for you to enjoy, like the famous story written about

15

the ancient land of Rome—called *Ben Hur,* written by none other than the Honorable Lew Wallace, governor of the New Mexico Territory. And we have the very recently published *Huckleberry Finn,* by the illustrious author of numerous stories, Mark Twain. A personal friend, I might add.''

McGill took a deep breath and a swig of his drink. Before he could continue, Emma called out, ''Boys. Go wash up. Supper'll be ready in a minute. Girls, set the table.''

Almost crestfallen, McGill sat back to let the others do their work. Zeus polished off his drink and walked outside with the young men to wash up.

''Can I help you with anything?'' Lila asked Emma.

''Heavens no, child. You're a guest. I'd be mortified if'n I had to put you to work. You just set and relax. You must be tired after all that travelin'.''

''But I feel I'm in the way, just settin' here doin' nothin'.'' She fidgeted, anxious to be doing something.

''Well you and Grandma Whitlock both deserve a rest, so's you just keep her company. We'll be done here in a blink.''

The table was set quickly enough and the young men returned. Everyone sat at the table, steaming plates and platters of meat, potatoes, vegetables and bread before them.

''Would you like to say grace, Doctor?'' Jonathan asked. ''After all, you're the guest of honor.''

Raising himself up slightly, McGill said, ''Thank you for the honor, Jonathan, but I'm sure you'd do it much better. Why don't you go ahead.''

''All right. Everyone bow their heads.''

''Oh, God, not this,'' Zeus muttered.

16

Lila pinched his thigh under the table. "Be respectful," she hissed.

Jonathan bowed his head and the short prayer was quickly over. Looking at the bountiful table, he said, "Let's eat."

He was happy. It was rare that they set so full a table. Their fare was usually simple; meat was scarce, and the extra garden produce was often sold. Only when an infrequent guest appeared did they enjoy such a plentiful, varied meal.

"What kind of medicine do you sell, Doctor McGill?" Emma asked.

"All kinds. I have medicines for almost everything—arthritis, rheumatiz, headaches, whooping cough—almost anything you can name. My best potion, though, is my own. It's my very special Doctor McGill's Patented Cure-All. I use it only on the most stubborn cases."

"What's in it?" Martha asked from across the table.

"Now, child, I can't very well give away the ingredients, now can I? That's my secret and will remain so as long as I live."

"Does he really use it only on the most stubborn cases?" Rebecca asked Zeus in a whisper.

"Sure," Zeus sneered. "Like on himself when he's got a hangover." Rebecca's eyes widened and she glanced suspiciously at McGill.

Not noticing, Emma said to McGill, "We may have need of your services or potions, Doctor. Martha's been feelin' a mite poorly of late."

"Yes," McGill said. "I did notice she looked a little peaked. Not quite as rosy-cheeked as her sister."

"She ain't really been sick, you understand. But she ain't been quite well, neither."

"Well, ma'am," McGill said with as much

17

dignity as he could muster, "I'd be right happy to examine Martha and do what I can for her. Free of charge, of course."

Zeus, his mouth stuffed with bread, snickered softly to Lila, sitting on his left, "I'd be more'n happy to examine her, too. But for different reasons."

Lila ignored him and continued eating.

"I don't reckon I need no examination, Ma," Martha said shyly. "I'll be fine. It's just a passin' thing."

Emma rose from the table and said, "We'll see, dear. Now, you'n your sister help me clean up."

McGill sat back and patted his stomach contentedly. He turned to Emma and said, as she worked, "That sure was a fine meal. Best I've had in many a day."

"Why thank you, Doctor." Emma turned away, her face flushed with pride.

Zeus also sat back with a full stomach. Looking at Lila he said, "Even I gotta admit it was a heap better'n some other cookin' I've had to eat lately." Giving her a knowing wink, he added, "Ain't that so?"

Indignantly Lila snapped, "You're just lucky we're in company, or—"

"Or what?" Zeus asked smiling.

Exasperated, Lila muttered between clenched teeth, "Or . . . or . . . or I'd take you over my knee."

Merrily Zeus said, "You'd take a shine to that wouldn't you? Almost as much as I would, I reckon."

Lila stood abruptly, almost knocking over the chair, and stalked away, sputtering mad. Walking up to Emma, she began to wash some of the piled-up dishes in the old wooden washing tub. Looking

18

at Emma, she said, "I have to help you, Mrs. Whitlock. I just can't bear settin' a moment longer not doin' anything."

"I understand. But call me Emma. You too, Doctor. Ain't no need for so much formality here."

McGill nodded as Jonathan shouted over the noise of dishes being washed: "Joshua. Charles. Go milk the cow and finish up the chores. Dark is nearly upon us. And remember to feed the chickens. Best bring in some wood and water too. We'll need it."

The boys rose from the table, grabbed their hats from the pegs by the door and walked out, a slight breeze whistling in through the open door.

The cleaning up was swiftly done and the women joined the three men sitting around the room. Emma sat at the small loom in one corner, weaving. The two girls—pale, frail Martha and the sturdy, red-cheeked Rebecca—took up their knitting. Grandma Whitlock sat near the fire, half asleep.

"Think you could break out that jug again?" Zeus asked. "I shore could use another taste of that tongue oil."

Before Jonathan could answer, Charles and Joshua clumped through the door. As Charles hung up his hat, he said, "Whooee! Shore is gittin' cold out there, Pa. Wind's comin' from the north."

"Well c'mon over here and set yoreselves by the fire a minute and warm yoreselves," their mother said.

As the young men settled themselves near the blaze, McGill said quietly, "Well, Jonathan, Emma. I'd sure like to repay you for all your hospitality and kindness. How'd you like it if my friends and I cut a shine; put on a little show for you? A little bit of high-steppin', hand-clappin' singin' and dancin'. Would that suit you?''

Jonathan pondered briefly before looking at his wife. Emma nodded almost imperceptibly, and Jonathan said, "That's mighty nice of you, Doctor. I think that'd be right nice. Yes, I do. We git so little entertainment 'round here that it'd be a welcome diversion. It's been quite a spell since we had us a real shindig.''

He stood. "C'mon, boys. Let's git this here furniture moved so's Doctor McGill and the others got some room.''

As the three men began clearing the room, pushing the chairs and other meager, handmade wooden furnishings out of the way, McGill said, "Zeus, go on out to the wagon and fetch the instruments. And be quick about it.''

Zeus, looking stormy, headed for the door, muttering to himself, "Zeus do this. Zeus do that. Fetch this. Run here. That's all I ever hear. Damned long-legged—" The rest of his tirade was cut off when he slammed the door behind him.

A few minutes later the midget returned, arms laden with a banjo, small hand-accordion, harmonica, and fiddle. Dumping the instruments on the floor at McGill's feet, Zeus snarled, "Here. Hope you're happy.''

Calmly McGill said to him, "Mind your manners, Little One. Remember, we are guests here.''

"Yessir, General," Zeus said sarcastically.

"Just pick up your squeezebox and prepare to play." McGill smiled and handed Zeus a cup brimming with homemade corn liquor. "Here," he said, "maybe this'll help.''

Zeus took a long gulp of the drink, his eyes
20

beginning to water a little. He set the cup down and grabbed his instrument, stationing himself near Grandma Whitlock, close to the fire. Taking the old lady's hand, the midget kissed it. "Ah," he sighed. "I am blessed by being so near a delightful creature as yourself. Indeed, I am the luckiest man in the room."

The old woman, a product of frontier life in the rough and tumble lawless Missouri settlements, and the equally lawless frontier farms of her home here in Wyoming, was not much impressed. "It ain't gonna work, Shorty," she chuckled.

"Nasty old hag," Zeus mumbled below her range of hearing. Aloud, he said, "I'll change your mind, madame."

"Pay attention, Zeus," McGill said. "We're about to begin. Ready, Lila?"

The woman, standing in the middle of the empty room, ringed by the eager members of the Whitlock family, sitting in old chairs, nodded.

"All right, then. One and two and—" He began to fiddle a furious dance, Zeus joining in on the accordion. Lila glided back and forth the room in graceful movements. Despite the intensity of the music, her dancing, slow and steady, fitted in perfectly. Gradually the tempo of the music changed, slowing down. When it did, Lila's dancing also slowed—to a sensual, soft dance.

She began to sing: a lilting, haunting ballad, about places and people far away from the lonely vastness of the Wyoming plains; of days gone by; of mythical and wonderful heroes and their ladies.

Quietly the song drifted to a conclusion. Lila sank to one knee in a curtsey, her full skirt spread out around her. She bowed her head, and her long, red hair covered her face, almost touching the floor. The Whitlocks sat in awed silence, quiet with

21

reverence, watching Lila, breathing heavily in the center of the room.

Finally Grandma Whitlock shouted out, "Well clap for the girl. She earned it."

The Whitlocks, broken from their stunned silence, gave Lila a rousing round of applause. The boys whistled and clapped harder than anyone else, both now in love with the beautiful visitor.

"I ain't ever seen anything so beautiful," Rebecca gasped.

Lila stood and then bowed happily, pleased at the response. The clapping died down, and McGill began another spirited tune, an old standard on the frontier, used at gatherings everywhere for what the folks called square dancing.

The lovely Lila again began dancing, abandoning herself to the music. Her skirts flew in the air, and the youthful Whitlock men watched in fascination, eyes glued on the lithe young woman, and the brief flashes of stockinged legs they saw.

While Lila's petticoats whirled and flashed and twirled, Zeus bent over and said to Grandma Whitlock, "What's a kindly, frolicsome young woman like you doin' in this godforsaken place?"

Elizabeth looked at him with displeasure and even a little surprise. Accustomed to a frontier life that was looser than that of civilization, she was nonetheless not ready for a proposition from a three-and-a-half-foot-tall stranger.

Nonplussed by her attitude, Zeus continued, "Why don't I spirit you away from all this? Just you'n me. We'll take the wagon and burn the breeze. Yep, just the two of us, all alone on the wide prairie. Ridin' happily into the sunset. Just picture it. . . ."

With a look of annoyance, Elizabeth picked up the old, weatherbeaten rocking chair and moved it a few feet away. "Horrid little man," she muttered. "Oughtn't to be let out amongst regular folks. Freak."

Plunking the chair down on the opposite side of the hearth, as far away from Zeus as she could reasonably go, she sat back down. Reaching into her apron pocket, she pulled out the old corn-cob pipe that had been her companion since her early married days back in Missouri. Filling it, she pulled a burning twig out of the fire and lighted the pipe.

Zeus, much amused at the old woman, chuckled as he watched her. With a glint of derision in her old eyes, Elizabeth spit into the fire, and settled more comfortably into the chair, rocking gently, puffing contentedly on her pipe.

All the while, the music carried on. Zeus hadn't missed a beat. Lila twirled around the room, while McGill fiddled furiously. Without warning, the music stopped and Lila sank gracefully into another curtsey.

The Whitlocks again cheered and whistled, the elderly Elizabeth happily leading the applause.

"Thank you," Lila smiled.

"Would you like to hear another?" McGill asked.

Charles stomped his feet and hollered, "We shore would. Play us another. Please?" All the while, he had his eyes on Lila.

"Zeus, are you ready with our favorite?" McGill asked.

Edging his way in front of the hearth toward Elizabeth, Zeus stopped halfway across. He quickly slid back to his original position. "Sure am, Chief. Fiddle on."

"Ready, Lila?"

The woman nodded, having caught her breath. She straightened up and waited for the music to begin.

Building up the suspense, McGill took a few patient seconds to ensure that his fiddle was in perfect tune, while the Whitlocks waited expectantly. Finally he was ready. With a quick nod, he began playing. The music began slowly, building as the notes drifted up toward the ceiling of the sod and wood house. The melodious grating of the fiddle floated in and out of the hammering strains of the accordion. Lila sped around the room, heels kicking high in the air, skirts and petticoats flying in abandon.

Joshua was the one who started for the Whitlocks. Timidly at first, but gaining in conviction, he began to clap and stomp along with the music. Soon the others had joined in and were merrily keeping time to the music.

McGill grinned and fiddled even harder. On her next swing past the Whitlocks, Lila paused long enough to pull Jonathan to his feet. With the encouraging whoops and hollers of his sons, Jonathan began to swing around the room with the beautiful young woman, happily holding onto her thin waist.

On the next circumference, Lila let go of Jonathan and grabbed the oldest son. "C'mon, Charles," she shouted gaily, "Dance with me."

Without argument the boy did, clumsily, but joyfully dancing around the room, dazzled by the lush-figured woman in his arms. Jonathan, still in a dancing mood, snatched up his wife and whirled her around the floor.

Joshua, too, got into the act, as Lila danced with him and they all began to dance together, the two Whitlock girls dancing with their brothers. The only Whitlock not joining in was Elizabeth, the grandmother. Tightly clenching the old corn-cob pipe between her few teeth, she stomped, clapped and occasionally cheered the others on.

Even Zeus was caught up in the excitement. Violently he pumped the accordion, his stumpy arms working furiously, beads of sweat forming on his brow and upper lip.

On and on they flew, dancing wildly, the sound wafting outside to lose itself on the ragged, empty prairie.

Swinging her younger brother around in a reel, Martha was happy. She felt hot and flushed, but she thought it was the unaccustomed exercise and the excitement. Suddenly she collapsed, crashing to the dirt floor, gasping for breath.

The dancers stumbled to a stop and the music scraped to a halt. Emma was the first to react. Rushing to where her daughter lie, still struggling for air, she shouted, "Doctor McGill, do somethin'! Please, hurry!"

Emma squatted down, taking the prone girl's head in her lap. "Martha, child. What's wrong with you?"

Everyone else slowly drew around, crowding closer and closer. Again Emma implored, "Doctor McGill, please do somethin'. Hurry!"

"All right. Everyone stand back," McGill ordered. "Come on now, move. Can't you see she's got enough trouble breathin' without all of you hangin' 'round takin' up all the air?"

McGill knelt next to the girl. Silently he checked her pulse and felt her forehead, flushed like the rest of her face. "Warm," he mumbled. He watched her ragged breathing, muttering all the while under his breath.

"Well, Doctor," Jonathan said, "what is it?"

Rising somewhat painfully to his feet, McGill looked at the Whitlock men. "Get her in yonder

25

little room and onto the bed. I can't do anything for her here.''

"But what is it?" Jonathan persisted.

"I said get her into that other room and on the bed. Quickly. This's no time to dally.''

"Boys, move your sister," Jonathan said. He went to Emma and gently lifted her from where she sat, still holding Martha. "Come now, Mother. Let the boys move her. Doctor McGill cain't do nothin' for her if'n you don't do like he says.''

Fearfully she tore herself away from Martha and threw herself, sobbing, into her husband's arms. As he comforted her, Charles and Joshua gently picked up the comatose girl and carried her into the small room that served as Elizabeth's bedroom.

The room was sparsely furnished, outfitted only with a rickety bed, an old, lopsided chair, and a small table holding a washbasin. The two young men softly placed their sister on the dilapidated old bed and stepped back.

McGill looked down at the girl with pity. The look changed to outrage. "This bed's filthy. There's bugs crawlin' all over it." He whirled around and pointed an accusing finger at the Whitlocks. "How d'you expect this girl to get better when you put her in an infested bed?"

Everyone looked down in shame. McGill calmed down a little and continued. "Now, quickly. Someone get some water. And one of you boys go and fetch some fresh hay for this tick. Emma, get some fresh clothes or, better yet, some linens, if you have any, to make a coverlet for this bed.''

Grandma Whitlock, standing in the doorway, looked at the rest of the family, standing dumbfounded. "Well, you heard the man. You cain't git no work done standin' there gawkin'. An' if you don't git crackin', the doctor cain't help our

26

Martha, can he? Now skeedaddle!"

The grandmother's explosion was enough to get the family moving. Emma hurried out of the room to search for some clean material to use on the bed, while the two boys ran outside to gather up the hay. Rebecca pushed past her grandmother into the room and snatched up the basin and left to fill it.

"Anything I kin do, Doctor?" Jonathan asked.

"Not right now. Just make sure anything I need is gotten in a hurry." Jonathan nodded.

"How 'bout me, Chief?" Zeus piped up. "Anythin' I can do? Maybe help you examine Martha?"

"Yes there is something you can do, my friend." The midget's eyes gleamed; he thought he was going to be given over a good job. "Yes, Zeus. You can go pick up the instruments from where we dropped them and put them back in the wagon where they belong. That way they'll not get abused."

"Yessir, Chief," Zeus said sarcastically. "You got any more little tasks for me while I'm at it?"

"Not right at the moment," McGill answered almost absentmindedly. "But if you insist on acting up, I'm sure I can find a few more chores for you."

Zeus began to make a smart remark, but was pushed out of the way by Lila, to make room for the returning Whitlocks. Emma and Rebecca rushed in together, water splashing from the basin onto the floor.

Joshua and Charles ran in right after the women, loose pieces of straw trailing them. They dumped the straw on the floor. While they held Martha, her father quickly cleaned off the bed and replaced the old straw with the new. Emma quickly but neatly covered it over with a large piece of linen she had been saving since her wedding. Finally the girl was

27

laid back down. "Take that old linen and straw and burn it," McGill ordered. "To kill the bugs. We can hope we get no more."

"She looks to be breathin' a mite easier now, Doctor," Emma said as she rose away from the bed.

"Yes. Yes she does, Emma." He surveyed the room before continuing. "Now, please, everyone leave the room. I must examine the girl and shouldn't be disturbed while doing so."

"But—" Jonathan started.

He was stopped by McGill. "Please, Jonathan. We can't afford to waste time. Just take your family and wait in the other room. I can work more quickly and efficiently if you follow my instructions."

Jonathan stalled for a moment and Emma looked ready to protest, but Jonathan moved. "C'mon now, Emma. We'd best leave the room and let the doctor do his work. We cain't do nothin' but git in the way here."

Jonathan shooed his family out of the room. He was the last to leave and, as he walked out, he turned back to say, "Please make her well again, Doctor McGill."

"I'll do everything I can, Jonathan. Now, please."

Whitlock walked out. McGill turned and said, "You, too, Zeus. Out."

"But I want to stay and help."

With a sigh, McGill said, "Lila, please take him out of here. And keep him out. Just stay close in case I need you."

"Sure, Winthrop. C'mon, Zeus, let's go." The midget started to protest, but Lila grabbed him by the hair and tugged him forcefully from the room.

Silently McGill shut the door and turned toward Martha.

Chapter 4

"What's takin' him so long? He's been in there for hours."

"Calm down, Emma," Jonathan soothed. "It's not been that long. I'm shore the doctor's doin' all he kin to help her."

Lila walked up and sat on a chair next to Emma. Taking the woman's hand in hers, she said, "Your husband's right, Emma. Winthrop'll do everything he can to help her. Now try to relax."

"Oh, I reckon you're both right, but . . ."

The door to the bedroom creaked open and McGill stepped out, sleeves rolled up. He looked worried. "Zeus!" he shouted.

"Yes, Master?"

"Don't smart mouth me, little friend. This's no time for humor. The girl is sick and needs our attention. Go on out to the wagon and fetch a bottle of the special medicine. And hurry."

"Sure, Doc," Zeus said a little contritely. "Right away."

Zeus hurried out of the room, slamming the door behind him, as the Whitlocks swiveled around to stare at McGill. Emma broke the silence. "What's ailin' her, Doctor?"

"Just stay calm, Emma. I must go back and tend to Martha. I will explain everything in due time."

"But, Doctor," Emma insisted.

"Please, Emma. I must return to your daughter.

Everything will be all right." Without waiting for further comment, McGill spun and went back into the bedroom. As he began to shut the door, he turned back. "When Zeus returns, tell him to come straight in." He turned away and closed the door behind him.

Without much success, Lila and Jonathan tried to comfort Emma, who sat softly weeping. Grandma Whitlock sat with the other children grouped near the fire. Quietly she said, "Becky, please fetch my knittin'. I feel the need of somethin' to keep my hands busy."

"Yes, ma'am," the girl said. She rose from her seat on the floor.

"Maybe you should also fetch yore books, child. An' you boys should git somethin' to occupy yoreselves with. There ain't no use in settin' here frettin'. An' there's a heap of chores kin be done."

"Yes'm," the three answered in unison. Rebecca started across the room for the knitting basket and her books, while the boys headed off on various chores.

Zeus burst into the room breathing hard. "Where's McGill?" he asked without thinking.

"In the bedroom with Martha," Lila answered. "He said for you to go right on in with the medicine."

Zeus nodded and scurried across the room. Displaying rare good manners, he knocked on the bedroom door and waited until he heard McGill's muffled, "Come in," before entering.

"Here you go, Doc." Zeus handed the bottle to McGill. "What's wrong with her?"

"Don't really know just yet. I may never know." He paused to wipe the light sheen of perspiration from his forehead. "I think it's serious though."

30

"Think that'll help?" Zeus asked, pointing to the bottle McGill now held. "This ain't like a game of bunko, you know. This girl might really be sick. Bad sick. You can't sell the family on no snake oil if she's really ailin'."

"I know, Zeus. I know," McGill said wearily. "I don't know whether it'll work or not. But I don't know what's ailin' her so I hate to dose her with anything specific. I figure this might help her around. Until I can find out what's wrong with her—if I ever can—this's all I can do."

"Well, it'd best work."

"If you have any better ideas, I'd be obliged if you'd let me in on them, my little friend."

"Naw, guess not. You'd best go on ahead with it."

"Yes, I guess I must." He turned back to the comatose girl and knelt at the bedside. Gently he lifted her head. "Come here," he said to Zeus.

The midget hurried over. McGill extended his arm, holding the bottle. "Open it," he commanded.

Zeus did as he was told. McGill carefully poured a few drops of the liquid onto the girl's lips. He waited until they had seeped into Martha's closed mouth. Again and again he repeated the process until Martha had swallowed almost a fourth of the bottle's contents.

Finally McGill sat back. "If nothing else, Zeus, it'll help her to sleep some. Maybe that's all she needs."

Zeus walked back over to the side of the bed and looked down at the girl. "It would be a shame if'n somethin' happened to her, wouldn't it?" In another unusual gesture, Zeus softly put his hand on McGill's shoulder. "Don't worry, Doc. She'll be all right. You can fix her up." He winked.

31

"After all, they don't call you the Curandero for nothin'."

McGill smiled a little. The Mexican term could mean either quack or healer. It was usually given to an unqualified doctor, one with some training in herbal medicine, or maybe someone they thought was a medicine man.

"I surely hope I can do something for her, Zeus. I really do." Wearily he rose. "Well, Zeus, guess I'll go on out and tell the family something. This'll have to be the best job of sellin' I've ever had to do."

He began rolling down his sleeves, and then reached for his coat. "Just one thing, little friend. Not a word of what's really going on in here. One peep out of you about me not really knowin' what's wrong with Martha and I'll make you sorry you ever opened your trap. Understand?"

Zeus nodded again and they headed for the door.

As they stepped into the main room of the house, McGill switched on his most appealing smile. Emma and Jonathan looked at him expectantly.

"Well, I've given her a good dose of the medicine and she's sleeping soundly. I reckon she'll be better by mornin'."

"Really?" Emma shouted happily, tearfully. "Will she really be all right?"

"Well, I'm not positive, but I think everything'll be just fine. Now don't you fret. I think it's best you all get some sleep, too. It's been a long day for all of us."

"Cain't we go in an' see her, Doctor?" Emma pleaded. "Just for a short spell. We won't bother her none."

"I don't think that'd be very good for Martha right now, Emma. She's asleep, and even the slightest disturbance could prove harmful. Tomorrow is soon enough."

"Doctor McGill is right," Elizabeth said. "I think she's best left alone. Now everybody git to sleep. Dawn comes early an' there's lots of work to be done come daybreak."

"Good night, everyone," McGill said. "Lila, Zeus, come on. We'll sleep in the wagon outside."

The others said their goodnights and Lila, McGill and Zeus walked out into the starlit night. Although summer, the late-night air had a real chill to it and Lila shivered a little.

"Won't be much longer before the snows come," McGill said.

They walked slowly toward the wagon, parked next to the barn. Of the three buildings on the Whitlock property, it was the only one made entirely of wood. The other two, including the house, were made mostly of sod, mud, and some wood planking. The house was cut into a hillock, which formed the rear wall. The roof was mostly dirt and was covered with grass. During the day, the Whitlock's two cows and three sheep could often be seen on the roof, placidly munching the grass.

McGill lifted Zeus into the back of the wagon and the midget lit the kerosene lantern. McGill helped Lila climb up, and then followed her. Inside they quickly unrolled their blankets and settled in among the clutter of pots, pans, rolls of wire, bolts of cloth, and other merchandise.

Zeus was asleep almost instantly and began snoring softly. Lila and McGill lay quietly for a few minutes, unable to sleep. Finally Lila said, "Winthrop? You awake?"

"Yes, Lila. I am."

33

"Winthrop, what's wrong with the girl? You maybe can fool them folks in there, but I've seen your game too many times to believe it. I know you weren't tellin' them the truth. Or at least not all of it."

"Very perceptive, my dear." He sighed deeply. "I don't know what's wrong with her. I know she's bad sick, but I don't know what from. If Martha's not better by tomorrow, we're going to have to hightail it out of here and tell these folks to find someone to tend to her. Or fend for themselves."

The farm seemed to come awake all at once. The cocks crowed and the sheep bleated. Birds chirped their twittering songs, and smoke issued from the house's chimney. Bustling noises came from within the house and, shortly after, the door opened and Charles came out wiping the sleep from his eyes.

The young man gathered up a small armload of firewood and went back into the house. He returned a few minutes later with Joshua. The two entered the barn to milk the cows.

Zeus awoke at the first noises. Angrily he shouted, "Damn it. Keep the noise down out there. Folks're tryin' to sleep."

There was no response from outside the wagon.

Lila awoke, too, but lay quietly, enjoying the morning sounds, not wanting to disturb McGill. The soft warmth of the summer morning reminded her of days long ago, during her childhood, and it pleased her. It reminded her of her early days in the solid brick house in St. Louis, the sun beaming in through the glass window on a fine sunny morning like this one.

But that was many years ago now. She sighed. Yes, so many years ago. Before the trouble that had so changed her life. She thought back on those times now, as she occasionally did in quiet times.

It was ten years ago that she had met McGill, way back in 1874. She was sixteen years old then and cold, standing outside one of the bawdyhouses that still lined one of the old side streets of St. Joseph, Missouri. She was debating whether to go in or not when she heard the deep, refined voice, "That's no place for a nice young lady like yourself."

She whirled around to see a man in his midthirties, dressed in finery that showed the ravages of time and distance. He was smooth-shaven and, despite his somewhat shabby clothes, rather handsome.

"What do you know about it?" she had asked.

"Nothin' more'n to know you don't belong in there."

"Well you don't know nothin'," she said. She started to turn back toward the brothel, determined now to go in and ask for work. But something held her. She kept hoping the man would offer her an alternative.

But she also knew her options were limited. It was a little more than a year before that her family had thrown her out of the comfortable brick house in St. Louis. At fourteen she had been wooed and won by a man of twenty-one. When he found out she was pregnant by him, he had stowed away on one of the many riverboats plying the broad Mississippi.

Frightened, she finally confessed to her parents. But instead of the expected sympathy, she had been stunned by their anger. Her father had humiliated her when he gave her the twenty-dollar gold piece and told her to get out and never return.

In despair, she had wandered through the dirty

streets of St. Louis, not knowing where to go or who to turn to. Finally she made up her mind and bought a ticket to Defiance, Missouri. Its name made her think she would be allowed to fit in.

She found jobs cleaning houses and doing laundry. It allowed her enough money just to live. She slept in barns and, sometimes, out in the open. She saved the money her father had given her, except for what it had cost for the ticket to Defiance. But that town soon paled, not living up to its name.

Her next stop was Jefferson City, and again she worked at menial chores. But by now her condition had become obvious and work was harder to find. She was finally taken in by a kindly preacher, the Reverend Josiah Lanshire, and his wife, Mary, who needed her to help around the house and the small church.

There she had been lectured and preached to incessantly about the error of her ways by the well-meaning people. She endured it because the child was near due and she had nowhere else to go. The day arrived, and the old people called in a midwife to assist in the birth. There were no complications, and soon, Theodore William O'Shaughnessy was born to Lila. To get back at her parents, she had kept her father's name for both herself and for her son, refusing to name the child after his father.

"It's a beautiful child," Mary said happily. "And we will raise him to be a true Christian."

On the birthing bed, Lila was not sure she wanted her son raised as a true Christian by these pious people, but she had not the strength to worry about it then.

Lila was up and about the next day, busy at her chores, but now with the added burden of caring for her newborn son. Things went smoothly for two months, Lila happily working, joyfully accepting the Lanshire's lectures. She was fiercely proud of her motherhood.

Then the child got sick. Lila rushed in a panic into the sitting room where the Reverend Lanshire and his portly Mary sat before the fire. "The baby!" Lila screamed. "The baby!"

But it was too late. By the time the doctor arrived, the child was already dead. The physician could give no reason for the sudden sickness or its severity.

Lila wept, berating herself. On Mary's shoulder she had cried, "Am I so bad? Have I done so much wrong that God would do this to me?"

Josiah and Mary tried to comfort her, but their talk of redemption and sin and the will of God had little affect on her. Time did. And before long she decided it was time to leave.

"I feel I must move on now," she told Josiah and his wife. "The memories of my son are too strong here and I cannot face them. I think it best if I leave."

They said they understood and gave Lila a little money and food to tide her over. They did not know that Lila had not told them the entire reason she was leaving. Lila could not bear to tell the kindly old couple that their piousness and overbearing religiousness was stifling to her free spirit. But they had been nice to her in their own way, and so she left them, glad she had met them, but happy to be shed of them. She bought a stage ticket to Sedalia and worked herself across the rest of the state until she reached St. Joseph.

All this had flashed through her mind as she stood in front of the St. Joseph bordello. She had lost some of her money and spent the rest of it to live. Jobs had been too short and too infrequent to help much. So now she tried to gather up her nerve to enter the bawdyhouse.

The man had stared silently at her for a few moments and then said again, "Maybe I don't know too awful much, but I do know you're not cut out for such work."

Still she hesitated. He stepped a little closer. "Come on," he said. "There's a nice little restaurant down the street yonder. Why don't we go on down there and get us something to eat."

He noticed her hesitancy and added, "I'll pay for it, and," he paused, "there's no strings attached."

She finally nodded. He took her arm and, without a trace of embarrassment, jauntily led her down the street, nodding to many of the people they passed on the dusty thoroughfare.

It was over the meal that he had propositioned her. But it was not what she had expected. Instead, he had asked her to become a member of his traveling troupe.

"What do I have to do?" she asked.

"Dance a little. Sing a bit. Help sell my medicine, and some merchandise. Maybe trifle with the men a little to get them to part with some of their money."

"That's shameful," she said, seemingly shocked.

"It's not half as bad as what you were thinkin' of doin' back down the the street yonder."

"Guess not."

"All I'm askin' you to do is smile pretty at the fellers, maybe take an occasional dance with them."

"Don't sound too bad," she said between mouthfuls of steak, potatoes and peas. "But I can't dance. Or sing."

38

"Don't you fret. We'll change all that. Before long we'll have local fellers fallin' all over themselves to pay you compliments."

Filled with good, warming food, dazzled by McGill's gentlemanly manner, she quickly agreed.

The meal over, they walked through the afternoon heat toward the wagon being looked after at the town's large, odorous livery stable.

It was then that she had met the midget for the first time. Drunk as a lord, the little man was sitting atop a pile of hay, loudly and poorly singing a lively tune that was popular in those days. When he spotted Lila and McGill, he stopped the song in mid-verse and wobbled to his feet. In a thickly slurred voice he announced, "Ah'm Zeush." He tried to bow gracefully and almost found his short length sprawled on the floor. Quickly and unsteadily he righted himself. Then he said, "At your servish. Care to join me—" he hiccuped—"here on the hay?"

The young girl had not known what to do. This was beyond anything she had ever seen, despite all her travels. Worriedly she looked at McGill. McGill was staring heatedly at the midget, but he turned to face Lila with a calm face.

"Lila, meet Zeus. Zeus, Lila. Excuse my little friend, Lila. He seems to have been in the cups again, a rather common occurrence."

"But who is he?" Lila asked, grasping McGill's arm tightly, still frightened.

"He," McGill said, still hiding his anger, "is the other member of our little troupe."

McGill left her and picked up Zeus and tossed him in the back of the wagon, which was already showing signs of wear. The midget did not like the treatment and complained vociferously about it. But McGill ignored him.

Before long, the wagon was hitched and Lila was seated next to McGill. The man clicked to the horses and turned them out of town while the midget snored heavily under the canvas covering in back, oblivious to the clanking and rattling from the sundry goods stored there.

They traveled southward for days, until they reached the dusty, sprawling, wicked, beautiful city of New Orleans. It was unlike anything Lila had ever seen: different even than St. Louis, the wonderful port city of her childhood.

The delightful French accents, the food, the strange architecture astounded her and rendered her almost speechless. McGill installed her in a quiet little room in the old French section of town and went off. He returned shortly and said, "It's arranged. You'll start your singing and dancing lessons in the mornin', so you'd best get some rest tonight."

McGill went off again, and it wasn't until days later that Lila learned he had, in his own eyes, lowered himself, taking a job tutoring the children of some of the city's wealthier residents in reading, writing and sundry other subjects. He had also forced his unwilling little colleague into a job cleaning stables. He had done all this, she learned, to support his little group. Even then, money was always in short supply for the three.

But the first night she knew none of this and so had enjoyed a fine French dinner with McGill and had gotten to bed early after a hot bath in a tub brought to her in her room by a young, talkative girl whose parents had not long ago been slaves.

The next morning she started her lessons with a stern taskmistress who brooked no foolishness during the sessions. Lila took to the older woman, as harsh as she was, and looked on her as a mother, or maybe an older sister. She learned quickly, showing a natural talent for movement and body grace. Within a few short months, she had learned all the old woman, Clarissa could teach her.

Clarissa told McGill, "There's nothin' more ah kin show that young gal, Winthrop. Y'all best take her away now."

So they packed their meager belongings in the wagon, already loaded with jumbled merchandise, and sadly pulled out of New Orleans.

That was when her education had really begun. As a child she had not had much of an opportunity for schooling; her parents had not believed in it much, especially for a girl. She had learned the rudiments of reading, writing and arithmetic, but little else. So McGill set about teaching her. This, too, she learned easily.

There were other subjects also—the ones not taught in school. She learned the friendly art of cheating, through sleight of hand and the use of the quickly turned phrase; the knack of making people, especially the men, hand over their hard-earned cash for a smile, a dance, or just the promise of beauty never to be held by them. She learned the fine art of picking pockets, a talent suited to her because it was so easy; the men were taken by her beauty and charm and were usually befuddled in her presence, making them easy marks for her new skills.

Other talents, too, McGill and Zeus taught her. The little man, she decided, was not as bad as she had originally thought and, as the years passed by, she developed quite a fond feeling for the irascible, troublemaking, aggravating, friendly, helpful little man.

The group traveled far and wide over the plains, from the Dakotas to the New Mexican Territory, from the Mississippi River to the Rocky Mountains. Their traveling was aimless. McGill turned the horses and wagon wherever the whim struck him. They brought their medicine, as Lila learned to call it, to the lonely people populating the remote reaches of the frontier.

Along the way they cured some of the sickness with their herbal potions, and carried a wagonload of new and useful gadgets and objects from such places as the store opened by Mr. Montgomery Ward and the recently opened Sears and Roebuck Company store. They also brought a more important commodity to the people of the western plains. They brought welcomed company and entertainment to the lonely homesteaders and townspeople who had little chance for such diversions.

Because of this, the people often overlooked or did not seem to mind that they had been mildly, efficiently swindled, or, as it was called, gigged or gouged. They did not mind that they had been sold "medicine" which was really nothing more than alcohol and flavoring, diluted with water; they did not care that there was no guarantee on the products they bought.

Yes, thought Lila, lying next to McGill in the cramped wagon, it's been a fine ten years: a time of adventure, excitement and warmth. Like her childhood. The rest could be overlooked.

Chapter 5

McGill rose up from sleep slowly, fighting against consciousness. Throughout the night he had slept poorly, tossing and turning, worried about the girl. Even in his sleep he had been afraid he would be unable to help her, and now he fought against waking. With a new day, he knew, would come decisions that would not be easy.

Finally he gave up the fight and sat up. Wearily he rubbed his bloodshot eyes. Despite his nervousness, McGill, always gracious, bid a fine good morning to his two friends. Standing, he stretched and said, "Lila, best get the coffee pot goin'. I reckon I'll need some good, hot Arbuckle this mornin'."

Lila stood and pecked McGill on the cheek. "All right. But I think we're out of Arbuckle Coffee."

"Anything'll do."

With McGill's help she climbed out of the wagon. He handed her a large, battered tin pot and she started off toward the well to fill it. Halfway there, she saw the two young Whitlock men coming out of the barn, milk pails full.

"Good mornin', boys," she called out.

"Mornin', ma'am," Joshua said shyly. His brother echoed the statement, but a little more boldly. "You'd best hurry, ma'am," Charles added. "Breakfast is nigh 'bout ready. Y'all don't wanna be late."

"I didn't know we were invited for breakfast. I was just on my way to the well to fetch some water for coffee. But we'd be mighty obliged to you for a good home-cooked meal. I'll get the others and join you right away."

"Fine," Charles said. "We'll tell Ma you'll be in straightaway."

The two men continued on to the house, and Lila retraced her steps to the wagon. "Winthrop, we've been invited to breakfast with the Whitlocks. I think they're expecting us, so you'd best hurry.

43

You, too, Zeus."

"I'm ready, Lila," McGill said. He clambered out of the wagon. "C'mon, Zeus. Hurry up."

"I'm comin'. I'm comin'. Just hold your horses. They'll wait for us."

"If you're not out of this wagon in one minute, I'll tell them nice Whitlock folks not to feed you. Then you'll have to make your own breakfast. Or go hungry," McGill said good-naturedly.

"All right, all right!" Zeus shouted. He rushed to the back of the wagon. "Help me down."

McGill lifted the little man down onto the ground. Zeus scurried ahead, anxious to fill his stomach. Zeus always ate big. It came from his childhood. Before they had put him in an orphanage, his parents had forced him to eat large meals, vainly trying to make him grow.

McGill and Lila followed along more sedately, arm in arm. As they strolled along, Lila asked, "Still worried 'bout Martha?"

McGill nodded. "I dread having to go in and see her, not knowing what to expect. I just have to remember to keep smilin'."

"It'll work out, Winthrop. Don't you fret so much."

They entered through the rickety wooden door of the shack the Whitlocks called home. "Good morning, everyone," McGill called out. "Hope you are all well this mornin'."

The Whitlocks nodded, as Jonathan answered for the family. "Mornin', Doctor. Ma'am. We're jist fine. 'Cept for Martha, of course."

"Yes," McGill said. "I think she'll be all right for now. If you don't mind, I'd rather set to breakfast first and see to Martha afterwards."

"Well," Jonathan said, "if'n you think she'll be all right, I reckon we don't mind none."

44

"I don't feel there's any need for concern. We'll just let her sleep a bit longer. It'll do her good."

"Come and get it," Emma called.

As everyone took their places at the table, Emma and Rebecca rushed between stove and table setting out the platters of simple, hearty fare.

The Whitlocks, farmers that they were, generally ate a large breakfast to keep them going through the day. They feasted on fresh eggs, flapjacks, bacon from the hog they killed the previous fall and smoked, home-baked bread and biscuits, fresh butter churned weekly, fresh milk from the two cows, and cup after cup of coffee, lightly sweetened with their precious small hoard of sugar or a little honey and molasses.

Breakfast on the farm was a serious affair and little talking was done during the meal. What conversation there was, centered around the work that had to be done that day. And Martha's condition.

Zeus stuffed his little frame with a vast amount of the tasty food, while McGill and Lila ate sparingly. Finally McGill pushed back his chair. He knew he was simply delaying the inevitable, but it must be done.

"That was sure a fine meal, Emma," he said, standing. "But now I think I'd best tend to Martha. If you'll excuse me."

"Want us in there with you, Doctor?" Jonathan asked.

"No, Jonathan. My examinations may take some time, so I'd suggest you go about your chores and try not to worry too much. If I need you, I'll just holler."

Jonathan nodded and rose. "Well, sons. We ain't gittin' no work done settin' here. Let's go." He and his sons took their hats and left.

"I ain't gettin' nothin' done whilst I'm settin'

here, neither," Emma said. She rose and began clearing the table.

McGill paused at the door of the bedroom. "Lila, you help Emma." When she nodded, he said, "Zeus, you help out here as much's you can. But keep close by in case I need you to fetch something. Understand?"

"Sure I can't help you, Chief?" Zeus had spent a number of years among the Indians of the Great Plains and in the Southwest. Because of it, he had early on taken to calling McGill "Chief." Though he often used it sarcastically, it was meant as a term of respect.

"No, that will not be necessary," McGill said, his irritation and worry beginning to surface. With a deep sigh he opened the door and stepped into the small room, closing the door behind him.

"Hello, Doctor," Martha whispered.

"You're awake," he answered, unable to think of anything else to say. He recovered quickly and stepped to the side of the bed. "How're you feeling?"

"Weak. Still tired." She paused briefly. "But I still can't breathe none too easy."

McGill's hopes rose a little. "Think you can eat something?"

She nodded. "Not very much maybe, but a little, I think."

"Good. You look a little pale, but some food ought to help get some color back into your cheeks." He began checking her pulse. "Want to eat now and get examined later, or the other way 'round?"

"I'm kinda hungry, Doctor. If'n it's all right with you, I'd ruther eat first."

"That's fine. Need to go outside first?"

"No, Doctor. I think I can wait till later for

46

that."

"Good. I'll be back in a few shakes with your breakfast. You just stay put till I get back," he smiled.

"Yessir," she said, also smiling. But as he left the room, Martha fell back on the scrawny pillow breathing heavily and going through a small spate of coughing.

As McGill walked back into the main room of the house, the bustle from the women stopped. Emma looked at him, expectant, worried. McGill smiled. "Fix up a small plate of food, Emma. We have a hungry patient on our hands."

"Then she's all right?"

"Well, I can't say for sure. But she's awake and a mite hungry. She's still very weak and she looks awful pale, but she's shown some signs of improvement."

"Oh, thank God," Emma whispered. She rushed about, readying a plate of food.

"Take it easy," McGill scolded gently. "She's not that hungry. Give her about half that much."

Emma started to laugh. "Guess I am bein' a mite foolish." She cut down the amount of food and asked, "Is it okay if'n I feed her, Doctor? I'm so almighty worried 'bout her."

"Oh, I reckon that'd be all right. Just take it easy with her."

"I will." She started for the bedroom and then stopped and turned. "Becky, run out to the fields and tell your pa and brothers what's happened. And tell 'em there ain't no use in them comin' back jist yet. They kin see Martha later."

"Okay, Momma." She started untying her apron.

"Before you go, Rebecca," McGill said. The girl stopped. "You can tell your father it'll be near

47

noon before he can see Martha. Maybe longer. After Martha's been fed, I must examine her and that'll take some time. So just tell him Martha's awake and eating."

"Yes, Doctor." She ran happily from the room.

Emma entered the small bedroom and McGill slumped tiredly in a chair. He rubbed his eyes. Lila walked over to join him, kneeling by the side of his chair and taking one of his hands.

"See, Winthrop. I told you everything'd work out."

"She's not out of the woods yet, Lila. I still have a feelin' she's very sick. But I don't even know what she's got. Maybe I'll have a better idea of what's ailin' her later."

"I think you just worry too much, Winthrop."

"Maybe so. But I still have a bad feelin' about all this."

"Everything'll work out. I keep tellin' you that, but you don't want to believe me." She paused as McGill smiled wanly. "Want some coffee?"

He nodded and she moved off to fill a cup from the pot of coffee she had waiting on the stove.

McGill sat sipping the steaming coffee. Before long, Emma came out of the bedroom carrying the almost empty platter. "I'm worried, Doctor," Emma said. "She don't seem too well."

McGill snapped straight up in the chair. "What's wrong?"

"Well, I'm not tryin' to be the doctor, you understand. But it seems to me Martha has a slight fever. She's also havin' a right hard time breathin' and she told me she's awful weak."

"That's not very good. But maybe now she's eaten she'll gain a little strength. I'll go back in and have another look."

He drained the last of the coffee and softly

48

walked back into the bedroom. "Well, young lady," he said as he closed the door. "How're you feeling now that you've got a full belly?"

"I'm still feelin' purty poorly, Doctor. I ain't ever felt so weak before. And hot, too."

McGill gently placed his hand on the girl's forehead. "You do seem to have a touch of fever." He frowned before saying, "And you're beginning to sound a little hoarse, too. Is your throat bothering you?"

"It ain't to say really botherin' me, Doctor McGill. My voice jist seems to be comin' out wrong."

"Well, then. Since you're not doing quite so well as I hoped, I'll have to give you another examination. Maybe this time I can find out what's wrong with you." He smiled down at her and she weakly returned it. "But first, I think you'd best go on outside for a few minutes. Don't you?"

"Yes, Doctor. I think I'd best."

McGill stepped to the door and opened it. "Lila," he called. "Rebecca. Would you both come here, please."

Lila nodded and started walking toward the bedroom, but Rebecca turned to look at her mother. Emma looked worriedly at McGill, who smiled and said, "It's all right, Emma. I just want them to take Martha outside for a spell. She's too weak to go herself."

Emma heaved a sigh of relief and nodded to Rebecca. "Go ahead, child. Help your sister."

The two young women walked into the bedroom. With care and tenderness they helped the ailing Martha sit and then stand at the side of the bed. Out of breath, the girl rested for a few minutes. "Ready?" Lila asked after Martha caught her breath.

The sick girl nodded. With her sister holding on one side and Lila on the other, Martha shuffled out of the room. Weakly waving to her mother as she passed through the main room, she made it to the other door and outside.

McGill and Emma passed the time in cleaning and straightening the small bedroom. The straw on the bed was freshened and the linen aired for a few minutes to freshen it, too. More water was brought in and poured into the basin.

"Zeus," McGill called, and the midget came running. "We have any of Sir William Burnett's Disinfecting Fluid made up?"

"I ain't sure, Chief. I think we used it all the last time we tended someone."

"All right, then. Hurry out to the wagon and fetch back the bottles of zinc and muriatic acid."

"Sure enough."

"And bring a pail and a good-sized hunk of that old flannel we have laying around."

Zeus hurried out of the room, and McGill called after him, "Bring a stick about three feet long, too."

"What're you aimin' to do, Doctor?" Emma asked, worried.

"Disinfect this room. It'll help Martha and maybe keep everyone else from catchin' what she's got."

Zeus ran back in just before Martha and her helpers entered. "You two girls set Martha down out there a few minutes. There's work yet to be done in here," McGill ordered.

As Lila and Rebecca helped Martha into a chair in the main room, McGill poured some of the acid into the pail. Then he added the zinc a little at a time, stirring it with the stick. When it was done, he tied the flannel rag to the stick, dunked it in the solution, wrung it out some and then waved it like a flag all around the room.

"Take a rag and wipe down that bed and the walls," he told Emma. "Zeus, you sprinkle some of it on the floor."

It was soon over, and Martha was brought back in. Martha was sucking in huge gulps of air trying to catch her breath. The short walk and its exertion were enough to exhaust her.

Even McGill was shocked at her state. "Get her right back into bed," he ordered. "And then leave the room. There is no time to waste."

Lila and Rebecca quickly but delicately laid Martha back onto the bed.

"Should I stay, Winthrop?" Lila asked.

"No, I don't think that'll be necessary. Just stay close to hand in case I need you."

"I will." Lila hurried the other two women and Zeus out of the room and firmly closed the door behind them.

McGill turned to the small, lopsided table and reached for the bottle of medicine. As he picked up the bottle, his attention snapped back to Martha, who started coughing frantically.

The spate of coughing finally ended, and she lay there, spent and wheezing for breath. "How long's this been going on?" McGill asked.

Martha's answer came out in gasps. "I first started coughin' 'bout a week ago, but it was only this mornin' it began to git read bad. I been spittin' up some, too."

"Well, then. Let's take another look."

The coughing spells became more frequent and delayed the examination. But then he was through. "I'll be back shortly," McGill told the girl. Sadly he turned toward the door.

McGill opened it and looked out over the Whitlock family, who turned to face him at the sound of the opening door. The men had come in from their work for lunch and to check on Martha's progress.

"Well, Doctor, how is she?" Jonathan asked anxiously.

"Yeah, how is she?" Zeus shouted from his seat near the door. "You been in there a right long time." Zeus chuckled at his own wit and was surprised when no one else did.

McGill ignored him. Quietly he said, "I'm afraid your daughter is very sick. I have tried everything I can think of at this point, including my patented medicine."

He paused to take the cup of coffee that Lila handed him. He took a few sips while everyone waited expectantly. Finally he continued, "But it has been of no use. And I doubt it will. In all truthfulness, I'm afraid it's above my bend. I doubt there's much I can do for her. I think you'd best send one of the boys for a doctor."

The Whitlocks sat in stunned silence for a few minutes before a shocked Jonathan said, "But ain't you a doctor?"

Zeus started to chuckle again. Cockily, he said, "He ain't no more of a doctor than I am. It sure took y'all long enough to puzzle it out."

McGill and Lila shot black looks at the midget, who realized his mistake. He started edging closer to the door, ready to make a break for it.

"He tellin' true?" Jonathan demanded.

"What my *little* assistant means," McGill said as persuasively as he could, "is that I never did quite finish medical school. I—"

Zeus, still hoping to make a joke out of it, interjected, "What he means is he flunked out."

The looks McGill and Lila shot at the midget were venomous. Lila made a move toward the little man, but she stopped at a wave of McGill's hand. "Leave him be, Lila," he said.

He turned back to face the Whitlocks. In a conciliatory tone, he said, "The impudent little whelp was incorrect. I was forced to leave medical school before I could complete my studies because of personal reasons."

Jonathan stood to his full height squarely in front of McGill. He looked down at the rather frail doctor. In tightly controlled anger, he said, "You're the closest thing to a real doctor we got 'round these here parts. The nearest town with a doctor's more'n five days ride from here. Leastways, they used to have a doc over to Powderville in the Montana Territory."

He paused to glare at McGill, to let the importance of his words sink in. "So you're it, *Doctor* McGill," he continued. "We ain't got no choice. And neither do you. You must make my daughter well again."

Whitlock turned on his heel. Striding to the mantlepiece, he reached up and pulled down the shotgun, a deadly weapon at this close range. He gestured sharply and his two sons moved toward the door. Joshua picked up Zeus, who squealed and cursed.

"Shaddup, or I'll stick you in the fire," Joshua growled.

Charles placed his big back firmly against the front door, effectively cutting off any means of escape.

Jonathan turned back to McGill. Pointing the double-barreled weapon at the doctor, Jonathan, still angry, snarled, "Like I said, *Doctor* McGill, you're the closest thing we got to a real doctor in these parts. So use your medicine. Or your prayers. Or anythin' else you got in that worn-out old

53

wagon of yours. Do whatever you have to. But cure my daughter."

He paused again, for effect. Then he said, "If'n you don't, I'll kill you and the others. Now git back in the other room and heal my daughter. And take them with you."

McGill looked around the room, searching for sympathy. But the Whitlocks were stone-faced, staring boldly back at him or down at the floor. With a sigh, he said, "Lila, Zeus, come into the other room. We will do what we can."

Lila moved toward McGill, but Zeus started to protest when he was put back on the floor. He thought better of it, though, when he saw the large muzzles of Jonathan's shotgun. He hastened over to hide behind McGill.

McGill spun and grabbed the midget by the shoulders. Propelling the little man into the other room, he said, "Hurry it up, my friend. You've caused quite enough trouble already."

Inside the small room they all breathed a sigh of relief. Zeus, happy about being away from the presence of three angry men and a loaded shotgun, tried to be cheerful. "Looks like we're in sort of a fix now, don't it?"

McGill, nerves tight from worry and fear, advanced threateningly toward the midget. Menacingly he said, "Why you saddle-broke, ungrateful little monster. I ought to . . ."

Zeus scurried to hide behind Lila's skirt. He peered out from behind her as she tried to push him back around in front.

Softly Lila said, "Now, Winthrop. Let him be. There's no time for that. Think of the girl. We've got to do something for her and soon. You can discipline this fourflusher later. I may even help you."

McGill nodded. "Yes, dear Lila. You're right. But what can I do? It's been years since I left medical school, and I didn't even have much of that. I may have known some of this once, but it's been too long. I haven't kept up with any of the developments. Nothing."

He walked over to the little table and picked up the bottle of his "special" medicine. "All I have now is this," he said, holding up the bottle. "And maybe some herbs."

Lila looked affectionately at McGill. Quietly, speaking only to him, she said, "Well, it's a start."

Chapter 6

McGill sat slumped in a chair near the fire. Darkness was falling rapidly and Emma went about the room lighting the two lanterns. Grandma Whitlock sat at the other end of the hearth, smoking her inevitable corn-cob pipe.

Lila sat near one of the two small, glassless windows, still trying to read by the day's last light. Zeus and the Whitlocks sat quietly around the room, working at various chores. The three Whitlock men now wore holstered, .44-caliber Starr six-shot revolvers strapped on their hips.

"Ain't you folks uncomfortable wearin' them guns?" Zeus had asked the day before.

"Shore it's uncomfortable," Charles had answered, patting the three pounds of iron hanging in a leather holster over his right leg. "But sometimes it's gotta be done. Like last fall when we had us an Injun scare."

"Injun scare, huh? I thought there weren't no

more Injuns 'round here.''

"There ain't, really. But a small band of Crows come through lookin' for game. So we strapped the guns on. Didn't really need 'em, but we all shore felt a heap better whilst we was wearin' 'em.''

"Just like now, huh?''

"Yep. We don't intend to use 'em this time neither. But we will if'n we have to. It's as much for you as it is for us. So long's we got 'em on, we know it and you know it and things'll go along right and proper.''

"I think I see what you mean," Zeus had said.

So the Whitlocks sat around the room, armed and ready for trouble from the three visitors.

Suddenly McGill sat bolt upright and shouted, "Zeus!''

Everyone stared at him. Even Grandma Whitlock snapped out of her doze, the corn-cob pipe falling out of her mouth and onto her lap. She quickly grabbed it and stuffed it back in her mouth, brushing the few smoldering ashes from her apron.

Holding the pipe stem in her almost toothless gums, she snorted, "What in tarnation's goin' on 'round here, with all this hootin' and hollerin'.''

"Sorry to have startled everyone," McGill said. "Zeus, go on out to the wagon and fetch me that pile of old medical journals I've been gathering up. Quickly.''

Zeus rose slowly. "All right, all right. Just hold your horses.''

As Zeus headed out the door, McGill shouted after him, "And bring them all.''

Zeus returned in a few minutes, staggering under a large load of magazines. He dropped them on the floor at McGill's feet. "Here," he puffed. "Hope you're happy.''

McGill ignored him, as he had the Whitlocks, who continued to stare at McGill with anxious looks. McGill just looked down at the pile of magazines, hope flickering briefly in his eyes. There on top was a three-month-old copy of the *American Journal of Science and Arts,* and underneath a year-old issue of the *Druggist's Circular and Chemical Gazette.* Further down in the pile, poking out a bit, was an issue of the *Hamburgh Pharmacopaeia,* now two years old.

He picked up the first one and sat back. Lighting one of his rare cigars, he opened the magazine.

"What d'you expect to find in them magazines, Doctor?" Emma blurted out.

"Maybe something. Maybe nothing." He settled a little further down into his chair. "Now, please. Let me be. I must get on with this."

"Well, then," Jonathan said, "it's gettin' late and we'd all best be in bed. Charles, d'you think you can stay awake through the night?"

"Sure, Pa. 'Sides, if I get tired 'long 'round mornin', I'll just wake Josh."

"Fine. If you'll excuse us, Doctor, we'll be headin' off to sleep. If you need us for anything to help Martha, don't fret none 'bout wakin' us. Charles'll be 'round to keep you company. But, please, don't try'n leave."

"We won't," McGill mumbled. "Good night." He went back to his reading while everyone else found their beds in the small shack.

When the Whitlocks settled in, Lila asked, "Charles, do you mind if Zeus and I go out and sleep in the wagon? It's mighty crowded in here."

"I don't know," Charles said shyly, still taken by the beautiful Lila. "I don't know's Pa'd like it much."

"You'll be in here with Winthrop. Do you really

think I'd hitch up the wagon in the dark and drive out leavin' him here?''

"Naw, guess you wouldn't." He pondered the request for another minute and then decided. "Sure, it'll be all right, I reckon. But," he pointed to Zeus, "don't let your little friend here make no foolish moves." He patted the butt of the big Starr pistol and said, "I know how to use this, so you'd best remember, we still have *Winthrop.*" The last was said nastily.

"I'll keep an eye on him." She rose. "C'mon, Zeus. Just remember what this nice young man said. Mind your manners. Good night, Winthrop. Try'n get some sleep."

McGill looked up. "I will. Good night." Before Lila and Zeus were out the door, McGill was again immersed in the journal, oblivious to almost everything else.

Throughout the night McGill read—page after page of medical reports and research. The latest medical testimony available in the West. Some were months, even years, behind, but still the most recent he had available.

He sat quietly through the night with the journals, rocking gently in the rickety old rocking chair, pausing only long enough to pick up a new journal or a cup of coffee.

While McGill read, Charles paced the floor. He, too, drank a lot of hot, black coffee. Twice during the night Mcgill had to go outside. Charles escorted him both times, his hand resting lightly on the Starr hanging from his waist.

"That's not necessary, son," McGill told him on the second trip.

"Don't reckon it is," Charles answered. "But I ain't takin' no chances."

When the cock crowed, McGill was halfway

through the stack of magazines. The house began to awaken. McGill stretched and yawned.

Elizabeth was the first to rise, as was her custom. She shuffled to the fire and lit a pipe, then warmed herself by the fire for a few minutes. Aloud she said, "Well, guess that's enough of warmin' for these old bones. Time to git breakfast a'goin'. Everybody'll be awake soon."

"Come on, Charles. I need another trip outside. And your grandma needs some working room." McGill stood and stretched again, then headed for the door with Charles close behind.

As they stepped outside, McGill said, "You can take your hand off the gun, Charles. I'm not going anywhere. Besides, after we finish our business out here, I think we ought to bring in some wood or something for the fire."

"I reckon. Promise not to try'n get away?"

"Of course. Look at it realistically. You probably know by now I'm what they call a fourflusher. You know, a sham, a bluffer." He looked directly at Charles.

Charles stared back in alarm, and his hand flashed back to the weapon at his side. McGill smiled and continued, "But I've been up all night and I'm not quite as young as I used to be. Now, do you think I could rush off after knocking a big feller like you down, get all the horses out of the barn, hitch up the wagon, make sure Lila and Zeus are aboard and take off before you, your pa and your brother caught up with us? Even if I could do all that, how far would I get before you ran us down?"

"Not very far, I reckon. But I gotta be careful."

"I know, Charles. Now, let's get us some firewood."

Warily Charles kept his eye on McGill as they

gathered up an armload of firewood each. McGill smiled at him and shook his head. Without hurrying, he carried the wood into the house.

Dropping the wood on the floor, McGill looked at Charles. "See," he said. "I'm still here." Charles breathed a small sigh of relief, enforced by the fact that Jonathan and Joshua were up and about.

"Guess I'll see to Martha while breakfast is being set," McGill said.

Weariness settled over him as he stepped into the tiny bedroom. Trying to be cheerful, he smiled and said, "Mornin'."

Martha weakly smiled back. "Mornin', Doctor."

His examination was cursory and he found little change except that she was coughing more frequently and for longer periods. Her breathing was still ragged and difficult.

The examination over, he said, still trying to keep her from worrying, "I still can't figure out exactly what's wrong with you, but I think I've almost found the solution. You just keep resting. Your mother'll be in soon to feed you."

As he turned away from the girl to head back into the main room, his facade dropped and the weariness returned. Dragging his feet, he shuffled slowly out of the small room.

He shut the door softly behind him and then noticed that everyone was looking expectantly at him. Sadly he shook his head. Rubbing his face, he slumped into one of the old wooden chairs lining the table.

The room bustled into activity. Pots and pans clashed and clanged as the women hurried about. The two young men came in, each carrying a pail of milk. Plates clacked onto the table, and outside the cocks raised a ruckus.

The outside door opened again and Zeus and Lila walked in, quietly for once. Zeus seemed subdued and Lila had never seemed more beautiful to McGill.

She walked over and pecked McGill on the cheek and put her hand on his shoulder. By the look on his face, she already knew Martha's situation had not changed. "Is she any better at all?" Lila asked so quietly that no one but McGill heard her.

"Afraid not," he answered in the same tone. "I think she's getting worse."

"Come and get it!" Emma yelled.

Lila gave McGill's shoulder one last squeeze and went to the other side of the table, taking a seat between Zeus and Charles. Jonathan said grace after everyone was seated and breakfast started with a rush.

With the day's work facing the Whitlocks, the meal went quickly and quietly.

When it was over, the men readied to leave. "Emma," Jonathan said, "we'll be out near the bend of the stream. Them three stumps need pullin' and we been puttin' it off too long now." To McGill he said, "One of us'll be near to the house all day, Doctor, so don't git no ideas of leavin'."

"I wouldn't think of it."

"Yeah," Zeus butted in, "especially since you're all still wearin' them damn guns."

Jonathan just nodded tightly and walked out, shutting the door quietly behind him and his sons.

"Emma," McGill said, "I think you should go on in and feed Martha now."

"Go 'head, Ma," Rebecca said. "I'll clean up the dishes."

"I'll help her," Lila added.

Emma nodded. "All right." She hustled around the kitchen area preparing a small plate of food for her ill daughter.

While Lila and Rebecca cleared the table and began preparing water to wash the dishes, McGill sat dully at the table, hardly moving, staring straight ahead.

Emma returned soon, seeming a little happier. "She ate a bit better this mornin', Doctor," she said.

McGill nodded. "That's a good sign."

Emma went to join the other women and McGill turned toward the midget. "You're mighty quiet this mornin', my friend."

Zeus's face screwed up like it did when he was about to make a sarcastic remark, but he stopped before the words came. McGill saw the sidelong look that Lila gave the midget and realized she must have had a long talk with the little man during the night. He wondered how long the effects of the lecture would last.

"I'm just a little tired," Zeus said finally.

"Well I hope you're not too tired. I may need your help. Like now. Go on back out to the wagon and fetch another bottle of the medicine. And get that old medical book I keep stashed away under the seat. It's pretty old, but maybe it'll help some."

"Okay, Chief," Zeus said. He jumped off the chair and threw McGill a salute.

As the midget ran out the door, McGill thought, wryly, that Lila's lecture would have few long-term effects.

He rose. "Lila, when Zeus gets back, send him in. I'll be with Martha."

Involved with her work, she only nodded.

McGill was bending over the child, bathing her face and arms with cool rags, when Zeus entered.

62

"Here's the stuff, Chief. How is she?"

"About the same."

The girl drifted off to sleep and McGill sat in the only chair, looking pensive.

When she awoke, McGill forced some of the liquid down Martha's throat. She choked a little and her eyes watered.

"Now, now," McGill soothed. "Just a wee bit more and it'll be all over." Gently he held her head and forced another spoonful of the tart liquid between her lips.

Standing beside him, Zeus asked, "How come you're usin' that junk? You oughta know it ain't gonna do her no good. 'Bout all it might do is get her drunk."

"Of course I know it won't do anything for her illness, Zeus. But it does serve a few purposes. First, the alcoholic content will keep the pain down some, if she has any. With the medicine in her, she might not feel so poorly."

He paused briefly to wipe a hand wearily across his face. "But more importantly, it makes the family think I'm really doing something for her. Keeps them happy and gives me time."

"But we both know it ain't gonna do nothin', so why try'n fool her folks?"

"Because it gives me *time*. Not just time to keep those folks out there from killing us, but time for me to maybe find out what's ailing her and do something about it."

"Suppose you can't?"

"Then, my friend, we're in serious trouble. And the few extra days I've bought with our patented medicine will be even more precious, won't they?"

"Yeah, guess so." He looked down at the girl and then back to McGill. "Think you'll be able to fix her?"

63

McGill shrank into the chair. "I don't know, Zeus. I really don't know. I thought I might find something in all those medical journals you brought in last night."

"Then you didn't?"

"No, not yet. But I haven't finished going through all of them yet. I wanted to check this first," he said, holding up the medical book.

"Expect to find anything?"

"I hope so." He sighed. "I just wish I had kept up with these things a little more. What bothers me is, I know that somewhere I've seen something about whatever this girl's got. I remember reading about it in some book or journal. But I can't remember when or where or in what book or even what the disease is." He sighed again. "So many years gone. So much I've missed, never paying attention."

"Can I help?" Zeus interjected.

"That's very noble of you, Zeus. But no, I don't think you can do anything at this point. Maybe you should see if you can help the Whitlocks somehow."

"What're you gonna do?"

"See what I can find out in this book. Maybe the answer will be in there."

Zeus started for the door, calling over his shoulder, "Well, if you don't need my help, I'll go see if'n I can keep all them ladies happy."

McGill shook his head, smiling at the little man's impertinence. As the door closed behind the midget, McGill opened the heavy black book and began reading.

He took a break for lunch, eating sparingly. After the light repast, he fed Martha a little and then talked her into swallowing a few mouthfuls of the potent medicine. She was still coughing badly and so McGill walked out to the wagon, grateful to be outside despite the blistering heat and the unwavering sun. At the wagon he mixed up a batch of cough medicine from pine needles and sugar.

Back in the house, he made Martha take some of the liquid. Then he went back to his chair and his medical book.

The door opened and Lila poked her head through. "Winthrop, supper's almost—" She stopped when she saw him slumped in the chair, asleep.

Quietly she walked over to the sleeping man. With a soft smile on her lips, she looked down at him before gently touching his shoulder. She shook him, calling his name a few times.

McGill started awake, almost rising out of the chair. Then he recognized Lila. He smiled in embarrassment, rubbing the sleep from his eyes. "Sorry, Lila. Must've dozed off."

"That's okay, Winthrop. You needed it."

"What time is it?" he asked, startled.

"Shank of the afternoon. Supper's near ready."

"I didn't realize it was so late." He stood and stretched. "You go on out and help Emma. I want to take another look at Martha."

She started to protest, but he stopped her. "I'll be out directly. I just want to look Martha over. Now, go on."

Dinner was more quiet than usual. Neither the Whitlocks nor their visitors relished conversation; the Whitlock men were tense and the women worried.

McGill, too, was worried. He knew he had to do something soon or it would be too late for him, his friends, and Martha.

Listlessly McGill picked at his food, only half listening to the desultory conversation going on around him. Finally he had had enough. "Excuse me," he said abruptly. He stood and walked back into the small bedroom.

A light rap on the door startled McGill, who was bending over Martha, wiping her face and forehead with a cloth. The girl was sweating profusely and was racked by choking coughs.

McGill turned his face toward the door. "Who is it?"

The door opened and a head poked in. "It's me, Doctor," Emma said. "Can I feed Martha now?"

"I'm sorry, Emma. But I think she's not got the strength to eat right now. Let me spend a little more time with her and we'll see how she's feelin' then."

Emma's face saddened. "Well, if you really think it best," she said unconvinced.

"Yes, I do." He turned back toward the girl. Over his shoulder he called, "Bring in some more towels or cloths. These here can be washed."

He heard the door close quietly behind him. "Dammit," he muttered, barely audibly. "You got to get better, girl. Come on, Martha, pull through." The seriousness of the girl's sickness was wearing on him; it was only on the rarest occasions that he resorted to oaths.

Emma returned with some new pieces of cloth and rags. She left with the old, sweat-stained ones and the dirty linens.

McGill did what he could for the girl and made her as comfortable as he could. With the same nagging sense of worry and frustration, he went silently back into the main room. There, without a word, he took a seat near the fire and opened one of the journals, an old copy of *Christianson's*

Dispensatory he had not read the previous night. Ignoring the Whitlocks' questioning looks, he settled in to read.

The evening passed slowly and, before long, Grandma Whitlock yawned and stretched. " 'Bout time I went and rested these old bones," she said. "It's gittin' late and the sun comes early to these parts. Rest of you best be gittin' off to sleep too."

"Guess you're right, Ma," Jonathan said. "All right, Joshua, you take over the watchin' tonight. And keep a close eye on our friends here. Becky, you go on and go to sleep now. You too, Charles. You was up all last night and you got a long day ahead of you tomorrow."

"Be glad to, Pa," Charles said.

"Me, too," Becky nodded.

"Now you just 'member what I said, Josh. Keep your eye on our guests. And not just the doc here, but the others, too. You hear me?"

"Don't worry, Pa. I'll watch 'em. I don't much reckon they're gonna give us no trouble."

"Just make sure they don't. You need anything, you just call me or your brother."

"I will, Pa."

Josh settled himself down and took to whittling. McGill paid scant attention to the exchange, pausing only to toss down the one journal and pick up another, a back issue of the *Boston Medical and Surgical Journal.*

As soon as the Whitlocks had gone to bed, Lila stood and grabbed Zeus. "C'mon, Zeus. Time to go to the wagon."

"Let me go," he squawked.

"Just hush up and march. It's gettin' late and Winthrop has work to do. He don't need you 'round to act up like you usually do."

With a grip on the little man, Lila walked over

and kissed McGill on the cheek. " 'Night, Winthrop," she whispered.

He looked up and smiled wanly. " 'Night, Lila. Good night, little friend."

"Good night," the midget muttered, still squirming in Lila's tight grip.

Lila dragged the wriggling midget outside.

Silence descended and reigned. Except for the crackling of the small fire, there was quiet. McGill had wondered aloud early that morning about the wood being used for the fire, asking Charles where it had come from.

"Couple miles down the creek there's a stand of cottonwoods. Every onc't in a while me'n Josh'll go on down there with the wagon and haul us up a load for the fire. Mostly we just use booshwa, you know, cow chips."

"I didn't reckon there was so much wood 'round here you could use it all the time," McGill had said. "Most folks out in places like this do use cow chips. Wood's too dear to throw it away on every-day use."

"Ma's just usin' it cause you're company," Charles said. "We ain't got very much left in the pile by the house."

As McGill tossed down the second journal of the evening, the fire caught his attention and he thought, I must remember to tell them to go back to using chips in the morning.

The hours of darkness dragged on. McGill sat rocking slowly, reading page after page of the journals he had been saving for months. Occasionally Joshua, the heavy six-gun looking incongruous on his youthful frame, would doze off. Seconds later he would snap out of it, anxiously looking around.

Chapter 7

It was edging toward the darkest pre-dawn hours when McGill snapped straight up in his chair. The sudden action shook Joshua out of a light doze and, frightened, he nervously searched the room. "What's wrong?" he asked, worried.

McGill ignored him, but his face had regained some of the animation it had lost recently. McGill's breathing came faster and he almost shook while reading through the pages of the journal. Without warning, McGill tossed the journal high in the air and whooped, "I found it! By the Lord, I found it!"

The noise woke the household and the Whitlocks came tumbling into the room. "What'n hell's goin' on here?" Jonathan bellowed.

Bleary-eyed, he stared around the room at the rest of his family gathered there, blinking in the dim lantern light.

"I don't know what's goin' on, Pa," Josh said. "All's I know is I was just settin' here and he was settin' there just as quiet as could be. Next I knew, he threw that there magazine up and took to shoutin'."

The front door opened and Lila and Zeus stumbled in, breathless. "What's going on?" Lila gasped. "We heard shoutin' all the way down to the wagon."

Everyone turned to stare at the newcomers, and Lila suddenly became conscious of her lack of dress. The noise had so startled her that she had scrambled out of the wagon, across the yard and into the house clad only in her nightdress.

"Oh, dear," she muttered. "I didn't realize—"

Grandma Whitlock hurried over to her and handed the younger woman the long shawl she almost habitually wore. "Here, child," she wheezed, "take this. Ain't nobody here wants to look at these old bones anyway."

"Thank you," Lila said shyly as she accepted the garment and draped it around her shoulders.

"I liked it the other way," Zeus grumbled.

From the look on their broad, handsome faces, it was evident that Charles and Joshua felt the same. But everyone ignored the midget and turned back to face McGill. They were wide awake now, and Jonathan asked, for them all, "Now, Doctor. What was all that hollerin' 'bout?"

McGill, almost forgetting his dignity, scrambled around until he found the journal he had been reading. When he did, he held the paper volume up for everyone to see. "I think I've found it!" he said excitedly. "I think I've found what's been ailing Martha."

He fairly beamed. "I'm not sure yet. But I think I've found the answer. I knew I had read something about the symptoms she's got. That's why I had Zeus bring all these in," he said, pointing to the stack of magazines. "I was pretty sure I had read about it in one of them."

"But what is it?" Becky asked.

"I don't want to say anything before I'm sure," McGill said thoughtfully. "I need to make some tests on Martha first, and read a little more on it. It'll take a bit longer before I'm sure."

"Well," Jonathan said, "dawn'll be breakin' soon anyhow. We might's well just git breakfast over and git an early start. Charles, Josh, bring in some firewood. Becky, fetch some water. And take

70

one of the lanterns so you can see."

"Oh," McGill interjected, "that reminds me. I know how dear firewood is 'round here, so why don't you just go on back to using booshwa. We've been here long enough not to be considered company."

"That's right thoughtful of you, Doctor," Jonathan said. "All right, boys. Leave the rest of the wood where it is and fetch a wheelbarrow full of the cow chips."

McGill, his composure regained, stood. "Now, if you folks will excuse me, I have work to do." With that, he stepped into the small room.

When the door shut behind McGill, the others burst into activity. "We'll be back in a bit," Lila said. She grabbed Zeus and headed back to the wagon to dress.

The Whitlocks, too, hurried off to dress and to begin preparing the morning meal.

Meanwhile, McGill sat in the rickety chair in the little room finishing his reading of the journal article. On the bed, Martha lay gasping for breath. The perspiration ran off her face in rivulets.

At a new severe spate of coughing, McGill dropped the magazine on the floor and rushed over to the bed. The girl's condition had worsened, he saw, and he felt a surge of pity for her. "Poor girl, poor girl," he muttered over and over.

Quickly he wiped the sweat from her as best he could and then began taking some of the tests that had been described by the doctor in the journal article.

Realizing he was missing some instruments, he ran to the door and bellowed, "Zeus! Fetch the kit from the wagon. Quickly!"

He slammed the door and went back to Martha. Within minutes, the midget, puffing heavily from his run, stormed into the room carrying the kit of medical instruments and chemicals that McGill had not used in more than a decade.

"Thank you," McGill said distractedly.

"Don't mention it, Chief. How's it comin'?"

"Fine, fine," McGill said absentmindedly.

He finished his work almost at the same time as he heard Emma hollering out the front door to the boys down at the barn: "Come and get it!"

Martha was now awake and coughing steadily. Her temperature had dropped slightly, but she was still weak. "I feel terrible, Doctor," she said in a voice barely above a whisper.

Trying to be cheerful, he said, "You don't look so chipper neither."

Not knowing he was fooling, she came near to crying. "Wait, Martha. Don't cry," he said. "I was just joshin', just trying to make you feel a little better. Just to cheer you up."

"Really?"

"Really. I just made some tests and now I'm going to get a bite to eat. By the time I finish, the tests should have some reaction and I'll be able to tell." He paused, then remembered the girl did not know about his discovery. "I think I've found what's ailing you." She perked up a little and he continued, "I'm not sure yet, but I took the tests and in a little while we'll know."

"Thank you," Martha whispered.

McGill walked out of the little room wiping his hands on a rag. "Well," he said, "it'll be a little while before I can tell anything." He was smiling for the first time in days. "What's for breakfast?"

"The usual," Emma said, also smiling for the first time in quite a while.

"That sounds right fine." McGill sat down and began piling a plate high with food.

72

The conversation was lighter now, less tense. There was even some laughter, and everyone paid little attention to Zeus's normal outbursts of sarcasm and underhanded remarks.

But it seemed over far too soon for McGill. And although he had kept on a happy facade throughout the meal, he was still worried. He was not at all certain he had found the disease. More importantly, he worried about what he would, or wouldn't, be able to do when he found it; he seriously doubted his ability to cure Martha.

However, he kept up his joviality through the meal, knowing the family needed it more than he did. When the meal was over, he said: "Well, folks. I mustn't stay any longer." He stood. "As usual, Emma, you have outdone yourself with this fine meal."

"It seems the old man is back to normal," Zeus said in a stage whisper.

Charles and Joshua chuckled a little, but McGill, retaining his dignity, did not acknowledge the remark. "Time is drifting by and there's work to be done," he said. "If you will excuse me."

He left the table, knowing everyone's eyes were on him.

Although it was not a long time, the minutes seem to stay suspended for the waiting people. Jonathan had not the heart to send the two sons out to tend the crops when word on their sister could come at any time.

Even the usually hardworking Emma left the dishes to sit on the table long after the meal had been finished. She was too anxious to clear them away herself and could not bring herself to order Rebecca to do it. So she sat with eyes glued to the bedroom door.

Lila got a start on the cleaning after a while,

despite Emma's protests. But her efforts were only half-hearted.

Every few minutes, the waiting people turned their eyes toward the door of the little room. Half expectantly, half nervously, they watched the door that held the secret. The time seemed interminable, but a bare half-hour passed before McGill walked out of the room where Martha lay sick. This time he did not look so happy. The weight of the problem seemed to rest heavy on his shoulders.

He stood, hand on the door latch, seemingly unwilling to go farther into the room. Finally Emma broke the silence. "Tell me!" she cried in an agonized shout.

McGill started to speak, but could not get the words out. He rubbed a hand over his face, stalling for time. "It's something called tuberculosis," he said sadly. "It was discovered about two years ago by a doctor named Robert Koch who studied bacteria."

"Can you do anything for her?"

"I don't know, Emma. From what he said in the journal, Doctor Koch didn't hold out much hope. There are a few suggestions I can try, but I don't know as it'll do much good."

McGill slumped into a chair. "I'll try them anyway. It can't hurt. And maybe I can find some other remedies I can use in my other books and journals. Right now I need to think a bit. Maybe there's a solution somewhere."

Jonathan exploded, leaping from his chair, his face masked in anger and frustration. He took the few steps separating him from McGill. His towering bulk shaking with fury, Jonathan grabbed a huge fistful of McGill's shirt and yanked the doctor to his feet.

Fairly lifting McGill off the floor, Jonathan

shook him and shouted, "You'd damn well best come up with a solution! I'm right good and ready to run outta patience with your high-falutin' ways. You'd best do somethin' right quick."

He broke off as Zeus, moving faster than he ever had, sped across the room, dinner knife in hand, and stabbed him in the thigh.

With a grunt of surprise, Jonathan slammed McGill back into the old chair, which splintered, landing the doctor on the floor. With the quickness of a cat, Jonathan swung a slab-sized hand that caught Zeus full across the face. The midget flew backwards, smashing against a chair and falling heavily, the knife flying harmlessly out of his hand.

Jonathan looked down at the blood trickling from the gash in his leg. Then he looked at McGill and Zeus, lying in different spots on the floor. Slowly he pulled the three-pound revolver from its leather holster and cocked it. Deliberately he brought it to bear on the midget, who was lying frozen, too frightened to move.

"I don't take kindly to folks stickin' knives in me, little man. You'll never do so again. I'll make damned sure of that."

"Jonathan!" Emma screamed. "Stop it!"

The big back muscles, which had tensed with the heat of the moment, relaxed some and he turned his head slowly to look at his wife. But the gun did not waver.

"This ain't your concern, Emma."

"Don't you tell me it ain't none of my business, Jonathan Whitlock. You're standin' there fixin' to kill that little feller right here in my house. That makes it my concern, and don't you forget it, either. Now you just stop this foolishness."

"But, Emma."

"Don't you 'but Emma' me. I ain't havin' no

killin' done here."

"Emma," he barked, "now you just listen to me. I'm plumb tired of all the tall tales these slick city folks keep givin' us. Martha's in there dyin' and these here folks keep on makin' light of it. I reckon if we kill this here little feller, then he," Jonathan nodded his head in McGill's direction, "just might do somethin' that's gonna save Martha."

"And if'n he does," Emma snapped, "what're you gonna do then? You promised to let him go if'n he can fix Martha. But if'n you do that after killin' his friend, he's gonna go straight to the sheriff. Where will we be then? Unless, of course, you figger on killin' him and Lila once Martha's back on her feet again."

Jonathan's shoulders slumped. With the utmost care, he eased the hammer of the big pistol down and reholstered the weapon. Then he stormed out the door, kicking the midget out of the way as he went.

He returned within minutes, calmer now, and took a seat at the table.

Quietly, not looking at the others, McGill picked up the pieces of the chair and threw them into the fire. As he worked, he wondered what he could do for the girl to help her, to save her life. And, he thought, in so doing save the lives of his friends as well as himself.

Finished with the small cleanup, he took another chair and placed it close to the fire and sat. His mind worked furiously, trying to come up with a remedy or potion that would work.

Lila came and knelt beside him while Zeus crouched on the hearth nearby. Emma faced McGill, a few feet away. The silence grew until Jonathan finally rose and began working around the room. The two young men took his lead and began working around the room also. Charles grabbed a worn leather harness and spread it out on the table. With his brother, he began replacing a broken section, with grim-faced determination.

"Becky," Emma said, "please finish clearin' the table. I'll be with you directly."

"Okay, Ma."

Zeus scuttled a little closer to where Emma sat. With a deadpan expression, he whispered, "Why don't we do something to get your mind off this for a while?"

She looked at the midget with dull eyes. "It'd be nice if I could. It purely would. But I'd keep thinkin' of Martha."

"Oh, I think I could get your mind off her for a spell. I got an idea. Why don't we take a quick trip out to the barn? You know, just you and me." He winked at her and continued, "We could get cozy down in the hay—"

Shocked, Emma looked toward where her husband and sons worked. She hesitated, not sure she believed what she just heard and trying to decide whether to tell her men.

McGill rose from his chair and moved toward Zeus like an avenging angel. But the midget was too fast. He scurried across the hearth away from the doctor. He kept going, then, across the room and out the door.

McGill settled back into his chair, shaking his head. Softly, almost sadly, he said, "I'm sorry, Emma. I'm truly sorry. Zeus sometimes forgets his manners. He has been terribly abused by the world because of his size, and so he often acts without regard for the feelings of others. He sometimes acts toward some people without thinking, like so many

77

others have acted toward him.''

"Well . . .''

"So many people have degraded him,'' McGill continued, "that their injustices have twisted his mind some. Often he acts, not with malice, but without thinking of the consequences of his actions. I'm sure he meant ho harm.''

Emma sighed. A little distractedly she said, "I'm sure he didn't, Doctor. But it was somethin' of a shock.''

"I reckon it was.''

"Is there any hope at all, Doctor? For Martha, I mean.''

"I really don't know right now. I know there are some things I can try, if I can find the right herbs or potions.'' He paused to collect his thoughts, then said, "Lila, where'd I put that big book on herb medicine and pharmacopeia?''

"It's in the wagon, packed at the bottom of our big trunk, I think. Why?''

"It may give me some clues as to what I can use.''

"Want me to fetch it?''

"Yes, that'd be nice. And tell our little friend I haven't quite forgiven him yet for his latest episode. But if he's willing to behave, he can come on back in.''

"I'll tell him.''

McGill settled back into silence, awaiting Lila's return. She hustled in through the front door toting a heavy, leather-bound book. Although old, it was in excellent shape.

Lila handed it to McGill, who took it almost reverently. "Ah,'' he said, "just what I've been looking for. Maybe this will hold the answer.''

Lila went across the room to help Rebecca with the dishes and other chores. As she did, she saw

Zeus slip in through the front door. He remained near it, just in case.

Again McGill sat back with a book in his lap, ready to try to find the answer to the riddle.

"Do you really expect to find the answer in there, Doctor?" Emma asked.

He glanced up and was instantly sorry he could not keep the frown of worry from her. He knew Emma had seen it and he was dismayed. "Not sure," he answered truthfully.

Emma nodded slowly. "I was afeared there wasn't nothin' you could do. I shoulda knowed there wasn't much hope." She started to rise. "Reckon I'd best go tell Jonathan and the rest of the family. They should know there ain't much we can do."

McGill gently, but urgently, reached out his hand and caught Emma's arm, stopping her. "Wait, please," he said anxiously.

With a questioning look, Emma sat back down. McGill looked toward where the men sat, working, at the table. Despite the passage of time, they were still alert and determined looking. Nervously McGill said, "Have you forgotten that your husband has promised to kill me and my friends if Martha dies?"

Emma shook her head and McGill continued, "Well, then. If he hears we don't have any hope, he might decide to finish us off right now." He paused briefly. "It's not that I care for myself, you understand. But I do care for my friends. Especially Lila. It's unfortunate that they have to suffer because of me." His voice started to fade. "She is so young, so beautiful . . ."

Sudden recognition crept across Emma's eyes. Slightly disbelieving, she asked, "She's not your wife, is she?"

"No."

"How sinful."

"Is it?" McGill asked, smiling a little.

There was a short pause. "I guess not." Another short pause. "Do you love her?"

McGill nodded. "Very much. But I have not told her. I am afraid to." He dropped his eyes to stare vacantly at the open book in his lap. "She is so young and beautiful. And I am too old. It would not be right to burden her with it."

Emma started to reply, but thought better of it. After a few seconds of silence, McGill said awkwardly, "You will say nothing to your husband yet?"

Nervously Emma replied, "Jonathan ain't about to do what he said. He ain't like that. He only said it 'cause he's worried 'bout Martha. He wouldn't hurt nobody."

In a dignified tone, McGill implored, "That may be so, Emma. But for the sake of my friends, I'd prefer if we didn't put your husband's resolve to a test yet. And besides, if I'm dead, then we sure can't do nothin' for Martha. I still may be able to puzzle it out."

"Well," Emma said, giving in, "if you feel that strongly 'bout it, I reckon it's the least I can do."

"Thank you," McGill breathed. He sat back in the rocking chair and patted the heavy volume on his lap. "Yep, the answer just might be right in here. It does contain a right good bit of information. There is some hope."

Now it was Emma's turn to plead. "Please, Doctor. Do everything you can for her."

Darkness crept over the small sod and wood house on the empty stretches of the Wyoming plain. And with it came more wind. The wind blew almost constantly here, sometimes in gentle gusts and breezes, sometimes in blustery blasts that rocked the house. And even in the summer, the night winds sometimes came from the north, bringing with it a chill, down from the Canadian provinces.

Earlier in the day, Jonathan could feel the wind changing, starting to move in from the north. He sent his sons to the small cottonwood grove near the river to bring back some more wood. "What the hell," he had said, "the cold'll be comin' in tonight and we still got guests, so we might's well have us a real fire."

Now Lila and Emma sat on the dirt floor near the warmth of the fire. Rebecca and her grandmother were seated in the two creaking rockers close by. The men sat at the long wooden table, working at necessary small chores; sharpening the knives used in the house, whittling a new set of bowls, repairing the cracked leg of a chair with wet rawhide. Zeus was curled up in a corner near the door, half asleep.

Emma looked toward the closed door of the little room. "I sure hope he can do somethin'," she said. "My poor Martha's been sick so long."

Lila patted her hand. "Winthrop is doin' all he can. If he can't help her, I doubt much anyone else could either."

"You sound mighty sure of him," Rebecca said.

"I am." She paused. "He's a good man."

"Sounds like you're mighty fond of him," Emma said.

Lila looked at her, startled, and Emma smiled. "He told me this afternoon."

Lila nodded slowly, but Rebecca shot out, "Told you what, Ma?"

81

"We're not married," Lila whispered.

Rebecca was shocked. "Why, that's terrible."

"Hush yore mouth, girl," the grandmother snapped. "Don't you go speakin' on what you don't know."

"Thank you," Lila said softly.

"None needed," Elizabeth said. "What you do is yore own concern and we ain't got no place to judge you." The last was said while looking directly at Becky, who dropped her eyes, embarrassed.

"I'm sorry," she said.

But her grandmother was not finished yet. "You oughta be. 'Sides, they ain't done so much wrong. There's lot worse bein' done in the world today." She looked at Lila. "Love him?"

No longer so ashamed, Lila nodded. "Yes."

"Well, then, that makes up for a lot now, don't it?"

"But he don't know it," Lila said in her soft voice.

"Well, why not?" Elizabeth asked.

"I've never told him."

"Why not?" Elizabeth asked, exasperated.

" 'Cause it ain't proper for a lady to be so forward."

The grandmother's cackling laughter rippled out. "But you're sharin' his bed, girl. Ain't that forward?"

Rebecca gasped in shock. "Grandma!"

But Elizabeth continued to cackle. Lila sat and stared. Then she grinned, finally joining in the old woman's laughter.

"Guess there's no foolin' you, is there?" Lila laughed. Then she said, "I've never told him 'cause it don't seem right somehow. He's never told me neither. I know he's fond of me, but he ain't ever spoke of it, so's I reckoned it best to keep my trap shut and let things be."

Emma was tempted to speak, to tell Lila how McGill felt about the beautiful young woman. But she thought better of it.

But Becky asked, "Why?"

Lila thought for a minute before answering, trying to choose her words carefully. "Well, he's had a hard life. Doesn't anything ever seem to work out for him the way he planned it. And I don't want to burden him with somethin' like that. It just don't seem right to put that on him."

"Well I think you should tell him," Becky said firmly.

Lila smiled, a little sadly. "Maybe someday, Becky. Maybe someday."

Emma finally brought the conversation to other areas. "How'd you meet up with him anyway?"

Lila, haltingly at first, then with more conviction, told the other women of her young years in St. Louis and her troubles, and finally her meeting with McGill in St. Joseph.

"It must've been excitin'," Emma said when Lila had finished. "All that travelin' an' all."

"Oh, it was," Lila said. "Once in a while I'd miss not havin' a house and a family. But the excitement of seein' new places and different people was wonderful."

"The people never got mad when you took their money?" Becky asked in wonder.

"Well, sometimes," Lila laughed. Like the first time they had been arrested after she joined McGill and Zeus.

They had passed through Shreveport, Louisiana, and on into Texas. McGill wanted to go to Houston, a town that was growing by leaps and bounds. Once in Texas, they headed south. A little more than halfway to Houston, they stopped in the small town of Loveland.

The residents of that little town had not been pleased when they discovered they had been gigged by the trio, and set out to catch them. The crooked sheriff arrested them outside town, but on the short ride back, Zeus escaped.

It was lucky for them that the little man did. McGill was thrown into the windowless adobe jail that stood bulkily alone in the middle of town. Lila was locked in a room at the mayor's house. There she was given a choice; submit to the sheriff and mayor, and her friends would be released. Refuse and they'd die.

They left her alone to think. The choice was not hard, especially since she had expected it. But then Zeus popped his tiny head through the window. "I paid some younker to get the wagon and horses and take 'em outta town," Zeus said. "Now c'mon. We gotta go spring the Chief."

"What can I do?"

"Just follow me."

She slipped out the window to follow Zeus. As they skirted the rear of the building lining the mud-caked main street, he outlined his plan.

At the jail, Lila entered the tiny office. A lone deputy sat there, bored, playing solitaire. He looked up in surprise when she entered. She smiled and said, "The sheriff's had his fill of me and told me to c'mon over here. Reckon he thought you'd like to join the fun."

The deputy looked at her questioningly. "I figured I might as well get into the spirit of it and try to enjoy it," she said, moving closer to him. "That way, everybody has a little fun."

The man's eyes lit up and Lila suppressed a shudder. As he stood and embraced Lila, Zeus slipped in the door carrying a heavy hammer stolen from the blacksmith's shop. Silently he clambered on top of the old wooden desk. Lila stepped back, tossing her long red hair, batting her lashes over the startling blue eyes.

The deputy stood transfixed, mouth slightly agape, staring hungrily. Zeus swung the hammer with all his might.

The deputy slumped unconscious to the floor. Zeus and Lila hurried to the back to free McGill. The three moved quietly out the door and, keeping to the shadows, made their way to the outskirts of town. There the boy was waiting with the wagon.

McGill gave the boy a few more coins and they leaped aboard the wagon and hurried back north and then west, crossing some small rivers trying to cover their tracks.

They never learned what had happened to the deputy and had avoided the area ever since, not taking chances.

"He deserved it," Grandma Whitlock cackled. "I'm glad you walloped 'im."

Lila laughed a little. "So was I at the time."

"Was that the only time?" a wide-eyed Rebecca asked.

"No," laughed Lila. "There was Dodge City a few years back. That time we were arrested not 'cause of what we were doin', but 'cause we didn't pay off the marshal. And Laramie and Yankton, over to South Dakota way, and Lawton down in Indian Territory, and a dozen other towns."

"Sounds like you've led a right checkered life," Emma said somewhat in awe and shock, not sure whether to condemn her guest.

The old lady cackled. "Sounds like a right lot of fun to me. Too bad I ain't a little younger, I just might take to joinin' up with you folks. It'd do my

85

old bones some good." She lit her old corn-cob pipe and sat back in her rocker, cackling her deep wheezing chuckle as she dreamed of it.

Lila smiled softly. At first she had felt a little twinge of shame for her life, but with the old lady's obvious joy in the harmless chicanery, she felt more relaxed.

"Yep," Lila giggled, "we been through some times together, the three of us. There was some good times and some bad times, some fun and a spot of trouble here and there. But I sure did learn a lot from Winthrop. And when all's said and done, I wouldn't change the life I've had for any other in the world."

Elizabeth's eyes popped open. "I wouldn't neither was I you, young lady. Leastways not so long as you're young. Onc't you git to be as old as I am, well then you can settle down some. But enjoy yourself whilst you can." Her eyes dropped closed again and she was silent except for the soft sucking sounds she made as she puffed her pipe.

"Did you ever go back to any of them places where you was arrested?" Rebecca asked.

"Why sure we did," Lila said. She laughed a little. "Most of them places don't hold a grudge. Besides, most of them towns go through a lot of sheriffs."

"You ever been back to Dodge City?" the young Whitlock girl asked eagerly. "We've heared a lot about it."

"Mostly bad," Emma sniffed. "It's a most wicked place from all accounts."

"It's that and more," Lila chuckled. "Yes, it most certainly is a wicked place. There's any kind of evil there you want to look for—gamblin', drinkin'. . . ." Her voice tapered off. She had come close to telling of the whoring that went on in

86

Dodge in front of the impressionable young girl and had only caught herself just in time. "But," she finally continued, "there's a lot of fine, godfearin' folks there now. It's changin', and for the better, I reckon. It's becomin' more civilized since the cattle drives slowed down some. Without all them cowboys comin' through regular, the saloons and gamblin' halls ain't got so much business."

"When was you there last?" Becky asked, still wide-eyed.

"Just a bit ago. Fourth of July. And what a time it was, too. You'll never believe what they had there."

Both Emma's and Rebecca's eyes implored Lila to tell them of the wonderful sight. Finally Rebecca blurted out, "Tell us. Tell us, please?"

Lila laughed. "Well, they built this big arena on the outskirts of town kinda. And they had—" She started to laugh again, thinking of the spectacle.

The others waited expectantly. Seeing them watching her, she finally said, "Well, they had themselves a bullfight."

"You're joshin'," Emma said, not believing.

"No I ain't. It was an honest-to-goodness, full-fledged, rootin'-tootin', all-dressed-up Mexican bullfight."

"That must've been some sight," Rebecca gasped.

"It most certainly was," Lila chuckled. "There was folks from miles around come flockin' to Dodge City that day. There was more people there that day nearly than I ever did see before. Even more than last year in Nebraska."

"What happened then?" Emma asked. She, too, was now wide-eyed, involved in the story.

"Well, on the Fourth of July last year. Least I

think it was last year." She sat back and did a little mental calculation. "Yep, 1883, last year. Anyways, we was in Platte, Nebraska, to celebrate. We didn't know it beforehand, but Buffalo Bill's Wild West Show was in town."

"Really?" Rebecca asked incredulously.

"Yep," grinned Lila. "And, oh it was so excitin'! All the horses and buffaloes and Indians and shootin', and carryin' on. It was all noise and color and excitement."

"Was Buffalo Bill there himself?" Rebecca asked.

"He sure was, Becky. Ridin' right out front of everybody on that big white horse of his. And he was decked all out in fine buckskins. I never seen nothin' like it."

Lila sat back a minute and then leaned forward again. "And there was real Indians there, too. Some of them that was there was even them that fought General Custer."

Rebecca's eyes grew even wider. "Really?"

"Sure enough. It was a sight I might never get to see again."

She leaned back in the chair again, a wistful look crossing her face. "Yep, I've seen a piece of this country. Even been back east a little. As far east as Chicago one time."

"It as big as they say?" Emma asked.

"Bigger. Buildings all clumped up together and all hustle and bustle. Seems amazin' they got so much put back together after that big fire they had ten, twelve years ago." Again her mind drifted back. . . .

It had been in March of 1883 that Lila, Zeus and McGill had arrived in the big city of Chicago. It had been bitterly cold on the plains that winter and they headed east finally to get away from it. Once

88

in the city, they had taken rooms at a hotel and spent the next few days in sightseeing. Even St. Louis and New Orleans seemed small places compared to this and the big lake on the east side startled them.

On March 23 they heard about the historic event scheduled for the next day—the first telephone line was to be opened between Chicago and New York. They were excited at the news, and Lila remembered she had told McGill it would be something worth seeing.

McGill had dropped Lila and Zeus off at the hotel and then left, returning a few hours later, beaming. And she had asked him what he was so happy about.

"I," he said, proudly puffing himself up, "have received invitations for the three of us to attend the momentous event taking place here in this fine city tomorrow."

She was excited, but remembered asking him how he had managed it. He would not tell her. And he never did.

It was not like her to worry about where the tickets had come from. She only knew she was excited about being there. Hardly able to contain her excitement, she clung to McGill's arm with a fiercely tight grasp. It was over rather quickly.

"What's a telephone?" Rebecca interjected.

"Well," Lila said. "It's kinda hard to explain. It's this little box and it's got a little thing you hold up to your ear. And a teeny bell on it. You just kinda hold the one thing up to your ear and talk into the little box part. And people real far away can hear you talkin' to them just like I'm talkin' to you. You can hear them too, and talk back to them."

"You're not tellin' true," Emma gasped.

"Really. It's true. You just turn this little crank handle on the side of the box and somebody else with one of them will hear the little bell ringin'. Then you just pick up the hearin' part and they can talk to you and you to them. All the way to New York!"

"How can they do that?" Emma wondered, still skeptical.

"I don't know," Lila said. "All's I know is I seen it with my own eyes and heard it with my own ears. It's like magic."

"What was it like? Bein' there, I mean," asked the ever-inquisitive Rebecca.

"It's hard to remember," Lila laughed. "I was so excited about bein' there that I can't really remember much of it. I do remember it was a lot more excitin' waitin' for it than was the actual happenin'. I reckon it was really borin'."

Rebecca gasped in shock. "How can you say that? It must've been one of the greatest things."

"I'm right proud I was there and I wouldn't have missed it for anythin'. But I've seen so many excitin' things it's hard to keep all of them straight in my mind."

Chapter 8

The door to the bedroom opened and McGill stepped out. His coat was missing and his sleeves were rolled up above the elbow. The once-fine vest was open, and underneath it his shirt was soiled and wrinkled. His face had gone unshaved for the past few days; he was bleary-eyed and looked pale and weak. But hope flickered in his eyes.

"Lila," he said, voice cracking as if from disuse, "some coffee please."

He turned to look almost dully around the room. Spotting Zeus, he said, "Ah, there you are, my little friend. We got any skunk cabbage in the wagon?"

"Yea, Chief, I think we do."

"Then I'd be obliged if you'd fetch me a handful of it and another bottle of our medicine." No use letting the Whitlocks know the patented medicine was little more than flavored alcohol, he thought.

"Well, Chief, I don't know as if I'm ready to go outside just yet. Maybe I'll grab me a handful of it when I'm out that way."

Without a word, Charles rose from his seat at the table and with one large hand grabbed the midget by the back of the shirt and lifted him off the floor. "We'll fetch it," he said quietly to McGill.

"Just like I said, Chief," Zeus remarked with a nasty gleam in his eyes, "I was just leavin'."

"Thank you," McGill said, turning to take the steaming crockery cup from Lila.

Charles started out the door with Zeus and the people inside could hear the big young man's easy voice, "Feel like walkin', or should I fetch you there?"

They could also hear Zeus's subdued voice answer, "I reckon I'll walk if you don't mind."

McGill slumped into the rocking chair Lila had vacated. "Have you found somethin'?" she asked.

He was aware of all the eyes in the room focused on him, but he answered calmly and slowly, "Not sure yet. I've found something in the book which seems to have been used with some success in the past."

91

Emma was excited. "Thank the Lord," she said.

McGill's cold stare could not completely hide his sympathy. But it calmed the woman a little, as did his words. "I'm not sure it'll work, but it seems to be the most successful thing I've found in the books so far."

He sat sipping the hot, black coffee, the steam curling around his graying temples. His eyelids drooped.

The door burst open and Zeus came strutting in, followed closely by Charles. The midget was carrying a small pouch and a bottle of medicine. "Here 'tis," he exclaimed.

"Good." McGill stood and handed Lila the empty cup. "Come," he said to Zeus. "I'll need your help."

"Yes, sir," Zeus snapped, throwing McGill a salute.

McGill ignored him, walking into the bedroom. The midget followed. Inside the room, McGill was all haste, the calm, even manner gone. "Quickly now, Zeus. There is no time for foolishness. I don't know whether this'll work, but it's been too long now for her to be this way. The quicker we get her dosed, the quicker we'll know if it'll do her any good."

He glanced hurriedly around the room. "The water basin. Empty it."

The little man complied. "Now," McGill said, "help me crush some of this skunk cabbage into the basin."

Zeus untied the pouch and opened it. The dried, shriveled leaves gave out a musty odor. They each grabbed some of the leaves and began ripping and shredding them into the basin. Finally, McGill said, "That's enough. Now give me the alcohol."

Zeus looked dubious. "Don't argue," McGill

snapped. "That's what the book says—skunk cabbage mixed with whiskey. That's what this is, isn't it?" he asked, holding up the bottle.

Zeus nodded. "Good," McGill said. "Look, Zeus, according to the book on pharmacopea, this is a remedy used by herbalists back east in Maine and other places."

"All right, Doctor," Zeus said seriously.

The mixture was completed quickly. "Well, here goes," McGill said, carrying the potion toward the girl.

Martha was worse than ever. She was coughing almost constantly, occasionally spitting up a little blood. Her breathing was ragged, strained and uneven. Her face was ashen and her hair was matted to her forehead by sweat.

Although urgently, McGill spoke calmly and soothingly to the girl. "Okay, Martha, I think I've got the solution. So we need to get as much as this into you as we possibly can. Okay?"

Barely noticeably, she nodded, choking and gasping.

Softly McGill raised her head and tried to plump the feather pillow up behind her, but was only partially successful. Propping her up, he had both hands free to spoon feed her the potion. With tenderness, he gave her more than she really wanted, but when he finally decided she had had enough, she seemed a little calmer and more relaxed.

"It's probably the bug juice that did it," Zeus whispered.

"Yes, I reckon it is the whiskey," McGill whispered in return. "Maybe that's why you're supposed to mix the skunk cabbage with whiskey. The alcohol calms the patient down and helps him to sleep, allowing the herb to work."

"Maybe so. How long's this supposed to take if it's gonna work?"

"Don't rightly know. The book doesn't say." He looked thoughtful. "But if it's going to work, we ought to see some kind of results pretty soon, I'd say."

"It'd best be soon. Them folks out yonder ain't gettin' no friendlier. I reckon they might just kill us anyway, no matter what happens."

"Don't get carried away, little friend. They're really nice folks. They're just worried about their kin."

"I reckon. But I still hope that stuff works. And soon. I got a hankerin' to be on the move again."

"Me, too."

McGill looked at Martha. "Well, she's asleep now. We'd best go on out and let her be."

Quietly the two stepped into the main room. Everyone glanced at them. "She's asleep now and seems to be breathing a bit easier," McGill said. "Now all we can do is wait."

It was another long night for McGill, who began to show the strain of many long days and nights without sleep. His escort this night was Jonathan. The girl's father said hardly a word to McGill all night, preferring to sit quietly puffing a pipe and bending his mind to the work before him.

McGill was glad he had a quiet companion. Unsure of the effectiveness of the medicine he was using on the girl, he delved deeper and deeper in the book on pharmacopea, as well as into some of the journals he had not read.

He, too, puffed a pipe, or an occasional cigar. And again he forced cup after cup of hot black coffee down his throat, fighting off the effects of too much worry and too little sleep.

Only once during the night was the silence

broken. "How's your leg?" McGill asked Jonathan.

"Fine," the big man grumbled.

Hours after the ruckus a few days earlier McGill had poulticed and bandaged Jonathan's leg. The wound was shallow and not more than a few inches long. It should, McGill had told him, heal quickly.

"Want me to check on it?" McGill asked.

"Don't reckon it's needed." Jonathan had been surly since his eruption and McGill wondered why. He knew Whitlock was worried about Martha and had to be frustrated at being taken down by his wife in front of the children and the guests. But McGill had a feeling it was more than that, something deeper that was eating at him. But he would not ask it.

"You're probably right," McGill said, "but I'd like to take a look anyway. Make sure it's healing properly."

Jonathan started to argue, but held his words back. Silently he stood and dropped his trousers. "Git it done," he said.

McGill checked the wound, freshened the poultice and rebandaged it. "Looks to be healing right well. Few days you'll be as good as new."

They went back to their chores, wrapped in silence.

The creeping coolness of pre-dawn made McGill shiver and he huddled into a blanket for warmth. His eyes drooped and closed, and his head sank onto his chest. His breathing was long and deep.

The cock's crowing snapped him out of the light stupor. Guiltily he looked around the room. Jonathan, a little more mellow after the quiet night, smiled a little at the doctor, pushing aside the wooden bowls he had been carving.

McGill smiled back. "How long was I out?"

"Not too long. 'Bout an hour, best I can figger."

McGill shook himself out of the blanket and stood, rubbing the weariness out of his face. "Sorry," he mumbled.

"What fer? You was plumb bushed. You been pushin' yourself purty hard these days, Doc." His hard, seamed face turned almost soft as he looked at McGill.

The doctor looked at him in surprise. "That sounds a mite strange comin' from you. Considering the circumstances."

"Well, Doc. I'm still worried sick 'bout my little girl. But I kin see you're doin' all you're able for her and I reckon you deserve some credit for all you been through the last few days."

McGill filled the coffee pot with water from the wooden bucket and poured a bunch of loose coffee in after it. He threw a handful of cow chips on the fire and then some wood, building up the blaze. The pot went on next and he swung to face Whitlock.

"That's mighty nice of you to say that, Jonathan. I don't reckon, though, that you've changed your mind?"

" 'Bout what? Killin' you?" McGill nodded and he continued. "Naw, Doc. I ain't changed my mind. I kin respect you fer what you been tryin' to do, but if you ain't successful at it, then the respect don't mean a damn thing. It's my daughter that counts. Can you understand that?"

"I reckon I can," McGill said, nodding slowly, sadly.

The subject was dropped when Grandma Whitlock shuffled into the room. "Mornin', boys," she said. "Hope you both passed a peaceable night."

They mumbled good mornings. Jonathan put

away the newly carved wooden bowls and headed for the door. "I'd best fetch up some booshwa. Comin', Doc?" The last was almost an order.

McGill shook his head. "I'd best go in and see to Martha." He saw Jonathan hesitate in indecision. "Don't worry, Jonathan. I'm not going anywhere."

A small smile slipped across Whitlock's lips. He nodded curtly and walked out.

When McGill came out of the bedroom, everyone else was gathered in the kitchen area. The pleasant aroma of fresh-brewed coffee, sizzling bacon and baking biscuits floated through the room.

"My, that smells good," McGill said.

"It'll be done in a jiffy, Doctor," Emma said. "We'll be set to eat in a few minutes." A pause and then, "How is she?"

"Seems a little better. She's not coughing as much and her fever is down a mite. But she's not out of the woods just yet. It may be a time before we'll know for sure whether the medicine's takin' hold." He smiled and gently laid his hand on her shoulder. "It's no use in worryin'. We've made progress. Now you just take your mind off it and serve up some breakfast. We're all hungrier'n buzzards and that's smellin' better with every passing minute."

Emma quickly wiped a few tears from her eye with a corner of her apron. She smiled thanks. "Then you'd best get outta my way so's I can get crackin'."

He gave her shoulder a soft squeeze and then sat.

The day went along like the others in the previous week. The Whitlock men went outside to work, at least one of them always keeping close to the house, ever watchful of the visitors.

Jonathan fluctuated between barely contained rage and his usual jovial self. The frustration and worry would grow within him, building until he snapped, taking out his frustrations on a tree he was chopping or by working furiously to uproot a stump. But always it was away from the house and away from the others.

McGill, Lila and Zeus, attuned to the feelings of others because of their profession, could tell these times, and they worried, wondering when the explosion would again be directed at them.

While the men worked outside, mostly away from the house, usually far off in the fields, the Whitlock women worked on various chores and projects in and around the house, with Lila lending a cheerful, efficient helping hand. Zeus lazed around, or created mild consternation when he could.

The work amazed McGill, as it always did on the lonely, out of the way farms. There never seemed to be an end to it for either the men or the women. Without rain for a few weeks, the men had to carry buckets of water to the crops from the fast drying out stream. Carefully the precious liquid was poured on the ground, being hungrily absorbed by the dry soil and the thirsty crops.

The crops—wheat and corn, mostly—had to be sprayed with water also. And it had to be done fast and early, before the brutal sun rose too high.

There was other ground to be plowed and turned, stumps and rocks to be pulled and removed. The men spent hours hauling fresh, wet horse and cow manure from the barn to the fields where it was used to fertilize the crops. Ripe produce had to be harvested and made ready for sale.

It was backbreaking work and McGill wondered

where they got the strength and energy to fight the brutal land day in and day out. These people, McGill saw, were valiant in their battle to wrest a living from the harsh land, facing heat, drought, insect plagues, loneliness, hungry wildlife, and even rare Indian scares. And they faced up to them steadfastly, rejoicing at the small victories and banding even more tightly together at the defeats and hardships.

The women had it no easier. There was cloth to be spun because store-bought clothes were too expensive, and darning of the old clothes to make them last longer. They cared for the garden patch near the house—the beans and pumpkins, peas and lettuce, potatoes and herbs, and the squash, beans, turnips, beets, and all the rest. They still made candles because kerosene for the lanterns was scarce and expensive. And they fed the two hogs, as well as the many chickens and ducks, and sheared the sheep. There was a never-ending and mostly futile battle to keep the sod house clean and free of dust, spiders, snakes, mice and insects. The loneliness, especially for the women, was devastating, and the sun, wind, heat and cold cracked and weathered their skin making them look old long before their time.

McGill wondered how they could live with it all and still remain cheerful and pleasant.

McGill, though, had his own work. And while it was not the backbreaking labor of the men, or the ceaseless routines of the women, it was, at least for now, the most important. He was in and out of the sick room. When he wasn't tending to Martha, he was poring through the medical books and journals. His searching was calm and studied, but in its own way frantic. He seemed to be seeking a miracle.

The men came back in at the noon hour for a light meal and a brief rest. With the heat of the day full upon them, and an already long day behind them, the talk around the table was desultory.

Finally Jonathan shrugged off the tiredness he had been carrying. "C'mon, sons. Time to git back to work."

He headed out the door, the young men following.

The women, too, struggled up and began clearing away the remains of the meal. McGill and Zeus were the only ones to remain at the table. Reaching for his plate, Lila looked at McGill and gasped. He was ashen with fatigue and worry. Gray circles sagged under his eyes and his face was puffy with exhaustion. His whole body slumped and he seemed unable to move. Unshaven and in rumpled clothes, he looked near collapse.

"My God," Lila whispered, shocked. Although she had sat near him at breakfast and lunch, she had not realized how badly he looked and how exhausted he was.

McGill had not looked up at her comment, but sat staring straight ahead, eyes glazed. "Winthrop," she snapped. "Winthrop!" Dazed, he looked at her. "Snap out of it," she ordered.

With a visible effort, he shook the dullness from him and looked up at her. "Winthrop," she said, brushing her fingers across his cheek, "you can't go on like this. You must get some rest. And soon."

"I can't. Martha—"

"You ain't gonna do Martha any good if you collapse just when she needs you the most. Now you go on out to the wagon where it's quiet and get yourself some sleep."

He started to protest, but she cut him off. "I'll

take no arguments. Now get."

Slowly the wisdom of her advice got through to his clouded brain. "Yes, I suppose you're right." He paused, then said, "But you'll have to take care of Martha for a while."

"Of course I will. Just tell me what to do."

McGill perked up a little. "Every hour, I want you to go in and check her temperature. If it seems to be going back up, come and get me." Lila nodded. "Every two hours, give her as much of the skunk cabbage medicine as she'll take. Usually a few large swallows is enough. If you run out, get Zeus to make you up some more. It's very simple."

"All right, Winthrop. I'll take care of it."

McGill creaked to his feet. "If you see anything out of the ordinary, any changes, fetch me right away."

"I will. Now shoo."

He hesitated. "Get," she ordered.

He nodded and, without further comment, shuffled out the door, plodding slowly toward the wagon.

It was a fine early September day, so Lila accompanied the Whitlock women outside where they all sat on the rickety porch. As usual, they kept their hands busy as they sat and talked. The door to the house remained open, not only to let the stuffy sod building air out, but also to allow them to hear any sound from the sick room. While they sat, Emma repaired some tattered clothes, Grandma Whitlock crocheted, and Rebecca churned butter. Emma asked Lila about McGill.

Lila sat thoughtful for a few minutes, as if debating whether to answer. She did not mind talking about herself, but she was not so sure about revealing the past of her man. She sat silently, snapping beans, thinking.

101

Finally she answered, "What would you like to know?"

"Well," Emma said slowly, "is he really a doctor?"

"Sort of," Lila answered cryptically.

"That ain't much of an answer. A while ago, there was some talk he might not really be a doctor at all. Somethin' Zeus said 'bout his not bein' able to pass medical school."

"He never finished medical college. But it wasn't 'cause he couldn't do it."

"Oh?" Emma's eyes emphasized the question.

"Guess I'd best start back at the beginnin'. I've learned a lot about Winthrop's early years over the past ten years."

While they worked, the sun slid slowly across the high, blue sky, and Lila unfolded her tale. . . .

McGill had been born, Lila estimated, in 1839, but she wasn't certain. She did know, though, that he had been born of fairly well-off parents in the town of Worcester, Massachusetts. He was the oldest of five children—three boys and two girls—and the favorite of his father.

The older McGill was a tinsmith, offering the finest quality craftsmanship, a man proud of the work he did. His customers came from miles around, some even from Boston, to purchase the exactingly detailed work turned out by Josiah McGill. Josiah was also a tinkerer, a hobby he passed on to his firstborn child—Winthrop.

Winthrop's childhood was a happy one. In the thriving town, there were always many playmates around. Because his father was quite well respected, Winthrop received the finest education the small town could offer. He was happy and healthy, full of fun and of laughter, and often the perpetrator of sundry practical jokes. With his intelligence, natural wit and his proclivity for tinkering and gadgetry, he was the natural selection by his peers for pulling practical jokes.

But they sometimes backfired on him. Like the time he rigged up a complicated little cuckoo clock that, when the hour struck twelve, would begin to strike again. The second time, it was rigged to strike thirteen. After the thirteen cuckoos were over, there would be a short pause, just long enough to allow someone to get close enough to the clock to begin investigating its strange behavior. At this time, the clock would douse the prying soul—in this case Winthrop hoped it would be his youngest sister, Mary—with a thick stream of black ink. The ink, too, McGill had prepared especially for the project; it was designed to stain and be unwashable for at least a week. But like many great schemes, it not only failed miserably in its appointed duties, it even got back at its originator.

The scheme started precisely on time. Twelve healthy cuckoos chirped out across the warm, sun-mottled living room. The last one echoed away and, on schedule, thirteen little cuckooing sounds rushed out across the room.

Winthrop could hardly contain his giggles as his inquisitive four-year-old sister skipped across the room to find out what was wrong with the "silly birdie clock."

Eagerly, he said, gasping to fight down the gales of laughter aching to break out, "Go on, Sis. See what's wrong. The clock ain't supposed to do that."

Merrily she climbed up on a chair to see the clock, while eleven-year-old Winthrop waited expectantly, holding his sides against the laughter threatening to erupt. But nothing happened. The young girl looked and looked, but nothing happened. After a few minutes, she climbed down and ran outside to play.

Winthrop, stunned that his carefully thought-out plot had failed, strolled over toward the clock. He, too, climbed on the chair to reach the device. Pulling the clock from its hanger on the wall, he opened the back to check the inside workings. As he did, a heavy, dark gush of liquid spurted out. It missed most of his face, but it splattered over his hair. Before he could move, the inky material dripped down one temple and across his cheek, leaving a thick black streak. Not thinking, he grabbed his shirttail and tried to wipe the offending ooze from his cheek. Too late he realized that it was the special formula he had prepared.

Now, instead of a ragged black streak, his face was adorned with a large ebony smear which he would have to explain to his parents. The explanation was difficult, but soon made. His punishment followed even more swiftly; while everyone sat around the dinner table that night enjoying homemade apple pie, young Winthrop sat across the room all alone, watching the feast.

But that was not to be the end of his punishment. The ink stayed on his face for more than a week. Within twenty-four hours of the incident, his brothers and sisters had spread the word and for as long as the stain lingered on his face he had to live with the humiliation of his unsuccessful stunt.

There were other failures, but there were many successes, too. He managed to accrue a small savings from money he charged his playmates for various devices and gadgets he made for them to use as practical jokes on their friends.

Despite his humorous side, and that part of him that enjoyed the fun and games, he studied hard.

He learned quickly and often easily, and his studious side often caused his teachers to overlook some of his pranks.

Winthrop grew more serious as he grew older, although he kept his wit as well as his love of gadgetry. He enrolled at Harvard College in nearby Cambridge, unsure of what he wanted to do. Before long he was attracted to medicine and switched to Harvard's medical college where he avidly pursued his studies. He was now a fine figure of a young man, moderately tall and angular, if still somewhat ungainly. Although his parents had never achieved great wealth, they were well-off enough to provide him with a fine, though small, wardrobe of quality clothing, to fit his burgeoning image as a doctor.

But ill fortune soon befell him. A series of poorly conceived investments had failed and left the McGills in severe financial straits. Josiah put off telling his son for as long as he could; but finally he could do so no longer. He had a note delivered to Winthrop at the school, telling his son to return home with all possible haste.

When he got to the small frame house, Winthrop was told, bluntly: "We're broke, son." Winthrop was shocked. Though he had known his family did not have unlimited funds, he had not been overly worried about money. There had always been enough.

Winthrop surveyed the sad faces of the family members sitting around the sparsely furnished living room. Most of the furniture was gone, and for the first time he realized that it had been sold off to pay creditors. The faces gave scant color to the dull surroundings, and were haggard and drawn. Grim lips were compressed, showing a prideful display of a willingness to fight.

With a straight back, he stood. In a voice tight with determination, he said, "I must return to Cambridge for my things. I'll return as quickly as I can."

His father's firm resolve seemed to disappear and the older man looked shaken. He reached out to touch his son. "I'm sorry about medical school, son. . . ."

He tried to continue, but Winthrop silenced him. "It's all right, Father. My place is now here with you. What must be done must be done. I am needed here now and there will be no more talk about it. I'll just go and collect my things and then look for work here. I can take up my studies later when we have cleared up this matter."

His mother also dropped her stern-faced determination with which she had first faced her son. She began to weep.

He went to her and grasped her shoulder. "It's all right, Mother. Right now it's important that I be here. You've done so much for me and now it's my turn to help out here. I've not gone so far in medical school that I'll lose much by taking some time off now. After all, it's been only little more than a year since I entered medical school. In a year or so I'll go back. I won't forget what I've learned in that short time."

She looked a little brighter. Winthrop turned to face the rest of his family. "Now," he said, "I want to see a smile on everyone's face. There's no need for looking so beaten down. We've had a spell of hard luck is all. We'll soon have our rightful place in society again. I'll hear no more talk about it."

McGill left, not willing to take the time to sleep. He mounted the tired horse and set out for Harvard.

It was not as difficult as he had at first thought to face the dean and relay the family's misfortunes. He maintained his composure and his pride and was done with it. The dean said he understood and hoped to see McGill return again soon.

"You're one of our finest students, Winthrop," the dean told him. "We would do well to have more like you. You are not too far in your studies of medicine and it should be of little trouble to you to regain your ranking."

"Yes, sir. Thank you. It is my hope to return before too long. God willing."

Stiffly he returned to his small rooms across the quadrangle and packed his meager belongings. He was glad that the young man with whom he shared the rooms was not there. They had been classmates and had spent many hours together, but now McGill was glad to be alone. It had been difficult enough to face the dean. He did not want to face his friend as well. Satchel packed, he took a long last look around his small, sparse room. Briefly he considered leaving a note for his friend, but then decided against it. With a ragged sigh, he walked out.

With even the relatively brief amount of college to his credit, Winthrop had little trouble finding work. Although the pay was lower than he would have liked, it was a big help to the family. Clerking for a mercantile firm was not really suitable, Winthrop often thought, but he persevered and within a year he was in charge of almost all of the company's incoming merchandise.

Along with his good fortune, his family's luck also improved. Winthrop settled in, taking his job seriously, putting off plans to return to the college. He even began courting a young woman, the daughter of a successful town merchant.

But his orderly life was not to last. Before two years had gone by, the Southern states seceded and shots were fired at Northern troops at Fort Sumter, South Carolina.

Winthrop continued with his work, steadfastly trying to ignore the raging war fever that surrounded him. A younger brother, though, did not feel the same and enlisted in the Union Army, proudly marching away with a Massachusetts brigade, his bright blue uniform still stiff from newness.

His pride was short-lived. Winthrop entered the house one evening a few months after his brother had marched off to war. A weeping mother and sisters, and a grim, ashen father greeted him. Woodenly he took the thin, crinkly piece of paper his mother handed him, knowing before he read it, what it was. The words in the letter blurred and floated in front of his vision. He didn't see all the words, but he saw enough; words like *dead, Bull Run, bravery.*

Wordlessly he hugged his mother and then went to his room, the one he had once shared with the youth now dead, to think. There was, he knew, nothing he could do until the funeral was over. But after that . . .

Since coming home, Winthrop had kept quiet about his short medical training career. Only those friends and neighbors who had known him when he had left home knew the story, and they respected his wish for silence.

He had been proud that he never spoke of his training and that he had never taken advantage of it. But now he began to reconsider. He still thought war a hellish thing, but he saw its necessity. And he couldn't help but think that if he had joined along with his brother, he might have been able to use his knowledge and skill to save the boy's life.

He loved medicine and while at school he had often studied far beyond what was required of him. He had a natural propensity for it, too. He was not a doctor, he knew, but he had studied hard and perhaps if he had been with his brother . . .

Never before had he so regretted not having finished his training. He knew he could have done well. But maybe, he thought, it is not too late.

As was his way, he kept his thoughts to himself. The body was soon returned home to Worcester and the funeral shortly after was over. The family went back to life and work, saddened, but knowing they must go on.

The day after the funeral, Winthrop went to see the Union Army recruiter in an old shop on the main street. He started to lie, trying to tell the recruiter he was a doctor. But the military man seemed unconcerned.

"Where'd you get your medical training?"

"Harvard."

"Good. When can you leave?"

McGill was dazed by the rapidity of it all. "Well," he said, "I'll need about two weeks to put my affairs in order."

"Good. Sign here." He shoved a paper across the desk toward McGill, who scrawled his name on the line indicated.

The recruiter, a sergeant, McGil now saw, took the paper and glanced at it. "Good," he said again. "Report to the train station two weeks from today. Eight in the morning."

McGill stood there waiting for more. The sergeant looked up. "That's all, Doctor."

Stunned, McGill turned and retraced his steps to

home. It wasn't until much later, after wading through the gore and blood of innumerable bodies in countless battles, that he realized they would have taken anyone who had any medical training at all.

But as he walked home that day he thought only of how hard it would be to break the news to his family; how difficult it would be to tell his mother that he, too, was going off to war so soon after they had buried young Ezra. It was almost too much for the woman to bear.

All McGill's arguments about going so that he could save lives, not to take them, nor even to lose his own, fell on deaf ears. After two hours of pointless, tear-filled arguing, Winthrop stalked off to his room in desperation.

The next two weeks were the most difficult he had ever spent. Life in the house was uncomfortable now for him, with its stony silence, and stony, unseeing faces.

The night before his scheduled departure, he stepped into the sitting room. The family members looked up at him and then back to their individual tasks. Winthrop walked to the center of the room. When in distress, he spoke even more formally than usual, and he did so now.

"There is something I would like to say, if I might have your attention."

He waited until they had all reluctantly turned their eyes toward him. Then he began. "You all have made my last two weeks here very difficult. It has been hard on all of you, I know, but it has also been very hard on me. However, your anger and your silence will not stop me from doing what I feel I must do.

"You," he said, looking at his parents, "have lost a son and are afraid of losing another. But I have lost a brother, and I do not want anyone, anywhere to lose another."

His father started to interrupt, but Winthrop silenced him. "I can, I think, in my own small way, try to make sure that no one else must endure the agony that we, our family, endured when Ezra was killed."

He paused to draw a breath. "I had hoped you would be able to see that, but in these last two weeks you have not done so. My affairs are in order and, barring death or the end of the war, I will be on that train tomorrow morning."

"But you are not a doctor, son," his father said softly.

Winthrop looked pained, but said with dignity, "I'm more of a doctor than some of them who call themselves so. I can do my share."

Defiantly he looked at his father and then at his mother. He was a little surprised to see her crying. He started to walk back toward his room, but she stood in his path.

She threw her arms around him and wept, mumbling, "We're sorry, son, we're sorry."

His anger dissipated and he hugged her, whispering, "It's all right, Mother." His father, brother and two sisters joined them in the center of the room, hugging each other, the few remaining tears drying in the face of the smiles of closeness.

The family threw an impromptu party for Winthrop that night and in the morning, tired and worried, they escorted him to the train station.

He had no chance to return home during the more than three years that remained of the war, but he wrote frequently. And often, the letters were filled with the pain and anguish he felt at his helplessness when he could not help a young soldier. Other letters, too, reached the family;

letters that offered thanks from young men he did save. And letters containing newspaper accounts that detailed the bravery of one Doctor Winthrop McGill who had, on occasions too numerous to count, waded into the thick of battle to repair the damaged bodies of fighting men.

Winthrop had never considered himself a brave man, and did not so now. His father, however, who once wondered on the young man's backbone, walked proudly through the town almost arrogant about the courage displayed in the face of danger by his favorite child.

He came home when the fighting was all over to a hero's welcome, a sadder, more quiet, more solemn man. But he was more self-assured, too, and proud of what he had done.

The war had brought many changes; including the marriage of his former sweetheart. He had known about it, from letters he had received. Despite his valor during the war, the young woman had not been content to wait for McGill's return, choosing instead the wealthy son of a Boston banker, a man who had the money to pay someone to take his place on the battlefield.

It was the impetus McGill needed to leave Worcester for good.

Although he had forged a considerable reputation for himself as a doctor during the war, too many people in Worcester knew his true circumstances. It was too risky to try to start a practice in his home town.

He had resolved to stay in the medical profession, but he was loath to return to the medical school. He had little money left, having sent most of it home to help the family. There was not enough for him to pay for the expensive schooling. In addition, he felt himself above the young medical students he would encounter there. He had gone through too much, had seen too much horror, too many mangled limbs, and too many dead men to be able to sit in a classroom all day.

No, he thought, he would leave Worcester, go someplace else. Far away. There he could use the reputation he built up as a wartime surgeon. He would be known there only by his military record. He thought that he would return to medical school later, to refresh himself, learn new techniques, and make it official at last.

Packing a light wagon with his few belongings, he bid his family goodbye and headed west. His travels brought him to a small town in southeastern Minnesota. Taking a look around the narrow, dusty streets, he thought he had found the place. Hanging out his freshly painted shingle, he felt only a twinge of guilt at calling himself *Doctor* Winthrop McGill. After all, he thought, I earned the title.

Despite his newfound solemnity, McGill had kept his wit and his manners. It was a combination that quickly won over the townspeople. It also helped that the next nearest doctor was more than a day's ride away.

Business flourished and McGill settled into small-town life easily. He was respected and soon won the eye of a number of eligible young women. His own eye turned toward one of them, the dark-haired daughter of a wagon-shipper.

Even in small towns news arrives, and one day McGill was confronted with the rumor that he was not really a doctor. It was not something he wanted to answer to, but the local civic leaders wanted the question addressed.

With all the pride he could muster, he faced a panel of those prominent individuals. The local saloon had been set up in something that McGill could see clearly resembled a courtroom. The meeting room, as the leaders called it, was packed not only with people from town, but also with many from the outlying farms. They all had a stake in what was going on.

The mayor of the small town, a pompous, self-righteous banker who had grand plans for both himself and the city, rapped for silence. Without further talk, he asked pointedly, "Doctor McGill, is it true that you are not really a doctor? That you are only posing as one?"

McGill stared up at the pudgy, balding man, whom he once considered a friend. Winthrop wondered where the rumor had started, and he wondered why the mayor was making such a show of the matter. But he was tired of living under the facade.

"No, Mr. Mayor," McGill said quietly, "I am not officially a doctor. I have had some medical training, but never finished medical school. I have no degree."

The room erupted into noise, some of the people arguing for McGill's arrest, but far more yelling that it did not matter.

The mayor banged the gavel on the stout wooden table until he was red in the face. Sputtering, he shouted for order, which was long in coming. When it did come, he said, "Have you anything to say for yourself?"

McGill drew himself up to his full height. "Mr. Mayor, I have never tried to deceive anyone. Most of my medical training came from doing. On the field of battle. It is, I believe, the best training a doctor could receive. Yes, even better than spending years in a college, listening to lectures and watching demonstrations. I have, I feel, fulfilled my duties.''

The mayor grunted in annoyance, and said, ''We'll recess this hearing so the panel can deliberate. We must decide what to do with this impersonator.''

McGill knew something was afoot, beyond the obvious. He had been given no real chance to defend himself, and apparently no one was to be allowed to speak on his behalf. So he waited stoically, outwardly calm, raging inside.

While the town leaders were away, the room rode through a noisy debate, occasionally vehement. Through it all, McGill sat quietly, hands folded in his lap, at the front of the room.

The gavel rapped again, and the crowd, almost argued out, quieted quickly. The mayor cleared his throat and then said, ''Mr. McGill.''

Winthrop stood, noting the use of mister instead of doctor. It's been a long time since anyone's called me that, he thought. He faced the panel.

''Mr. McGill, we have decided that it is in the best interests of this town that you immediately cease the practice of medicine here.'' A shocked gasp fluttered through the room as the mayor continued, ''We think it only fair, and in the best interests of the people of this town. It is not necessary that you leave, but you must stop practicing medicine here. We are sure you can find another suitable position.''

''But, Mr. Mayor,'' McGill interjected.

''Please, sir. Allow me to finish,'' the mayor shot out. ''As I said, we think we are being fair. There are laws in this town that prohibit unqualified people from posing as doctors. They are made to protect the people. We could have prosecuted you, but we don't think that'll be necessary.''

McGill nodded glumly.

"Have you anything further to say for yourself?"

McGill just shook his head. As usual, when things were gloomy for him, he reverted to introspection, keeping his thoughts to himself.

"Then I declare this meeting over." The mayor rapped his gavel with finality, and people began filing out.

McGill held his head high as he pushed through the crowd of shouting people. They followed him into the streets and along them to his spacious frame house, where they remained outside, shouting.

A rap on the back door got his attention and he opened it to let his fiancee in. "You've drawn quite a crowd out front," she said uneasily.

"Yes, it seems I have."

They stood facing each other. "I'm sorry," he said.

"And I am too."

He looked at her in surprise. "Why?"

She looked at the floor. "I'm afraid I won't be able to marry you now, after all this. It's too—"

"I understand," he said, turning away.

She looked up. "Maybe you don't. I can't marry you and go out there to face those people every day. I've known most of them all my life. It would be too humiliating."

"I see." He decided to try one last time. "We could move away where no one would know."

"I would know. And I would not want to live with the shame. Besides, if they found you out here, they could find you out anywhere. It could happen all over again."

"I understand," he said again.

"You're not angry with me?"

He was amazed at her audacity, but kept it to
116

himself. "No," he said curtly. "But I think you'd best go."

She started for the door, then hesitated, looking back at him. But he had turned away again, lost in his thoughts. She left quietly, out the back door.

Once again McGill packed his belongings in the old carriage, hitched up the single sorrel horse and rode out. As he headed down the main street, the town stared at him. Some of the people watched in contempt, but most looked on in sadness. He still wondered how they had found out, but the reason soon became at least partially clear. In one of the windows of the small hotel he spotted a familiar face; the face of a not-very-well-liked former Harvard schoolmate.

While at Harvard the man behind the face had antagonized McGill unmercifully. The wealthy scion of an old Boston family, William Strathington had constantly berated McGill for his poor upbringing. He had often pointed out McGill's lack of breeding, or so Strathington called it. McGill had taken heart, though, in knowing that he was not the only one who suffered at the hands, and mouth, of William Strathington.

Past the edge of town, McGill saw a trusted friend, one of the many who wanted McGill to stay. McGill pulled the horse to a stop. "Howdy, Jake."

"Howdy, Doc. I figgered you'd be leavin', so I thought to stop you and let you know what happened. Less'n you know already."

"Nope, Jake. Don't know. Reckon I know who's responsible. But I don't know why or how."

"Well, then, Doc, I'll just tell you," Jake said, climbing up next to McGill. "Drive on a ways." McGill started and Jake said, "Seems there's a feller here who says he knew you back in doctorin'

117

school.''

"I thought as much," McGill nodded. "His name's William Strathington.''

"Yep. That's the name he gave. Seems he knew you and knew you never did finish up at doctorin' school. From what I hear, his pa threw him out of that big fancy house they got back to Boston, I believe it was, and told him to make somethin' of himself. So, he got the idee he wanted to start doctorin' here and you was in the way.''

"Why in tarnation would he want to open up a practice here? With all the money his family's got.''

"That he has. From what I heard, his pa didn't throw him out of the house broke. From what people been sayin' he tried practicin' in New York, then Philadelphia. But it seems he ain't much of a doctor and nobody was comin' to see him.''

"Still, why here?''

"From what's been said, he thinks this area's gonna be growin' a heap before too long and he wants to be the only doc around when it happens. Out here, folks ain't got as much schoolin' as they do some places back east, so's they don't often know a bad doc when they see one. All they know is he's got schoolin' and he's a doc so he must be all right.

"Anyway, this feller met the mayor and knew he had himself somebody he could use for his own purposes. All he did was tell the mayor and his sidekicks he'd build 'em a hospital right here and give 'em all some money come election time if they'd just get rid of you.''

"I see.''

"Yep. It warn't hard. He knowed you in school and he did some checkin' to find out you never did finish. That, some fast talkin', and the mayor's

118

greed was all he needed."

McGill just shook his head sadly, while Jake continued, "It's a shame you thought to be leavin', Doc. Most of us 'round here'd sure like for you to stick around."

"I can't do that."

"Sure you can. Just move your practice on over to Shakopee. Everybody'll be glad to travel a little ways to see you. Most of us trust you, Doc, and we ain't none too happy with what that feller's done to you."

"I'm obliged for the offer, Jake. But I reckon I got to be movin' on. I'd only bring trouble stayin' on around here."

"Reckon you're right, Doc. But we'll miss you just the same. Well, why'n't you let me off right here, then. I can mosey on across the field to the house."

McGill stopped the carriage and Jake hopped down. He faced McGill and held out his hand. They shook. "Well, Doc, best of luck to you."

"Thanks, Jake. Same to you."

With soft clucking noises, McGill headed the sorrel away from the old farmer. He traveled the Middle West not knowing what to do with himself. He considered settling down in another small town to start up a medical practice again, but he was too weary for that now. So he roamed.

Until the day he saw a traveling medicine-show wagon. It was in a typical Mississippi River town, far to the north, where he saw the crowd. He strolled over to see what the spectacle was and became enthralled.

Later that day he thought hard about it. He had noticed the streams of voyagers bound for the limitless expanse of the West and thought he could make his fortune there. He also thought back on how haggard and poor the traveling medicine man had looked. Then it dawned on him—the man wasn't making any money because the people here were too used to charlatans and tricksters. But out West . . .

That night he found the man in a local saloon, half in his cups. He introduced himself and they talked until the early hours and until they were both quite drunk.

With a pounding head, McGill pulled out with the old man, heading for the next town. It was then that he began learning the tricks of the trade. Within months, he had learned all the old man could teach him.

"Listen, Enos," he said one night while they camped on a river bank in Illinois. "You're gettin' a little too old for all this travelin' around. Wouldn't you like to settle down somewhere?"

"Well, I've thought of it plenty, but I don't know's if I can afford it. And I don't know if I'd be very happy tied down to one place. I like travelin'."

"But you're not makin' any money this way."

"Got somethin' in mind?"

"I thought if we'd cross the Mississippi and headed out west, maybe up the Missouri, we could do a lot better. Towns're a lot farther apart than they are here and those folks don't get to see somethin' like this too often. They'd be happy to get some company once in a while, I'd say. Least most of them would."

"I don't like travelin' that much," Enos snorted. He glanced over at McGill's perplexed face. "Got somethin' else on your mind, Winthrop?"

"Well, Enos, I didn't really want to say it."

"Go on ahead, son."

"Well, I thought you might like to sell me your wagon and supplies. Then you could retire to some place where you want and live out the rest of your days in peace."

"I'll have to do some thinkin' on that one."

"Take your time, Enos. I'm in no hurry."

As usual, Enos was up earliest and had breakfast cooking. McGill hunkered up to the fire, trying to ward off the early-morning chill. They grunted greetings and Enos said, "You got yourself a deal."

He handed the stunned McGill a steaming cup of coffee.

Still half asleep, McGill said, "What?"

"All we gotta do is agree to a price," Enos said happily.

Recognition dawned on McGill. "You mean it?"

"Sure do. You was right. I'm gettin' a mite too old for all this bouncin' 'round these parts. Towns're gettin' real civilized and they're startin' to run folks like me outta town more and more often. It ain't like the old days. Headin' west is the way to do it, I reckon. But I ain't got the stamina for it. I ain't hankerin' to face down no hostile redskins, nor face maybe travelin' weeks all by my lonesome between towns. Yep, you was right. It's time for me to settle down."

A week later McGill dropped Enos off back in Indiana where he had a married daughter. Then he turned the team of horses leading his newly purchased wagon toward the setting sun.

With a new life facing him, McGill gave up all thoughts of returning to medical school. He was too soured by past events. And he thought himself too old now for that. This was, he knew, what he would do now; ride through the open West, selling

121

a few wares and offering his "medicine" along the way.

He arrived in St. Louis and, using most of the precious few dollars he had left, bought a new cover for the old wagon. The bright white canvas was festooned with his name and new occupation in gleaming red, gold and blue letters.

He headed north, catching a ferry across the Mississippi near St. Charles, Missouri, and then began following the river that gave the state its name. He had no particular direction. He just drifted along, sometimes joining a wagon train for safety, at other times risking his life detouring across the emptiness of the prairie that held little but animals and often-hostile Indians.

Though infrequent, the encounters with the formidable Plains tribes were frightening. But by passing out small goods and dispensing some medical care, he was generally left alone to go his own way. And from them, he learned some of their secrets for herbal medicine. But he would learn more of that from the little man he would befriend in later days.

Chapter 9

"It's about time you was checkin' Martha's temperature, now ain't it?" the old voice cackled.

Lila sat up, instantly erect. She had been absorbed in telling the Whitlocks of McGill's life and was lost in her own thoughts. She looked over at Elizabeth. The old lady was holding out an old, beat-up pocket watch so Lila could see the time.

The watch, scratched and dented, was a legacy from her late husband and she cherished it.

"Oh my," Lila fluttered. "I completely forgot the time. Winthrop will be so disappointed in me."

"Hush up, girl," Grandma Whitlock said, lighting her pipe. "You ain't but a few minutes past the time and them few minutes ain't gonna make the least bit of difference. 'Sides," she laughed, "I ain't about to tell your doctor man."

She chuckled a bit and winked at Lila, who smiled. "Thanks. I'll be right back. Soon's I tend to Martha."

While she was gone, the other women took the time to take on other chores, grateful for the small breeze that cooled them.

When Lila returned, they were again busy; all that is except the old woman. It seemed to be her place to just sit and pass judgment on people, places and things, and to settle disputes and dole out advice, whether wanted or not.

Lila looked over at the dozing old woman and thought of the adventures old Elizabeth must have had in her long life.

She smiled and asked, "Grandma Elizabeth, how'd you come to be way out here?"

The eyes popped open. "Well, child, it's been a long road with a sight of country between." She looked back into her memory, checking her facts before telling the attentive Lila.

She had been born in Kentucky about 1805, as best she could figure it and, though she didn't voice it, was a true pioneer woman. Kentucky was still a frontier when she was born, but it was filling up fast. Her parents, among the earliest settlers to drift into the new territory across the Cumberland Gap, felt the pressure of the increasing population and, when Elizabeth was ten, headed west.

First they had settled in Ohio, then Indiana, and then Illinois. She was married there, at age eighteen, to a man five years older and who had as much wanderlust in his heart as had her father. With her new husband, she set out for Missouri, a place still raw. The youngest of twelve children, she was the last to leave home.

Times were hard as she and her husband moved around, usually following the river. Most of the time, Jeremiah Whitlock was off on the river, a roustabout for one of the many steamers side-wheeling their way between New Orleans and the blossoming city of St. Louis.

When the Civil War came, Jeremiah was too old for the fighting. But they watched four of their sons go off to war. Only their youngest, Jonathan, barely sixteen when the war began, remained at home to help.

Not wanting to choose up sides, Jeremiah packed up his wife, Jonathan and three daughters into a wagon and pulled up stakes. They tried settling in Kansas first, but tension there was even as great as it had been in Missouri, so they moved north, following the Mississippi for mile after mile. Then they angled off west along the Minnesota River. It was there that they stopped.

Life went on and the war ended. Only one of the four sons they had seen go marching off returned. He soon married and left for the Southwest to make his fortune supplying goods to the miners flocking to the area and to the soldiers in the many forts.

Jonathan, too had grown, and married a local farm girl named Emma Washburn in 1865, only a month after the war ended.

Old Jeremiah had died less than a year after Jonathan's wedding, and the farm was failing.

Jonathan, now the head of the family, packed his wife, newborn son, and mother, with all the belongings they could carry, into an old wagon.

They settled in Colorado, but were driven out, almost losing their lives, when the Southern Cheyennes and the Arapahoes took to raiding farms. It was only two years since Black Kettle's band was destroyed on the banks of Sand Creek and the Cheyennes were still on the prowl.

They moved on to the area now known as Wyoming, and there they settled for good. Although their first son had died on the trip, the Whitlocks had quickly started a family with another son. A first daughter died in infancy, but the other three children they produced were fine and healthy.

So Elizabeth sat now, near eighty, rocking and passing on her judgments, telling tales and giving advice. And, yes, rocking some more. Always rocking, usually with the old corn-cob pipe stuck between almost toothless gums.

Having always lived on a frontier, or the fringe of one, she was less than severe when morals were overlooked and she was not as quick as some to condemn others. She regretted many of the changes she saw coming, but knew she could do little about them. She had lived many years, and they had been full ones, earning her the right to do little more than she did.

Something the old lady had said had caught Lila's attention. She, too, knew something more than just worry about his daughter was wearing heavily on Jonathan. Here, she thought, might be a clue. But she wondered how to bring it up.

"It must've been terrible losing your grandkids," she finally said. And, turning to Emma, she added, "And you your young 'uns."

"Happens, I reckon," Elizabeth said. "Seen it many a time in my day."

But Emma's eyes had misted over. Softly, she said, "You should know how it feels, after what happened to your child."

Lila smiled softly and reached over to pat Emma's hand. "Yes, Emma, I know." She paused and then said, "How'd it happen?"

Emma started to protest, but stopped. It had been so many years ago now that the pain, while still there, had faded considerably. It would be all right to talk about it now—especially to this woman, who shared the same loss.

Emma took a deep breath and said, "The first was the hardest, especially for Jonathan. It was on the trip out here like Grandma Whitlock said. It was a hard trip and more'n once I didn't reckon we'd make it. It was plumb hot the whole time; hotter'n I ever seen it.

"That was bad enough, but if'n that was the only problem, we might've still made out all right. Water was plumb scarce, but there was just 'bout enough. Then we was attacked by Sioux just after crossin' the Missouri."

"You never told me that, Ma," Rebecca interjected.

"Didn't see no reason to."

"Was that how the baby died, Ma? Killed by Injuns?"

"No. The Injuns only killed one of the men. Older feller as I recall, but I can't remember his name. A few others was hurt. The real damage was done when them Injuns run off most of the cattle we had for food and for milk for the younkers. And, with all the fightin' goin' on, some of the wagons caught fire. When it was all over, we was right low on food."

"What about huntin'?" Lila asked. "There should've been at least a few fellers that could've bagged some game."

"Wasn't much game to be found," Emma said. "Reckon it was so hot and had been for such a spell that most of the game must've moved on lookin' for fresh grass and some water. Some of the men managed to bring in an old buffalo or a elk, or a few rabbits once in a while. But there was just too many mouths to feed and the meat never went none too far."

She paused to put down her finished work and pick up another chore. "We was too far out to turn back, though a few folks did so. Most of us decided to keep pushin' on ahead. Few days later little Elijah took sick. There was a doctor along with us, but he said there wasn't nothin' he could do for us."

"Did he even try to do anything?" Lila asked.

"No. Just said that there was no hope less'n we got more food and milk. Blamed it on me sorta. Said if'n I had ate better and drank more milk, I could produce enough milk for the baby. He told me the baby got sick 'cause I wasn't makin' enough milk."

"But there was no food and the cattle was all took by them redskins," Becky shot out, eyes flashing with anger.

"I know that, child," Emma said softly, "though it was hard for me then. Your pa, though, he knew it wasn't my doin's. Your pa tried to force that old doctor into doin' somethin', but wasn't much he could do, I reckon."

Lila's eyes widened a bit at the last, but she kept it hidden from the others.

"Anyways," Emma continued softly, "Elijah died 'bout a week later."

Lila bit her tongue, cutting back the words of rebuke that ached for release. She wanted so very badly to revile the man who had called himself a doctor, the man who had let the child die through laziness or ineptitude or maybe fear. But to do so would reopen the box of fear and frustration about Martha's health and McGill's inability to help the girl.

So she kept silent on it, asking, "What about the other child?"

"That was Amanda, the first daughter," Emma said. "It was after we come here from Colorado." She looked sad again, and pointed out to a lonely tombstone standing starkly against the horizon across the stream on the upper bank. "She's buried right over there."

She looked back to Lila. "After Elijah died, I borned Charles. Then came Amanda. She was less'n a year old when she took sick with fever and her neck got all swole up. Soon's it happened, Jonathan lit out for the Montana territory. It was the closest place we knew of what had a doctor. But it was too far."

Emma paused to dab at the corners of her eyes with her apron. Taking a deep breath, she continued, "Jonathan made the trip in three days, though it usually takes five. His horse was near spent so Jonathan traded it for a fresh one. But the doctor had took that night to likker hisself up. It wasn't a usual thing from what folks said, but he was in no condition for travelin'.

"Jonathan got him sobered up the next mornin' and they left right out. Jonathan said more'n once he had to put a gun to the doctor to keep him movin'. They got back here more'n a week after Jonathan left, but by then it was too late."

"Amanda had died?" Becky asked.

"No, she was still holdin' on when they got here. But she was so far gone there wasn't nothin' the doctor could do. Lord knows, he tried, though. He really did. We kept on thinkin' that she could've been saved if'n only the doctor had been closer."

"It's really sad," Lila said.

Emma just nodded, and Lila decided it was time to speak up. "That why Jonathan don't take kindly to doctors?" she asked.

Emma's eyes widened in surprise. "What makes you think that? He's not—" Her lips clamped shut. Then she dropped her eyes in embarrassment. "Yes," she said softly. "It was bad enough when Elijah died, but when Amanda's time came, Jonathan took a real distrust to doctors. He just can't hold reliance in 'em anymore."

Lila nodded. "I'd wondered why he got so wild the other day. He don't seem to be that way regular-like."

"He ain't. But then again, ain't none of the young 'uns we got now ever been this sick."

"I can understand how you and Jonathan feel, Emma. I've lost a younker of my own. But killin' us ain't gonna make your daughter well. And," she added pointedly, "it won't bring her back if she don't get well."

"I know," Emma mumbled. "I don't reckon he'd really kill nobody. He ain't no murderer."

"I don't say he is. But he was almighty close to puttin' a bullet in Zeus the other day. If you hadn't of stopped him, we'd have buried poor little Zeus."

"Well I did stop him, and I'll keep on stoppin' him as long as I can."

"I do hope so, 'cause if Jonathan kills Zeus or me, Winthrop won't do nothin' to help you. He's doin' the best he can."

"I know. If'n only Martha'd get better." Then she remembered. "Lila, I plumb forgot. We got to talkin' so quick after you come back, you never did say how Martha's doin'."

"She's got no real fever and she seems to be restin' some easier. She looks to be purty comfortable, though she's still coughin' quite a bit."

"That's good," Rebecca said eagerly. "She must be gettin' better if she ain't got no fever."

"I wouldn't go so far as to say that just yet," Lila said, smiling down at the girl. "But we can hope."

She sat. "How about if I take over that churnin' from you, Becky? Then you can help your ma with the darnin'."

"Okay." She passed over the heavy wooden churn and cleaned her hands on a piece of cloth. Then she got the sewing materials and started repairing a shirt.

Lila fell to working the churning handle slowly through the heavy cream. They all sat silent, engrossed in their work and listening to the sleepy sounds of late summer.

Finally Emma broke the silence. "Your Doctor McGill sure has been around some, ain't he?"

"That he has," Lila smiled. "He's just about seen everything there is to see. And there's been some sights, too. He saw the first subway in New York and—"

"The first what?" Rebecca interrupted.

"Subway. Winthrop told me they call it a pneumatic subway system. It's a big tunnel underground and these things like railroad cars go whizzin' along through them.

"You're just joshin' us," Rebecca snorted. She wasn't about to let these educated folks think she could be fooled so easily. She couldn't be made a fool of.

Lila laughed. "No, I ain't joshin' you. It's for real. I ain't ever seen it myself, but I've seen photo pictures of it and I trust Winthrop not to tell me tall tales."

Rebecca looked reluctant to believe her, but let it go.

Trying to gain a little more acceptance in the girl's eyes, Lila said, "He was there at Promontory Point, too. When they drove in the golden spike that linked the East and the West for all time. I 'member him tellin' me about it, how it was in Utah that mornin', with all the noise and confusion. People came from miles and miles and government folks came all the way from Washington. Wish I had been there with him, but that was a ways before we met up."

They fell back into silence again, before Emma asked, "How'd Doctor McGill meet Zeus? He seems such an odd little feller."

"He is that," Lila smiled. She pumped at the churn, thinking back on what she knew of the midget.

"Come to think of it," Lila mused, "it was right about the time of the ceremony down there in Utah that they met up. Yes, 1869. It was a little later that year. Late summer. . . ."

McGill had drifted down from Utah, through Arizona Territory and east across the New Mexico Territory until he passed in Texas. He did well in El Paso and thought he'd try his luck into San Antonio, a flourishing town, still wild and rambunctious.

The old wagon clattered down the dusty street past the Alamo, and weaved along the banks of the

131

slow-moving river that gave the city its name.

It was McGill's first trip to the glittering oasis surrounded by the small rolling hills in the midst of the flatness, and he was pleased with its soft, earth-brown friendliness. An American city for the past twenty years or so, it retained much of its earlier Mexican heritage. As he clopped down the main thoroughfare, McGill wondered at the unusual amount of bustle going on in the town's business district. It was siesta time and normally the town would be quiet.

Pulling up at a livery stable, he asked about a hotel. Leaving the horses and wagon with the stable man, McGill walked slowly toward the inn, taking in the sights and sounds of the city.

A tall, slender Mexican greeted him at the door with a pleasant, "Welcome, señor."

"I'd like a room for a few days," McGill said, knocking the dust from his worn black hat. "Don't know how long exactly, but at least two days."

"Certainly, señor."

McGill looked around at the once-lavish hotel. Although still grand, it had lost much of its former elegance. "By the way," McGill asked, "what's all the commotion about?"

"A circus has come to town, señor." He grinned widely. "Si, a circus. With animals and silly men in costumes and pretty señoritas." He grinned even more widely. "Everyone in town will be there, señor."

"Certainly sounds like a good time," McGill smiled. "I may even go myself." He collected his key and clumped up the stairs thinking how nice it would be to be entertained by someone instead of having to do the entertaining. Yes, I will go, he thought.

After freshening up, he walked over to the stable

and checked on his rig. Then he strolled down the street letting the sights, smells and sounds of the city envelop him. He enjoyed them all despite the dust and the stench of sewage and rotting meat. McGill was too full of excitement to rest, although his long journeys had tired him, so he continued to casually stroll along the almost deserted streets.

He arrived back at the hotel tired from his walk, now ready for a nap. Rested, he walked over to buy a ticket for that night's performance. His expectation rose with the swelling excitement of the city and, when the hour arrived, he joined the festive throng of people flocking to the arena. And it was every bit as much fun as he had thought it would be.

One particular attraction had caught his attention. A funny, little man who juggled and played music and made jokes, most of them rather vulgar. He also performed stunts of many kinds in between the main acts. The little man had a sharp wit and his pointedly ribald jokes were a hit with the earthy audience, and his juggling was superb, as was his music.

Winthrop attended the performances every night, intently watching the midget. The night before the circus was to leave town, McGill weaved his way through the crowds after the show to the rear area where the performers had their quarters.

Already the burly men were tearing down equipment and loading it on wagons for the trip to the next town. Not knowing where to look, he wandered aimlessly, trying to stay out of the way of the sweating, swearing men. A boisterous confrontation caught his attention and he drew nearer.

"Why you little hornswaggler," McGill heard a burly cowboy holler. "I'll tear you limb from limb!"

A small figure darted out of the crowd, shouting, "You're gonna have to catch me first, you tinhorn."

Not looking where he was going, the midget bumped into McGill, who grabbed him and held tight. "Hold on a minute."

"Let me go," the little man squealed. "That big galoot's gonna kill me."

"No he's not," McGill assured him. "Just wait right here."

By now the big cowboy was in front of McGill. "What seems to be the problem here?" McGill asked calmly.

"That little varmint stole a jug of my best sippin' whiskey, and I ain't gonna let him get away with it."

"Now hold on," McGill said calmly despite the cowboy's towering menace. "No need to get yourself all riled up." He pulled a few coins from his pocket and handed them to the cowboy. "Here, this should cover it. Go and get yourself another bottle."

The cowboy's eyes gleamed at the unexpected largesse. "But what about him?" he asked, pointing to the midget.

"I'll take care of him. You got what you wanted, so why don't you just drift on over to the saloon."

The cowboy and his cronies drifted away, heading for the saloon. The little man looked up at McGill when they had left. "That was a close one," he said. "Be seein' you."

McGill grabbed him by the collar. "Just hold on a minute there, young fellow. I'd like to have a little chat with you."

The midget tried to wriggle out of the grasp, but to no avail. "What for?"

"Just about things. How about we get us some-

134

thing to eat and a few drinks?"

"You payin'?"

"Of course."

"Okay then. Let's go."

McGill still held his collar. "Sure you won't try'n make a getaway?"

"Why sure. Now let me go."

McGill released him. They walked in silence, McGill slowing his strides to match the tiny steps taken by the midget.

When they were seated in the dining room of the hotel, McGill finally asked, "What's your name?"

"Zeus."

"Zeus what?"

"Just Zeus." He looked angry at the question, but then softened. "It's the only name I ever had. Just Zeus. Never had a last name. Or even a proper first one."

"Well then, Zeus will do."

They ate in silence for some time, McGill looking over his new acquaintance. Zeus, for his part, cast occasional furtive glances at McGill while wolfing down large bites of steak and potatoes.

"Slow down," McGill said. "There's more where that came from. When's the last time you ate anyway?"

"Yesterday, I guess. I don't eat too regular."

"I reckoned." A pause. "How do they treat you over there?" McGill asked, nodding toward the circus grounds.

"Fine," Zeus said smoothly. "Couldn't be better."

"I think you're lyin' to me."

"How do you think they treat me?" Zeus snapped. "Look at me. I'm a damned freak. That's all those galoots over yonder know and so that's the way they treat me."

135

"Why don't you get out? Leave the circus."

Zeus looked up in amazement. "And just what would I do outside the circus?"

"Come with me," McGill said simply.

"And do what? Be a parlor maid to some Eastern dandy that shouldn't be out here in the first place?"

"What makes you think I'm an Eastern dandy?" McGill was smiling, amused at the little man's assumption.

"Look in a mirror." Zeus wiped his hands on his shirt front. "And listen to yourself talk. It's funny."

McGill laughed. "You think that just because someone speaks properly, dresses well and has a little schoolin' he's a dandy?"

"Well ain't they?"

"Not exactly. I, for example, was born and educated in the East. Harvard to be exact. But I served as a doctor in the Civil War. I am not unused to hardship."

"Oh, so you're a doctor, are you? Is that why you want me along? To take me apart and see what makes me what I am?"

McGill vehemently shook his head. "No. No, you have me all wrong. I'm not exactly a doctor." He paused. "It's rather difficult to explain. Finished?"

Zeus nodded and McGill said, "Good. Then come with me. There's something I want to show you."

They strolled down the street, McGill again matching his pace to that of the midget. They turned into the livery stable and McGill pointed across the yard. There sat the old, hulking wagon.

McGill reached down and lifted Zeus, placing him on the top rail of the split fence. "Now what

136

do you say, Zeus?"

"What do you expect me to do?"

"Same as you've been doing for the circus."

"What's my cut?"

"I think we can work out an equitable arrangement."

Zeus stared across the yard, an almost wistful look on his face. Finally he smiled. "When do we leave?"

"Soon's you're ready."

"Then let's go. It won't take me long to get my gear together."

McGill helped him down and they started back down the dusty street. Zeus set a much faster pace than he had earlier. They stopped at the circus grounds and Zeus slipped into a tent. He scurried and scrounged, flinging things into a trunk that was nearly as large as he.

Finished packing, he started dragging the trunk out of the tent. "That's quite a load you got there," McGill said.

"I know," Zeus puffed.

"You sure you only have your own things in there?"

"Yep." His face was turning red.

McGill laughed. "Put it down. We'll get someone else to carry it." Looking around, he spotted a large boy lounging against a circus wagon. McGill called him over. Giving the youth some coins, he told him to carry Zeus's trunk over to the livery stable and tell the man there to hitch up the wagon.

The boy looked at the coins in his hand, his eyes gleaming. "Sure, mister." He started to hoist the trunk, but McGill stopped him.

"When you get done at the livery stable, stop by the hotel. I have some things there you can take to the wagon for me."

"Yes, sir." Trunk on shoulder, the youth hurried off.

McGill packed his things and paid the hotel owner, and was long finished when the boy returned. He hurried off ahead of McGill and Zeus.

McGill settled his bill at the stable and helped Zeus onto the wagon seat. "Ready to go?"

"It ain't no time for dawdlin'."

McGill clicked the horses forward up the street. As they passed the Alamo, Zeus looked back toward the colored tents that still stood. He continued to watch, eyes wary, but McGill could see him grow easier with each step they took away from the city.

In bits and pieces over the next few years, McGill learned about the little man's tortured past.

He had been taken, without love or ceremony, to an orphanage by his parents because of his abnormality. In his rare moments of candor, Zeus would relate the alienation he felt and the cruelty he suffered at the hands of the other children at the orphanage. And, yes, from those who ran the house, too. Bitterly he recounted the mental torture by those less-than-kindly folks, the master and mistress he came to hate with a soul-warping ire. It was mental torture that twisted his otherwise normal sense of propriety and decency.

McGill pitied Zeus when he heard these tales, knowing that it must have been very difficult for the little man. And he would treat Zeus more kindly than usual after one of the midget's soul-baring sessions.

It was on these days, when McGill went out of his way to be nice to Zeus, that the midget took advantage of him, showing some of the cruelty he had inherited from his tormentors at the orphanage. But McGill took it in good humor, and after a while, it became a game with them—a badinage of gentle insults.

McGill's kindness did take its toll, and Zeus became fiercely protective of his only friend. He often silently berated himself when he took advantage of the kindly McGill, knowing he had done it without thinking, but also realizing he had hurt his friend and benefactor.

It was the cruelty of the orphanage that forced Zeus to run away from it when he was fourteen, only to find his lot was worse than that of the normal runaway. The outside world was even more hostile than the orphanage had been. He was humiliated, abused and set upon by most of the people he met. This unfriendliness served to shape his own hostile personality even more. He attacked the big people even as they were attacking him. They could not understand this strange little man and, after a while, he refused to try to understand them.

He was near starvation when the circus stopped in New Orleans, a city he had drifted to thinking the free-wheeling port city would find him more acceptable. It did not and he was beginning to think he would die from hunger. Trying to steal food from the open shops got harder and harder, particularly since the shopkeepers, after catching him at it a few times, were wary of him. He snuck into the large circus area, thinking he could find a new market for his petty thievery and pickpocketing. But a brawny guard grabbed him and carried the squealing Zeus off to face the owner of the show.

"Well, I'll be damned," the owner said when Zeus was brought before him. "A real live midget.''

"I caught him sneakin' in, Mr. Simpson," the guard reported.

"Broke?" Simpson asked.

Zeus nodded, surly, on the defensive.

Simpson looked him over. "We been lookin' for someone like you. Ever think of joinin' the circus?"

"Not really."

"I reckon you ought to. Can you do anythin'?"

"Pick pockets," Zeus said sarcastically. But he saw Simpson's face go stern and quickly added, "I can play music and juggle some."

"What can you play?"

"Harmonica, squeezebox. Some fiddle." He now saw a little salvation in his musical talents. It was one of the few worthwhile things the orphanage had taught him, and he had learned it well. It had been his only escape as a child.

While on the road he had sometimes made money by playing on street corners and in saloons with instruments he had stolen, found or made. But they were always lost or broken, or sold, and he would go back to picking pockets, begging or theft.

He had also learned to juggle while he was on his own. It was in Pittsburgh when he first saw a circus, not long after he had left the orphanage. The juggler fascinated him, and he took it up, practicing when he could with whatever he could find, often with rocks or pilfered eggs.

Simpson's voice startled him. "I'll overlook this little incident, Zeus. If you decide to join us. How 'bout it?"

"Ain't got much choice, do I?"

"Nope."

"Then I accept," Zeus said graciously, bowing.

140

And so he joined the circus. But it was not as idyllic as he might have hoped. Many of the other performers disliked him because of his thieving ways and his ill humor.

The mutual dislike and distrust was wearing on him and as soon as he had an opportunity he ran off. He snuck aboard a ferry in St. Louis and then headed out across the plains, alone.

Heedless of the danger, not really knowing if the accounts of hostile Indians were real and not really caring, he pushed his stubby legs across the wide emptiness. When he was lucky, he found food, shelter and a taste of safety with a family or wagon train heading west.

When he wasn't so lucky, he sweltered or froze as the weather saw fit to treat him. He was drenched, pounded with hailstones, and fought the almost ceaseless wind. And the constant walking punished his short arms and legs. For weeks he wandered, reveling as much as he could in the lonely peacefulness he felt. Until the day he thought his luck had run out.

A band of roving Sioux caught him flatfooted. With shrieks and howls, the fiercely painted warriors, armed and scowling, reined their horses in a lathered frenzy around the little man. Zeus stood frozen, frightened like he had never been before. He had heard the stories about these red devils and how they treated captives. But he hadn't really believed them; he had always thought them the overactive imaginings of timid souls. But confronted with the reality of a dozen caterwauling, greasy savages, as he saw them, his doubts fled. Unable to speak or protest, he stood, face blank, as one of the Indians prodded him gently with an iron-tipped war lance.

The warriors were quiet now, staring at him with

coal-black eyes. Zeus expected to die; he had the terrible feeling that his short, pain-packed life was about to end. And he realized that he did not want to die. There was time yet, he knew, to live and to do and to be.

But still the Indians stared. Zeus could stand it no longer. "C'mon, git it over with, you red heathens!"

The Indians burst into excited jabbering Zeus couldn't understand. They argued and gesticulated wildly. Zeus had the feeling that some of the warriors wanted to kill him on the spot and the others wanted to wait.

Their talk stopped with a final, forceful epithet from the one who seemed to be leading the small band. With a brawny left arm, that same one reached down and grabbed Zeus by the back of his tattered shirt and hoisted him up and across the horse's neck. With a piercing shriek, he wheeled his horse and raced off, the others following wildly behind. They roared into the Sioux camp in a swirl of color and dust. The village was noisy, dirty and, despite the danger Zeus felt, exciting. The warriors jammed to a stop in front of a large, painted tipi. A gaunt, ancient Indian stood in front. Seams creased his face giving him the appearance of weathered bark. His long, plaited hair, decorated with otter skin, was mostly white. The Indian holding Zeus flung the midget into a heap at the feet of the old man. Zeus scrambled upright, but was afraid to move further.

The Sioux talked among themselves and Zeus guessed they were discussing his fate. The palaver ended abruptly and with a grunt, the old man hauled Zeus inside the tipi.

Zeus was astouned at its size. Despite a tangy aroma of smoke, grease, and unwashed bodies, it seemed comfortable. The Indian made Zeus sit and then had him fed. The midget ate with relish, fearing it might be his last meal.

But he was wrong. The old Indian meant no harm. Walking Eagle, as Zeus learned to call him, was the band's medicine man. The men of the war party had turned Zeus over to him because they thought the little man touched by the Great Spirit. They had never seen a man such as Zeus before and, because of his fearlessness, thought he was in some way special. So they had brought him to Walking Eagle.

Now Walking Eagle began teaching Zeus the ways of the Sioux.

Zeus learned fast, learning the language and many of the customs quickly. And once he had a grasp of the language, he began learning the ways of medicine from the old man. He learned the songs to be sung and the prayers to be prayed. He learned the dances and the ways of making medicine bundles for the warriors to carry for protection. He learned, too, of the root medicine; the different roots, herbs and berries to use in curing sickness. He learned which ones to use for what ailments and how they were to be made.

It was the happiest time of his life and he enjoyed each minute of it. Until Walking Eagle died.

Many of the warriors distrusted the funny little white man who made medicine for them. And Bear Claw, grandson of old Walking Eagle, hoped to take over as the band's medicine man and spiritual leader.

Zeus decided it was time to leave the Sioux. With a few warrior friends he packed a few small items in a parfleche bag—some herbs and roots mostly—and was escorted out by the warriors he called his friends. He traveled aimlessly over the prairie, this time on horseback and with head held high. Many of the other tribes had heard of this tiny white man of medicine and even the enemies of the mighty Sioux paid him respects. From other tribes he learned of other root medicines, becoming quite adept in their use. His life was carefree and generally easy, though he longed for the companionship he had enjoyed with Walking Eagle.

But the travels and the rough life in Indian camps finally took its toll on Zeus and he fell ill. Frightened, the Kiowas with whom he had been staying tried what they could to remedy him, but to no avail.

In desperation, they bundled him into a travois and hauled him to the nearest white man's town. There they left him in the night on the doorstep of a doctor.

With the physician's help Zeus quickly recovered, but was now in debt. To pay the debt he took a job at the general mercantile store, accepting the abuse and humiliation heaped on him by the ungrateful owner and rude customers.

Hate boiled inside him, fueled by frustration. He suffered and fumed, often plotting revenge against his employer and those others who tormented him the most. But he persevered.

As the months passed, he thought more and more about escaping. He was watched closely by his employer, who had found a gold mine in the small man who was so dependent on him for the miserable wages. The doctor, too, kept a tight rein on him as did the local saloonkeeper to whom Zeus was also indebted. He had run up quite a bill at the saloon in trying to drink away his frustration and the pain of being what he was.

144

Zeus was sitting on a bench, head throbbing and stomach turning from a hangover when he heard the noise. Looking up through bleary eyes, squinting into a blistering orange sun, he saw the first wagon turning onto the short main street.

It was followed by another and another and again another. Music blared forth and people stumbled out of buildings to investigate the cacophony.

Zeus sat bolt upright. His eyes bulged and his breathing grew ragged. "My way out of here," he breathed.

The circus set up its tents on the edge of town and stayed for three days. Zeus pretended indifference, not even going out to the grounds.

But when it had packed up and pulled out, Zeus was aboard one of the wagons. He had managed to sneak under a pile of costumes and props in the back of one of the huge, painted wagons. There he snuggled deep into the pile and slept.

He awoke to the jouncing, but kept under cover until the caravan stopped for the night. He crawled out under cover of darkness and scuttled around until he found the leader.

Approaching the man, Zeus said without preliminary, "Need an extra hand here?"

The man was startled. "Who are you?"

"Name's Zeus and I stowed away on your wagon after you left the last town. I'm lookin' for a job. I been with a circus before, so I know the ropes."

"What d'you do?"

"Juggle, sleight of hand. Some music. I can even do a clown act if it's necessary."

The man looked at Zeus for a while as he munched a hunk of roasted meat. Finally he wiped his hands on his trousers. "Sure. I can use you.

Go set yourself down over at yonder fire and have yourself some vittles. We'll talk about pay later."

Zeus turned away but was called back. "Just remember one thing. I expect a full day's work for the pay I give you. Part of the job is helpin' set up and take down and carin' for the animals. You don't pull your weight, I'll dump you on the road somewhere."

Zeus, hungry, just nodded and moved off to the fire.

Life with the circus was little improvement over his stay in the small Texas town or his time with the other circus, now some years in the past. Still an oddity even among the other strange circus performers, he was not well liked. With his sarcastic wit, his growing fondness for alcohol and his love of pranks, he was highly unpopular with almost everyone in the troupe.

His anger was worsened when the circus owner right off decided that Zeus's small size required a correspondingly small salary. This insult festered within the bothersome midget and, combined with the other factors, led Zeus into practicing his sleight of hand on more than the locals in the small towns they played. He often picked the pockets of some of his working partners, and he used it well in the card games with the other circus men.

He had no other alternative. To leave the circus was to court a life of deprivation. At least here, he thought, he was regularly fed. And, despite their dislike of the little man, the circus performers at least accepted him. So he hung on, month after month, seeking solace and friendship in the bottle and with those few boomtown dancehall girls who would spend the night with anyone who paid.

Until one day a slight, well-spoken man found him after a performance in San Antonio. . . .

All this McGill learned over the first few months he and Zeus traveled together. They complemented each other well. McGill tried to teach Zeus the use of proper English and the use of proper manners. In return, Zeus taught McGill his knowledge of herbs and roots, until McGill could earn from Zeus the sobriquet of *curandero*—one who cured.

Zeus also afforded McGill safe passage through Indian territory.

They visited the camps of buffalo hunters and the boomtowns of mining camps. They entertained and "cured" miners, farmers, buffalo hunters, sodbusters, travelers, and ranchers.

Yes, the two men complemented each other. Their wit was constantly tested with sharp retorts. They entertained together and got drunk together. They got into scrapes and, mostly, got out of them intact. Zeus lost some, though not most, of his bitterness. He mellowed a little and his pranks were now more in fun than in revenge. Zeus also began to copy McGill's style of dress. He often sported colored caps and bright vests. And he turned his eye toward the ladies; without much success to be sure, but he kept his humor about it.

Chapter 10

"Poor little Zeus," Emma muttered, breaking off Lila's reverie. "He's sure had some sad life now, ain't he?"

"That he has, Emma." Lila set aside the churn. "I think this's just about ready. And I gotta go check on Martha again. I'll be back directly."

She was not gone long. "Well, Martha's lookin' a little more lively and the fever seems to be gone.

She may be mendin'."

"Oh, thank God," Emma whispered.

Grandma Whitlock leaned over toward her daughter-in-law. "See, I told you everything'd be all right."

"Don't get your hopes up too high now. I just said she seemed a little better. I didn't say she was cured."

Lila retook her seat and began pumping the churn again. It was getting late and the sun was beginning to dip. The air, hot and muggy, was still. The women sat in silence, working, not needing to speak.

Emma eventually stood. "C'mon, Becky. We'd best be gettin' supper on before the men git back."

"All right, Ma." They put down their work and entered the house.

After they had left, Lila said to Grandma Whitlock, "Guess I'd best go on down and fetch some water."

Elizabeth nodded, clamped her teeth a little tighter on the pipe stem and closed her eyes. "Think I'll just rest here a bit," she said smiling.

When she carried the water into the house, Lila stayed, helping Emma and Rebecca prepare the meal.

Zeus came in carrying some wood. Lila considered scolding him for it, wishing he had brought in some cow chips instead. But to scold him would only ruin his humor; it was not often that he voluntarily did some work. She settled for, "Where've you been hidin' all afternoon?"

"Out in the barn cleanin' the wagon." The wagon had been pulled into the barn days before, Jonathan thinking to prevent the three guests from escaping before Martha was well again.

"All afternoon?"

Zeus gave her a sheepish grin. "Well, I must confess I did stop off to take a wee small nap."

Lila smiled fondly at him. "That's good. Now why don't you go on out and fetch up another load of wood and some booshwa? That oughta be just about enough."

"Yes, ma'am," he said with a courtly bow, and left.

The simple supper was ready quickly. As Emma and Rebecca began setting plates and bowls out on the scarred wooden table, Lila said, "I'll be back in a minute. I want to go wake Winthrop. He'll be hungry and I reckon it's time he looked to Martha."

Emma just nodded, wiping her flushed, sweating forehead with the bottom of her apron.

When Lila returned with McGill, who still rubbed the sleep from his eyes, everyone was seated around the table waiting patiently. The men, knowing the meal would be ready, had come in minutes before.

"My apologies everyone," McGill said. He looked more cheerful and healthy than he had in days. "Sorry I've kept you all waiting." He sat. "Please dig in."

The meal was almost cheerful, with a lot of polite banter and talk being passed between mouthfuls of turnips, salt pork, squash, beans, and homemade bread laid heavy with fresh-churned butter.

McGill finally stood, wiping his mouth with a cloth. "As usual, Emma, you have surpassed yourself with this fine meal. But I'm afraid I must take my leave. It's past time I was tending to Martha."

"Of course."

It seemed an eternity to McGill since he had last stepped into the small, sparse room. And he was pleasantly surprised. Martha lay partially propped up against the wall, looking out at the warm darkening sky through the tiny window. A hard, brittle cough racked her frail body.

"That's a mighty big cough for a little girl, young lady. You don't sound none too good, but you're looking a bit better. How do you feel?"

Martha had whirled at the sound of his voice. "You startled me." She struggled weakly to sit up, succeeding with McGill's help. "Thanks, Doctor. I feel some better. I'm still coughin' a lot. Not as much as before, but still a lot."

McGill felt her forehead. "Seems your fever's broke, too."

"Yep. I think it has. At least I ain't been sweatin' so much today even though it's hotter'n a fried egg."

McGill checked the girl over and then called Zeus. In a corner of the room he whispered to the midget, "You got any liverwort in your sack of herbs?"

Zeus nodded. "I think so. Why?"

"Well, the skunk cabbage seems to've worked some. But not as much as I hoped. I read somewhere that the Indians back in Maine used liverwort for things like this. I reckon that with the skunk cabbage we already gave her and the liverwort, she ought to come around."

"Okay, Chief. Anything else you need with it?"

"Bring in another bottle of our medicine. We don't need to mix it, but it should make the liverwort more palatable. Also fetch all these other things. Maybe you'd best write them down so you don't forget."

He fished a crumpled piece of paper and a stubby pencil out of a vest pocket and handed them to Zeus. "Now take this down. I need some lobelia, only an ounce, and a couple ounces of Iceland moss, and some capsules of white poppies. Weigh all that up on the scale out in the wagon. There's no need for doin' it in here.''

"That all?"

"No. I also need some pearl barley and molasses. And some of that sugar candy we give out to the young folk. Bring in a small bag of it. What we don't use now we can pass out as treats. Might help keep everybody happy.''

"What're you fixin' to do with all this stuff?"

"Make up some cough syrup. We've got to do something about this cough Martha's got. It won't cure her, but it'll ease her and let the other potions do their work.''

"Okay, Chief.'' Zeus, still in an amiable mood, hurried from the room and returned quickly. He placed a small satchel full of bottles and little sacks of herbs on the table and handed McGill a sack of mossy material.

Zeus sat and watched as McGill scurried about doing various unimaginable things to the mossy liverwort. Finally he mixed it with the patented "medicine" and turned toward the girl. "Okay now, Martha. I'm going to dose you again with something a little different. It'll probably taste worse'n alkali water, but you got to drink quite a bit of it down. Think you can do it?''

She wrinkled her nose, but said, "Reckon I can. Ain't too much can be worse'n this godawful coughin' all the time.''

"We'll do something about that, too. A little later. Now, let's get this over with.''

He sat and held her as she gamely drank the foul-tasting concoction. "That's enough,'' he finally said. "You did real fine. Hungry?''

She nodded, still trying to get the taste of the

151

medicine out of her mouth.

"Good. We'll get you something to eat and get this bed cleaned up a little."

"That'd be right nice," Martha said fervently. Again she had a fit of coughing.

McGill went to the door and called Emma. "Get Becky to take Martha outside for a spell. She probably needs it anyway. And I want to get this room cleaned. Besides, the fresh air just might do her some good."

As Becky supported Martha out of the room, McGill said to Emma, "Now get that bed cleaned up. It needs new straw and some fresh cloth if you have it. The poor girl fouled the bed while she was unable to get up. So scrub it down real good. There's still some of the disinfectant left. You know how to use it."

"Yes, Doctor."

"Lila will help you. And once you get the bed cleaned up, fix her a plate. She's hungry and a full stomach ought to do her a world of good."

The women hurried about cleaning and scrubbing, McGill pitched in by fetching a load of fresh straw from the barn. As the bustle swirled around him, Zeus piped up from his seat in the corner chair, "Reckon I'll go see Martha outside. She might be needin' some help."

"You'll do no such thing," McGill wheezed, winded from his trek to the barn. "What you'll do is fetch clean water for the washstand and some drinkin' water in the pitcher."

"Aye, aye, General," Zeus snorted.

"Just go do it."

The tasks done, Martha was brought back in. The brief turn outside had brought some color back into her face and the food helped even more. When she was finished, McGill shooed everyone

152

out of the room, except for Zeus. "Now," he said to his little friend, "it's time to get to work." He grabbed a large basin, one big enough to hold a lot of medicine.

"While I'm mixin' up some of these things," McGill said to Zeus, "I want you to bash up them poppy capsules you brought in."

Into the large bowl, McGill dumped the small sackfuls of lobelia tincture, Iceland moss, two tablespoons of barley malt and two ounces of molasses. When Zeus was finished, McGill added the poppy capsules to the others and mixed it together with his hands.

Wiping his hands on an old cloth, McGill said, "C'mon, Zeus. We've done all we can here." He picked up the bowl and the two of them walked out of the room. "Have you an extra cook pot?" he asked Emma.

As Emma went to fetch the pot, McGill ordered, "Zeus, build up that fire a bit. Becky, fetch me a pail of water."

McGill poured the contents of the basin into the large pot and added two quarts of water. As he was doing so, Emma asked, "What're you doin', Doctor?"

"Makin' cough syrup."

McGill let the concoction boil a few hours, occasionally checking its progress. Then it was ready. "There ain't much of it left, is there, Doctor?" Emma said.

"That's the way it's supposed to be. Zeus, fetch the sugar candy." Rebecca's eyes lit up at the mention of the sweet and McGill smiled. When Zeus handed him the sack, McGill gave a piece of the candy to Becky. Seeing the looks given him by Emma and Elizabeth, he also handed each of them a hunk.

He poured most of the remaining candy into the boiling pot. It was probably more than he should have added, but he wanted to sweeten it as much as possible for the sick girl.

It boiled merrily away until the sugary confection was dissolved. Carefully he carried the concoction into the small room. Martha looked up in apprehension, not wanting more medicine.

He set it down and let it cool a few minutes before tasting it. "This ought to do the trick," he said happily.

He smiled at Martha. "This'll be some better than the last. It's a sweet cough syrup to ease that tickle in your throat."

The girl gulped some of it down and lay back. "It feels better already."

"That's good. Now you get some rest."

Throughout the night, McGill kept an eye on the girl. Three times more he made her drink of the medicine, and twice more the cough syrup. He dozed intermittently, catching a nap when he could, waking in fits and starts each time the girl coughed. Joshua sat quietly at the table, his work-hardened fingers quickly, efficiently mending a leather harness.

The cock crowed and morning slowly broke. The girl had slept well, despite frequent coughing spells. She no longer seemed to suffer from night sweats, and she seemed the tiniest bit stronger when she woke.

Grandma Whitlock straggled into the main room, yawning and already filling her pipe. She nodded toward the bedroom. "How's she doin'?"

"Seems to be some better. Can't be sure yet, though."

The day droned by, sweltering, much like the previous ones. The women worked around the house and the men outside. McGill napped and forced Martha to take her doses of the medicine and cough syrup off and on during the day. Zeus floated from place to place; sometimes watching the men in the fields, at others sitting on the porch making ribald remarks to the women.

It was a blistering hot day, the sun hanging low and heavy in the sky, the mugginess oppressive. Everyone and everything seemed soggy and wilted.

Once during the day, when McGill went in to check on Martha, Lila tagged along. McGill had tried to argue, but Lila shushed him. Inside, Martha was sleeping and Lila seized the chance.

"Winthrop, I've got to talk to you," she said anxiously.

"Not now, Lila, I have work to do."

"It can't wait. Now listen to me."

Having his attention, Lila told him about the two Whitlock children that had died, and how their deaths had affected Jonathan.

"So you've got to do somethin' to fix Martha," she concluded. "Because there ain't no tellin' just what he'll do if she dies."

"I'm doing all I can, Lila."

"I know you are. But it's not makin' Jonathan any easier to live with."

"I understand. And don't worry about Jonathan. I'll handle him."

Lila looked skeptical, but said, "All right," and then left. McGill turned to Martha.

Martha at times seemed to be getting better. But then she would cough and choke, spitting up phlegm. When she did, she sank back on the bed weakened, gasping for breath and sweating. It was then that McGill worried the most.

And it was after one of these spells that he again sought out Zeus. "You got anything in your sack

155

called pippsissewa?"

"What in blazes is that? I never heard of it before."

"Don't know it by any other name. It was something else used by Indians back east. You should pay more attention to these things. It isn't only the Indians out here use herbs for curing. Anyway, they made a tea out of it and dosed their people with it to cure consumptive disorders."

"Sorry, Chief. I ain't ever heard of it. Or anything else like it. You're gonna have to do with what you got."

"I don't know if that's good enough."

"From what you've said, it seems to be workin'. Give it more time." For the moment he grew serious. "That's somethin' I tried to teach you about herb medicine years ago. Herbs and roots and primitive medicine don't work overnight. They take time. Give it a while and see what happens."

"I reckon you're right."

Zeus's bantering tone returned. " 'Course I'm right. I'm always right."

McGill patted him on the back and smiled distractedly.

The night passed slowly, too. It was cooler than the day, but still hot. McGill catnapped again, waking frequently to wake Martha and force more medicine and cough syrup into her.

Not only did he give her the liverwort mixture, but he went back to using the skunk cabbage potion, too. He alternated between them, hoping the combination would work.

Another brutally hot morning broke. But this one was different. McGill could sense right away that although the heat would be staggering, it would be dry. The soggy moisture had disappeared overnight.

156

When the family was up and about, McGill ordered, "Emma, as soon as breakfast is over, feed Martha. When she's had her fill, I want her taken outside."

"Outside?"

"Yes, outside. The weather's so hot and dry it'll be good for her."

"Are you sure?"

"Of course I'm sure," McGill said, his temper short. He was frustrated by Martha's lack of progress and he was becoming irritable. "Of course I'm sure," he repeated. "It's a disease of the lungs she has. The dry air will help them dry a little."

"If you say so, Doctor, it'll be done."

"Good." He turned toward Jonathan. "I've a favor to ask you, too, Jonathan."

"Do so," the brawny man said, finishing his meal.

"Since the weather's so nice after bein' so damp for such a spell, I'd like to get the wagon out in the sun a while. Kind of let it air out some. Get the mustiness out of it."

Jonathan looked thoughtful. "Thinkin' of makin' off with it when I ain't lookin' maybe?"

McGill drew himself up straight. "You should know better."

"I gotta think of my daughter, you know." He still watched McGill closely. Then he shrugged. "Aw, hell. Sure. I'll have the boys haul it out of the barn, over near the chicken coop."

"That'll be fine. Thank you."

McGill went to give Martha another dose of medicine before she was taken outside. The women cleaned up after the meal while the men headed out to work after pulling the old wagon out of the barn.

McGill took a nap and joined the women on the porch where they were joined by the men at the noon hour. The men had eaten only a light meal; it was too hot for anything more. As usual, the women's hands were busy.

Jonathan gazed over at the wagon sitting across the yard. "Looks like you got a mighty full load on that old wagon, Doc. What do you have in there? Anything interestin'?"

McGill's eyes lit up. "Well, sir," he said, sitting a little straighter. "I got somethin' for everybody in yonder wagon. From your toes to your head, and things for your bed. I got tools and spools and wire and thread, pails and nails, and things for when you wed. I got fancy things and plain things and clothes of all colors and styles. New things and old things and more things. You name it and I got it. Nothin's too small and nothin's too big. I got—"

"Whoa. Whoa," Jonathan laughed. "Hold your horses, Doc. I just asked what you had in there. I didn't want a whole lesson."

McGill and the others joined in the laughter. "Okay, then. I'll tell you straight. Just doin' that ought to be enough to sell you something."

"We'll see," Jonathan smiled.

"Well, I have the usual merchandise found on a peddler's wagon—pots, pans, bottle goods, cooking utensils, seed, small farm tools, axes, a full stock of Bull Durham tobacco."

He saw old Elizabeth's eyes light up, but he continued, "A fine selection of jackknives, lump oil, even some airtights."

"What in tarnation's airtights?" Emma asked.

"Canned foods, ma'am. Mostly I got what's called love apples—canned tomatoes. But I got a few others, too. I got whatever you might need

158

'round the house.''

"I have far more than that, thought. Yonder wagon holds delights the likes of which you have never seen. Some are useful and some are just for fancy. Some you haven't even heard of yet.''

"Just get on with it," Jonathan laughed again. "You can talk more'n a whole sewin' bee full of women who ain't had no company in six months.''

McGill stuck with his salesmanship—the way he did to pump the customers to buy more. "Can't sell nothin' without I give it a big buildup first.''

Jonathan laughed some more. "Who says I want to buy anything from you? I just want to know what you're carryin' in there. It appears to be bulgin' at the seams.''

"All right. All right," McGill chuckled. He looked thoughtful for a minute. "Well, like I said, I have all the usual things you might expect a peddler to carry. But I also have all the latest gadgets and inventions.''

"Like what?" Jonathan asked.

"Like an electric fan.''

"A what?"

"An electric fan. It's a propeller-like device powered by the new-fangled electricity. Helps keep you cool in summer. It was invented by somebody named Wheeler. Along about two years ago.''

Jonathan looked a little dubious. "Reckon I've heard a little about this here electricity thing. But I can't say as I know it'll work. It seems like we're foolin' with things we got no business messin' 'round with.''

McGill chuckled. "Electricity is a right strange thing, but it can do some wonderful things— operate trains, make lights, do any number of wondrous things.''

Jonathan still looked skeptical. "Well, I doubt

159

much if we'll get that electricity stuff way out here for quite a spell."

"You're right on that. But if you had it, you could use some of the other gadgets I'm carryin'."

"Like what?" Emma asked.

"Like an electric flat iron for one. Instead of havin' to keep heatin' an iron on the stove, electric power keeps this one hot all the time you use it."

"That sounds wonderful," Rebecca exclaimed.

"Don't get your hopes all set on gettin' one, girl," Jonathan said.

"I do have many items that are much more practical," McGill interjected. He waited until he had their attention, then said, "Like steel-cut nails, just invented last year. They're made by the Riverside Iron Works in Wheeling, West Virginia."

"Now that's somethin' I might be able to use," Jonathan said. He turned to his sons. "That'd sure make buildin' the new wood house we been talkin' about a heap easier."

"I'm also carrying some new woven fence wire, straight from the factory in Lenawee County, Michigan. Just came out last year, invented by J.S. Page, up there in Michigan."

"Wow, Pa," Joshua interjected. "That'd keep them cows from strayin'."

"Yep," Charles said, "and it'd keep them cattle from over on the Double Bar D from tramplin' our crops every year."

"Sure would," Jonathan nodded. "We just might have to take a look-see at some of that fencin' before you leave, Doc."

"If we leave," Zeus muttered under his breath from his seat near the porch's edge.

McGill pretended he didn't hear. "I thought you might be interested. And I have some other things that might interest you. And the ladies."

160

"Such as?" Jonathan asked.

"Well, I think I just heard you mention you might be building a new wood house to replace this old soddy?"

"That's right."

"Well then, I got just the thing for your new home." He paused to make sure the Whitlocks were attentive. "Some new-fangled plate glass direct from the manufacturer. Finest glass you can get, and it's from the New York Plate Glass Company."

Emma's eyes widened. She stared at McGill in wonderment and then turned to her husband, eyes pleading. Jonathan looked thoughtful. Finally he said softly, "We'll see, Emma. We'll see. But I cain't promise."

She nodded, half happily, half sadly.

"You're really temptin' us, Doc," Jonathan said, knowing he would not be able to afford half of what he needed or wanted from McGill's wagon.

McGill smiled. "I have other things that might be of interest. Many of them are frivolous, but some, although they are fancy, are quite useful."

"We heard the others, so we might's well hear the rest. We can't be any more desirin' than we already are," Jonathan said.

"One thing that might strike your fancy is the new fountain pens we're carrying. First really practical one ever invented. It was patented just this year by L.E. Waterman in New York City. And I got some stuff called malted milk. Fellow named William Horlick came up with it just two years ago."

"What in the world is malted milk?" Emma asked.

"It's some crazy powder stuff you mix in milk to

get a chocolate-flavored drink." He looked at Jonathan. "And for you, I have a cigar-rolling machine so's you can make your own cigars. Came out just last year."

Jonathan looked interested. "It makes real ceegars?"

"The finest kind. I also have a list of books and magazines for your reading pleasure. I have some new ones, like *The Adventures of Huckleberry Finn*, written by my friend Mark Twain. I hear tell it's pretty good. I haven't come to read it yet. It just come off the presses earlier this year.

"And I have every copy of the *Ladies Home Journal* since it began last year. I also have older books, magazines, and even some old newspapers, includin' some from as far back east as New York and Philadelphia."

"I'm afraid," Jonathan said, "that we ain't got much use for no books. Ain't none of us can read so well. Nor write too well, neither. Ain't got much time for such foolishness neither."

"A pity," McGill said. And he meant it. "There's a lot of things can be learned from reading. A lot of pleasure too."

"Where do you fit it all in?" Becky asked in wonder.

McGill chuckled, enjoying his role in the lime-light. "Do it long enough, young lady, and you learn how to pack a tight wagon. After all, the more I can get in my wagon, the more I can sell. If I packed a light wagon, I'd have little to sell and wouldn't be able to visit folks like you way out here away from everything. It's not like back east where everything's all jammed together. You folks out here seem to like your space."

"That's true enough," Jonathan said. "Bein' cramped up's no good for a man. Drives 'em plumb crazy. I been in the big city once or twice. Back to St. Louis. All them folks was rushin' 'round like chickens that had their heads took off. Helter-skelterin' ever' which way. It like to drive me crazy myself.''

Everyone laughed. "You got a point there, Jonathan," McGill said. "It's enough to make almost anyone loco.''

"How'd you get into sellin' all them things, Doctor? I thought you was just an entertainer and a doctor sellin' mostly fake cures," Emma asked.

McGill winced a bit at the reference to the fake medicine, but said, cheerfully enough, "That's how I started out mostly. But I wasn't makin' much money at it. And, once the three of us got together, expenses went up.

"I always carried a few small items with me. Then one night we were sittin' 'round the fire tryin' to figure out how to make some more money and I thought back to when I was a younker back in Massachusetts. You ever heard of Yankee peddlers?''

Elizabeth spoke for the first time. "Sure, I heared of 'em. They was called Yankee peddlers, but we had 'em in Kaintuck, too. Some of 'em even drifted west in the old days, 'fore it got settled and they started settin' up them general stores.''

"That's right," McGill nodded. "I thought back to the peddlers that used to stop in town to pick up supplies from the stores there. I used to talk to them and help them pack their wagons. So I knew a little about it. So I took a trip back east and hauled back a small load of things and they sold pretty well. The next load was bigger. Now you can take a look in there and see what kind of things we're carrying.''

"Well, it sure is a blessin' for people like us livin'

so far away from everything. To git supplies now we got to travel to town, nearly sixty mile away. And that general store is most always outta everything we need," Emma said.

McGill smiled and bowed as best he could from his seat. "Our aim is to please."

Jonathan stood and stretched. "It's been good just settin' here jawin', but that ain't gettin' our chores done. We'd best be gettin' back to work. C'mon, boys."

The three strode purposefully off into the blazing heat. Emma stood and said, "Reckon it's about time I got back to work, too. There's a heap to be done yet. Becky, fetch up these plates and things and get to washin' them."

"Okay, Ma."

"I'll help you," Lila said.

McGill stepped over to where Martha sat bundled up leaning her chair against the cabin wall. "How're you feelin'?" he asked.

"Much better, Doctor."

"I thought you might. You have more color in your face and you're not coughing up so much."

She nodded. "That's purely been a relief. But I still feel almighty weak."

"You'll get your strength back soon. But now I want you to take some more medicine for me."

She wrinkled her nose at the thought, but said, "If I must."

McGill chuckled. "Yes, you must."

He went into the house and returned with the concoction he had made the night before. She drank some of it down, gagging on the nasty liquid. McGill relented and let her take less than he had been forcing her to drink.

He went back into the house, this time returning with a cupful of cold, clear water. "Here, drink this. It'll help wash the taste of that medicine out of your mouth."

Gratefully she gulped it down. "Better," she gasped.

McGill and Zeus spent the rest of the afternoon making small repairs to the wagon. "Why're we doin' this?" Zeus asked.

"You should know the answer to that."

"You think they're gonna let us outta here?"

"If the girl gets better."

"Reckon she will?"

"She seems better already. She's not cured yet, but she's a lot better off than she was yesterday. She'll be all right."

Zeus laughed, but it was dry. "You must certainly think so. You've got your hopes up mighty high."

"Just keep working, little friend."

"Aye, aye, Captain, sir."

The sun started to dip a little, lengthening the shadows, and a slight breeze sprung up. Its brief coolness was noticed by McGill. "I'd best get Martha inside before she catches a chill. No use letting her do that just when she's getting better. You finish up here. Shouldn't take you but a few more minutes."

"How come you get all the fun? Why'n't you stay here and finish off while I go and help Martha? I could do her more good than you." The last was said with a wink and a leer.

McGill smiled fondly at his companion. "You never change, do you, Zeus?"

Zeus laughed. "You wouldn't like me no other way."

McGill joined in the laughter. "You're probably right. Now just make sure you finish up fixing that rip in the canvas before you come back to the

165

house."

"Maybe I oughta just make a break for it."

"Don't you dare," McGill said in mock menace. Zeus feigned resignation. "You don't never let me have no fun."

"Just get back to work." McGill smiled. "Come on, Martha," he said, stepping onto the little porch, "time to go back in."

"Okay, Doctor. I am gettin' a mite tired. I think I'd like to take a nap now."

"Good. Let's go." He pulled her gently to her feet. Slipping an arm underneath hers and across her back, he helped her shuffle into the house.

Halfway across the big room she lost power, slumping heavily against McGill, nearly crumpling to the floor. Although caught unaware, he held on and managed to pick her up in his arms, ignoring a gasp of fright from Emma. He struggled with his burden into the little room and placed Martha down on the bed as gently as he could, after kicking the door shut behind him, closing out Emma and Becky.

Puffing, he looked down at Martha, worried. But it was she who spoke first. "Reckon I was some weaker than I thought, Doctor. I'm sorry."

"Don't be sorry," McGill wheezed. "Wasn't your fault. I just asked you to do a little more than you could handle."

McGill plopped into the chair, breathing heavily, looking to give both of them a short rest. He listened in frustrated silence as Martha choked and gasped through another spate of coughing.

Rising, he went to her and stroked her perspiring forehead. Softly, almost as if talking to himself, he whispered, "Poor girl. Poor Martha. Wish there was sometin' more I could do for you . . . to stop this infernal coughing."

166

She had heard. "You're doin' the best you can, Doctor," she gasped. "You been with me 'most every minute, tendin' to me, tryin' to get me fixed up. A body can't ask for no more."

Amazed at her fatalism, McGill turned away. "You're not going to like this, but it's time you had some more medicine."

"Do I have to?"

"Yes. Now don't argue. The quicker you get it over with, the quicker you can forget about it."

As easily as he could, McGill poured some of the foul potion down her throat. She gasped, sputtered and choked until finally McGill, feeling pity and guilt at the same time, relented.

"Here, quick, take this," he said, handing her a cup of water to ease the bitterness in her mouth.

"Thanks," she mumbled.

McGill took the cup when she had finished and filled it again, placing it on the table within reach. He pushed a stray hair away from her forehead. "Now, you just take some of this cough syrup and try to get some rest. It's still early and you have enough time for a short nap before eating." He looked at her and a small smile creeped across his lips. "And, another dose of medicine."

Martha made a face at him, but quickly smiled. "Whatever you say, Doctor."

"Get some rest now," he said as he left the room.

He faced a worried Whitlock family gathered around the table. He looked at them and put on a brave front. Smiling, he said, "She's all right. Just very weak. The heat, the excitement, even the small walk to the porch, were a little too much for her."

He sat and continued. "She's resting right now. I dosed her again. She'll sleep for a while. Then we can feed her and dose her again. I'll spend the night up just to keep an eye on her. Make sure she spends a peaceable night.''

The Whitlocks looked relieved and went back about their business; the women preparing the evening meal, the men to finish their chores outside. The men had come in at Becky's call when Martha collapsed.

As Jonathan reached the door, he said, "Want us to put your wagon back in the barn? Your little friend seems to be finished with whatever it was he was doin' to it.''

McGill looked thoughtful. "I'll be out shortly to make sure the work is done. But I think we can leave it outside overnight. The weather appears it'll stay fine till morning. So I reckon we can just leave it where it is. That is, if you don't mind.''

It was Jonathan's turn to look thoughtful. Then he grinned. "Don't see no harm to it. I don't reckon you'll be goin' very far. I think I can trust you after all this time.''

"Thank you," McGill said softly as Jonathan walked out.

Dinner was routine, with enough banter and conversation to almost keep their minds off the sick girl in the next room.

When it was over, Emma took a small plate of food into her daughter. Waking her gently, she spooned Martha, who was still groggy from sleep.

By the time she had finished her meager meal, Martha was full awake and had prepared herself for McGill's appearance. He smiled when he saw the look of determined acceptance on her face.

When he had finished pouring the medicine into her, he gave her more water, and then some cough syrup. Sitting back on the edge of the bed, he said, ever so softly, "If only you'd get better, little Martha. Then you'd not have to take this foul stuff any more."

"I'm tryin', Doctor. I really am."

He lightly brushed her cheek. "I know, Martha. I know." He stared sadly into her pale blue eyes.

The vigil through the night was a strange one for McGill. He dozed and woke, over and over. Sometimes he felt light-hearted, feeling deeply that Martha would get better. At other times he was certain she would die, and he and his friends would be killed.

The little sleep he did get was fraught with strange and often frightening dreams. He saw Martha wasting away to a skeleton, the flesh dripping from her bones, melting before his eyes.

He awoke, covered with sweat and trembling. Later he slept again, only to dream that he stood before a judge. Martha lay on a white-sheeted bed near the judge's bench. He saw himself surrounded by gun-carrying Whitlocks, male and female.

The judge's sonorous bass boomed out for all the world to hear, "Why, Doctor McGill, have you not cured the girl?"

"Because, Your Honor," he answered timidly, "I am not really a doctor and I cannot save her."

McGill shook and trembled at the resounding voice. "You should have finished medical school, instead of making fake cures and fooling with useless herbs and weeds. You had the talent, and the training, once. But you let it slip through your fingers in a wail of self-pity. Had you used the talents given you, you would have been able to save her. You have failed."

McGill sank to his knees, weeping in fright and frustration at his helplessness. "No, no," he whimpered and moaned, over and over, covering his face with his hands.

He jolted awake, finding himself kneeling on the

dirt floor of the old sod cabin. Charles sat across the room, looking at him strangely. Shakily he got to his feet. Pulling a worn red bandanna from his pocket, he wiped his face. Without a word to Charles, he walked outside and lighted a cigar, drawing the smoke deep into his lungs before expelling it sharply with a cough.

He could feel Charles's eyes on his back and he turned to face the young man. "A nightmare," was all he said in explanation.

Charles nodded and stepped back into the house.

The cigar served to calm McGill's jangled nerves and he decided it was time to give Martha more medicine. He felt guilty when he woke her; she had been sleeping so soundly. She was still half asleep when she took the dosage, and it was over quickly. She was asleep again before he had laid her head back down.

Despite the warmth of the evening, McGill stoked up the fire with some cow chips and he put on a coffee pot to boil. The coffee, he knew, would keep him awake. He was afraid, now, to go back to sleep; the thought of the terrible dreams filled him with dread. He knew he was being irrational, and even laughed a little at himself for his childish fears, but he could not bring himself to face another moment's sleep.

So he sat and thought, and read, and drank cup after cup of harsh black coffee while puffing a cigar. He fought off the fatigue, his drooping eyelids frequently betraying him.

Once more in the darkness he stumbled into Martha's room, woke her, and forced the bitter liquid down her unwilling throat. From her room he went back outside, breathing deeply of the hot, dry air, softened only by the faintest touch of a breeze. It would be dawn soon, he knew, as he peered through the inky blackness that belied the nearness of the new day.

He took another deep breath, exhaling some of the worry and nervousness that had plagued him throughout the night. Looking up at the blur of stars, he somehow felt everything would work out. With renewed vigor, he went back into the house, determined to remain awake and alert through the waning hours of the night. Filling the crock cup once more from the large pot of strong, black coffee, he flopped into the rocker and lifted the thick medical book he had been reading sporadically during the past few days.

Grandma Whitlock's rummaging around the kitchen, getting together the beginnings of the family's morning neal, awoke him. Startled, he sat straight up, the book falling from his lap with a soft thud.

"Mornin'," the old lady cackled. "Hope you had a good night's rest."

He stood and stretched, feeling the weariness of long hours and lack of care. He laughed at Elizabeth's statement. "It was right wonderful. All thirty minutes of it."

"I reckon. How's Martha?"

"Can't rightly say just yet. She's slept soundly through the night. She barely woke when I dosed her."

Elizabeth grunted in response as she continued her chores. McGill tried again to rub the weariness from his face. "I'll be back directly," he said.

Elizabeth nodded. "Bring in some booshwa with you."

"Sure enough."

Charles didn't even bother to follow him out this time. When he came back in, arms loaded with dry cow dung, the rest of the Whitlock family was up and about. "Mornin', folks," he said cheerfully, dropping the armful of fuel.

As the morning business of preparing breakfast went on, Lila and Zeus came in. Their arrival seemed to animate the still sleepy Whitlocks and conversation grew considerably.

Breakfast was soon served. By that time, the sun had fully risen, bringing a little light into the dim soddy.

And with the sun came the heat. The kind of baking, broiling heat that could scorch the Wyoming prairie in the waning days of summer. The small room sweltered, although it was cooler inside than out. The men grumbled through breakfast.

"Hope this heat don't damage the corn, Pa," Charles said. "It's likely hot enough to roast the ear right on the stalk."

"We'll be lucky we don't lose half the crop if'n it stays like this another few days," Jonathan commented. He nodded glumly. "We sure do need some rain plumb bad. That's certain." He pushed his plate away and stood. "Well, there's nothin' can be done about it now, 'cept try'n tend to things as best we can. The good Lord will provide for us."

"Guess you're right, Pa," Charles said, also rising. "I'll fetch in some extra water, Ma. You'll like as not need all you can get today."

"Thank you, son," Emma said, wiping her already soaked face. "Just make sure you fill some jugs from the well before you head on out to workin'. You'll need it worse'n us and that stream ain't fit to drink from with that mud stirred up and all."

"I'll do so, Ma."

The three men took their hats from pegs by the

door and filed out. Charles returned a few minutes later with two buckets of cold well water and then left, hurrying to catch the others.

As the women cleaned up, McGill looked in on Martha. Breakfast had cheered him and even made him more alert. But it faded when he saw the girl. Martha was bathed in sweat. Still asleep, she seemed uncomfortable, breathing heavily and coughing without seeming to notice.

"She looks worse," McGill mumbled. Afraid to wake her, he stood looking sadly down at the valiant young woman. He opened the door and called out, "Emma, don't make Martha any breakfast now." Emma looked up sharply, fear and worry gripping her face. McGill smiled as warmly as he could. "No need to fret, Emma. Martha's still asleep and I reckon she can use all the rest she can get, so I'm not going to wake her just yet."

The lines of worry slid from Emma's face. "Okay, Doctor."

"Lila," McGill said, "bring me in some fresh water."

Lila gasped, nearly spilling the water, when she saw the girl on the bed. "She looks terrible."

McGill's shoulders sagged. "I know. I'm afraid we've lost her. She seemed to be getting better yesterday, but now she's worse than she ever was. I don't know what more I can do for her."

"Maybe it's just the heat," Lila said hopefully.

"I doubt it. I just don't know what's wrong." He slumped into the chair. "No, I'm afraid I've failed her."

"Stop it, Winthrop," Lila snapped, her green eyes flashing. She shook him, hard. "You'll not be able to help her if you keep on like this. I know you can help her."

With a visible effort McGill shook off the weariness and the feeling of defeat. "I reckon there still are a few things left I can try. We're not finished yet."

"That's the spirit," Lila said smiling. "That's more like the Winthrop I've known all these years."

Their talking woke Martha. McGill noticed her first. "Mornin'," he said, feigning cheerfulness.

But she could not speak. She gasped and choked and coughed, trying desperately to gulp in air.

"Oh, you poor child," Lila murmured. She rushed over to the bedside. She dipped a clean piece of cloth, torn from the hem of her petticoat, in the water and began wiping Martha's forehead.

"Let me give her some medicine," McGill said, leaning over Lila's shoulder.

"Let her be." Lila wet the rag again and, leaving it sopping, brought it to the girl's lips. She squeezed some of the fluid off and Martha eagerly licked up the drops. Lila patiently repeated the process until Martha finally croaked, "Thank you."

"Now you can dose her," Lila said.

McGill quickly, efficiently, gently forced some of the liverwort, skunk cabbage and whiskey combination into her. Martha sputtered and choked, but McGill gave her some water to ease her.

"Feelin' any better?" he asked without much hope.

"A bit," she replied bravely.

Lila turned to McGill. "Now get yourself out of here for a while. I have work to do."

"What're you going to do?"

"I'm goin' to bathe Martha with some cool water to try'n stop this infernal sweatin'. And I need to take her clothes off to do it properly. Ain't no need for you to be here for it."

174

McGill backed off. As he turned for the door, he said to Martha, "I'm leaving you in very capable hands. You just do whatever Lila tells you."

"Okay," Martha whispered.

McGill left. "All right, now," Lila said, "let's get you out of these here clothes. You'll feel a sight better."

But while the cooling bath seemed to soothe Martha, it did little to help her. The staggering heat only served to drench the young invalid as quickly as Lila wiped the perspiration from her cough-racked body. Lila fretted over her, but talked calmly and softly, hoping her sing-song voice would serve to succeed where the medicine and bath had failed.

Still Martha worsened. Her body, wasting away, struggled valiantly for air, the shrunken chest lifting and falling weakly. She coughed almost constantly now, stopping only to spit up or to gasp for oxygen. Lila finally gave up. She managed to force Martha back into her thin cotton dressing gown, and then cleaned up the room and bed a little. With trepidation she called McGill.

He came into the room with a look of expectation. Without acknowledging it to himself, he had pinned a lot of faith on Lila's caring ministrations. The hopeful look dropped from his face like a stone when he saw Martha. "Oh, my God," he gasped.

He rushed over to the bedside and checked her pulse while listening intently to her ragged, tortured breathing. He knew it would do little good, but he could think of nothing else to do. He felt helpless and the activity at least gave him something to do.

"Leave us be," he said to Lila.

When Lila had left, McGill paced back and forth

at the side of the bed, flinching at every cough that racked the poor girl's body. The feeling of helplessness grew. He picked up the jar of the medicine he had concocted, but he put it back down. "Useless, useless," he muttered. He paced, worrying, a frown creasing his forehead.

Despite the gnawing worry, his mind raced, flicking back over the years, past pages and pages of dusty medical books and journals, seeking an answer. But he found none; and he knew he had to go face the Whitlocks, tell them their daughter had become even more ill and there was nothing more he could do. He would have to tell them he had failed. And he would plead for the lives of his friends.

Yes, he thought, he would plead for their lives, but not his own. He had failed, not they; there was no need for them to suffer because of him. He owed them that much.

His mind made up, he went for the door. But his resolve faltered and then disappeared when he saw the faces of Martha's family looking on, expectantly, at him. It would do them no good, he thought, to know of their kin's impending death. Haggard and drawn, he managed at least a small smile. He closed the door behind him. "Martha seems to have taken a turn for the worse," he said without preamble. He held up his hand to stop their questions. "I don't think it's anything to worry about. I just think the strain of moving about so much and all the heat yesterday were too much for her."

McGill could not bring himself to look at Lila, knowing she had seen the wretched condition of the young woman. "She's back asleep again, and I think we ought to let her be. Me or Lila will feed her when she wakes up."

The Whitlocks looked disappointed, but before Rebecca could complain, Emma said, "Well, then, we'll just leave her be for now. Let's get on with the chores. There's a heap to be done."

McGill breathed a sigh of relief. He was glad no one had questioned him too closely. "Excuse me," he said abruptly, and walked outside. He needed to get away for a while, so he sought the refuge of the wagon, where he sprawled among the scattered items of his trade, dreaming and hoping for a miracle.

The day dragged on and McGill finally realized he could not stay in the wagon forever. Without much hope, he went back to the house and forced Martha to swallow more of the medicine. He had said nothing to Lila, Zeus, or the Whitlock women as he walked past the porch and into the house.

Martha looked as bad as she had earlier and pity welled up in McGill. He now knew the medicine would not work, but he was at a loss for anything else to do. Wearily he trudged outside and squatted on a small stool near Emma. "Where'd Zeus and Lila go?" he asked. "They were here when I came up."

"Down to the wagon, I think. They were headed that way."

He just nodded, closing his eyes against the glare of the sun and the fatigue he felt. He slept.

Chapter 11

The back of the big wagon was down and Lila and Zeus sat on it, dangling their feet over the edge. The early afternoon sun blistered the landscape. The air was still, no trace of wind disturbing the solemnness.

The heat and stillness lulled the two of them, and they sat drained, immersed in their own flights of fancy. They had tired of sitting on the porch, working, always working, and so had sought the shade and solace of the friendly wagon.

"I wonder if Martha'll ever get better," Lila wondered distractedly.

"I doubt it," Zeus snapped sarcastically. The heat and the immense boredom that swamped him brought out the devil in him. "And it's a pity, too. We could've made delightful music together." He leeringly winked at Lila. "Know what I mean?"

"You disgusting little creature. You have no heart, do you?"

"Nope," Zeus giggled. "Leastways I try'n avoid it much's I can. It only gets in the way."

Lila ignored him. Wistfully, she said, "I wish there was somethin' I could do. Poor Winthrop. He's so tired. And he's tried so hard. It ain't fair."

A sly grin slithered over Zeus's face. Cheerfully, he said, "There is somethin' we can do."

Lila brightened. Expectantly she looked at Zeus, waiting to hear the plan.

The grin broadened into a smile. "You and I could quietly hitch up the wagon and burn the breeze." He gloated openly at the shocked expression that had grown on Lila's face. "They don't care about us. Just your sweetheart Winthrop. Just think," he said, waving his tiny hands in the air for emphasis, "We could change the name to Doctor Zeus's Traveling Medicine Show and Dance Troupe—Gadgetry a Specialty."

His eyes seemed to get a faraway look, as if he was viewing in his mind's eye the picture he was creating with words. Lila sat and stared, stunned.

"We could get hitched somewhere," Zeus continued. "Maybe have us a few younkers. Big ones, of course. You know, regular size. And then—"

Lila's voice of shocked rage split the still air. "Why you wretched little devil!" Her fists tightened as she leaped to the ground and spun to face him. "Winthrop has given you everything you have. You were nothin', less than nothin', before he picked you up. Everyone hated you until Winthrop found you—you ungrateful little monster." She looked around wildly.

"I have a good mind to pick you up and feed you to the chickens right over yonder," she sputtered. "Let 'em peck your beady little eyes out."

Zeus knew he had gone too far. With some apprehension, he said, "You wouldn't dare . . . would you?"

Lila appeared not to have heard the midget. "In fact," she said tightly, "I think I'll do that."

Zeus jumped up to stand on the back of the wagon, knowing for certain he was in deep trouble. He started edging backwards toward the inside of the wagon, looking for a means of escape. But Lila was too quick for him. Lashing out with a rapidity neither of them knew she possessed, she grabbed a tiny foot and hauled the little man toward her.

Lifting him up, she carried him roughly toward the chicken pen, enclosed by wire, near to the barn. Zeus squirmed and squiggled heartily, but to no avail.

"Lila! Lila!" he squealed. "Put me down! Please? I didn't mean it. Honest. I really didn't. I was only joshin'. I just wanted to cheer you up some. Take your mind off everythin' that's been goin' on. You know I'd never really say nothin' against the Chief."

179

Lila continued her steadfast march toward the rickety, foul-smelling enclosure. Zeus's squeals turned to pleas. "C'mon, Lila. Let me go! I was only makin' a joke. Really! You gotta believe me!"

Lila tightened her grip on the struggling midget. It was her only response to his pleas. Zeus, looking up from his precarious position, saw how near the enclosure now was. He became more agitated.

"Lila, put me down. You don't wanna do this. Really! You don't!" It did no good. He had never seen her so furious. He had often kidded her about her flaming red hair and the temper that should have gone with it, but that had never been seen. Now it appeared that it had been there all along—buried or hidden maybe, but there. And it frightened him.

His mind worked overtime, trying to come up with something that would get through to her; get her to put him down, safely far away from the chickens. He couldn't stand chickens; the smell of them and their filthy habits affected him to his core. He would be in torment for days if he allowed her to put him in that small enclosed pen.

Something flickered in the recesses of his brain. It had been fluttering there for a few days now, but had not bloomed into a full-fledged idea. Yet he knew he had something of vital importance there. Something . . .

"Lila, wait!" he shouted. "I can help the girl!"

The words were like a splash of cold water across her face. She stopped dead in her tracks. With a firm grip on her struggling captive, she looked down at him. She placed him on the ground, still holding his collar, and knelt so she could be face to face with him. With hope in her voice, she asked, "Can you really help the girl? Can you cure her? Oh my, if you could, Winthrop would be saved."

She paused for breath. "Can you do it? If you can, I'll forgive everything."

Feeling he now had the upper hand, Zeus said cockily, "Everything?"

Lila tightened her grip on Zeus's shirt, and her face grew hard. Menacingly, she said, "Don't push your luck, little one. Can you really cure the girl?"

Her grip and threatening manner took some of the starch out of him. Trying to placate her, he said, "Well, I ain't certain, you understand. But maybe. You know how much stuff I got in my herb sack, don't you?"

She nodded and he continued, "I just remembered, there's somethin' I got in there that the Comanches use to cure this stuff called tuberculosis. It's called Black Nightshade and I got some."

"Will it work?"

Nervousness crept into Zeus's voice. "Like I said, I ain't sure. The Comanches swear by it, but I ain't ever really seen it used, so I don't know how good it really is. Some of these Indian concoctions work miracles. Others ain't worth a plumb nickel. You can't never tell till you try 'em."

"Is it worth a try?" Lila implored.

Regaining some of his cockiness, Zeus said, "Anything's worth a try if it's gonna save my hide." Seeing Lila's suddenly stern face, he quickly added, " 'Sides, nothin' else's worked so far, so's it can't hurt none."

"I reckon you're right." Lila stood. Taking Zeus's hand, she started walking back toward the wagon. Suddenly she stopped. "Why didn't you think of this before?"

"Wish I had." He grew serious. "I don't like bein' here no more'n you do. I've had an idea

181

rattlin' 'round in my head now for the past couple days. But I couldn't figure out exactly what it was. But it all started with somethin' the Chief said the other day."

"What was that?"

"Well, he said the girl's sickness was somethin' called tuberculosis. I never heared of it before."

"He did say it was discovered just a few years back."

"Yep. That's what threw me. I didn't have no idea what was wrong with Martha till the other day when the Chief said somethin' about her havin' a lung disease, a consumptive disorder. That's what got me thinkin'. But I couldn't place it. It was familiar, but it just got stuck up here." He pointed to his head.

"Then," he continued, "I was so worried you was gonna throw me in with them chickens that I came to think of it." He scowled at her.

"Sorry."

"You ain't too awful sorry." He paused. "So, like I said, that's when my old head started to work and it all fell into place."

"What did?"

"The word. I knew there was somethin' awful familiar 'bout the words he used. It finally dawned on me. What he meant was Martha had the old sickness we always called consumption. Leastways, somethin' mighty similar to it."

"So?"

"The Comanches ain't ever heard of tuberculosis. But they use this Black Nightshade for what we always called consumption."

"Then this tuberculosis and consumption are the same thing?"

"I ain't sure exactly. Consumption is a lung disease, I know that much. If the doc calls what

Martha's got a lung disease, it's either the same thing or else close enough not to worry about.''

Lila continued her interrupted walk toward the wagon. "I'm certainly glad you finally thought of it.''

Zeus felt a little remorse. Contritely, he said, "You really love him, don't you?''

"Very much,'' she answered sadly.

"Does he know?''

"I don't reckon so. I never said anything.''

"Why not?''

She was tired of saying it, and she didn't know if she even believed it any longer. "Wouldn't be right for a lady to be so forward.''

Zeus snickered. "Since when ain't you been forward? Any woman who threatens to throw me to the chickens can't be all that refined.''

She giggled a little. "That's different.''

With a devilish grin, Zeus said, 'I'll be glad to tell the Chief for you.''

For the second time Lila stopped short. "You'll do no such thing,'' she said sharply. "If you so much as open your mouth about this, to anyone, it's back to the chickens for you.''

"Open my mouth about what?'' Zeus asked slyly.

"That's better,'' Lila snapped, again starting to walk.

At the wagon, Lila picked Zeus up and placed him on the broad back flap. He turned to her, serious now. "I ain't quite so retirin' as you and the Chief, but I ain't ever said this before.''

"Yes?'' Lila thought she knew what was coming.

"You know I love you, don't you?''

Lila met his gaze. "I've known for some time.''

"And you don't love me?''

183

"Not that way." She shook her head sadly. "I love you like a brother. I really do. I'd do almost anything for you. But I can't love you the way you want me to."

Zeus looked a little crestfallen. "Least I know where I stand now," he said with dignity. He turned toward the inside of the wagon.

"Zeus," Lila called softly. He turned to face her. "I'm sorry," she almost whispered.

He walked back the few steps and looked down at her from his infrequent position of height. "So am I."

"I don't know what to say. It's just that—"

She looked perilously close to tears. "Hush up now," he said soothingly. "There's nothin' neither one of us can do 'bout it now. So we'll just go on. It won't change nothin'."

"Are you sure?" she asked tearfully.

He smiled a true smile and she knew everything would be all right. "Yes, I'm sure."

He went back into the wagon, looking for his bag of herbs, while Lila stood in the sun, wiping the tears from her eyes.

Zeus pulled out the well-worn, black satchel with its cracked leather sides and almost rusty hinges. "Aha! Here it is," he exclaimed, dragging it out.

He sat on the open flap of the back of the wagon and dangled his legs over the edge. Opening the sack, he mumbled to himself as he extracted the contents.

Lila stood, watching in awe. It was the first time, to her knowledge, that Zeus had ever opened the sack in front of someone, and she was amazed at the contents. Zeus pulled out small vials and bottles of liquid, clumps of herbs and roots, tied with string or rawhide thongs. There were other vials, jars and bottles of mysterious powders, and unidentifiable packets of rawhide and cloth containing only Zeus knew what.

"Here it is," he exulted. He held up a rather small bottle containing a plant with purplish-colored berries, and flowers that were once white. Now they looked dead and sadly wilted.

"That's it?" Lila asked dubiously.

"What's wrong?"

"It's just . . . just not quite what I expected is all."

"It ain't the looks that count, you know."

"I guess you're right."

Zeus started repacking the satchel. He felt he now had the upper hand. Lila was counting on him, and he could afford a little cockiness. And some fun.

"Why don't you forget about the old doc," he said, standing. He pulled himself to his full height and looked down at her from his position on the wagon. "You need a *real* man, young and healthy. Like me." He smiled sardonically at her, an eyebrow raised.

Acidly, Lila replied, "The chickens're too good for you. Maybe I'll just turn you over to the Apaches so they can use you for a little target practice."

She smiled sweetly up at him. "As I seem to recall, the Apaches have a few scores to settle with you. I reckon they'd just love to have you visit for a spell."

The Apaches were the one tribe that Zeus had had trouble with. They had welcomed him warmly enough to be sure, but shortly after his arrival, the small band of Mescaleros had been stricken by a strange disease, the likes of which they had never seen before. They had heard of the spotted sickness that had devastated vast tribes to the north years

185

before, but had never encountered it. So they blamed it on the little man who had so recently come to their village with his little bag of herbs and his medicine. They called on him to cleanse the village of the demons that had descended, to cure the people of the illness.

But there was little he could do. He tried a few potions, knowing they would not work, but wanting to buy himself time in hopes the disease would run its course. He prayed to the gods of many tribes, and he called upon his special spirit power to help him. And he danced the dances. It was to no avail. The small band grew weaker and weaker, as death stalked through the camp. With no natural immunity, they were helpless in the face of the white man's disease.

To make it worse, a few members of the band slipped away to warn other small bands in the area, thus carrying the strange malady with them.

Zeus managed to steal a horse and some food one night, and slipped away. It had been a long, dangerous, frightening horseback ride across the treacherous mountains and arid flatlands of the New Mexico Territory.

He eluded the grief-crazed, vengeful warriors that had set out after him, and finally he made it to the safety of a village of Comanches, ones he had visited before. It was there that he learned the disease had come from tainted blankets traded to the warriors by roving Mexican traders.

The knowledge did little to reassure him. The word had gotten around that the Mescaleros considered him bad medicine and would kill him when they found him. But first, they would practice some of their reknowned tortures on him.

Zeus shuddered at the thought. "Sorry," he mumbled, moving hastily back into the wagon to replace the satchel. "It was just a small idea I had."

"Small idea is right," Lila smiled.

"I get the point. Help me down from here."

Lila did as she was told and the two strolled toward the house. As they neared the sod structure, Emma looked up and said, "Well, land sakes, if it ain't two strangers. Haven't seed you two 'round here in quite a spell. Been up to somethin'?"

Lila started to tell her about the new medicine, but a kick from Zeus stopped her. "Oh, we just been cleanin' the wagon up a bit," she said lamely. "We hope to be leavin' here soon and I want the wagon ready."

Emma looked at her a little suspiciously, but Grandma Whitlock piped up, "Sounds like a right good idea to me. Ain't much else a body can do on so hot a day."

"What you got in your hand there, Zeus?" Becky asked.

"Oh, this," he said, holding the bottle up to plain sight. "Just a plant specimen I picked up. It may have some use one of these days."

Zeus plopped himself down on one of the stools, looking like he had not a care in the world. Lila stayed standing, an anxious look on her finely chiseled face.

"Siddown, Lila," Zeus said calmly. "It's too hot to be standin' 'round. 'Sides, I reckon one of these fine ladies could use some help with their chores."

He gave her a stern look and she sat. Absentmindedly she picked up an old shirt and began darning a jagged hole in a sleeve. As the women worked, Zeus sat, happily whistling a cheerful tune, looking unconcerned. When he saw an opportunity, he leaned over to Lila and whispered, "Just keep shut 'bout this whole thing. I don't wanna get their hopes up no more than they already are. So just go 'bout your business like nothin's changed."

She nodded and set about her work more vigorously. Zeus sat whistling a while longer before nonchalantly rising. He stretched. "Reckon I'll go see if I can be of any help to the Chief."

Lila looked up slyly from her darning to see what the others' reactions would be. But they thought nothing of it, only nodding and going about their work.

Once inside the house, Zeus moved with more speed. He rapped at the door of the sickroom and said, "It's me, Chief. I came to help you."

McGill's voice from within sounded exhausted. "Go 'way, Zeus. I'll talk to you later."

Zeus was not to be put off. Boldly opening the door, he stepped in, finding McGill, drawn and haggard, sitting on the edge of the bed, bathing the girl's face with cool rags.

"I thought I told you to stay outside," McGill snapped in an uncharacteristic tone.

Zeus ignored him. He came closer to the bed and saw Martha. He took a deep breath. "I don't know who looks worse, Chief, you or her. I never seen you lookin' so poorly and she ain't looked this bad in days. The two of you make a lovely pair."

McGill just shook his head. "Please go, Zeus."

"But, Chief. I got somethin' here that might help her."

"Go away, Zeus," McGill said wearily. "I'm in no mood for one of your pranks."

"This ain't no joke, Chief." He held out the bottle. "Look."

McGill stared at it with glazed eyes. "What's
188

that?'' he asked, a look of distaste coming over him.

"Black Nightshade."

"Fine. Just what we need. A nightshade."

Zeus's patience, never at a high level, was quickly running out. "You don't understand. It may cure Martha." Fighting against agitation, he explained what he had told Lila earlier, but it seemed to make little impression on McGill.

"Thanks, Zeus. It's a nice thought, but I don't think it'll work." He had lost hope and it showed in his face and voice.

Zeus's patience fled altogether. "A fine lot you know. Everything else we tried ain't done no good. Them big fellers out yonder are goin' to shoot us dead if she don't get better and you sit here worryin' 'cause this is somethin' different. Hell,'' he shouted, "nothin' else's worked, so why not give it a try? It might amaze you. 'Sides, maybe you don't care 'bout yourself, but I aim to do whatever I can to save my hide."

McGill was still unconvinced. "Here I am supposed to be the doctor, or the next thing to it, and a sideshow juggler is trying to tell me how to cure a patient. You and your Indian medicine cures,'' he snorted.

"You seen many of them work before, ain't you?"

"Yes, I guess I have."

"And you've used a heap of 'em before this, ain't you?"

"Yes." It was said slowly. "But . . ."

"But nothin'. You know danged well a lot of your fancy medicine cures was developed from herb medicine. So why ain't you willin' to try this? You already tried two Indian remedies already. Or are the Indians back east better at doctorin' than

189

the ones out here?"

"It just don't seem right is all. She's dyin' and we're pourin' one crazy concoction after another into her. I feel sorry for her."

"You'll feel even sorrier if she dies."

"You really think you'll cure her with that stuff?" McGill snapped. His exhaustion and frustration had gotten the better of him. Zeus had never seen him so angry and had never heard him speak this way. "And I suppose you're going to dance around her with rattles, too, while you're at it?"

Zeus's face condensed into fury. "You illiterate oaf. Maybe your life don't mean much to you, but Martha's life is important. And so's mine and Lila's. If you don't give a hoot for yourself, at least think of someone else for a change."

McGill was taken aback by Zeus's anger. He hung his head. A shudder passed over him and his shoulders slumped. Then he lifted them with an effort and brought his gaze to Zeus. "I am truly ashamed. Will you forgive me? I never spoke to you like that before. I don't know what came over me."

Zeus was still rankled. "I know what's come over you. You ain't had no proper sleep in days and you been worried sick about the girl. That's understandable. But you ought not to take it out on your friends."

"You're right, my friend. And I'm sorry. I'll make it up to you some day. If we ever get out of here."

"Will you try this, then?"

"Think it'll do any good?"

Zeus shrugged. "What've we got to lose?"

"You have a point there, my little friend. Well, then, let's get started with it. What do you want me

190

to do?''

"Just keep on doin' what you were. My medicines're my secret and I'd like to keep it that way.''

"Anything you say. Just hurry.''

Zeus began his mysterious preparations, crumbling this, sorting that and mixing it with something else. McGill stole an occasional glance at his small assistant, but could not fathom what was being done.

There was a knock on the door. "Doctor McGill,'' Emma called. "Doctor McGill, may I come in?''

McGill threw a worried look at Zeus and ran to the door. He opened it a crack. "I'm sorry, Emma, but you can't come in right now. We're preparing a new medicine for Martha and we need privacy.''

"What do you mean a new medicine? Ain't she mendin'?''

"Yes, she's gettin' better. It's just a more potent mixture of the same medicine we were giving her before. But we need privacy and quiet to do it right.''

"Well . . .''

"She also needs all the sleep she can get. She's been dozin' and wakin' all along. It's best she's not disturbed.''

"Well, if you're sure,'' she said doubtfully.

"Course I'm sure. Now hush and let us work. Everything'll be fine. You just go on and wait outside.''

She acquiesced and left. McGill closed the door and breathed a sigh of relief. "That was a mite close.''

Zeus just nodded, engrossed in his work.

McGill went back to the bed and continued applying cool wet cloths to Martha's forehead and cheeks. He was startled when suddenly Zeus was standing next to him, holding the glass bottle, now filled with a sickly looking, purplish-colored liquid.

McGill took the bottle and contemplated it. "This had better work, friend Zeus. Or the Whitlocks may not get a chance to kill you." He smiled wryly.

He turned to the comatose girl and gently lifted her head. "Wake up, Martha. Come on, wake up," he called softly.

She groaned and opened her eyes. A coughing spell caught her and she choked and spit. She gasped for air, eyes clouded with pain and bewilderment.

"Feelin' all right, now?" McGill asked, knowing the answer, but needing to reassure her with his concern.

She played along. "Yes, Doctor. A mite."

"Good. Now I got another medicine here for you to take. It's pretty much the same as the last one, 'cept it's a mite more powerful. I thought the last medicine would be strong enough to fix you up, but it wasn't so we're going to try this one."

"Does it taste as bad as the last batch?" She knew the question was silly, but she couldn't help it, she had to ask.

"Not quite," he lied. "Ready?"

She nodded weakly, spitting up again after coughing harshly. McGill held her through the spell, feeling the helplessness of not being able to do anything to ease her.

When she was over it, McGill held the bottle to her lips. "Quick now. Drink some before you start to coughin' again."

He forced a few swallows of the liquid down her throat, stopping when she again began to cough.

Once more he held her while she coughed, talking to Zeus while he did so. "How much of this do I use?" he asked nervously.

"Couple more swallers ought to do it," Zeus answered, now also showing signs of strain.

McGill nodded at Zeus. The girl stopped coughing and McGill said, "Okay, Martha. Just a few more swallows."

Hurriedly McGill poured the fluid into her mouth, easing off periodically to allow her to swallow. Finally he pulled the bottle away. "That's enough for now." He laid her head back on the worn, lumpy pillow. "You get some sleep now. I'll be back directly to see how you're comin' along."

She nodded and he continued, "If you're feelin' a little better later, we'll get some supper into you. A good meal will probably work wonders."

McGill capped the bottle and handed it back to Zeus. "I know it's hot, Martha, but keep this sheet on you. I don't want you catchin' a chill on top of everything else."

She nodded again, struggling for breath. She looked terribly wasted; a frail fragment of the robust young woman who had danced so carefree not so long ago.

McGill was also drenched in sweat from the heat and the tension of the past few days. "C'mon, Zeus," he said, standing. "It's time we let her be. We've done all we can for now. It's up to the medicine, time and God now. I reckon we best hope for the first, wait for the second and pray to the third. With any luck, we'll get a miracle."

"Guess you're right, Chief." For the first time, it seemed that the seriousness of the situation had gotten through to the midget. He shook his head sadly looking at Martha. To McGill he said, "I really do hope she gets better, Chief."

193

He looked at Zeus. "You mean for once you're thinking of someone else? You're not just worried about your own hide?"

A tiny smile crept onto Zeus's lips. "Must be gettin' soft. Or else old. But I am worried 'bout her."

"I think I've worried enough for the both of us. So let's try'n put it from our minds for a while."

Zeus nodded acceptance and the two walked toward the door. Outside, the sun was searing; blinding them with its brilliance. McGill had not realized how cool it was inside the soddy interior compared to the furnace-like atmosphere outside.

The women looked up as they walked onto the porch. "She's sleepin' again," McGill said before they could question him. He continued, "Have you any soft soap, Emma? I'd like a bath down to the stream, but all I have is hard cake soap. Soft is best."

"Why sure," she said, befuddled. "Got some fresh made up you can use." Although she did not ask, her eyes pleadingly questioned him. He said nothing.

"Becky, go on in the house and fetch the doctor a dishful of soap," she finally said.

"All right, Ma." She put down her sewing and hurried inside.

"Thank you," McGill said. "Zeus, please fetch me some clean things from the wagon. I'll change down there by the stream."

"Sure, Chief."

As Zeus ran off, Rebecca returned, handing McGill a wooden bowl, half-full with squishy, yellowish-white soap. "Thank you," he said. And to Emma, "Martha's asleep and should stay that way for a while. I'd be obliged if, while I'm gone, you just leave her be. If you go in there, you might

194

wake her."

Emma, hoping for some good word on Martha's condition, was crestfallen. But she agreed to McGill's request.

"Good," McGill said. Turning, he trudged across the hard-packed ground, baked dry in the sun. Reaching the grove of trees, he put down the dish of soap, shucked his clothes, piling them in a heap, and jumped naked into the cool water.

He splashed around, enjoying himself. He was happier now than he had been in days. He saw Zeus up on the bank. "Come on in!" he shouted.

Zeus felt the devil rising in him again. "Naw," he said happily. "I think I'll just take off with all your clothes. Leave you here the way you are."

"That wouldn't be very nice, now, would it?"

"Naw, it wouldn't." He smiled, cat-like.

"I'd also advise against it," McGill called out, still enjoying the water. But he edged a little closer to the shore.

"Why's that?"

"Well, for one thing, I can outrun you even in my bare feet."

"And your bare everything else, too?"

"Yep. That's right."

Zeus and McGill had plunked down on chairs vacated by the women and spent the time chatting with each other and Elizabeth.

Soon the men came trudging back, hot, tired, agitated, thirsty. "How's Martha?" Jonathan asked.

"Holding her own," McGill answered calmly.

"Can we go in and see her?"

"I'd prefer you didn't just yet."

Jonathan nodded tightly. McGill could see the anger boiling just below the surface. The heat only intensified the steadily building fury within the burly farmer.

McGill could also see that it was only by the sheerest force of will that Jonathan kept the raging storm inside. But there was little he could do to ease the man's fear and worry.

Jonathan and his two sons washed up briskly from a pail outside. By the time they finished, supper was on the table.

As they ate, Emma said to her husband, "Doctor McGill and Zeus went for a swim down to the stream a while back. They took some soap with 'em to get cleaned up. Seems to me it's a right good idea and you three should do likewise."

Jonathan looked up sharply. "Somethin' wrong with us?"

She looked him squarely in the eye. "Nope. Wouldn't say that exactly. But it'd sure make you all feel a sight better."

Charles jumped in. "It sure would. How 'bout it, Pa? Before it gets too late, why'n't we all run down there and take us a swim. It's been godalmighty hot these past days and a swim would be right pleasurable."

Jonathan's hard look softened and he grinned. "I reckon you think it's a good idea, too," he said to Joshua.

"Sounds good to me, Pa."

"Seems like I been out-voted. All right, we'll do it. But all the chores still gotta be done before we turn in."

Dinner went quickly, the young men, anxious for their swim, setting the pace. The two finished first and waited impatiently for their father to finish. Jonathan, knowing they were waiting for him, deliberately took his time, delaying, sopping up the last of the gravy with a hunk of fresh bread.

But after what seemed like an eternity to the two

young men, Jonathan stood, pushing his plate back. "Okay, boys. Charles, fetch us all some clean shirts. Joshua, you dish up some soap."

They hopped up and hurried about. Prepared, they waited for their father. Getting into the spirit of it, Jonathan opened the door. Turning to his two sons, he yelled, "Last one to the stream has to clean the chicken pen!" He raced out the door.

Charles and Joshua screeched in surprise. Then they, too, raced out the door, whooping and hollering.

They were back soon, talking, laughing and roughhousing in high spirits. "Who lost?" Emma asked as they walked in.

"Charles," Joshua said joyfully.

They joshed the eldest son about the unpleasant chore he would have to perform the next day, and he took it manfully. It helped in knowing that his father and brother would be there to help. It was their way—the sharing of everything, joy and sorrow, fun and work.

"Guess I'll see to Martha," said McGill, who was happy to see that the cool dip in the stream had not only refreshed Jonathan, but had wiped away his anger, too.

When he left, the women started their seemingly endless task of cleaning away the remains of the meal. The men, with work still to be done, went about their business; Jonathan making some needed repairs on some tools, the young men heading toward the barn to tend to the animals.

McGill popped his head out of Martha's room. "Emma, please fix up a small plate for Martha. But let Lila bring it in."

Emma looked alarmed. "She's fine," McGill reassured her. "She just needs a bit of extra care and Lila is better trained to handle it."

Emma nodded, tight-lipped. She did not like being unable to help her daughter, but she would not argue with the doctor.

Lila soon joined McGill in the small room, again unclean and pungent. McGill propped Martha up so she could be fed.

"Hungry?" Lila asked.

Martha coughed and gasped, sitting back heavily, choking. "Yes," she finally managed to say.

"That's a good sign."

Lila began feeding the girl, patiently waiting out the frequent attacks of hacking coughs. During the coughing spells, Lila looked on sadly, knowing Martha looked no better. But she knew the girl looked no worse either.

After Martha's meager meal, Lila left. McGill stayed in the room until dusk, when he again called Lila. "Get her outside for a while," he told Lila when she had come in and closed the door behind her. "I'll get the bed and all cleaned up as best I can." Lila nodded and started to lift the girl off the bed. She halted in mid-lift at McGill's words. "Lila, try'n get her past her folks as quick as you can. Martha don't look so good and I don't want them getting too worrisome."

Lila nodded again and bent to her task. When she had shuffled out with Martha, McGill worked hurriedly. There was a small pile of fresh straw in the corner of the room, left there the last time the bed had been changed. McGill cleaned most of the old straw off the bed, throwing it out the window, knowing it would be carted away by the young men the next day.

Placing the new straw on the rickety wooden bed, he shook out the two thin sheets as best he could to clean and air them.

The sheets were back in place and the rest of the room tidied up when Lila returned with Martha. Lila helped the young girl back onto the bed, both breathing heavily from exertion.

"How was it?" McGill asked.

"Not too bad. They were all purty busy and we were halfway 'cross the room before they realized we were there. They all began askin' questions, but I just kinda ignored them, telling them I was in a hurry."

"They left you alone?"

"Becky followed us outside, wantin' to help. But it's well onto dark now, so she couldn't see none too well."

"What about comin' back in? They must've been ready for you. And what about Becky?"

"I'd sent Becky in, tellin' her I could get by better without her. She wasn't too happy about it, but she went. The rest of them were waitin' for us, but Martha has that long, beautiful hair. It covered most of her face and everyone knew we was both winded, so they let us be."

"Good, I'll go talk to them directly. Calm them."

"I reckon you'd best. They're gettin' a mite itchy with all this secrecy. 'Specially Jonathan. He puts on a good front, but down inside he's worried sick about his little girl."

McGill looked dubious, but Lila continued, "That's what she is to him, Winthrop. His little girl. And she's sick and he can't do nothing about it. He's near ready to explode. He's been holdin' himself on a purty tight rein, but it ain't gonna last forever."

"There's not much I can do."

"Just keep doin' what you're doin'. And wait. Time is probably what we need most right now."

McGill nodded grimly. "That's what we have too precious little of now."

The statement needed no answer, so Lila turned and fiddled with the bed, trying to make the sick girl more comfortable.

"That's enough, Lila," McGill finally said. "You go on outside. I want to give her more medicine and make sure she's all right. I'll be out directly."

"All right, Winthrop." With light footsteps, she left.

McGill sat on the edge of the bed and, with kindly motions, helped Martha take the medicine. He dawdled, wasting time. He knew there was nothing more he could do for the girl, but he was loath to face the Whitlocks.

He knew he would have to continue the lie to them, telling them Martha would get better. But he was not so sure. She had been sick a long time and, despite the short spell when she seemed to be recovering, had grown steadily worse.

The kindly medicine man did not like to lie. He would stretch the truth until it screamed for mercy, but out-and-out lying did not set well with him. Throughout all the miles and all the towns he had seen since coming west, he had never been in such a tight spot.

He shook his head in disgust. You're getting old, Winthrop, he said aloud, softly to himself. Afraid to go gig a few sodbusters, to play the game till the end.

He chuckled to himself. Standing, he straightened his shirt and brushed the graying hair back from his forehead. Squaring his shoulders, he walked out of the room. "Well," he said, smiling. "Martha is resting comfortably. That little turn outside did her a lot of good, 'though it wore her plumb out. She's still pretty weak.''

"Why wouldn't Lila let us see her when she was on her way out?'' Jonathan rumbled.

Despite his reluctance to lie, McGill could do it easily when it was necessary. ''Couple of reasons.'' His smile broadened until he was almost gleaming. It was, he knew, almost guaranteed to melt the hostility. ''One reason was because she is still very weak, and if they had stopped long enough to chat, Lila might not have been able to get Martha outside and back.''

"I would've toted her in,'' Charles said.

"I know. So would Joshua or your father. But it would have put an extra strain on Martha. And she's too weak for any of that. That's the same reason I've been keepin' you all out of her room. As much as you'd try to stay calm, you'd likely get her all riled up and then she'd get sicker.''

He could see their irritation dwindling. ''But the important reason why Lila wouldn't slow down out here long enough for you to talk to Martha was that Martha asked Lila not to.''

Everyone in the room, including Lila, gasped, though she managed to cover up pretty well.

"Is that right, Lila?'' Emma asked.

"Well, yes, I guess it was,'' Lila sputtered.

McGill smiled benevolently. ''Since Martha's been laid up sick so long, she really hasn't had a chance to pretty herself up. She just thinks she looks kind of bedraggled and doesn't want anyone to see her that way.

"I told her she was being foolish 'cause we're all her family and friends, but she wouldn't have none of it.''

Jonathan slapped his thigh, laughing. ''Well if that don't beat all. Danged fool woman. They're all the same. Here she is lyin' on her deathbed more'n likely, and all she can do is to worry 'bout her looks.''

"Oh, hush up, Jonathan," Emma scolded. "It's you men who're all alike. Don't care a blamed thing 'bout lookin' decent. You just don't understand a woman needs to look her best every once in a while. It's part of bein' a woman. But I don't know why we do it, you men never notice what we're lookin' like anyway. You just go on about your business without thinkin' about what we went through tryin' to look our best for you so's you'll have a woman you'd be pleased to call your—"

"Enough. Enough," Jonathan laughed. "I just reckoned she'd be more concerned with gettin' better rather'n what she looked like. We've seen her lookin' poorly before."

Emma prepared herself to give Jonathan another scolding, but Elizabeth cut her off. "Let 'im be, daughter. That lunkhead of a son'll never learn. It's best to let it drop."

Emma reached out a hand to hold one of her husband's huge paws. "Reckon you're right. He is kinda hardheaded, ain't he?"

"That's the truth," Elizabeth chuckled.

Chapter 12

McGill turned the lamp down low and settled comfortably into the rocker. He had a built-in wake-up system that was usually reliable, and he told himself to be up in three hours. He shut his eyes and drifted off into a land where he was once again free and unfettered, bouncing slowly along in the big, overloaded wagon. . . .

He awoke with a start. Rubbing his face, he looked at the old pocket watch he had carried for years. He smiled. "Right on time," he said. Jonathan glanced up briefly, but then bent back to the work spread out before him on the table.

In his stocking feet, McGill went silently into the bedroom, carrying a candle. As gently as he could, he roused Martha and made her drink some of the Black Nightshade medicine.

Despite the candle, it was still dark in the room and he could not see very well. But he noticed Martha seemed to be breathing easier and only coughed once while taking her medicine.

He left the room as silently as he had entered and went back to his chair. He went almost immediately back to sleep after warning himself to awake in another three hours.

He slept dreamlessly this time, again rising on time. Once more he made the quiet walk into the little room and woke the girl. In the dim light of the candle he looked her over carefully as she drank. He was pleased with what he saw, but tried to keep his hope in check. She no longer suffered through night sweats, but he was unsure of the reason; he could not be certain she was getting better, or whether it was just the relative coolness of the night after the searing heat of the day.

This time she did not cough at all while taking the dose of medicine and this sign gave McGill the most hope. She also breathed easier, not straining for each breath as she had been.

Dousing the candle, he slipped softly from the room and prepared himself for the few last hours of sleep before the coming dawn would bring the family.

McGill fought his way up from the dregs of sleep to the tune of Elizabeth's clanging and clanking of utensils. He shook his head, trying to clear the cobwebs of drowsiness. "Must've been more tired than I thought," he said when the old lady handed him a cup of steaming coffee.

"You most rightly was," she cackled.

The heat was already staggering by the time they all sat down to break their fast. "Damn, it's gonna be another scorcher," Jonathan grumbled.

"Hush your frettin', now, boy," his mother reprimanded. "We'll be gettin' a real goose drownder one of these days and then you'll be bellyachin' 'cause there's too much rain. You're never satisfied."

Winthrop thought it humorous to see the hulking Jonathan looking so hound-doggish, hanging his head in front of the frail old woman. "But we do need rain, Ma," Jonathan mumbled. "Bad."

"Well you'll be gettin' rain a mite soon now, I'm sayin'. I kin feel it in my bones and I kin feel it in the air."

She was right almost every time in one of her predictions, and no one made light of her now. It was too serious to make light of.

"Can you tell when it'll be here, Granny?" Charles asked.

"Naw. Can't be certain just yet. But it's a comin', sure as can be. You just mark my words."

"Will it be along before the crop's ruined?" Jonathan asked.

"It'll be a mite close, I'm sayin'. And them crops ain't gonna get saved all by themselves. They need all the help they can git. The longer you set here flappin' your gums, the worse off they're gonna be. So's I'd be suggestin' you get off your rumps and get out yonder where you can be doin' some good."

204

Jonathan grumbled, but stood, finishing the last of his coffee. "I'm goin'. I'm goin'."

Throughout the encounter, everyone else had watched with smiles. Zeus grinned the most. It was the kind of exchange that delighted him. With an endearing smile, he said to Jonathan, "It's a good thing we ain't had no rain in a spell."

"Why's that?"

" 'Cause then you'd be cooped up in this here little soddy with her all day," he said, nodding toward Elizabeth. "Then you'd have to listen to her flap her gums at you all day long, and there'd be nothin' you could do about it."

Everyone exploded into laughter. Even Elizabeth's high-pitched cackle bounced off the old sod walls. All, that is, except Jonathan. The big man advanced threateningly toward Zeus, but the laughter was infectious and soon he, too, joined in.

Refreshed, he said, "All right, boys. Time to go. Your grandma's right. We can't be gettin' nothin' done by settin' here all day. Give my love to Martha," he said, stalking out.

When the men had left, McGill said, "Think I'll take a short walk outside. Get a little fresh air. Then I'll see to Martha. Emma, would you please fix up a small plate for her. Lila'll take it in."

Emma looked disappointed, but nodded her acceptance of his order.

McGill breathed in the sweltering air outside the house. The sun was brutal, beating down unceasingly, cracking the already parched earth. McGill was sure the hot, dry air was good for the sickly girl, but he also sympathized with her father. A few more days like this one and the Whitlocks would face a winter of privation.

He still marveled at the strength and stolid determination of the poor dirt farmers scattered across

205

the broad expanse of the prairies. They fought wind, heat, droughts, horrendous rains, locusts, bitter cold in the winter, tornadoes, and every other kind of wretchedness nature threw at them.

But most of all, they persevered through loneliness. Utter, heartbreaking solitude. Months and months would go by and these people would see no one except the members of the family. It was hard on the men, who at least had an occasional trip to the nearest town to look forward to, but it was particularly difficult for the women. The land had driven more than one woman to the brink of insanity. It was not an easy life; not a life for everyone. It took a special kind of people. And many was the family that passed McGill on the road, headed back east, beaten and subdued—their dreams of making a new life in the West shattered. It was particularly true after the locust plague ten years earlier. The massive deluge of insects had devastated the land, laying the crops to waste over most of the plains. Known to most as the Year of the Locusts, it had broken thousands of people, many of whom had fled back east.

McGill was glad he had come to know people like the Whitlocks. He was glad he had brightened their lives a little. He was glad he could be a part of their experience, even if only for a few brief days. But he was even more glad he had not chosen that life for himself. No, it was not for him.

McGill turned his steps back toward the house. He could delay it no longer. He had to tend to the girl. Without a word, he walked through the main room of the house and into the small cubicle where the sick girl lay.

Lila was still there, kindly feeding Martha. She smiled at McGill and went back to her task. McGill paced the room, trying to stay out of the way while

Martha was fed. Lila finally left, and McGill knelt by the girl. "How're you feeling today?"

"A mite better, I reckon."

"That's good." McGill examined her, seeing what he wanted to believe were signs of progress. The uncontrollable sweats had subsided and she appeared to be a little stronger. He tried not to hope too much, knowing it could lead to disappointment, but it was hard. He was brought back to reality when she started coughing; a dry, hacking cough that seemed as if it would tear her apart.

She finally stopped off, gasping. Despite his frustration and worry, he was pleased to see she was breathing almost regularly within minutes. There's still hope, he thought.

He made her take some of the medicine and told her to rest, but Lila poked her head in. "The whole family's off in different places, so there's nobody around," she said.

McGill got her meaning immediately. "Good. Get her outside. She can use the trip, and the fresh air ought to benefit her." Lila nodded and entered the room as McGill continued, "But don't be too long about it. I still want her kept from them awhile."

When they were gone, McGill took to straightening the room. They were back before he was finished, forcing him to hurry.

The trip had winded Martha, but not as badly as the one the night before. This, too, encouraged McGill. "All right, Martha. I want you to take it easy now. You're still very weak. Lila and I will be near to hand all day in case you need anything. All right?"

"Yes, Doctor."

McGill and Lila left the room and went outside.

207

"She seems better," McGill said. "But that cough still worries me." He stood thoughtfully for a moment. "Lila, go put a heap of water on to boil. I need about three quarts. Zeus!" he shouted.

The little man seemed to pop out of nowhere.

"I need to make another cough potion for Martha. I'd be obliged," he said politely, "if you'd fetch me four ounces of blood root, boneset, slippery elm—"

"Wait a minute, Chief. I can't remember all this." He pulled out the stubby pencil and crumpled hunk of paper he had used a few days before. "Now tell me."

McGill repeated the first ingredients, then added, "Horehound plant, comfrey root, elecampane root, wild cherry bark, spikenard root, and penny-royal plant."

"That it?"

"Yep."

"Okay, Chief."

While Zeus was gone, McGill cleaned out the big bowl and the jar. When the midget returned, McGill dumped the herbs and roots into the bowl and poured the boiling water over them.

"I'm going out to the wagon to get some rest," McGill said. "This heat's really wearin' me out. Keep an eye on Martha and call me if she looks to be gettin' worse. That cough syrup's got to set three hours. Wake me then."

"Okay, Winthrop. You just go and rest now. Leave the girl to me."

McGill shuffled off. Lila, who stood watching him, saw more fatigue and frustration than he was willing to admit. The tension was wearing on him, she knew. She also knew that if the girl was not better soon, he would wear himself to a frazzle. The Whitlock guns would have little meaning for him then. She sighed and walked over to the garden to help the other women with their chores.

Throughout the morning, Lila would periodically check on Martha. She thought she could see signs of progress, but she could not be sure. Three hours later she woke McGill. "It's time," she said.

Tiredly he walked back to the house. There he strained the water from the herb-root mixture and set it to boiling again. When it was bubbling, he poured it back over the mixture.

"That's got to set another five, six hours," he said. "I'm going back to the wagon. Fetch me at the noon meal. But first I'd best see to Martha again, give her another dose." He did so and then left quietly.

When everyone gathered for the small noon meal, McGill joined them looking hot, but more alert. The heat, though, made everyone short-tempered and it was not an easy meal.

When it was over, the men straggled back to work, while the women stayed close to the house, working desultorily. McGill read for a while, then did some work on the wagon. At regular intervals he would look in on Martha, occasionally making her take another dose of medicine. He thought he saw signs of progress; more regular breathing, less coughing, and an almost imperceptible gaining in strength. But, like Lila, he was unsure. And he was afraid to hope.

But hope he did. Throughout the long, broiling afternoon and into the early evening. Eyes could be deceptive, he knew, but each time he checked, Martha seemed a little better.

In mid-afternoon, the cough balsam was ready. He melted down a bit of the sugar candy and added it to the mixture. Heating the whole thing up, he served a small cupful to Martha, repeating it as she needed it throughout the rest of the day.

Lila commented on Martha's condition that night, after she had fed the girl some of the pork, beans and cornbread the family had had for supper.

Jonathan overheard Lila's comment to McGill, and he commented himself. Jonathan was overwrought; the strain of working in the heat, his worry about losing the crops, and his concern for Martha combined to make him short-tempered. During the evening meal he had been surly, dampening the lighthearted conversation that had marked the meals over the past few days.

When he heard Lila's comment, he had finally had enough. Striding in front of McGill, he said tightly, "She damn well best be mendin'. Somethin' best happen soon. She's been lyin' in there sick for a right long time now and it don't seem like you been able to do too awful much. If'n she ain't better by sometime tomorrow . . ." He trailed off, pointedly patting the heavy sixgun hanging from his waist.

Emma started to reprimand him, but thought better of it. He was not like this often, but when he was, he was not open to argument.

The others took their cue from Emma and kept silent. Even the usually talkative Elizabeth sat quietly in her rocking chair puffing stolidly on her pipe, her eyes fixed on the ceiling.

McGill drew himself up to his full height and stared back at Jonathan, looking up into the big man's dark eyes. McGill's unwavering glare almost unnerved Jonathan. "You understand what I'm tellin' you?" the farmer asked.

"Yes." It was said simply, quietly.

"Good." Jonathan was still confused by McGill

and took the opportunity to break the gaze, walking back to the table where he plunked himself angrily down. With deliberate motions, he pulled the heavy sixshooter from its holster and emptied it, placing the cartridges one by one in plain view on the table. Then he slowly cleaned the weapon, letting the unsubtle movements emphasize his earlier threats.

McGill slept fitfully that night, dozing and waking regularly. During his waking periods, he checked on Martha, sometimes waking her to make her take some of the medicine, at others just making sure she was as comfortable as could be.

When he slept, his mind filled with nightmares and dreams that left him uneasy. Although he had kept his calm in front of Jonathan's onslaught, he was not all as confident as he seemed. He knew Martha's chances of recovery were slim, but he also knew it was amazing she was still alive. Usually in these cases, out here in the midst of nowhere, where sanitation was at a minimum, people who got sick rarely recovered. When they did recover, it was more often the person's own constitution that carried him through.

And that was what McGill was counting on. Although slim, Martha had always been a healthy, robust young woman. This, McGill hoped, might allow her to survive. All he could do was wait. And maybe convince Jonathan he needed a little more time.

Dawn floated in and the Whitlocks began to rise. Breakfast, eaten quickly this morning, was even more dismal than the supper the night before. As soon as they had finished, Jonathan, Charles and Joshua headed out into the blazing heat. McGill nodded to Lila, who understood. Preparing a small plate of ham and eggs, she brought it in to Martha.

She was back sooner than McGill had expected, a slight smile creasing her full lips. McGill gave her a questioning look, but she said nothing.

Knowing he could put it off no longer, McGill finally pushed himself away from the table and, without a word, went in to see the sick girl. He was pleasantly surprised to see her looking better. Her breathing appeared to be more regular and she coughed infrequently. He gave her some of the medicine, leaving only a tiny bit in the bottom of the bottle. When she had finished, he felt her forehead. It was cool to the touch. Then he noticed she could almost help herself to take some of the water he offered her.

Can it be, he thought. *Can it be?*

A small coughing spell served to dispel some of his enthusiasm, but some remained. Encouraged, he asked, "Need to go outside?"

She shook her head. "Not just yet."

"Good. I want you to get some more shuteye."

"Okay, Doctor." She closed her eyes and McGill stood over her watching the weak rise and fall of her chest.

The morning was not an easy one for McGill. He constantly wanted to check on Martha, watch her progress, if that's what it really was. So he held himself in check, knowing it would do her little good to disturb her.

He also knew that if he went into that little room he would have to dose her again, using the last of the medicine. And that was all there was; Zeus had already told him he had no more of the Black Nightshade left in his satchel. Worse yet, he knew of no place here to find more.

And so he sat and fidgeted, listening to the women talk as they worked, and talking to Zeus in quiet tones.

212

He and Zeus were still sitting on the single rickety step to the porch when the men returned for the noon meal. Jonathan was parched and his temper brittle.

"How's my daughter, McGill?" he snarled.

"Progressing."

Jonathan's temper snapped. "Progressin'," he snorted. "I been hearin' that damn fool statement for nigh on a week now and I am plumb tired of hearin' it. I want to know how she's really doin'."

"She seems to be getting better," McGill said, still calm.

"What d'you mean, seems? Dont' you know?"

"That's the best I can do, Jonathan, as far as telling you anything." He stood. "She's doing better than she was yesterday and the day before, but it might be quite a spell before she's fully mended."

Jonathan was almost beside himself in anger now. He had reached the point where he had to do something or burst. "I've had enough of your stallin'!" he shouted. "Charles, Joshua, hold your guns on the bunch of 'em. I don't want none of the three of 'em goin' anywheres. I think their time's about up."

The two young men, looking doubtful, did what their father ordered. They pulled their weapons and pointed them reluctantly at McGill, Lila, who stood with her head held high next to him, and Zeus, huddled between them.

"Just keep 'em covered," Jonathan said. "I'm goin' in and see to Martha."

"That ain't necessary." The voice startled everyone. They all spun as one toward the door. "And them guns ain't needed, neither," the young girl said. "I'm ashamed of you, Pa, for actin' this

213

way."

Emma jumped up, the initial shock over. "Martha!" she screamed. She ran the few steps and embraced her daughter.

McGill, beaming in relief, rushed over to the two, followed by the others. They clustered around the young girl. McGill tugged at Emma's arm. "Emma. Emma! Please. Let her be a minute. You're gonna smother her."

He tugged a little harder. "Come on now, Emma. Let her be. I know you're happy, but you're not helping her."

Reluctantly Emma let go of her daughter, tears streaming down her cheeks. Martha, still very weak, leaned against the doorjamb, smiling happily.

"Put them things away," she said joyfully, pointing to the guns the two young men still had in their hands.

Sheepishly they obeyed, looking embarrassed that they had ever strapped them onto their hips.

"Come on, Martha. Let's get you back inside and take a look at you," McGill said. "I want to see if you're really cured, or just feeling a mite feisty." He took her by the arm and led her inside. The others followed along, right to the bedroom door. "That's as far as you all go," McGill said. "Everybody get."

They turned away, anxiously heading for the table; the traditional gathering place in times of trouble.

All went, that is, except Zeus. The midget tried to slip into the small room. "You, too, Zeus. Get," McGill said happily, but sternly. He grabbed the little man and propelled him toward the table with the others.

"But I want to help you, Chief," he said,

protesting. "I can examine her real good."

McGill gave him another soft push. "I don't really need your help, thank you."

Lila, Zeus and the Whitlocks watched the door of the small room with varying displays of emotion. They were tense, happy, hopeful or scared at different times. The door opened after what seemed like an eternity. McGill's broadly smiling face told them the story, but they wanted to hear it from him.

"Well, folks, Martha seems to have come through this all with no lasting ill effects. She's still weak and needs more rest, but she'll be all right. The worst is over."

Emma and Rebecca began to cry. "Oh, Doctor," Emma wailed, "how can we ever thank you?"

Cheerfully, without hesitation, McGill said, "Well you might ask your husband to forget his little promise."

Silence hovered for a few seconds, before everyone began to laugh. Jonathan unstrapped the heavy pistol from around his waist and hung it on a peg near the door. His two sons did likewise.

"Make you feel better?" Jonathan asked.

"Sure does!" Zeus shouted from across the room.

"Can we go in and see her?" Emma asked.

"I reckon so. Just don't stay too long. Too much excitement's not good for her."

Jonathan threw one huge arm around his wife's shoulders. Together they walked into the small room, closely followed by the other members of the family.

McGill, Zeus and Lila stood near the door looking in. Emma greeted her daughter again and let her husband hug the girl. They stepped back

215

near to the door to let the rest of the family squeeze in and say a few words.

Zeus sidled up to Emma and tugged on her skirt. She looked down. With a leer, Zeus beckoned with a finger, requesting she bend over to be near his lips.

Emma recoiled at first, remembering the insulting proposals the little man had made in the past. Then she looked at her daughter, and remembered what McGill and his strange companions had done for Martha. She steeled herself and did as the midget requested, after moving a few small steps away from her husband.

With a smart-alecky whisper, designed to make Emma shudder, Zeus said, "He really was one of the best. Both in medical school and during the war." She looked at him in surprise. "Fooled you, didn't I?" he asked facetiously.

She nodded and he continued. "His marks was always high. He would've been one of the best. He *was* one of the best during the war. Saved more lives than you could count. But he had to quit schoolin' and later regular doctorin'. Nothin' he done seemed to work out. After a while it just got too late for him to go back."

Emma smiled. "I know all that. Lila told us the whole story a while back. But I thank you for tellin' me anyway. It shows the respect you have for him. In fact, now it's all over, I'll go and tell him what I think of him."

But Zeus grabbed her. "No," he said anxiously. "You can't do that. He would be right embarrassed."

"But—"

"You ever wonder why he never told you any of this? You got all you know about him from me or Lila. He don't like to talk about it. He reckons

216

people will think he's makin' excuses."

She nodded slowly and a little sadly. "I reckon I understand. I won't say nothin'."

But her sadness was momentary. As soon as she straightened, she saw her family clustered around Martha. Her smile grew again.

McGill called Zeus and said, "We'd best let them alone for a while. Come on."

He turned to shut the door behind them and reminded the family not to linger. "Remember, just a short while. She needs rest." He closed the door firmly.

Chapter 13

Lila and McGill sat on the big wagon, hitched and ready to roll. "Where's Zeus?" McGill asked impatiently.

Lila shrugged. "Don't know."

The Whitlocks, including the rapidly recovering Martha, stood outside the soddy in the warm morning sun.

McGill had wanted to stay at least one more night after Martha's sudden improvement. But the next morning, the rain that Elizabeth had predicted finally came. Torrents of rain cascaded down, leaking through the sod-covered roof, making life in the house muddy and miserable. Everyone was happy, though, because Martha was well, and they needed the rain. McGill had worried some that the dampness and cooler air would bring on a recurrence of Martha's ailment, but she grew steadily stronger.

It was a time to celebrate. The first day of the

rain, McGill brought out two bottles of the best whiskey he carried.

"Since we're all cooped up here together, we might as well make the best of it," he said, plunking the bottles on the table. "Emma, fetch some cups."

Everyone's cup filled, Jonathan said, "I'd like to make a toast." He stood. "To Doctor McGill and his two friends for savin' our Martha's life."

They drank heartily and then McGill stood. "Reckon it's my turn." He raised his cup. "To the rain that'll save your crops and make your winter less hard."

Again they drank, Grandma Whitlock and Zeus smacking their lips contentedly. And so the day passed.

The next day, with the rain drumming ceaselessly on the roof, McGill suggested some festivities to take their minds off the rain and the constant exposure to each other.

So it ended where it had started: with McGill fiddling furiously, accompanied by Zeus's banjo and squeezebox playing. Lila had started the dancing, but she was soon joined by Jonathan and Emma. Charles and Joshua, overcoming their shyness more easily this time, took turns spinning and reeling with Lila and Becky.

Even Elizabeth and Martha got into the act, keeping time with some furious foot-stomping and hand-clapping. Elizabeth's high cackling laugh frequently accompanied the hooting and shouting that went along with the music.

It was a rip-snorting jamboree and carried long into the night until, exhausted, they could dance, sing, and play no more.

"I ain't seed a knee-bender like that since I was a wee little girl back in Kaintuck," Elizabeth chortled as she headed off toward her bed.

Lila helped Martha back to bed. The girl was recovering quickly, but she was still weak and the excitement had left her a little short of breath. McGill, watching her disappear into the small room, hoped she hadn't overdone it.

Once Martha was safely asleep, Charles and Joshua thought it their duty to escort the flushed, puffing Lila out to the wagon, a move that both annoyed and amused Zeus.

McGill spent another uncomfortable night in the house, sleeping in the rickety old rocker, keeping it close to the door of the small room in case Martha should need him.

But she slept soundly, something he could not claim for himself. When he did sleep, he dreamed of leaving, of being off again on the prairie, the soft clump of the horses' hooves ringing in his ears; he dreamed of the drone of Zeus's incessant harmonica playing or talk. He dreamed of the faraway Southwest with its dryness and earth-warmth; and he dreamed of the East, along the shores of the muddy Missouri or the wide Mississippi.

More than once he awoke during the night and felt the constrictions of being tied to this house. He hoped it would be clear and dry in the morning so they could be on their way. He had spent enough time cooped up in the small soddy and he had had enough of company for the time being. He desperately wanted the relative solitude of the wagon.

But it was not to be. The rain beat restlessly down once more. The men did what they could, grumbling more about the rain that seeped down their collars inside their shirts than they had about the melting heat of a few short days ago.

They played cards and talked and worked at

219

what they could. And they traded, as McGill called it. He could not let a golden opportunity pass and, about midday, he and Zeus hitched up the wagon and pulled it as close to the cabin door as they could.

The others, sitting in the house, were unaware of his actions and were startled by his voice. "All right, step right up and see what we got here. There's no time to lose now; these fine quality goods won't last forever. I'm down to the last on some items and everything's goin' fast."

The Whitlocks tumbled out of the house to stand in wonder under the small overhang of porch roof, trying to keep the rain off their heads.

"That's right, folks. Step right up and take your pick of these fine goods. We got somethin' for everybody. How about you, ma'am?" he pointed to Elizabeth. "I have here the finest selection of domestic tobaccos, direct from the growing fields in the fine old state of Virginia."

The old woman looked interested and he turned from his perch on the wagon back. He had fixed up a small awning to keep the cold rain off him and he was in high spirits. He turned his spiel on, "And to go with this high-quality smoking tobacco, I have the finest assortment of hand-hewn pipes this side of the Mississippi River."

That was enough to do it. Elizabeth pushed her way forward. "Let me see some of them there pipes you got, Winthrop. I just might have a need for one."

McGill was surprised at her use of his first name, but he smiled and held out a box with pipes of various shapes and sizes.

She looked them over and finally selected one with a deep bowl and long, thin stem. "This'll do jist right," she cackled.

She turned over a gold coin, taken from an apron pocket.

McGill grinned and handed her another, a briar with a thick heavy bowl and curved stem. "My compliments, ma'am. For special occasions."

She also bought some tobacco.

Business picked up. He sold a cigar roller and more tobacco, and dress material and nails and fencing, and even a fountain pen. But he was not in his usual form. Instead of selling all he could, taking the last penny he could squeeze out of his customers, he gave away almost as much as he sold.

Zeus was surprised and even a little amused. "What're you doin', Chief?" he asked during a short lull.

"Hush up and get another bolt of cloth for Martha," he mumbled. He could not tell Zeus that he had spent so much time inside the walls of this home that he almost considered the Whitlocks family.

Nor could he tell the midget that he felt sorry for these brave people, stuck out here with no neighbors or company except travelers like themselves. He could not show his pity for the fresh-faced young girls who would grow old before their time, exposed to the harsh elements and perhaps forced into marriages with men they did not know and might not care for. He knew he could not mention the warmth he felt at the closeness of this family, of how they stuck together. How they would do whatever they thought necessary to protect each other.

No, he could not say these things. But he could help them in the only way he knew how. And so he gave of the things he had, the things that would make their lives a little easier, a little less harsh, a little more livable.

But he gave without being conspicuous, knowing charity would offend their independent pride. He sold things at half price, knowing these people would not know the real prices of most of the things. Or he sold them two for one. By the time he had brought out almost one of everything he had in the stocked wagon, it was well into evening and everyone was tired and wet. But happy.

The Whitlocks drifted off to sleep early; it had been a long celebration, and they had been up early. For the first time in days, McGill slept in the wagon in what was for him a comfortable bed.

The morning came bright and sunny. The rain had refreshed the earth and cooled the air a little. It was, McGill knew, the perfect day to leave. They had their last breakfast with the Whitlock family. Jonathan, joined by the others, had tried to get McGill, Lila and Zeus to stay on a while, but McGill remained adamant about leaving.

So now Lila and McGill sat atop the bulky wagon saying their last farewells and wondering where Zeus had gotten himself off to.

Finally an exasperated McGill shouted, "Zeus! Zeus! Where are you? Come on out. We're ready to leave."

The only noise to be heard was the slight breeze rustling through the stalks of corn. Until a smack was heard from around the corner of the sod barn.

From around the corner, Rebecca came running. She looked perilously close to tears. Zeus followed more slowly, sauntering toward the group rubbing his cheek, already reddening with the imprint of a hand.

Holding back the tears, Rebecca ran to her mother and said, "Momma, that little creature wanted me to . . . wanted me to . . . oh, I can't

even tell you."

Not knowing whether to laugh or be angry, Emma said sharply, "Hush up now, girl. Our company is leavin' and we must show them a proper send-off."

McGill, watching the exchange, glared at Zeus. Angrily he said, when the little man reached the wagon, "You impudent, little—" He paused and then said more calmly, "Just hurry it up. We've a ways to go before dark sets in, and we don't want to overstay our welcome."

The two men clasped hands and Jonathan said, more than a little sheepishly, "I don't know how to thank you, Doctor. All I can say is I'm mighty obliged and I'm sorry for some of the things I said."

Lila clamped her hand over Zeus's mouth before he could retort. Instead, McGill answered, "No thanks needed. I just did what was necessary. And so, I reckon, did you."

He let go of Jonathan's hand. "We'd best be movin' out. Goodbye, all."

He clucked the horses into movement. McGill and Lila waved back at the tight little family, while Zeus gallantly blew kisses to the Whitlock women.

As the wagon moved off, Jonathan thought he heard Lila's voice, "You'll never learn, will you, Zeus? You ungrateful, nasty heathen. Just remember we're still close to the chickens."